THE MORGAN MEN

LOOK FOR THESE EXCITING WESTERN SERIES FROM BESTSELLING AUTHORS WILLIAM W. JOHNSTONE AND J.A. JOHNSTONE

The Mountain Man
Luke Jensen: Bounty Hunter
Brannigan's Land
The Jensen Brand
Smoke Jensen: The Early Years
Preacher and MacCallister
Fort Misery
The Fighting O'Neils
Perley Gates
MacCoole and Boone
Guns of the Vigilantes
Shotgun Johnny
The Chuckwagon Trail
The Jackals
The Slash and Pecos Westerns
The Texas Moonshiners
Stoneface Finnegan Westerns
Ben Savage: Saloon Ranger
The Buck Trammel Westerns
The Death and Texas Westerns
The Hunter Buchanon Westerns
Will Tanner, Deputy US Marshal
Old Cowboys Never Die
Go West, Young Man

Published by Kensington Publishing Corp.

THE MORGAN MEN

William W. Johnstone
And
J.A. Johnstone

PINNACLE BOOKS
Kensington Publishing Corp.
www.kensingtonbooks.com

PINNACLE BOOKS are published by

Kensington Publishing Corp.
900 Third Avenue
New York, NY 10022

PUBLISHER'S NOTE: Following the death of William W. Johnstone, the Johnstone family is working with a carefully selected writer to organize and complete Mr. Johnstone's outlines and many unfinished manuscripts to create additional novels in all of his series like The Last Gunfighter, Mountain Man, and Eagles, among others. This novel was inspired by Mr. Johnstone's superb storytelling.

First Kensington Books hardcover printing: June 2020
First Pinnacle Books mass market printing: August 2024

ISBN-13: 978-0-7860-5125-0
ISBN-13: 978-0-7860-5127-4 (eBook)

10 9 8 7 6 5 4 3 2 1

Printed in the United States of America

CONTENTS

PART ONE
THE DRIFTER

To Debbie and Dent Sigh

CHAPTER 1

"Boy," the older man said, "I strongly advise you not to pull on me."

It seemed to those in the barroom there was not only a great weariness to the man's voice, but also a great sadness. Some of the spectators wondered about that. A few thought they knew why the sadness was there.

Outside, the early spring winds still had a bite to them on the late-afternoon day.

"You're nothin' but a damned old washed-up piece of coyote crap," the young man replied.

Old is right, the man thought. *Both in body and soul.*

"And you're a coward, too!" the young man added.

The older man smiled, but his eyes turned chilly. "Boy, you should really learn to watch your mouth."

The young man laughed. "You gonna make me do that, you old has-been?"

"I would rather not have to do that, boy. Besides, that's something your mother and father should have taught you."

"I never paid no mind to what they said."

"Obviously."

"Huh? Old man, you talk funny—you know that? You tryin' to insult me or something?"

"Not at all, boy. Just agreeing with you."

"I don't like you, old man. I mean, I don't like you at all. I think you're all talk and no do. And I don't believe all them stories told 'bout you, neither. I don't think you've kilt no twenty or thirty men."

"I haven't."

"I knowed it!"

"Closer to forty."

"You're a damn liar!"

"Boy, go home. Leave me alone."

"Naw. I'm gonna make you pull on me, Morgan. Then I'm gonna shoot you in the belly so's I can stand right here and watch you beg and cry and holler like a whipped pup 'til you die. That's what I'm gonna do."

"Is that really Frank Morgan?" a man in the crowd whispered to a friend.

"That's him."

"I thought he was a lot older."

" 'Nuff talk, old man!" the young man yelled. "Grab iron, you old buffalo fart!"

Frank Morgan did not move. He stood and watched the much younger man. "If you want a shooting, boy, you're going to have to start it."

"Then I will, by God!"

Frank waited.

"You think I won't?"

"I hope you don't, kid."

"I ain't no kid!"

"Pardon me?"

"I'm known around here as Snake."

"There is a certain resemblance."

Someone in the crowd laughed at that.

"What?" the young man yelled.

"I was just agreeing with you," Morgan said.

"Yore gonna die, Morgan!"

"We all die, kid. Some long before their time. And I'm afraid you're about to prove me right."

The kid cussed and grabbed iron.

Morgan shot him before the kid could even clear leather—shot him two times, the shots so close together they sounded as one. The kid's feet flew out from under him and he hit the floor, two holes in the center of his chest.

"Good God Almighty!" a man in the crowd said.

"He's as fast as he ever was," another man stage-whispered.

"You know Morgan?"

"I seen him once back in seventy-four, I think it was. He shot them two Burris brothers."

It was now April, 1888.

Frank slowly holstered his .45, then walked the few yards that had separated the two men. He stood for a moment looking down at the dying young man.

"I thought . . . all that talk 'bout you was . . . bullcrap," the young man gasped. Blood was leaking from his mouth.

"I wish it was," Frank said, then turned away from the bloody scene and stepped up to the bar. "A whiskey, please," he told the barkeep.

"I thought you only drank coffee, Mr. Morgan."

"Occasionally I will take a drink of hard liquor."

"Yes, sir. Mr. Morgan?"

Frank looked at the man.

"The sheriff and his deputies will be here shortly. Gunplay is not looked on with favor in this town."

"In other words, get out of town?"

"It was just a friendly suggestion. No offense meant."

"I know. None taken. Thank you." *Same old story,* Frank thought. *Different piano player, same song.*

Frank took a sip of whiskey.

"The kid's dead," someone said. "Reckon I ought to get the undertaker?"

"Not yet," a man said from the batwings.

Frank cut his eyes. Three men had stepped quietly into the saloon—the sheriff and two of his deputies. The two deputies were carrying Greeners—sawed-off, double-barreled shotguns.

No one with any sense wanted to take a chance when facing Frank Morgan.

Frank was standing alone at the bar, slowly taking tiny sips from his glass of whiskey.

"Frank Morgan," the sheriff said.

"Do I know you, Sheriff?" Frank asked. "I don't recall ever meeting you."

"I know you from dime novels, Morgan."

"I see."

"Them writers want to make you a hero. But I know you for what you really are."

"What am I, Sheriff?"

"A damn, kill-crazy outlaw."

"I've never stolen a thing in my life, Sheriff."

"You say."

Frank set the glass down on the bar and turned to face the sheriff. "That's right, Sheriff. I say."

The deputies raised the shotguns.

Frank smiled. "Relax, boys," he told them. "You'll get no trouble from me."

"You just can't keep that pistol in leather, can you, Morgan?" the sheriff said.

"I was pushed into this fight, Sheriff. Ask anyone here."

"I 'spect that's so, Morgan. The kid was a troublemaker, for a fact."

"And now?"

"You finish your drink and get out of town."

"I've got a very tired horse, Sheriff, with a loose shoe. He's at the livery now. You don't like me—that's all right. But my horse has done nothing to you."

The sheriff hesitated. "All right, Morgan. You can stay in

the stable with your horse. Get that shoe fixed first thing come the morning and then get the hell gone from here."

"Thank you. How about something to eat?"

"Get you some crackers and a pickle from the store 'cross the street. That'll have to do you."

"Crackers and a pickle," Frank muttered. "Well, I've eaten worse."

"Understood, Morgan?" the sheriff pressed.

"Perfectly, Sheriff."

"Some of you men get the kid over to the undertaker," the sheriff ordered. "Tell him he can have whatever's in the kid's pockets for his fee."

"Them guns of hisn, too?" a man asked.

"Yes. The guns, too."

Frank turned back to the bar and slowly sipped his drink. The sheriff walked over and leaned against the bar, staring at him.

"Something on your mind, Sheriff?" Frank asked.

"What's your tally now, Morgan? A hundred? A hundred and fifty dead by your gun?"

Frank smiled. "No, Sheriff. Not nearly that many. The kid there was the first man to brace me in several years."

"How'd you manage that, Morgan?"

"I stayed away from people. I mostly rode the lonesome."

"What made you stop here?"

"My horse. And I needed supplies. I lost my packhorse and supplies to some damned renegade young Indians last week. Down south of here."

"I heard about that. Got a wire from a sheriff friend of mine down that way. A posse went after those young bucks and cornered them. Killed them all."

Frank nodded his head. "They got what they deserved. That was a good horse they killed."

"Wilson at the livery's got a good packhorse he'd like to sell, if you've got the money. I don't think he wants much for him."

"I've got some money."

"I'll amble over there and drop a word on him to let you have the horse for his lowest price. Then you get supplies and ride on."

"Thanks, Sheriff."

Without another word the sheriff turned and walked away, his deputies following.

The swamper mopped up the blood on the floor and sprinkled sawdust over the spot.

The saloon settled down to cards and low talk. The excitement was over. Killings were rare in the town, but nobody had really liked the kid who called himself Snake. He had been nothing but a smart-aleck troublemaker. He would not be missed.

Frank Morgan pulled out early the next morning, after provisioning up at the general store. The man at the livery had tossed in a packsaddle for a couple of dollars, and Frank brought supplies, lashed them down, and pulled out before most of the town's citizens were up emptying the chamber pot.

Frank took it easy that morning, stopping often just to look around. It had been years since he'd been in this part of New Mexico territory, and things had changed somewhat. Hell of a lot more people, for one thing. Seemed like there were settlers nearly everywhere he looked.

For his nooning, Frank settled down in the shade by a fast-running little creek that came straight down from the mountains and had him a sandwich the lady at the general store had been kind enough to fix for him . . . for a dime.

Frank still wondered about the change in attitude of the local sheriff the day before. Some lawdogs could be real bastards, while others were fairly decent sorts once you got past all the bluster. But it had been many a year since any badge-toter had gotten too lippy with Frank Morgan. One tried to shove Frank around down in Texas—back around '75, he thought it was. Wasn't any gunplay involved that day, but Frank had sure cleaned the loudmouth's plow with his fists.

Frank ate his sandwich and then rested for a time while his horses grazed. Then he stood up and stretched. Felt good. Frank was just a shade over six feet, lean-hipped, broad-shouldered, with smooth, natural musculature. At forty-five years old, Frank was still a powerful man. Not the hoss he used to be, but close enough. His thick hair was dark brown, graying now at the temples. Pale gray eyes.

Frank wore a .45 Colt Peacemaker, right side, low and tied down. He carried another Colt Peacemaker in his saddlebags. A Winchester rifle was stuck down in a saddle boot. On the left side of his belt he carried a long-bladed knife in a sheath. He occasionally used that knife to shave with. He was as handy with it as he was with a pistol.

Frank reluctantly left the peaceful setting of the creek and the shade and rode on slowly toward the north. He did not have a specific destination in mind; he was just rambling.

Frank had worked the winter in a line shack, looking after a rancher's cattle in a section of the high country. He still had most of his winter's wages.

Frank did have a dream: a small spread of his own in a quiet little valley with good graze and water. He occasionally opened a picture book in his mind and gazed at the dream, but the mental pages were slightly torn and somewhat tattered now. The dream had never materialized. Twice Frank had come close to having that little spread. Both times his past had caught up with him, and the local citizens in the nearest town had frozen him out. Nobody wanted the West's most notorious gunfighter as a neighbor.

Frank let part of his mind wander some as he rode, the other part remained vigilant. For the most part, Indian trouble was just about all over, except for a few young bucks who occasionally broke from the reservations and caused trouble. Those incidents usually didn't last long, and almost always ended with a pile of dead Indians.

The Wild West was settling down, slowly but surely.

Bands of outlaws and brigands still roamed the West, though, robbing banks and rustling cattle.

In the northern part of New Mexico it was the gangs of Ned Pine and Victor Vanbergen that were causing most of the trouble. Frank Morgan knew both men, and they hated him. Both had been known to go into wild outbursts of anger at just the mention of his name.

Frank had, at separate times, backed each of the outlaw leaders down and made them eat crow in front of witnesses. They both were gutsy men, but they weren't stupid. Neither one was about to draw on Frank Morgan.

There were several names in the West that caused brave men to sit down and shut up. Smoke Jensen, Falcon MacCallister, Louis Longmont, and Frank Morgan were the top four still living.

Ned Pine and Victor Vanbergen had started their careers in crime when just young boys, and both had turned into vicious killers. Their gangs numbered about twenty men each—more from time to time, less at others—and they were not hesitant to tackle entire small towns in their wild and so far unstoppable pursuit of money and women . . . in that order.

Frank Morgan's life as a gunfighter had begun when he was in his midteen years and working as a hand on a ranch in Texas. One of the punchers had made Frank's life miserable for several months by bullying him whenever he got the chance . . . which was often. One day Frank got enough of the cowboy's crap and hit him flush in the face with a piece of a broken singletree. When the puncher was able to see again and the swelling in his nose had gone down some, he swore to kill the boy.

Young Frank Morgan, however, had other plans.

The puncher told Frank to get a gun 'cause the next time he saw him he was going to send him to his Maker.

Frank had an old piece of a pistol that he'd been practicing with when he got the money to buy ammunition. It was 1860, and times were hard, money scarce.

That day almost thirty years back was still vivid in Frank's mind.

He was so scared he had puked up his breakfast of grits and coffee.

Then he stepped out of the bunkhouse to meet his challenger, pistol in hand.

There was no fast draw involved in that duel. That would come a few years later.

The cowboy cursed at Frank and fired just as Frank stepped out of the bunkhouse, the bullet howling past Frank's head and knocking out a good-size splinter of wood from the rough doorframe. Frank damn near peed his underwear.

Young Frank acted out of pure instinct. Before the abusive puncher could fire again, Frank had lifted and cocked his pistol. He shot the puncher in the center of his chest. The man stumbled back as the .36-caliber chunk of lead tore into his flesh.

"You piece of turd!" the cowboy gasped, still on his boots. He lifted and cocked his pistol.

Frank shot him again, this time in the face, right between the eyes.

The puncher hit the hard ground, dead.

Frank walked over him and looked down at the dead man. The open empty eyes stared back at him. He struggled to fight back sickness, and managed to beat it. Frank turned away from the dead staring eyes.

"Luther had kin, boy," the foreman told him. "They'll be comin' to avenge him. You best get yourself set for that day. Make some plans."

"But I didn't start this!" Frank said. *"He* did." Frank pointed to the dead man.

"That don't make no difference, boy. I'll see you get your time, and a little extra."

"Am I leavin'?" Frank asked.

"If you want to stay alive, son. I know Luther had four brothers, and they're bad ones. They will come lookin' for you."

"They live close?"

"About a day's ride from here. And they got to be notified. So, you get your gear rolled up, son, and get ready to ride. I'll go see the boss."

"I'm right here," said the owner of the spread. "I was having my mornin' time in the privy." He paused for a moment and looked down at Luther. "Well, he was a good hand, but deep down just like his worthless brothers—no damn good." He looked at Frank. "You kill him, boy?"

"Yes, sir."

"Luther ain't gonna be missed by many. Only his sorry-assed brothers, I reckon. You got to go, boy. Sorry, but that's the way it has to be. For your sake. You get your personals together and then come over to the house. You got time comin', and I'll see you get some extra."

"I ain't even got a horse to call my own, Mr. Phillips," Frank said. "Or a saddle."

"You will," the rancher told him. "Get movin', son. I'll see you in a little while."

Frank rode out an hour later. He had his month's wages—twelve dollars—and twenty dollars extra Mr. Phillips gave him. He still had twenty-five dollars he'd saved over his time at the ranch, too. Frank felt like he was sort of rich. He had a sack of food Mrs. Phillips had fixed for him. He was well-mounted, for the foreman had picked him out a fine horse and a good saddle and saddlebags.

The other hands had gathered around to wish him farewell.

"You done the world a favor, Frankie," one told him.

"I never did like that sorry bastard," another told him.

"Here you go, Frankie," another puncher said, holding out Luther's guns. "You throw away that old rust pot you been totin' around and take these. You earned 'em, and you'll probably damn shore need them."

"What do you mean, Tom?" Frank asked.

"Frankie . . . Luther was a bad one. He's killed four or five men that we know of with a pistol. He's got himself a reputation as a gunman. There'll be some who'll come lookin' to test you."

"Test me?"

"Call you out, boy," the foreman said. "You're the man who killed Luther Biggs. They'll be some lookin' to kill you. Stay ready."

"I don't want no reputation like that," Frank protested.

"Your druthers don't cut no ice now, boy. You got the name of a gunman. Now, like it or not, you got to live with it."

CHAPTER 2

Frank drifted for a couple of months, clear out of Texas and up into Oklahoma Territory. He hooked up with two more young men about his age, and they rode together. Their parents were dead, like Frank's, and they just plain hadn't wanted to stay with brothers or sisters . . . as was the case with Frank.

By then the story had spread about the shoot-out between young Morgan and Luther Biggs. Frank never talked about it; he just wanted to forget it. But he knew he probably would never be able to do that . . . not completely.

The War Between the States was only a few months away, the war talk getting hotter and hotter. One of the boys Frank was riding with believed in preserving the Union. Frank and the other boy were Southern born. If war did break out, they would fight for the South.

The trio of boys separated in Arkansas when they received word about the beginning of hostilities between the North and the South. Frank joined up with a group of young men who were riding off to enlist in the Confederate Army. He never knew what happened to the other two boys.

For the next four years Frank fought for the Southern cause and matured into a grown man. He became hardened to the horrors of war. At war's end, Frank Morgan was a captain in the Confederate Army, commanding a company of cavalry.

Rather than turn in his weapons, Frank headed west. During that time he had been experimenting with faster ways to get a pistol out of the holster. He had a special holster made for him at a leather shop in southern Missouri: the holster was open, without a flap, and a leather thong slipped over the hammer prevented the pistol from falling out when he was riding or doing physical activities on foot. Frank practiced pulling the pistol out of leather; he worked at it for at least an hour each day, drawing and cocking and dry firing the weapon. The first time he tried the fast draw using live ammunition, he almost shot himself in the foot. He practiced with much more care after that, figuring that staying in the saddle with just one foot in the stirrup might be a tad difficult.

By the time Frank reached Colorado, his draw was perfected. He could draw—and fire—with amazing accuracy, and with blinding speed.

And that was where his lasting reputation was carved in stone. He met up with the Biggs brothers—all four of them.

He was provisioning up in southeastern Colorado when he heard someone call out his name. He turned to look at one of the ugliest men he had ever seen: the spitting image of Luther Biggs.

"I reckon you'd be one of the Biggs brothers," Frank said, placing his gunny sack of supplies on the counter.

"Yore damn right I am. And you're Frank Morgan. Me and my brothers been trailin' you for weeks."

"I got the feelin' somebody was doggin' my back trail. Never could catch sight of you."

"Our older brother, Billy Jeff, run acrost a man who knowed you. I disremember his name. That don't matter. He said you come out of the war all right and was headin' up to the northwest. Tole us what kind of hoss you was ridin', and what you looked like now that you was all growed up. But here and now is where your growin' stops, Morgan."

"Take it outside, boys," the store owner said. "Don't shoot up my place. Gettin' supplies out here is hard enough without this crap."

"Shet up, ribbon clerk," Biggs said. Then his eyes widened when the store owner lifted a double-barreled shotgun and eared both hammers back.

"I said take it outside!"

"Now don't git all goosey, mister," Biggs said. "We'll take it outside."

"You do that."

"You comin', Morgan, or does yeller smell? I think I smell yeller all over you."

"Don't worry about me, Ugly Biggs. You go run along now and get with your brothers, since it appears that none of you have the courage to face me alone."

The storekeeper got himself a good chuckle out of that, and a very dirty look from Biggs.

"Don't you fret none about that, Morgan. I'd take you apart with my bare hands right now, 'ceptin' that would displease my brothers. They want a piece of you, too. And what is this ugly crap?"

"You, Ugly. You're so damn ugly you could make a living frightening little children."

The veins in Biggs's neck bulged in scarcely controlled anger. He cursed, balled his fists, and took a step toward Morgan.

The store owner said, "I'll spread you all over the front part of this store, mister. Now back out of here."

"I'll be right behind you, Ugly," Morgan told him.

Cursing, Biggs backed out of the store and walked across the street to the saloon.

"You want to head out the back and get clear of town, mister?" the store owner asked.

"I would if I thought that would do any good," Frank replied. "But you can bet they've got the back covered."

"You can't fight them all!"

"I don't see that I've got a choice in the matter." Frank patted the sack of supplies on the counter. "I'll be back for these."

"If you say so."

"I say so." Frank looked at the shotgun the shopkeeper was holding.

The man smiled and handed it across the counter. "Take it, mister. I don't know you, but I sure don't like that fellow who was bracin' you."

"Thanks. I'll return it in good shape." Frank stepped to the front door, paused, and then turned around and headed toward the rear of the store. The shopkeeper walked around the counter and closed and locked the front door, hanging up the closed sign.

At the closed back door Frank paused, took a deep breath, and then flung open the door and jumped out, leaping to one side just as soon as his boots hit the ground. A rifle blasted from the open door of the outhouse, and Frank gave the comfort station both barrels of the Greener.

The double blast of buckshot almost tore the shooter in two. The Biggs brother took both loads in the belly and chest and the bloody, suddenly dead mess fell forward, out of the outhouse and into the dirt.

Suddenly, another Biggs brother came into view—a part of him, at least: his big butt.

That's where Frank shot him, the bullet passing through both cheeks of his rear end.

"Oh, Lordy!" he squalled. "I'm hit, boys."

"Where you hit, Bobby?"

"In the ass. My ass is on far, boys. It hurts!"

"In the ass?" another brother yelled. "That ain't dignified."

"The hell with dignified!" Bobby shouted. "I'm ahurtin', boys!"

"Hang on, Bobby," a brother called. "We'll git Morgan and then come to your aid."

"Kill that no-count, Billy Jeff!" Bobby groaned. "Oh, Lord, my ass end burns somethang fierce!"

"Can you see him, Wilson?" Billy Jeff called.

"No. But he's down yonder crost the street from the livery. I know that."

"I know that better than you do," Bobby yelled. "I got the lead in my ass to prove it! Ohhh, I ain't had sich agony in all my borned days."

Some citizen started laughing, and soon others in the tiny town joined in.

"You think this is funny?" Wilson Biggs yelled. "Damn you all to the hellfars!"

Morgan had changed positions again, running back up past the outhouse and the mangled body of Wells Biggs. He was now right across the wide street from Wilson Biggs.

He had picked up the guns from Wells and shoved them behind his gunbelt. He holstered his own pistol and, using the guns taken from the dead man, he emptied them into the shed where Wilson was hiding. The bullets tore through the old wood, knocking great holes in the planks.

Wilson staggered out, his chest and belly bloodsoaked. The Biggs brother took a couple of unsteady steps and fell forward, landing on his face in the dirt. He did not move.

"Wilson!" Billy Jeff shouted. "Did you get him, Wilson?"

"No, he didn't," Frank called. "Your brother's dead."

"Damn you!" Billy Jeff called. "Step out into the street and face me, you sorry son."

"And have your butt-shot brother shoot me?" Frank yelled. "I think not."

"Bobby!" Billy Jeff called. "You hold your far and let me settle this here affair. You hear me, boy?"

"I hear you, Billy Jeff. You shore you want it thisaway?"

"I'm shore. You hear all that, Morgan?"

"I hear it, but I don't believe it. You Biggs boys are all a pack of liars. Why should I trust you?"

"Damn you, Morgan, I give my word. I don't go back on my word, not never."

"Step out then, Billy Jeff."

"I'm a-comin' out, Morgan. My gun's holstered. Is yourn?"

Before Frank could reply, Bobby said, "I'm a-comin' out, too. Let's see if he's got the courage to face the both of us!"

"Bring your bleeding butt on, Biggs!" Frank yelled. "If all your courage hasn't leaked out of your ass, that is." He checked to see his own pistol was loaded up full, then slipped it into leather, working it in and out several times to insure a smooth draw.

Bobby was hollering and cussing Frank, scarcely pausing for breath.

Frank walked up to the mouth of the alley and stepped out to the edge of the street.

Bobby stopped cussing.

Billy Jeff said, "Step out into the center of the street, Morgan, and face the men who is about to kill you."

"Not likely, Biggs. The only way scum like you could kill me is by ambush."

That started Bobby cussing again. He paused every few seconds to moan and groan about his wounded ass.

The residents of the tiny town had gathered along the edge of the street to watch the fight. Some had fixed sandwiches; others had a handful of crackers or a pickle.

This was exciting. Not much ever happened in the tiny village, which as yet had no official name.

"Make your play, Biggs!" Frank called.

Billy Jeff fumbled at his gun and Frank let him clear

leather before he pulled and fired, all in one very smooth, clean movement. The bullet struck Billy Jeff in the belly and knocked him down in the dirt. Frank holstered and waited. He smiled at Bobby Biggs.

Bobby was yelling and groping for his pistol, which was stuck behind his wide belt. Frank drew and shot him in the chest, and forever ended his moaning and griping about his butt. Bobby stretched out on the street and was still. The bullet had shattered his heart.

Frank never knew what made him do it, but on that day he twirled his pistol a couple of times before sliding it back into leather. He did it smoothly, effortlessly, and with a certain amount of flair.

A young boy in the crowd exclaimed, "Mommy, did you see that? Golly!"

"I never seen no one jerk a pistol like that," a man said to a friend.

"He sure got it out in a hurry," his friend replied. "And a damned fancy way of holstering that thing, too."

Frank was certainly not the first to utilize a fast draw, but he was one of the first, along with Jamie MacCallister and an East Texas gunhand whose name has been lost to history.

Frank looked over at the crowd to his left. "This town got an undertaker?"

"No," a man said. "We ain't even got a minister or a schoolmarm."

"We just get the bodies in the ground as soon as we can," another citizen said. "Unless it's wintertime. Then we put 'em in a shed where they'll freeze and keep pretty well 'til the ground thaws and we can dig a hole."

"They ain't real pretty to look at after a time, but they don't smell too bad," his friend said.

"If you don't stay around 'em too long," another man added.

"You can have their gear and guns for burying these

men," Frank told the crowd. "And whatever money they have. Deal?"

"Deal," a man said. "Sounds pretty good to me. They had some fine horses. The horses is included, right?"

"Sure."

"I hope they ain't stolen," a townsman said. "Say, I heard them call you Morgan—you got a first name?"

"Frank."

"You just passin' though, Frank?" There was a rather hopeful sound to the question.

"Just stopping in town long enough to pick up a few supplies," Frank assured the crowd.

"All right. Well, I reckon we'd better get these bodies gathered up and planted."

"I'll help," a citizen volunteered.

"I'll get their horses," another said. "I got a bad back, you know—can't handle no shovel."

"Sure you do, Otis. Right."

Frank turned and walked away, back to the store to get his supplies and to return the shotgun to the man.

"Hell of a show out there, Mr. Morgan," the shopkeeper told him.

"Not one that I wanted the leading role in, though."

"I suppose not. Where do you go from here?"

"Just drifting."

"Back from the war?"

"Yes." Frank smiled. "My side lost."

"We all lost in that mess."

"I reckon so. Thanks, mister."

"Take care, Mr. Morgan."

Frank rode out, heading toward the northwest, his growing reputation right behind him. . . .

CHAPTER 3

Frank rode on toward the north and tried to put old memories behind him. But there were too many memories, too many bloody shoot-outs, too many killings, too many easy women with powder and paint on their faces and shrill laughter that Frank could still hear in his dreams.

And of course, there was that one special woman.

Her name was Vivian. Frank had met her in the town of Denver early in '66, and had been taken by her charm and beauty. Frank was a very handsome young man, and Viv had been equally smitten by him. She was the daughter of a businessman and lay preacher.

Frank was working at the time on a ranch in the area, and doing his best to stay out of any gun trouble.

Theirs was a whirlwind courtship, and they were married just a few months after meeting. Viv's father did not like Frank, and he made no attempt to hide that dislike. But after the wedding, Frank felt there was little Viv's father could do except try to make the best of it.

Frank was wrong.

Six months after their marriage, Frank found himself facing a drifter hunting trouble.

"I heard about you, Morgan," the drifter said. "And I think it's all poppycock and balderdash."

"Think what you want to think," Frank told him. "I have no quarrel with you."

"You do now."

There were no witnesses to the affair. The drifter had braced Frank on a lonesome stretch of range miles from town. Frank had been resting after a morning of brush-popping cattle out of a huge thicket. He was tired, and so was his horse.

"How'd you know I was working out here?" Frank asked.

"I heard in town. I asked about you."

"No one in town knew."

"You callin' me a liar?"

"This isn't adding up, friend."

"I ain't your friend, Morgan. I come to kill you, and that's what I aim to do."

"Who paid you to brace me?"

The drifter smiled. "You better make your mind up to stand and deliver, Morgan. 'Cause if you don't, I'm gonna gut-shoot you and leave you out here so's the crows and buzzards can eat your eyes."

"That isn't going to happen, friend. Now back off and ride out of here."

"I keep tellin' you, Morgan, I ain't your friend."

"Tell me who paid you to do this madness."

The drifter smiled. "On the count of three, you better hook and draw, Morgan. One—"

"Don't do this, friend."

"Two—"

"I don't want to kill you!"

"Three!"

The drifter never even cleared leather. As his hand dropped and curled around the butt of his pistol, Frank's Colt roared under the hot summer sun. The drifter's mouth dropped open in a grotesque grimace of pain and surprise as Frank's bullet ripped into his chest. He dropped his pistol and stared at Frank for a couple of seconds, then slumped to his knees.

Frank walked the few paces to stand over the dying man. "Who paid you to do this?"

"Damn, but you're quick," the drifter gasped. "I heard you was mighty fast, but I just didn't believe it."

"Who paid you?" Frank persisted, hoping the name would not be the one he suspected.

But it was.

"Henson," the drifter said. "Preacher Henson." Then he fell over on his face in the dust.

Vivian's father.

Frank turned the man over. He was still breathing. "How much did he pay you to brace me?"

"Five hundred dollars," the drifter gasped. Then his eyes began losing their brightness.

"You have the money on you?"

"Half of it. Get . . . the other half . . . when you're dead." The drifter's head lolled to one side.

"Talk to me, damn you!"

But the drifter was past speaking. He was dead.

"Dear father-in-law," Frank whispered, rage and disgust filling him. "I knew you disliked me, but I didn't know your hatred was so intense."

Frank went through the drifter's pockets and then loaded the man's body across his saddle and lashed him down. Leading the skittish horse—who didn't like the smell of blood—Frank rode into the nearest town and up to the marshal's office. The much smaller town was miles closer than the fast-growing town of Denver.

Frank explained what had happened, sort of—leaving out who hired the drifter, and why.

"Any reason why this man would want to kill you, Morgan?"

"No. I don't have any idea. I've never seen him before. As you can tell by looking at me, and smelling me, I suppose, I've been working cattle most of the day."

The marshal smiled. "Now that you mention it . . ." He laughed. "All right, Morgan. Did you go through the man's pockets?"

"Yes, I did. Trying to find some identification. I didn't find any papers, but he had fifty dollars on him. The money is in his front pants pocket."

Frank had taken two hundred and left fifty to bury the drifter and to throw off suspicion.

The marshal did not question Frank further on the shooting. "We'll get him planted, Frank. Thanks for bringing in the body. Most people would have just left him."

Frank rode back home, arriving late that night. He did not tell Viv about the shooting—how could he? She wouldn't have believed him. He spent a restless night, wondering how to best handle the wild hate her father felt for him.

The next day he went to see his father-in-law. Frank tossed the two hundred dollars on the man's desk.

"There's your blood money, Henson. I left fifty dollars in the man's pockets to bury him."

The successful businessman/lay preacher looked up from his desk. Frank had never seen such hatred in a man's eyes. "You filth!" Henson said. "Worthless gunman. Oh, I know all about you, Morgan. You're a killer for hire."

"That's a lie, Mr. Henson. I've killed men, yes. I won't deny that. But it was in self-defense. Not for hire."

"You're a liar!" Henson hissed. "And you're not worthy to even walk on the same side of the street as my daughter. You're a hired killer, a gunman. You're filth, and always will be."

Frank stared at the man in silence for a moment. "I'm going to prove you wrong, Mr. Henson."

"No, you won't. You can't. I've had detectives tracing

you all the way back to your miserable, hardscrabble beginnings, you white trash. And I know all about the rape charges that were brought against you in Texas."

"Rape!" Frank blurted. "What charges? There are no rape charges—there have never been any."

Henson smiled cruelly at Morgan. His eyes glinted with malevolence. "There will be when my men get through doing their reports."

Frank got it then. Viv's father was paying detectives to write false reports. He was speechless.

"Leave," Henson urged. "Leave on your own, and I won't use those reports against you. I give you my word on that. Just saddle up and ride away."

"Leave? Vivian is my wife. I love her."

"Love!" Henson's word was filled with scorn. "You don't know the meaning of the word. You're a damned rake! That's all you've ever been. I'll destroy your marriage, Morgan. I will make it my life's work. I promise you that."

Frank started to speak, and Henson held up his hand. "Don't bother begging, you trash. It won't do you a bit of good. Leave. Get out. Get out of my office, get out of my daughter's life, and get out of town." He smiled. "Before my detectives return and I have the sheriff place you under arrest."

"I'll tell Viv about this," Frank managed to say.

"Go right ahead. I'll just tell her I knew all about it and was trying to protect her. See who she will believe. Me, naturally."

"I can beat the charges."

"No, you can't. I'll see you tried, convicted, and carried away in chains, just like the wild animal you are. My detectives have found, ah, shall we call them 'ladies,' who will testify against you. And they will be believed."

Frank was boxed, and knew it. Henson had wealth and power and position, and could very easily destroy him. He sighed and said, "All right. But I have to know Vivian will be taken care of."

"Of course she will be. I'll see to that personally. She'll never want for anything. You're making a very wise decision, Morgan. Do you need money? A sum within reason, of course."

"I wouldn't take a goddamn dime from you, you sorry-assed, mealymouthed, self-righteous, sanctimonious son of a bitch!"

"Get out!" Henson flared. "Get out of town right now. Don't go home. Don't see Vivian. Just get on your horse and ride out of here. For Vivian's sake, if not for your own."

Frank almost lost it. He balled his big hard hands into fists, and came very close to tearing his father-in-law's head off his shoulders. Henson saw what was about to happen, and paled in fright. But at the last possible second Frank backed off.

Frank turned and walked out of the office.

Henson looked down at his trembling hands, willing them to cease their shaking. After a moment, he rose from his chair and got his hat. He just had time to go get his daughter and escort her to the doctor's office.

Vivian Morgan was pregnant.

"Come on," Frank muttered as he rode north. "Put the memories away and close that old door."

But that was not an easy thing to do. Even though it had been some twenty years since he had pulled out of Denver, twenty years since he had last seen Vivian, the memories were still very strong, and the image of her face was forever burned into his brain.

Frank had heard little bits of gossip about Henson: the man had become a millionaire through land deals in and around Denver, and a powerful voice in his church. He had sent his daughter, Vivian, back east to live with family. She had gotten married there (somehow her father had had her marriage to Frank annulled). She had a child by her second husband.

She and her husband had returned to Denver to take over her father's business when Henson's health began to fail. By that time, Frank had learned, the boy was in college somewhere back east.

Occasionally Frank ran across a weeks- or months-old Denver newspaper and read it. Sometimes there was something in there about Vivian Browning, and Frank would wonder what she looked like now, and for a time he would be lost in "what ifs?"

"Crap!" Frank muttered as he made camp for the evening in the timber of the Sangre de Cristos, east and a little north of Santa Fe. "Put it out of your mind, Morgan. Put her out of your mind. She hasn't thought about you in years."

But as many times as Frank thought that, he always wondered if it was true.

He certainly had never forgotten her.

Frank filled the coffeepot with water and set it on the fire to boil. He settled back with a book. Frank always made camp with at least an hour of daylight left him, so he could read. He was a well-read and self-educated man. There were always a couple of books in his saddlebags—history, government, sometimes poetry.

On this day he dug out a book by John Milton. He had bought the book weeks back from a traveling salesman. And while he would be the first to admit that sometimes he didn't know what the hell Milton was talking about, he nevertheless enjoyed his writings. Frank read for a time from something titled *Paradise Lost.* But he was not so engrossed that he did not know what was happening around him: the birds that had been singing so gaily had stopped, and the squirrels that had been chattering were silent. Frank put his hand on the stock of his rifle and pulled it close to him. Whenever he made camp for the night, he levered a round into the chamber of his rifle. All he had to do was ear back the hammer and let 'er bang.

"Easy, friend." The voice came out of the timber. "I don't mean no harm."

"Then why are you trying to slip up on me?"

" 'Cause I know who you are, and how quick you are on the shoot—that's why."

Frank smiled. "Fair enough. Come on into the camp."

"Let me get my horses—all right?"

"Bring them in."

The man looked to be in his sixties. He carried a rifle and wore a pistol at his side. He carefully propped his rifle against a tree and then saw to his animals. He joined Frank by the small campfire.

"If you ain't got no coffee, I got some in my gear."

"I have coffee. Waiting for the water to boil. What's on your mind?"

"Company for the evenin', that's all. If you don't mind."

"Not at all. I'm Frank Morgan."

"Jess McCready. I know who you are."

The water was boiling and Frank dumped in the coffee. "Be ready in a minute, Jess. What are you doing out here in the big lonesome?"

"Gettin' away from people, mostly." The older man sniffed at the heady aroma of coffee brewing and smiled. "I do like my coffee, Mr. Morgan."

"Frank. Just Frank."

"Thankee. Frank it is."

"Getting a little bit crowded for you, Jess?"

"A little bit?" The older man snorted derisively. "The territory is fillin' up. Towns sproutin' up ever'where you look. It's disgustin'."

Frank smiled and dumped in some cold water to settle the grounds. "I have noticed a few more people, for a fact." He got up and dug another cup out of his pack, then rummaged around and found the bacon and flour. "Stay for bacon and pan bread, Jess?"

"Oh, you betcha, I will. I got some taters we can fry up, and a couple cans of peaches in my gear. I'll fetch them, and we'll have us a regular feast."

"Sounds good to me."

Frank watched the man out of the corner of his eye as he got the peaches and potatoes. He made no suspicious moves and sat back down and started peeling the potatoes.

Jess grinned and held up an onion. "We'll slice this up and stick it with the taters. Gives 'em a good flavor."

"Sure does. I forgot to get me some onions when I provisioned up last stop."

"Frank, I ain't tryin' to meddle in your business. Believe me, I ain't. But are you by any chance headin' up toward Barnwell's Crossin'?"

Frank stopped his slicing of bacon to look at the man. "I never heard of that place."

"Well, it's called the Crossin', usually."

"Still never heard of it. What about it?"

"There was a silver strike there 'bout three years ago. Big one. Millions of dollars was taken out of them mines. But it was short-lived. Mines are about played out now."

"So? I've never mined for gold or silver."

"Ned Pine and Vic Vanbergen drift in and out of there from time to time."

That got Frank's attention. "Well, I see. You know about the bad feeling between Ned and Vic and me, eh?"

"Yep. I was there that time you made Vic back down. I know he's swore to kill you. And so has Ned."

"Those are old threats, Jess."

"But still holdin' true, Frank. Point is, one of the big company mines hit another strike. Got tons of damn near pure silver out and melted down. They're waitin' to transport the bars out. And the Pine and Vanbergen gangs are waitin' for them to try it."

"Why don't they hire some people to guard the shipment?"

"Don't nobody want the job. Ned and Vic done passed the word."

"I still don't see what that has to do with me, Jess."

"Well, I'll tell you. The minin' company is the Henson Mine Corporation. It's owned by Mrs. Vivian Browning. Old man Henson's daughter."

CHAPTER 4

The next morning, Jess headed south and Frank headed north, toward Barnwell's Crossing. When Frank questioned the older man, Jess told him he had learned about Frank's marriage years back, from a pal of his who had worked for a man in Denver who knew Henson. Henson, Jess said, had not been well-liked. He was ruthless in his business dealings, and few had mourned his passing some years back.

Jess had told him that Barnwell's Crossing was a dying town, although it still had a couple of hundred people eking out a living there. The silver was just about all played out.

Frank didn't know how he would handle matters once he got to the Crossing. He sure didn't know how he would react if he came face-to-face with Vivian. He wondered if Vivian had told her husband about him.

Probably. Frank felt that a marriage built on a lie would not last.

Jess had given him directions on how to get to Barnwell's Crossing. After listening to the twisted route, Frank had commented that it sure seemed to be in a very isolated section of the territory . . . not in an area that he was at all familiar with.

"Wait until you get there," Jess had said. "You'll think you've fallen off the earth into hell."

"That bad, eh?"

"Worser. One way in, one way out"

"A perfect setting for Pine and Vanbergen."

"You betcha."

After a week of hard riding after leaving the company of Jess McCready, Frank reached a narrow, twisty road that led off into the mountains. Miles later, at a crossroads, he saw a crossing sign. A crudely painted arrow pointed off toward the west. The road was literally cut out of the mountains in some spots, and some of the drop-offs were hundreds of feet, straight down.

Frank remembered some long-ago campfire talk about the town as he rode. He had forgotten it until now. The town had been established some thirty-five years back; Frank couldn't recall the original name. The Apaches had raided the tiny town and burned it to the ground. It had been rebuilt, and the Apaches had raided and burned it once more. It had sprung to life again, Frank guessed, when silver had been found.

Frank had no idea where the name Barnwell came from, unless it belonged to the man who hit the latest strike of silver.

After he rode for several miles on the twisty road the town came into view. A dozen or so stores had not been closed and boarded up: a hotel, a large general store, a saloon, a doctor's office, a barbershop/undertaker's, a livery, and several other false-front stores. On all sides of the town the hillsides were dotted with mine entrances and narrow roads, all leading down to the town and the mill. Frank stared at the mill for a moment. It was still operating.

Frank rode into town, looking at the homes on either side as he rode. Some were very nice. Others were no more than shacks, thrown together. There were tents of varying sizes scattered among the houses and shacks.

No one paid the lone rider the slightest bit of attention as he rode slowly up to the livery and swung wearily down from the saddle. He wanted a hot bath, a shave and a haircut, and some clean clothing; his shirt and jeans were stiff with the dust and dirt from days of traveling.

"Take care of my horses," Frank told the young man, handing him some money.

"Yes, sir. Rub them down, curry, and feed?"

"Yes." Frank looked across the street. The livery was the last still operating business at this end of town. The reasonably nice houses across the street looked empty. "Any of those houses over there for rent?"

"All of them. See Mr. Willis at the general store, and he'll fix you up." The young man pointed. "That one is the best. It's got a brand-new privy just a few steps out back, and the man who just left installed a new hand pump right in the kitchen. It's nice."

Frank thanked the young man. "My gear be safe here, boy?"

"For a dollar, yeah. I can lock it up."

Frank smiled and gave him a couple of coins. "See that it is."

"You bet, sir. I'll do it. What's your name?"

Frank hesitated and then said, "Logan."

"Yes, sir, Mr. Logan."

Frank walked up to the general store and made arrangements to rent the house for a time, after making sure the place had a bed and a cookstove. While at the store, Frank bought some new clothes: underwear, socks, britches, shirts, and a suit coat that fit him reasonably well. He took his new purchases and walked over to the barber shop. There, he had a hot bath and a shave and a haircut while his old clothes were being washed and his new clothes pressed to get the wrinkles and creases out. He also had his hat blocked as best the man could do it.

Feeling like a new man, having washed away days of dirt and probably a few fleas, Frank walked the town's business district. The marshal's office was closed and locked, and showed signs of having been that way for a long time.

"Haven't had a marshal for several months now," said a man passing by. "Can't keep one."

"Why?" Frank asked.

"They get shot," the miner said, and walked on.

"That's one way to get rid of the law," Frank muttered, and walked on.

Frank stepped into the small apothecary shop and asked if there was anything new in the way of headache powders.

"You got a headache, mister?"

"No," Frank said with a smile. "But I might get one."

"We don't have anything new here. But I hear there is something being developed over in Germany. Supposed to be some sort of wonder."

"Oh. What's it called?"

"Don't know. Big secret. Being developed by the Bayer Drug Company. It'll be available in a few years, so I'm told.* I got some laudanum, if you want it."

"Maybe later," Frank said. "Thanks."

Frank walked on down the street, stepping carefully along the warped old boardwalk that still showed signs of the times when the town had been destroyed by fire. He came to a café called the Silver Spoon and went inside for a bite.

Frank had the Blue Plate Special: beef and beans and a piece of pie. He lingered at the table for a few minutes, enjoying a pretty good cup of coffee and a cigarette, watching the people in the small town as they went about their business.

"You working a claim here?" the cook asked, coming out

*Aspirin went on sale in 1899.

to lean on the counter. There was only a handful of people in the café, for it was not yet time for the supper crowd.

"No," Frank replied. "Just passing through."

"You sure look familiar to me. I know you from somewheres?"

"Could be."

Frank was sitting at a corner table, bis back to a wall, as was his custom. He had a good view of much of the street and everyone in the café.

A woman came up and whispered in the cook's ear. The cook's mouth dropped open, and his eyes bugged out for a few seconds. He stared at Frank for a couple of heartbeats. "Good God! It really is him!" the cook blurted, then beat it back to the kitchen.

The woman—Frank assumed she was the waitress-—looked over at him and smiled. "Remember me, Frank?"

"Can't say as I do. You want to hotten up this coffee, please?"

"Sure." The woman brought the pot over and filled his cup, then sat down uninvited across the table from Frank.

"I was married to Jim Peters," the woman said softly.

Frank paused in his sugaring and stirring. His eyes narrowed briefly; then he nodded his head. "I recall Jim Peters. He tried to back-shoot me up in Kansas."

"That's him," the woman said with a sigh. "Coward right to the end. I left him a couple of years before that shooting. Moved to Dodge. He followed me. I still wouldn't have anything to do with him. You did me a favor by killing him."

Frank sipped his coffee and waited, sensing the woman was not finished.

"That was five years ago, Frank. But the man who offered up five thousand dollars to see you dead is still alive, and the money is still up for your death—to anyone that's brave enough to go for it."

Frank set his cup down on the table. "I never knew anything about any five thousand dollars on my head."

The woman studied Frank's face for a moment. "You really don't know, do you?"

"No."

"He's a lawyer. Works for the Henson Enterprises."

"They own a mine here in Crossing."

"The biggest mine, Frank. No telling how many millions of dollars of silver was taken out of that mine. One more shipment to go, and the mine closes."

"But they can't ship it because of the Pine and Vanbergen gangs, right?"

"That's right, Frank. And then here you come riding in, getting set to get all tangled up in something that doesn't really concern you."

"It's a long story, Miss . . . ah—"

"It's still Peters. We were never divorced. And please call me Angie."

"All right, Angie it is. And I assure you, it does concern me, greatly."

Angie shook her head. "Because of Mrs. Vivian L. Browning, Frank?"

"You know a lot, Angie. The question is, why?"

"Why do I know? I've owned cafés all over the West. People talk in cafés as much or more as they do in saloons." She smiled. "And I am a real good listener."

"I bet you are." Frank returned the smile as he studied the woman. A good-looking woman. Not beautiful, but very, very attractive. Black hair, blue eyes, and a head-turning figure. Frank bet that when Angie took a stroll men looked . . . and wives got mad.

"How many men do Pine and Vanbergen have?"

"No one knows for sure. Thirty or forty at least. Probably more than that."

"Do any of them ever come into town?"

"Quite often. But never Pine or Vanbergen. The men who come in for supplies are not on any wanted list . . . that anyone knows about." Angie looked out the café window.

"Frank, there are two members of the gang riding into town now."

Frank followed her eyes, watching as two rough-dressed men rode slowly up the main street. "I know them," he said. "They're related somehow. Cousins, I think. Both of them are wanted in Arkansas on murder charges. If this town had a marshal he'd be a thousand dollars richer by arresting those two."

Frank smiled and pushed back his chair. "As a matter of fact, I could use a thousand dollars right now."

"Frank . . ." Angie's voice held a warning note. "This isn't your fight. Don't get mixed up in this mess."

"Watch me," Frank replied, slipping the leather thong off the hammer of his pistol.

CHAPTER 5

Frank stepped out of the café and stood for a moment on the elevated boardwalk. It was built several feet off the ground due to a slope. The two riders stopped in front of the Silver Slipper Saloon and dismounted. They stood for a moment, giving the wide street the once-over. Their eyes lingered for a moment on Frank, and one said something to the other. The second man shook his head, and the pair of outlaws turned and walked into the saloon, apparently dismissing him as being someone who presented no danger to them.

Frank slipped the hammer thong free and walked across the street, his boots kicking up dust as he walked, his spurs rattling softly. He stepped up onto the old boardwalk and stood for a moment, thinking about his next move. He had some money on him, but he could also use a thousand dollars.

Frank was not a poor man by any means, but neither did he have money to throw around. He had some savings in a couple of Wells Fargo offices which were available to him by wire. He also had money sewn into a place behind the cantle of his saddle.

Frank was no stranger to bounty hunting. He'd done his share of tracking down wanted men for the prices on their heads. He did it only when he needed the money. The men he tracked down were always wanted for murder, and it nearly always ended in a shoot-out, for most of them would rather die from a bullet than dangle from the end of a rope with a crowd of gawkers looking on. Then Frank had to tote their stinking bodies back as proof, so he could collect the reward. It could be very unpleasant . . . and smelly.

Frank had been a lawman more than once. It was a job he liked. He'd carried a badge in towns in Kansas, Texas, and several other places. But once he'd cleaned up the towns, seems like the "good" people no longer wanted him around. Frank never argued about it—just collected what money was due him, packed up, saddled up, and rode away without looking back. He understood how they felt, and harbored no malice toward any of them. It was human nature, and Frank understood that well. Frank had done a lot of riding away without looking back in his life—most of his life, as a matter of fact.

Frank stepped up to the batwings and pushed them open, stepping inside the saloon.

The two outlaws were at the far end of the long bar, having whiskies. They did not turn around to look at Frank as he walked in. For that time of day the saloon was doing a good business. About half the tables were filled with drinkers and card players. The young man from the livery was seated at a table with several older men. Several heavily painted, rouged, and powdered-up soiled doves were working the crowd—without a lot of luck, Frank observed.

Frank walked to the bar and ordered a beer. He would have preferred coffee, but wanted to blend in for a few minutes without drawing undue attention to himself.

The talk was mostly about the mines playing out, the town slowly dying, and all the silver that was waiting to be shipped out. Frank could catch a few words here and there as he stood at the bar and sipped his beer.

Suddenly the talk died out, and the large room became silent. Frank sighed. He knew what had probably happened: somebody had recognized him.

"Hell," a man said, his voice unnaturally loud in the silence, "his name ain't Logan. I don't give a damn what he told you, Booker. That's Frank Morgan!"

Booker must be the young man from the livery, Frank thought. *Well, it's all out in the open now.*

The two outlaws at the far end of the bar turned to stare. Frank ignored them.

"Well, well," one of the outlaws said. "If it ain't the man all them books was writ about. I thought you had done up and died of old age, Morgan."

"Not hardly," Frank said softly, struggling to remember the man's name. Then it came to him: Davy something-or-another. Jonas was the other fellow's name. They were cousins.

"I know some folks who will be awful happy to hear you're in town, Morgan," Jonas said. He grinned, exposing a row of yellow teeth.

"I imagine so, Jonas. But how are you going to get the news to them?"

"Huh? Why I'll just ride out of here, you dummy!"

"You'll have to go through me to do that. You feel up to that?"

"They's two of us, Morgan," Davy said.

"I can count, Davy," Morgan replied, lifting the mug of beer with his left hand. His right hand stayed close to the butt of his .45. "But I don't care if there's five of you. You still won't get past me."

The men seated at the nearest tables began pushing their chairs back, getting away from what they were sure would turn into gunplay any second.

"You got no call to do this, Morgan," Jonas said. "We ain't done nothin' to you."

"Not personally, Jonas. But you both offend me."

"We both does what?" Davy asked, quickly adding, "What the hell does that mean?"

"You offend a lot of people, Davy. And you both are wanted by the law for murder."

"That's a damn lie!" Jonas said.

"No, it isn't, boys. I've seen the dodgers on you."

Davy's right hand started moving slowly toward the butt of his pistol. Frank's voice stopped him.

"Don't do it, Davy. I'll kill you where you stand."

Davy put his hand back on the bar.

Without taking his eyes off the two outlaws, Frank raised his voice and said, "One of you men go get the keys to the jail. Right now! Move!"

Several men rose from their chairs and left the saloon.

"What do you aim to do with us, Morgan?" Jonas asked.

"Put you in jail."

"Mayhaps we don't want to go to jail," Davy said. "What then?"

"Then I'll kill you," Frank replied, taking several steps closer to the pair of outlaws.

"You're just foolin' yourself, Morgan, if you think you're man enough to take both of us," Jonas told him.

Frank just smiled and moved closer.

"You stop right where you is!" Davy shouted. "We don't want no trouble, Morgan."

"That's up to you, boys," Frank said, stepping closer. "But if you don't want trouble, drop those gunbelts and stand easy."

"You go to hell, Morgan!" Jonas said, and he grabbed for his pistol.

Frank hit him with a fast, hard left, connecting squarely with the outlaw's jaw and dropping him to the floor.

Davy cussed wildly, then panicked and tried to run. Frank

tripped him as he attempted to push past, and he hit the floor. Frank jerked the outlaw's pistols from leather and, using one of them, popped Davy on the noggin, dropping him into dreamland for a few minutes.

Jonas was groaning and trying to get to his boots. Using Jonas's gun, Frank laid it against the man's head, and Jonas joined his partner, unconscious.

Frank took Jonas's gun from leather and laid all three pistols on the bar. The batwings were shoved open, and the men who had hustled from the bar reentered, one of them carrying several sets of handcuffs.

"The jail's unlocked, Mr. Morgan," one of the men said, placing the cuffs on the bar. "The keys to the cells are on the desk."

"And the mayor's on the way to talk to you," another citizen added.

"What's he want?" Frank asked, bending down and fitting the cuffs on the outlaws.

"Durned if I know. But he'll be along any minute now."

"Name's Jenkins," another citizen said, looking down at the two murderers.

"He's president of the bank," the third man offered.

"Wonderful," Frank said. "We'll wait until these two yahoos can walk, then escort them to the jail. There's a telegraph office in this town, isn't there?"

"Oh, you bet, Mr. Morgan. If the wire's up, that is."

"It's up," a citizen called from the tables. "I seen Mrs. Browning send some wires this mornin'."

Vivian, Frank thought as something invisible and soft touched his heart. . . .

"And that damn brat son of hers was with her," the citizen added.

"Way he keeps that snooty nose of his stuck up in the air, he's gonna drown if he's caught out in a hard rain," another citizen said.

"Sort of an uppity young man, is he?" Frank asked.

"Uppity?" one of the men blurted. "Conrad thinks he's better than everyone."

"Conrad?" Frank questioned.

"Conrad Browning. Sixteen or seventeen years old, I'd say. Big kid. And doesn't treat his mother with the proper respect, neither."

Another man summed it up. "He's a turd."

Vivian's father must have had a hand in raising the boy, Frank thought.

"You know, Mr. Morgan," a citizen pointed out, "them outlaws is rumored to be part of the Pine and Vanbergen gangs?"

Frank shrugged. "I know both of those no-counts. Why hasn't the law around here done something about them?"

"For one thing, the law can't catch them. For another, nobody is willin' to step up and point the finger at any of them. They always wear masks and dusters when they're robbin' people. The third thing is, law is scarce in these parts. We ain't had a marshal here in this town for months."

"And the pay is real good, Mr. Morgan. I'm Will Moncrief, a member of the town council. The town may not have long to live as a silver boom town. Another two, three months, maybe. But while it does, we pay good money for a badge-toter. Why don't you take the job? You've wore a badge before."

"And I'm on the council, too," another citizen said. "You want the job, Mr. Morgan?"

"Maybe. But it'll take more than the two of you to OK me, won't it?"

"There's four of us on the council, and the mayor," Moncrief said. "And—"

The batwings were pushed open, interrupting Moncrief. A man stepped inside the saloon. "And I'm the mayor of Barnwell's Crossing," the neatly dressed man said. "Mayor Jenkins. What's going on here?"

The crowd hushed up, and all eyes turned toward Frank.

"These two hombres on the floor are wanted men, Mayor," Frank said. "They're both murderers. Rewards out for them. I want to hold them in your jail until they're picked up."

"Sounds all right to me," Jenkins said. "You took them without firing a shot?"

"Yes."

"I know you. Seen your picture. You're Frank Morgan."

"That's right. You have a problem with that, Mayor?"

"Oh, no. Not at all. You're not an outlaw. You've never been wanted anywhere for anything, as far as I know. And you've worn a badge a number of times, as I recall."

"Yes, I have."

"Want to wear another one?"

Frank paused dramatically, for effect. "If the money's right, yes."

"The money will be right—I can assure you of that."

"Let me lock these two no-counts up, and we'll talk about it, all right?"

Frank jerked the two members of the Pine and Vanbergen gangs to their feet and shoved them toward the batwings. He would send a wire to Arkansas just as soon as he locked the two down. What the state of Arkansas did after that was up to them.

Crossing the street, Davy said, "The boys will come in here and tear this town apart, Morgan. They won't let us be held for no hangin'."

"If Pine or Vanbergen and their gangs come riding into this town hell-for-leather, there's a good chance they'll be buried here."

"You say!" Jonas's words were filled with contempt.

"That's right, Rat Face. I say."

"Rat Face!"

"Yeah. You look like a rat to me."

"You go to hell, Morgan!"

Frank laughed and opened the jail office door. He shoved the pair inside and over to the door that led to the cell block.

He carefully removed the cuffs from each and shoved them into a cell.

"I'll find blankets for both of you before night. And I'll build a fire in the stove that'll get the place warm before I leave."

"How about some food, you bastard?" Davy asked. "Or are you gonna let us starve to death?"

"You'll be fed. Probably from the Silver Spoon Café. The cook over there fixes good meals."

Frank took the time to inspect the jail. It was as solid as the rock it was made of—shaped rock two or three feet thick. The bars were thick and solid, set deep in the rocks. Davy and Jonas would not be prying or digging out. That was a dead certainty.

Frank found a rag, sat down at the battered desk in the front office, and wiped the several months' accumulation of dust from the top of the desk. He looked around the big room. Several rifles and shotguns were in a wall rack. He would inspect and clean them later. Frank began opening the desk drawers. He found dozens of dodgers and laid them off to one side. Two pistols and several boxes of .45 ammunition. The jail log book. The last entry was a drunk and disorderly, dated several months back. He found an inkwell, empty, and several pens and pencils. That was it.

The front door opened and the mayor stepped in, followed by a group of men. Frank was introduced to the town council. He shook hands, sat back down, and waited for the mayor to say something.

"We talked it over, Frank," the mayor said. "And we think you're the right man for the job of marshal."

"I'm honored," Frank said.

The mayor smiled and named a monthly salary that was astronomically high for the time and place, and Frank accepted the offer. Frank stood up to be sworn in by the mayor, and a badge was pinned to his shirt.

"If you can find a man to take the job, you're entitled to one deputy," the mayor told him. "Congratulations, Marshal. Welcome to Barnwell's Crossing."

The mayor and town council trooped out, closing the door behind them, and that was that.

"Marshal Frank Morgan," Frank whispered. "Too bad the town is dying. I might have found a home."

"Hey, Morgan!" Davy shouted from the cell area. "We're hungry. How about some food?"

"I'm cold!" Jonas yelled. "Where's them blankets you promised us?"

Frank ignored them and got up to set and wind the office wall clock. It had stopped at high noon. Frank wondered if that was somehow significant.

CHAPTER 6

Frank went to Willis's General Store and bought a few supplies for his rented house—coffee, sugar, bacon, flour, and the like—then began strolling the town, letting the townsfolk see him and get used to the badge on his chest. The Crossing was larger than Frank had first thought. There was another business street, angling off like the letter L, and many more houses than Frank realized, at the end of the second business street. The other business street had several smaller stores—including a leather shop, a ladies' store right on the corner, a smaller and rougher-looking saloon, and the doctor's office.

Frank smiled and touched his hat when meeting ladies, and he gave the men a howdy-do. Most of the people returned the greeting; a few did not. At the end of the street, Frank saw a sign for Henson Enterprises dangling from a metal frame.

The building was one story, and nice. Even though it was getting late in the day, with shadows already creeping about, darkening this and that, the office was bustling with people bent over ledgers and scurrying about.

Frank forced himself to walk on. He would run into Vivian sooner or later, and he had very mixed feelings about the inevitable meeting.

Frank had just stepped off the boardwalk when a very demanding voice behind him said, “You there, Constable. Come here.”

Frank stopped and turned around. A young man, eighteen at the most, was standing in the doorway of the Henson building, wagging his finger at Frank. “Yes, you!” the young man said. “I’m not in the habit of speaking to an empty street.”

Frank stared at the young man for a few seconds, stared in disbelief. He was dressed at the very height of fashion . . . if he were in Boston or New York City, that is. In the rough mining town of northern New Mexico territory he looked like a damned idiot.

“Well, come here!” the young man said.

Frank stepped back onto the boardwalk, his hackles already rising at the kid’s haughty tone. “Can I help you?” Frank asked.

“I certainly hope so. You’re the new constable, aren’t you?”

News travels fast in this town, Frank thought. “I’m the marshal, yes.”

“Marshal, constable . . . whatever,” the almost a man said, waving his hand in a dainty gesture that would damn sure get him in trouble if he did it in the wrong place. “There is a drunken oaf staggering about in our offices, cursing and bellowing, and I want him removed immediately.”

“All right,” Frank said. “Although I was just passing by, and didn’t hear a thing.”

“He’s calmed down for the moment, but I suspect he’ll be lumbering about and swearing again at any moment.”

“Oh? Why do you think that?”

“Because he’s that sort—that’s why. Now will you please do your duty and remove that offensive thug?”

“Lower-class type, huh?”

"Certainly. He's a laborer. They really should learn their place."

"Oh, yes, quite." Frank hid his smile and stepped into the offices. The front office seemed as calm as when Frank had first looked in only a couple of moments ago.

"In the middle office," the snooty kid said. He pointed. "That way."

"Thank you," Frank said, just as acidly as he could. Just then the shouting started.

"By God, you owe me a week's wages, and I ain't leavin' 'til I get it, you pukey-lookin' little weasel!"

"Do you?" Frank asked the young man. There was something about the kid that was vaguely disturbing to Frank. Something . . . well, familiar.

"Do I what?"

"Do you owe him money?"

"Heavens! I don't know. Take that up with the accounting department."

Frank walked to the middle office and shoved open the door, stepping inside. A big man in dirty work clothes stood in the center of the room, shouting at several men seated behind desks. When the door was opened the man paused and looked at Frank, his eyes taking in the star on his shirt.

"I eat two-bit marshals for supper," the miner told Frank.

"This one will give you a bad case of indigestion," Frank responded.

"This company owes me several days' pay," the miner said. "And I'll either get my money or I'll take this office apart."

Frank looked at one of the bookkeepers. "Do you owe him money?"

"He was off work for two days," the bookkeeper said. "He was paid for four days, not a full six."

"I got hurt in the mine!" the miner shouted. "That ain't my fault."

"Is that right?" Frank asked the bookkeeper.

"That doesn't make any difference, Marshal. He worked four days. He gets paid for the time he was on the job."

Frank looked at the miner. "Did you agree to those terms before you took the job?"

"I knew how it was," the miner said sourly. "But that don't make it right."

"I agree with you. It doesn't make it right. But you agreed to the terms. You got no quarrel. Get on out of here and cool off."

"And if I don't?" the miner challenged him.

"I'll put you out. Then I'll take you to jail. The doctor can see you in your cell."

The miner laughed. "You and how many others are gonna do that, Marshal?"

"Just me," Frank said softly.

"You really think you can do that, huh?"

"Oh, I know I can."

"With or without that pistol?"

"Either way. But if you want to mix it up with me, you'll be liable for any damage to this office."

The miner laughed at that. "How would you collect the money?"

"A day in jail for every dollar of damage. You really want to spend months behind bars? Then there will be your medical expenses. And they will be many—I assure you of that."

"You got a name, Marshal?"

"Frank Morgan."

The miner paled under his dark stubble of whiskers. He slowly nodded his head. "I reckon I'll leave quietly."

"Good," Frank told him. "You know the way out."

The miner didn't tarry. He nodded in silent agreement, left the office, and walked out of the building without saying another word.

"You certainly calmed that situation down in a hurry, Marshal," one of the bookkeepers said. "Are you really Frank Morgan?"

"Yes." Frank no longer wondered how so many people knew about him. He'd seen several of those penny dreadfuls and dime novels that had been written about him. Most of them were nothing but a pack of lies.

And he had never gotten a nickel for all the words in print about him.

"Have you really killed five hundred white men and a thousand Indians?" another office worker asked, his eyes big around.

Frank smiled. "No. Nowhere even close to either number."

"I do so hate to interfere in this moment of juvenile adoration," said the young man who had first hailed Frank. "But it's time for everybody to get back to work."

Frank had just about had enough of the kid, and came very close to telling him where to stick his lousy attitude. The only thing that saved the moment was the miner who had just left. He came storming back inside, yelling and cussing.

"No man orders me around like I was some damn stray dog!" he hollered. "Gunfighter or no, by God, let's see what you can do with your fists!"

He ran over and took a wild swing at Frank. Frank ducked the blow and stuck out one boot. The miner's forward momentum could not be halted in time, and he tripped over Frank's boot and went butt over elbows to the floor, landing with a tremendous thud. He yelled and cussed and got to his feet.

"You afraid to fight me kick, bite, and gouge, gunfighter?" he threw down the challenge.

"No," Frank said calmly. "But my warning still holds. Whatever this fight breaks, you pay for."

"I boxed in college," the haughty kid said. "And I was quite good. Allow me to settle this dispute. I can do it rather quickly, I assure you."

Frank and the miner looked at the young man, then at

each other, and both suddenly burst out laughing, all animosity between them vanishing immediately.

"Are you laughing at me, you lumbering oaf?" the young man asked the miner.

Frank verbally stepped in. "Boy, this isn't a boxing match with rules. Out here there *are* no rules in a fight. It's kick, gouge, bite, and stomp. I don't think you understand."

"I can take care of myself, Marshal. And I don't appreciate your interference."

"Fine," Frank said. "Then by all means, jump right in, boy."

It wasn't a long jump, and the young man didn't have but a few seconds to realize he had made a horrible mistake. He didn't even have time to get his feet planted and his dukes up before the big miner hit him twice, left and right. The young man bounced on the floor and didn't move.

The miner backed up and looked at Frank. "What else could I do?"

"Nothing. He attacked you." Frank knelt down and checked out the young man. He was all right, pulse strong and breathing normal. He was just unconscious, and probably would be for several minutes.

Frank stood up and told the miner, "Get out of here and stay out of sight for a few days. You might want to hunt for another job."

"I've 'bout had enough of this town, anyways," the miner replied. "At least for a while, even though I don't believe anyone's found the mother lode yet. It's out there. I know it is. I can feel it. But you're right. I'm gone for a while. No hard feelin's?"

"None at all."

"See you around, Morgan."

The miner left, and Frank looked at the office workers. They were all smiling, looking down at the young man sprawled unconscious on the floor. Frank was sure the kid was the son of Vivian—had to be. And he wasn't well-liked, for a fact.

Suddenly there was a shout coming from the street, followed by several other very excited shouts. Someone yelled, "They found it! Found it at the Henson mine. It's big. My God, it's big!"

"What's big?" Frank asked.

"They've hit another vein," one of the office workers said. "Has to be it. Our engineers said it was there. Said it was just a matter of time."

"Who is this kid?" Frank asked, pointing to the young man on the floor, who was just beginning to moan and stir.

"Conrad Browning," a man said. "Mrs. Vivian L. Browning's son."

"I thought so. Snooty, isn't he?"

"That's one way of putting it, for a fact."

"Where is Mrs. Browning?"

"She should be along any moment now. She always comes in just at closing time to check on things."

"Let's get Junior on his feet and walking around," Frank suggested. "If Mrs. Browning sees him like this she'll likely have a fit."

"Doubtful," an office worker said. "Mrs. Browning is well aware of her son's predilection for haughtiness. Conrad has been a sour pickle all his life."

Frank smiled as he heaved Conrad Browning to his feet. "A sour pickle . . . that's a very interesting way of putting it."

"Mrs. Browning's carriage just pulled up at the rear," a man said.

Frank plopped Conrad down in a chair and turned to make his exit—too late. The door to the rear office opened and Vivian stood there.

She recognized Frank instantly and gasped, leaning against the doorjamb for a moment.

Conrad broke the spell by blurting, "Mother, I have been assaulted by a hoodlum. I am injured."

"Oh, horsecrap!" Frank said.

CHAPTER 7

Frank and Vivian stood for several silent seconds, staring at each other, before Frank took off his hat and said, "Ma'am. Your son is not hurt much. He just grabbed hold of a mite more than he could handle, that's all."

"It was not a fair contest," Conrad objected. "That thug struck me before I was ready."

"What thug?" Vivian asked.

"Mr. Owens," one of the office workers said. "He was in here again about his money."

"The man I spoke with yesterday?" Vivian asked.

"Yes, ma'am."

"Did you give him his money, as I instructed?"

"Ah . . . no, ma'am . We didn't."

"I told them not to pay him," Conrad said. "He was adequately compensated for the work he performed."

Vivian closed her eyes just for the briefest second and shook her head. "Conrad, you go see Dr. Bracken. Your jaw is bruised and swelling a bit."

"Mother—"

"Now!"

"Yes, Mother."

"I'm pretty sure it isn't broken, ma' am," Frank said. "Just get some horse liniment and rub it on the sore spot. That'll take care of it."

"Horse liniment?" Conrad blurted. "I think not. I'll be back in a few minutes, Mother." He left the middle office, walking gingerly, rubbing his butt, which was probably bruised from impacting with the floor.

Outside, the excited shouting was still going on.

"A new strike, Mrs. Browning?" a bookkeeper asked.

"Yes. A big one. We'll be hiring again. And we need Mr. Owens. If he comes back in, pay him for the days he missed while hurt and put him back to work."

"Yes, ma'am."

"I'll probably see him around town, ma'am," Frank said. "I'll tell him to check back here."

"Thank you, Marshal. Would you please step into my office? I'd like to speak with you for a moment."

"Certainly, ma'am."

In the office, behind a closed door, Vivian grasped Frank's hands and held them for seconds. Finally she pulled back and sat down in one of several chairs in front of her desk. Frank sat down in the chair next to her.

"It's been a long time, Frank."

"Almost eighteen years."

"You know my father is dead?"

"I heard."

"Frank, I want you to know something. I knew within days that my father made up all those charges he was holding over you back in Denver. I also knew that you left to protect me—"

"Water under the bridge, Viv. It's long over."

"No. Let me finish. I did some checking of my own, and found out Father had paid those detectives to falsify charges against you. I confronted him with that knowledge. At first he denied it. Then, finally, he admitted what he'd done. He hated you until the day he closed his eyes forever. He threatened to cut me off financially if I didn't do his bidding. I didn't really have much choice in the matter. Or, more truthfully, I thought I didn't have a choice. When I finally realized Father was bluffing, it was too late. You were gone without a trace, and I was pregnant."

That shook Frank right down to his spurs. He stared at Vivian for a long moment. "Are you telling me that . . . Conrad is my son?"

"Yes."

Frank had almost blurted out, *You mean to tell me that prissy, arrogant little turd is my son?* But he curbed his tongue at the last possible second. He stared at Viv until he was sure he could speak without betraying his totally mixed emotions. "Did the man you married know this?"

"Yes, Frank. He did. My late husband was a good, decent man. He raised Conrad as if he were his own."

"Does the boy know?"

"No. He doesn't have a clue."

"Your father had a hand in raising him, didn't he?"

"Quite a bit. He spent a lot of time back east with us. Several years before he died, Father was with us almost all the time."

"Viv, ah . . . the boy . . ." Frank paused and frowned.

"Doesn't fit in out here? I know. He probably never will. He hates the West. He loves to ride. He's really very good. But he won't ride out here."

"Why not?"

"The way he rides, his manner of dress. He just doesn't fit in."

"He rides one of those dinky English saddles?"

"Yes."

"Don't tell me wears one of those silly-looking riding outfits."

"Yes, he does."

"I bet he got a laugh from a lot of folks the first time he

went out in public, bobbing up and down like a cork with a catfish on it."

Vivian smiled despite herself. "I'm afraid he did."

"I can imagine. Wish I'da seen that myself."

Viv's smile faded. "Why'd you come here, Frank? To this town, I mean."

"Oh, I didn't have anything else to do. Besides, I heard you were in trouble up here. Had a lot of silver to ship, and nobody would take it out for you."

"Tons of it, Frank. Tons and tons of it. Worth a fortune. But getting it out of these mountains and to a railroad has proven to be quite a chore."

"How many shipments have been hijacked?"

"Several. You have any ideas on how to get it out?"

"Oh, I imagine I could get some boys in here to take the shipments through. But they don't come cheap."

"I think I can afford them."

Frank smiled. "I 'spect you can, at that."

"Look into that for me, will you?"

"I sure will. I'll send some wires first thing in the morning."

"I would appreciate it. Frank? How are we going to handle this? You and I, I mean."

"How do you want to handle it, Viv?"

"I . . . don't know. I'm not sure."

"Did you love him? Your late husband."

She averted her eyes for a few seconds and said, "No. I liked him. But I didn't love him."

"There has never been another woman for me, Viv."

"Nor another man for me, Frank. Not really."

"And there it stands, I suppose."

"I suppose so, Frank."

"It would cause talk if I came calling, wouldn't it?"

"If you don't come calling, Frank, I'll have some of my miners come looking for you."

Frank smiled at her. Vivian had lost none of her beauty.

She had matured—that was all. "I'll drop by tomorrow, Viv. What time will you be in the office?"

"From seven o'clock on. We'll be working long hours for a while, now that the new strike is in."

"I'll try to get by at midmorning. You'll be ready for a coffee break by then."

"I'll be here waiting, Frank. And don't be surprised at how I'm dressed."

"Oh?"

"I've set many a tongue wagging in this town by occasionally dressing in men's britches."

"Really?" Frank smiled as he met Viv's eyes. "Now *that* I'd like to see." Viv was a very shapely lady.

Vivian returned his smile. "Midmorning tomorrow it is, Frank."

Frank picked up his hat from the carpeted floor by his chair and stood up. He looked at Vivian for a moment, then said, "What about Conrad, Viv?"

"Let's just let that alone for the time being. It's much too soon to even be thinking about that."

"As you wish, Viv. Tomorrow, then."

"Yes."

Frank left the office, closing the door behind him, and walked the length of the building to the front, ignoring the curious looks from the office workers. He stood on the boardwalk for a moment, listening to the excited whooping and hollering from the milling crowds on the main street. By this time tomorrow, the town would be filling up again. Closed and boarded-up stores would be reopening, and new merchants coming in. Surely there would be a couple more saloons. And there would be a lot of riffraff making their way to the town.

It was going to be a money-making place for some people for a while and, above all, a place where trouble could erupt in a heartbeat.

Frank had seen it all before, in other boom towns where precious metals were found.

Big strikes were both a blessing and a curse.

Frank's thoughts drifted back to Vivian, and he struggled to get the woman out of his mind. He could dream about her in quiet moments, but now was not the time. He had his rounds to make. And any marshal in any Western town who walked the streets at night and didn't stay alert ran the possibility of abruptly being a dead marshal.

Frank walked up to the corner of the main street and stood for a moment. He rolled a cigarette and smoked it, while leaning up against a hitchrail. It was full dark now, and both saloons were doing a land-office business. Pianos and banjos and guitars were banging and strumming and picking out melodies. Occasionally Frank could hear the sounds of a fiddle sawing away.

Frank walked up to the Silver Spoon Café and ordered supper for the prisoners, then carried the tray over to the jail. While they were eating, he made a pot of coffee and sat at his desk, smoking and drinking coffee. Then he took down the rifles and shotguns from the wall rack and cleaned and oiled them. He took out the pistol he'd found in the desk drawer and cleaned it, then loaded it up full with five rounds. It was a short-barreled .45, called by some a gambler's gun. It was actually a Colt .45 Peacemaker, known as a marshal or sheriff's pistol. Frank tucked it behind his gunbelt, on the left side. It was comfortable there.

A little insurance was sometimes a comfort.

Frank took the tray back to the café, then went over to the general store and bought some blankets for the cell bunks, charging them to the town's account. Back at the jail, he blew out the lamps and locked the front door. He did not build a fire in the jail stove, for the night was not that cool. Besides, if they both caught pneumonia and died that would save the state of Arkansas the expense of sending someone out here to take them back, plus the cost of hanging them.

He walked away, putting the very faint yelling and cussing of the two locked up and very unhappy outlaws behind him. They would settle down as soon as they realized there was no one to hear them.

Frank first stepped into the Silver Slipper Saloon and stood for a moment, giving the crowd a slow once-over. He spotted a couple of gunslicks he'd known from way back, but they were not trouble-hunters, just very bad men to crowd, for there was no back-up in either of them.

Frank walked over and pushed his way to a place at the bar, between the two men. "Jimmy," he greeted the one to his left.

"Morgan." Jimmy looked at the star on Frank's chest and smiled. "I won't cause trouble in your town, Frank."

"I know it. I just wanted to say howdy. Hal," he greeted the other one.

"Frank. Back to marshalin' again, huh?"

"Pay's good."

"I don't blame you, then."

"You boys bring your drinks over to that table in the far corner—if you've a mind to, that is. I may have some work for you both."

"If it's marshalin', count me out, Frank," Hal said.

"It isn't."

"OK, then. I'll listen."

At the table, Frank laid out the problem of getting the shipments of silver to the spur rail line just across the border in Colorado.

"I heard Vanbergen and Pine was workin' this area," Jimmy said.

"Big gangs," Hal added.

"That worry you boys?" Frank asked.

"Hell, no," Jimmy said. "You let me get some boys of my choosin' in here, and let us design the wagons, we'll get the silver through. Bet on that."

"All right. Get them in here."

"It'll take a while. They're all scattered to hell and gone," Hal said.

"We've got the time. And Mrs. Browning's got the money."

"Who is this Mrs. Browning, anyways?" Jimmy asked.

"Old Man Henson's daughter. He died some years back, and she's running the business."

"Any truth in the rumor I heard years back, Frank?" Jimmy asked. "'Bout you and Old Man Henson's daughter?" He held up one hand before Frank could say anything. "I ain't pushin' none, Frank, and I sure ain't lookin' for trouble. But the rumor is still floatin' around."

"Whatever happened was a long time ago, boys. Her father hated my guts. Now he's gone, and she's in a spot of trouble. That's why I'm here."

"That's good enough for me," Jimmy said. "I won't bring it up no more."

"I'll get some wires sent in the momin'," Hal said. "Then we'll see what happens."

"Good deal," Frank said, pushing his chair back. "Where are you boys staying?"

"We got us a room at the hotel," Jimmy told him. "We picked us up a bit of money doin' some bounty huntin' work. Brought them two in alive, we did."

Hal grinned. "'Course they was sorta shot up some, but they was alive."

"What happened to them?" Frank asked.

"They got hanged," Jimmy said.

Frank smiled and stood up. "See you boys tomorrow."

"Take it easy, Frank," Hal told him.

Frank left the saloon, very conscious of a few hostile eyes on him as he walked. He had spotted the young trouble-hunters when he first pushed open the batwings: three of them, sitting together at a table, each of them nursing a beer.

Frank did not want trouble with the young hotheads who were—more than likely—looking for a reputation. All three were in their early twenties—if that old—and full of the piss and vinegar that accompanies youth. But the youthful piss was going to be mixed with real blood if they tangled with Frank Morgan.

Frank walked up and down both sides of the main street of town. All the businesses except the saloons, the two cafés, and the hotel were now closed for the night. Frank turned down the short street that angled off of Main and paused for a moment, standing in the shadows.

The street and the boardwalk were busy, but not overly crowded with foot traffic. Judging from the noise, the Red Horse Saloon was doing a booming business. A rinky-dink piano was playing—only slightly out of tune—and a female voice was singing—also out of tune. Everything appeared normal.

But Frank was edgy. Something was wrong, something he couldn't quite put his finger on, or name. He had learned years back to trust his hunches. Over the long and violent years, that sixth sense had saved his life more times than he cared to remember.

Frank stepped deeper back into the shadows and waited, his pistol loose in leather, his eyes moving, watching the shadows across the street.

There! Right there! Frank spotted furtive movement in the alley between two boarded-up buildings across the street.

Frank squatted down in the darkened door stoop, presenting a smaller, more obscure target. His .45 was in his hand, and he did not remember drawing it. He eared the hammer back.

He watched as the shadows began to move apart and take better shape. Frank could first make out the shapes of three hats, then the upper torsos of the men as they stepped out of the alley and onto the boardwalk. He could not hear anything they were saying, if they were talking at all, because of the music and song from the Red Horse Saloon.

But he did catch a glint of reflection off the barrel of a rifle.

"They ain't huntin' ducks this time of night," Frank muttered.

But are they hunting me? he questioned silently. *And if so, why?* He was sure they weren't the three young hotheads he'd seen back in the saloon.

He was further intrigued as he watched the men slip back into the alley and disappear from sight. Just then a door opened on Frank's side of the street and bright lamplight flooded the street and illuminated the alley he'd seen the men walk into.

But they were gone without a trace.

"What the hell?" Frank muttered. "What in the hell is going on here?"

The door closed, and Frank sprinted across the wide street and darted into the alley. He paused, listening. He could hear nothing.

He moved on, to the end of the alley, stopping as he heard the low murmur of men's voices.

"I told you that bitch wasn't in her office this late. I told you both that."

What bitch? Frank asked himself.

"So OK, so you was right. We'll grab her tomorrow night."

"Oncest we get the big boss lady, that brat kid of hern will gladly hand over the silver."

"Yes," the third man said. "Shore a lot easier than waitin' for them to ship it."

Viv! They're after Viv.

"So what do we do now?"

Frank stepped out of the alley, his hands wrapped around the butts of both .45's. "You stand right where you are, is what you do."

The three men whirled around and the night exploded in gunfire.

CHAPTER 8

As soon as the words left Frank's mouth he side-stepped back into the alley. The three men fired where Frank had been, their bullets hitting nothing but the night air.

Frank hunkered down next to the boarded-up building and fired at the shadows to his right. One man screamed and went down to his knees. The other two fired at the muzzle flashes, and Frank was forced to duck back.

He crawled under the building. Built about two feet off the ground, it was damp, smelled bad, and was littered with trash. He slithered along like a big snake until he was only a few feet away from the two men still left standing.

"I think we got him!" one said.

"Think again," Frank said from the darkness under the building, and opened fire.

The two men went down in an awkward sprawl. Frank rolled out from under the building and got to his boots.

"My leg's broke," one of the men moaned. "Oh, crap, it hurts bad."

"I'm hard hit," another one said. "Where is that bastard?"

"Right here," Frank said. "And if either of you reaches for a gun you're dead."

"Sam?" the one with a broken leg said. "Sam? Answer me, boy."

There was no response. The only person Sam was going to answer to was God.

"He's dead," Frank told the would-be kidnapper just as a crowd began to gather, some of them with lanterns.

"Who the hell are you?" The other outlaw groaned the question.

Frank ignored that. "Get the doctor." He tossed the command to the gathering crowd. "And someone else get the undertaker."

"Who are these men?" someone in the crowd asked. "And what did they do?"

"They're part of the Pine and Vanbergen gangs," Frank told him. "They were attempting to kidnap Mrs. Browning for ransom."

"Good God!" a man said.

"How the hell did you know that?" one of the wounded outlaws asked. "And who the hell are you?"

"Somebody talked," the other outlaw said. "That's how he knew. Man . . . Ned is gonna be pissed about this."

"Who are you?" the outlaw persisted.

"Frank Morgan."

"Oh, hell!"

The town's doctor pushed his way through the growing crowd and ordered lamps brought closer to the wounded men. "That one's dead," he said, pointing. "This one's got a broken leg." He moved over to the third man. "Shot in the side. Bullet went clear through. Some of you men carry these men over to the jail. Where is Mr. Malone?"

"Right here," a tall thin man said, pushing his way through the crowd. "How many dead?"

"One. The other two will live, I'm sure."

"One is better than none," Malone the undertaker said. "If he's got the money to pay for my services."

"You bastard!" the outlaw with the broken leg said. "You give him a decent sendin' off, damn you."

"He'll get planted," Malone said. "How solemn and dignified will depend on the cash in his pockets."

"Get the living out of here," the doctor told the volunteers.

Frank spotted Willis in the crowd. "I'm going to need some extra blankets from your store."

"I'll get them and bring them over to the jail," the store owner said. "Anything else?"

"Laudanum," the doctor said.

"I'll get it from Jiggs at the apothecary."

Doc Bracken stood up. "I've done all I can do here."

"I'll be at the jail," Frank told him.

When the wounded outlaws were patched up and locked down, Frank went looking for Hal and Jimmy. He found them in their room at the hotel.

"Big doin's, huh, Frank?" Jimmy asked.

"Shaping up that way. How tired are you boys?"

"Not tired at all," Hal replied. "Matter of fact, we had just finished washin' up and was thinkin' of findin' us an all-night poker game."

Frank told them about the planned kidnapping, and that got their attention.

"What can we do to help?" Jimmy asked. "Name it, Frank. We owe you more'un one favor."

"You'll be well paid for this, I assure you. Want to stand guard at the Browning house?"

"Consider it done. Have you talked to Mrs. Browning about it?"

"I'll do that right now. You boys get dressed and we'll walk over together." Frank smiled. "That is, as soon as I find out where she lives."

* * *

It was the grandest house in the town, naturally, with a sturdy iron rail fence around it. The gate was locked. A cord was hanging out of a gap in the fence, and Frank pulled on it.

A man dressed in some sort of uniform came out and stood on the porch. "Yes? What do you want?"

"I'm Marshal Frank Morgan. Here to see Mrs. Browning on a matter of great urgency."

"I'll tell her, sir."

"Got to be one of the servants, I guess," Frank said to Hal and Jimmy.

"Must be nice," Hal said.

"I reckon," Frank replied.

"I never been in a house this grand," Jimmy said. "Y'all stomp your boots a couple of times to get any horseshit off of 'em."

Frank smiled. "Good idea. We don't want to leave tracks on the carpet."

Conrad came out onto the porch and down the walkway to the gate, and he took his time doing it. As he was unlocking the chain he said, "I do hope this is important, Marshal. We were in the middle of dinner."

"Hell, it's eight o'clock," Hal said. "Y'all hadn't et yet?"

"Eight o'clock is when most civilized people sit down for dinner," Conrad told him.

"Pardon the hell outta me," Hal muttered.

The interior of the home was elaborately furnished. There were paintings on the walls, and vases and various types and sizes of sculptures on itsy-bitsy tables and pedestals.

"La dee da," Jimmy muttered, looking around him as they were led into the dining room.

"Don't knock nothin' over, you clumsy ox," Hal told his partner. "And don't touch nothin', neither."

"Speak for yourself, you jumpy moose," Jimmy responded.

Vivian rose from the longest table Frank had ever seen

outside of a banquet hall. The chandelier over the table must have cost a fortune. Its glow made the room as bright as day. Vivian smiled and said, "Marshal Morgan."

"Evening, ma'am," Frank said, taking off his hat. "We're sorry to disturb you, but something came up I thought you ought to know about. This is Hal and Jimmy."

"How do you do, gentlemen?"

"Fair to middlin', ma'am," Hal said.

"OK, I reckon, ma'am," Jimmy told her. "Shore is a nice place you got here."

"Thank you. Would you gentlemen like something to eat, or some coffee?"

"Coffee would hit the spot," Hal said, ignoring the dirty look he was getting from Frank.

Viv picked up a little silver bell from the table and shook it. A servant appeared almost instantly. "Coffee for the gentlemen, please, Marion."

"Yes, mum."

"Sit down, please," Viv said. "Do make yourselves comfortable." She looked at Frank. "What is the matter of great urgency, Fra"—she caught herself—"Marshal?"

"Yes," Conrad said, entering the dining room and sitting down. "Do enlighten us."

Frank resisted an impulse to slap the snot out of Conrad. "Jimmy and Hal here are going to be your bodyguards for as long as you stay in this area, Vi"—damn, but it was catching—"Mrs. Browning."

"Oh?" Vivian said, staring at Frank. "Don't you think I should have something to say about that? And what makes you think I want or need bodyguards?"

"Yes. And I must say I quite resent your coming in here and giving orders. I am perfectly capable of looking after my mother," Conrad said haughtily.

"Shut up, boy!" Frank told him. "You couldn't look after a lost calf."

Conrad's mouth dropped open, and he started sputtering and stuttering.

"Close your mouth," Frank said, "before you swallow a fly." He turned his gaze to Vivian. "I just shot three men tonight, Mrs. Browning. Killed one, and wounded the other two. They were planning to kidnap you."

CHAPTER 9

Terms of employment were quickly agreed to, and Frank stayed with Vivian while Hal and Jimmy returned to the hotel to get their belongings. Vivian wanted them to stay in the house, but both gunhands shook their heads at that suggestion. They would stay in the carriage house, behind the main house.

Conrad, his feathers ruffled by Frank's blunt comments concerning his ability to protect his mother, stalked off to bed, leaving Frank and Vivian alone in the dining room. The candles and lanterns had been trimmed, leaving the room in very subdued light.

"If you had not heard I was having trouble shipping the silver—" Viv said. She shook her head. "I shudder to think what would have happened had you not been here."

"Well, I'm here, Viv. And Hal and Jimmy are good men. They'll get some wires off in the morning to some friends of theirs, and before you know it your silver will be safely shipped. Hal and Jimmy will design the wagons, and they'll be built right here in town. Until Vanbergen and Pine are taken care of, Hal and Jimmy will be your shadows, around the clock."

"And you, Frank?"

"I'll be around—you can bet on that. You couldn't run me off if you tried."

She touched his hand. "I'm counting on that."

"You've got it."

"Hal and Jimmy are certainly . . . well, capable looking. I have to admit that."

"They're both tough as wang leather. They're not the prettiest pair in the world, but they're one hundred percent loyal. They ride for the brand, Viv. And they're quick on the shoot. They'll stick no matter what."

"Why doesn't the law do something about this gang, or gangs, I should say?"

"You were living back east a long time, Viv. You've forgotten this is the West. It's slowly being tamed, but it's still pretty much wild and wooly and full of fleas. There isn't much law out here, not in most places. And it'll be some time before there is."

"I suppose so."

"I taught you how to shoot, Viv. Do you still have a pistol?"

"No. My husband didn't like guns."

"Can Conrad use a gun?"

"No. He doesn't like guns either."

Frank shook his head. "Maybe that's for the best. He'd probably brace somebody and get himself shot."

"He's lonely, Frank. That's his biggest problem. And I don't know what to do about that."

"He wouldn't be, Viv, if he wasn't such a stuck-up fuss-bucket."

Vivian tried her best to look offended at that, but couldn't quite pull it off. She gave up, and with a half-smile said, "He just doesn't fit in out here, Frank. I don't believe he ever will."

"Some folks never do. But those that can't are the folks who want someone else to do for them. You were raised out here, Viv. You know all this."

"The settled East is an ideal place to forget all that," she said gently.

"I guess so. Don't know much about the east. Never wanted to go there." Frank fiddled around with his empty coffee cup for a few seconds.

"More coffee, Frank?"

"No, thanks. This will do me. Soon as the boys get back I've got to start making my night rounds and check on the wounded at the jail."

"What will happen to those men?"

"They'll be held here for trial. I'll be checking dodgers to see if they're wanted anywhere else . . . and I'm sure they are."

"What if their gang tries to break them out?"

"I'll do my best to prevent that."

"You're just one man, Frank. The combined strength of those gangs, so I'm told, can be as high as forty."

Frank shrugged his shoulders. "I can't help that. I was hired to enforce the law and keep the peace. I intend to do just that."

The gate bell rang, and Marion went outside to let Hal and Jimmy in. Frank stood up. "I'll see you tomorrow, Viv. About midmorning, for coffee."

Frank stood outside the Browning estate for a moment and rolled and smoked a cigarette, then strolled up the boardwalk and stepped inside the Red Horse Saloon for a look around. It was noisy and rowdy, but that was a joyful sound. There were a few sour expressions at the sight of Frank, but that was to be expected whenever a badge showed up at a party.

Frank looked around for a moment, then quietly left the saloon without speaking to anyone. He walked the business area of the town, checking the doors of the closed-for-the-night businesses, making sure they were all secure. He stopped in at the Silver Slipper Saloon and stayed only a couple of minutes before walking over to the jail and checking on his prisoners.

The men were all asleep—the wounded ones in a laudanum-induced slumber. Frank quietly stepped back and closed and locked the heavy door leading to the cell area. He checked on his horses at the livery and then walked across the street to his rented house and went to bed. He had missed supper, but it wasn't the first time Frank Morgan had missed a meal—nor, he suspected, would it be the last.

He went to sleep and dreamed about Vivian, frowning whenever Conrad entered his dreams. Frank felt no closeness or affection for the young man. He felt nothing, and his sleep became restless because of that. As the boy's father, shouldn't he feel some sort of blood bond, some sort of paternal sense or awakening . . . something, anything?

Frank awakened with silent alarm bells ringing in his head. Men who constantly live on the razor edge between life and sudden, bloody death develop that silent warning system—or die very young—in their chosen, violent lifestyle.

Frank lay very still and listened. He could hear nothing. Perhaps, he thought, the sounds of silence were what woke him. No. He rejected that immediately. He didn't think that was it. Then . . . what?

Frank slipped from bed and silently pulled on his britches and slipped his bare feet into an old pair of moccasins he'd had for a long time. He picked up his gunbelt and slipped it over one shoulder. Frank had learned years back that it was not wise to run out of ammunition in a gunfight. The loops on his gunbelt always stayed filled. He didn't bother pulling on a shirt.

He padded noiselessly to the rear of the darkened house

and looked out through the window. He had not yet purchased material for some seamstress to make him curtains. He could see nothing in the rear of the house.

He walked to the front of the house and looked out. Nothing. He pulled his pocket watch from his jeans and clicked open the lid. A few minutes after four o'clock. This was the time when people were snuggling deeper into bed and blankets for that final hour or so of good, deep sleep. The best time of the night for murder.

He should get going. By the time he heated water and took a shave and a spot bath it would be five o'clock. Then he had to get over to the jail and make coffee and empty and rinse out all the piss pots from the cells. Then he had to see about breakfast for himself and the prisoners. After that, he had to see if there was any reply from Arkansas about the reward money. He would be busy for a couple of hours, at least. And he didn't want to forget to check on any bounty on the men he'd locked up last night and the one he'd killed. Yes, it was shaping up to be a busy morning.

Banker Jenkins, also the mayor, had told him as soon as he received confirmation about the reward money he would advance Frank the money and have Arkansas authorities send it directly to his bank. That sounded good to Frank.

Walking about the still dark house, Frank bent down to pick up some kindling wood from the box by the stove. He heard a tin can rattle in the backyard, followed by a soft curse.

OK, Frank thought. *Whoever you are and whatever you want, boys, you just queered the deal.*

Frank slipped to the back door and waited. There was no way he was going to open that door and step into a hail of bullets. He heard the soft creak of boards as someone stepped onto the small back porch. Frank carefully backed up until he could get the large stove between the door and himself. He eased the hammer back on his .45.

Frank heard the sound of someone carefully trying the

doorknob. It was loose, and rattled when touched. "Come on in," he whispered.

But the man on the porch obviously had other ideas. He backed away, stepped off the porch, and silently faded into the coolness of night.

"Now just what in the hell was that all about?" Frank questioned.

The night was silent, offering no explanation.

Frank slipped through the house to the front room and peered out. The street was silent and empty.

He decided he'd shave at the jail. He did not want to risk lighting a lamp. He finished dressing. Then, taking a change of clothing with him, he slipped out the back of his house and cautiously made his way up the side of the house to the street. He neither saw nor heard anyone.

"Strange," Frank muttered. "Very odd, indeed."

At the jail, he rolled out the prisoners and collected the bed pots. Then he made coffee and shaved and dressed: black trousers, new red-and-white-checkered shirt buttoned at the collar, string tie, and the suit coat he'd bought at the general store the day before.

"How about some coffee and some breakfast, Morgan?" a prisoner called.

"Coffee is almost ready. I'll get your breakfast in a few minutes."

At the café, which was doing a brisk business, he asked Angie to fix some trays—beef, fried potatoes, cornmeal mush—and to cut up the meat and leave only a spoon for each prisoner to eat with.

"You going to feed them lunch, Frank?" she asked.

"Biscuits and coffee. I'll be back around noon."

The prisoners fed, Frank turned up the lamps, sat down at his desk, and brought his jail journal up to date. Then he wrote several wires to send about his new inmates and the dead man.

Dawn was busting over the mountains when he finished.

Frank checked on the prisoners, then walked over to the café for his own breakfast. He took the empty trays with him, after carefully checking to make sure all the spoons were there. With a little work a spoon could be turned into a deadly weapon.

It was past six now, and the café had cleared out some.

Frank ordered breakfast and sat at a corner table, drinking coffee until the food arrived. It was pointless to ask Angie if she'd seen any strangers in town, for the town was full of newcomers. And during the next few weeks, there would be hundreds more streaming in.

Frank made up his mind to hire a deputy, and he asked Angie if she knew anyone.

"Yeah . . . I think I do, matter of fact. He ought to be coming in here anytime now. He's a man in his mid-fifties, I'd guess, and he's steady and dependable. I think he's done some deputy work in other places."

"Sounds good to me. What's his name?"

"Jerry. Jerry Dobbs."

"Introduce me when he comes in."

"I'll do that."

Frank was just finishing his breakfast when Angie called out, "'Mornin', Jerry. Got someone here who wants a word with you."

"Oh?" the big man said just as Frank was pushing his chair back and rising to his boots.

The men shook hands, and Jerry sat down at the table with Frank. A few minutes later, Frank had hired a deputy.

"I'm no miner," Jerry explained while eating his breakfast. "Didn't take me long to figure that out. I've worked a lot of things in my life, but lawing is something I enjoy the best."

"It can be rewarding," Frank said. "Until the town is cleaned up. Then the people want to get rid of you."

"For a fact," Jerry agreed. "I've sure seen that happen a time or two."

"This town is going to boom for a while," Frank said. "I'm going to ask the mayor if I can hire a second deputy."

"Might not be a bad idea. I've seen these boom towns go from a hundred people to five thousand in a matter of days. The way I heard it, this is a major strike, too."

Frank liked the older man almost instantly. Jerry was big and solid and well-spoken. Frank could sense he had plenty of staying power, and once he made up his mind it would take a steam engine to move him.

Frank told Jerry about the planned kidnapping attempt against Vivian and his hiring of two bodyguards for her.

"Hal and Jimmy are known throughout the West as men who'll brook no nonsense," Jerry replied. "Not killers, but damn sure quick on the shoot. They'll take care of her."

"I'm counting on that. Jerry, there's a small living area in the jail. You want to use it?"

"Yes," the big man said quickly. "Sure beats payin' a weekly rate for a room with two other guys."

"As soon as you finish your breakfast we'll go over to the jail and see what you need for your living quarters, then go to the store for provisions."

"Sounds good to me."

"By that time the mayor should he in his office at the bank, and we'll get you sworn in. Jerry, you haven't asked about salary."

Jerry smiled. "I know what boom towns pay their lawmen. It will he more than adequate, I'm sure."

"I'll see that it is."

Angie came over and refilled their cups. The customers all had been served and were chowing down, and no one was calling for anything, so she pulled out a chair and sat down.

"Gonna be a law dog again, Jerry?" she asked.

"Beats the mines, Angie."

"I'm sure. Unless you're the owner."

"Frank Morgan!" the shout came from out in the street. "Get out here, you bastard!"

"What the hell?" Jerry asked.

Frank got up and looked out the window. A man was standing in the center of the wide street. He was wearing two guns, something that was becoming a rarity in the waning days of the so-called Wild West.

"You know that man, Frank?" Angie asked, standing just to Frank's left.

"I never saw him before, but he sure as hell is no kid."

Jerry joined them at the window. "I've seen him around town a time or two. Don't know his name."

"Morgan!" the man called. "You murderin' pile of coyote puke. Get out here and face me!"

"I don't think that fellow out there likes me very much," Frank said.

Jerry looked at Frank and smiled and shook his head at the marshal's calmness. "I think you'd be safe in sayin' that, Frank."

"Did you see anyone with the guy, Jerry, anyone at all?" Frank asked.

"No. Never. I never even seen him talkin' to anyone."

Both sides of the street had cleared of people within seconds. The few horses at hitch rails that early in the day had been quickly led away by their owners in anticipation of lead flying about.

"You either come out and face me or I'm comin' in there and drag you out, you yellow bastard!" the man in the street hollered. "By God, I mean it, Morgan!"

Frank slipped his pistol in and out of leather a couple of times. He didn't have to check to see if it was loaded. He knew it was. "Time to go see what that fellow wants," Frank said.

"Hell, Frank!" Jerry blurted. "You know what he wants. He wants to kill you!"

"Lots of people have tried that over the years, Jerry. I'm still here."

Angie put a hand on Frank's arm. "He may have someone in hiding, Frank. Not many men would face you alone. It's something to consider."

Frank cut his eyes to her. "I always take that into consideration. That's one of the reasons I'm still alive. But I'm marshal here. I can't afford to let something like this get out of hand. And it could, very easily. If it did, that would be the end of law and order in this town."

Angie opened her mouth to speak. Jerry held up a hand. "He's right, Angie. I know you've got a shotgun behind the counter. Give it to me, and I'll back him up."

"All right." Angie hurried behind the counter and returned with a long-barreled scattergun.

"It's got light loads in it," the cook said. "But at close range they'll sure put someone out of commission."

"Good enough," Jerry said, breaking open the scattergun to make certain both chambers were loaded up. He looked at Frank. "You ready?"

"You sure you want to do this, Jerry? Hell, man, you're not even on the payroll yet."

Jerry grinned at him. "Maybe you can arrange a bonus for me."

"Count on it."

"Come on out, you chicken-livered has-been!" the loudmouth in the street hollered.

"That does it," Frank muttered through suddenly clenched teeth, and moved toward the café door.

None of the principals noticed the young man across the street stop on the boardwalk and stand and stare. Dressed in his stylish business suit, he was as out of place as a buffalo turd in a crystal punch bowl.

"What in the world is going on?" he asked a clerk who had been sweeping the boardwalk.

"There's gonna be a gunfight."

"Why doesn't someone call the marshal?"

"Someone just did, boy. That fellow standin' in the street."

"My word!" Conrad said.

CHAPTER 10

Frank stepped out the front door of the café, taking his time while Jerry hustled out the back door and made his way to the street, coming up the narrow space between the two buildings. The small crowd that had gathered on the boardwalks moved left and right, out of the line of fire . . . they hoped.

Frank looked more closely at the man in the street. He did not recognize him, and did not believe he had ever seen him before. "What is your problem?" Frank called.

"You! You're the problem, Morgan."

"Why? I've never seen you before. I don't know you."

"I know you."

"How?"

"You killed my brother up in Wyoming. Jim Morris was his name . . . remember?"

"Can't say as I do. What's your name?"

"Calvin. The man who's gonna kill you, Morgan."

"Doubtful, Calvin, very doubtful."

"You callin' me a liar? Damn you, you back-shootin' lowlife!"

"I never shot anyone named Morris. Not in the back or anywhere else."

"You're a liar, Morgan. You ambushed him one night and shot him in the back!"

"Not me, Calvin. You have the wrong man."

"You're both a liar and a coward, Morgan!"

"You're wrong on both counts. Think about it. Don't throw away your life."

"Enough talk, Morgan. Walk out here and face me if you've got the guts."

That settled the question in Frank's mind about a second, hidden gunman. He and Morris were in full, open view of each other. So the hidden gunman must not, as yet, have a good shot at Frank. He hoped Jerry got the message.

"What's the matter, Calvin?" Frank asked. "Can't you see me? You need glasses, maybe?"

"I can see you, Morgan," Calvin said sullenly. "I don't need no damn glasses."

"Then let's get this over with. I'm tired of trying to save your life."

"Huh?"

"You seem determined to end your life this morning. I've tried to keep you from doing that. But you won't listen. So let's do it, Calvin. Enough talking."

Calvin looked up for just a second. That was all the signal Frank needed. The second gunman was on the roof of the café, or one of the buildings just left or right of the café. As long as Frank stayed under the awning, he was safe from the sniper.

"I knowed you was yeller, Morgan. I'm challengin' you to stop all this talk and step out here and face me."

"Hook and draw, Calvin," Frank said easily. "You can see me."

"You're yeller. I knowed all along you was yeller. Told everybody I'd prove it."

"And you're a loudmouth son of a bitch," Frank said without raising his voice.

That got to Calvin—if Calvin was his real name, which

Frank doubted. The man tensed, and Frank could see his expression change.

"You'll pay for that, Morgan."

"How? You going to have your buddy on the roof shoot me in the back?"

"Take him, Lou!" the man on the roof shouted. "Take him now. He's on to us!"

Calvin/Lou hesitated for just a second, then grabbed for his pistol.

Frank shot him twice just as he was clearing leather. He placed his shots fast but carefully, knocking both legs out from under the man. Jerry's shotgun boomed, and there was a scream from the gunman on the roof.

"Oh, my ass!" the sniper squalled. "You done ruint me. Oh, sweet Baby Jesus!" Then he fell off the roof, crashing through the awning and landing on the boardwalk.

Frank took a quick look at the man. His ass was a bloody mess. He had taken both barrels of Jerry's scattergun in the butt. He had landed on his belly on the boardwalk, and the wind had been knocked out of him.

Jerry stepped out of the alley, a six-gun in his hand. "Watch him," Frank said, pointing to bloody butt. Then he walked over to the fallen man in the dusty and now bloody street.

"Calvin, or Lou?" Frank asked him.

"Lou. You bastard! You done broke both my legs."

"That was my intention."

"Damn your eyes!"

"Lou what?"

"Lou Manning."

"Well, well, now. I have a dodger on you over in the office. Another five hundred dollars in my pocket."

"That's an old dodger. It's a thousand now."

"That's even better. How about your buddy over there?"

"Bud Chase. He ain't got no money on his head. You gonna get me a doctor, Morgan?"

"I see him coming now. Was that you prowling around outside my house this morning?"

"Huh? No." He groaned in pain. "I don't even know where you live, Morgan. I wish to God I'd never seen you. Where is that damn sawbones?"

"Taking a look at your buddy's butt. He's got two loads of bird shot in his ass."

"To hell with Bud's butt! My legs is busted, goddamn it."

Doc Bracken came over and looked at Lou's wounds. "Neither leg seems to be broken, but you won't be doing much walking around for a while."

"I really hurt something fierce, Doc," Lou said. "Can you give me something for the pain?"

"When we get you settled in the jail," the doctor told him.

"How's the other one?" Frank asked.

"Very uncomfortable," Bracken said with a half-smile. "And he's going to be even more so when I start probing around for those shot."

Frank waved at some men. "Get these two over to the jail," he told them. He looked at Doc Bracken. "Unless you want them in your office."

Bracken shook his head. "Jail will be fine. Neither one of them are in any danger of expiring. Your jail is getting full, isn't it, Marshal?"

"I'll have two cells left after these two are booked."

"Ummm," Doc Bracken said. "What happens if your jail gets full?"

"I'll chain prisoners outside to a hitch rail."

Bracken gave him a hard look. "And you would too, wouldn't you, Marshal?"

"Bet on it."

The doctor chuckled. "I think you'll be the best marshal this town has ever had, Morgan. Providing you live long enough, that is."

"Thank you, Doc. How soon can I ask these two a few questions?"

"A couple of hours, maybe. Probably longer. I'm going to sedate them heavily. I'll let you know."

"Good enough."

The wounded were carried off to the jail. Dirt was kicked over the bloody spot in the street, and Frank told Jerry to locate one of the town's carpenters and have him get busy repairing the awning and the broken boardwalk. He sent another man to find the mayor and arrange for a meeting.

Conrad had not moved from his spot in the doorway across the street. Frank spotted the young man and walked over to him.

"How is your mother this morning, Conrad?"

"Very well, Marshal. Thank you for inquiring. That was quite a performance a few moments ago. Do you always twirl your pistol after a shooting?"

Frank did not remember doing that. It was just something he did automatically. "I suppose so, Conrad. It's just a habit."

"Very impressive, I must say. You are quite proficient with that weapon."

"I try."

"Tell me, Marshal, if you will, how long have you known my mother?"

Frank had no idea what Viv had told the young man, but he wasn't going to start off whatever relationship that might develop with a lie. "I knew her years ago, Conrad. For a very brief time."

"Before she married my father?"

"Oh, yes."

"I see. Well, at least you both have your stories straight. Good day, Marshal." Conrad turned away and walked off toward the Henson Enterprises office building without another word.

"Boy damn sure suspects something is not quite right," Frank muttered. He also knew that he and Viv had better get their heads together and plan something out, and do it quickly.

Mayor Jenkins strolled up, all smiles. "Well, Marshal," he said, grabbing Frank's hand and shaking it, "congratulations. I was just informed about the incident. I was told that was quite a dandy bit of shooting on your part. Knocked the pins out from under that gunman quicker than the eye could follow. And I'm told you have a new deputy. Jerry, ah, what's his name? Consider him on the payroll." He named a very generous monthly sum of money—about twice the going rate, even for a boom town. "You can swear him in. That goes with the office, Marshal. I should be hearing something from Arkansas in about a week. I'll let you know immediately. Good day, Marshal. Great job you're doing. Yes, indeed."

"Most happy fellow," Frank muttered. He went in search of Jerry to swear him in.

Frank did not notice Conrad peeping around the corner of a building, watching his every move.

CHAPTER 11

Frank swore Jerry in as deputy marshal and pinned a badge on him. Then they went over to Willis's store and bought provisions for the small private room at the jail. Back at the jail, Frank fixed a pot of coffee and the two men talked while Doc Bracken worked on the wounded in the cell block.

"Never married, Jerry?"

"Once. Had two kids. Boy and a girl. She didn't like the West, and she really didn't like me, I guess. We lived in Kansas. Took the kids and left one day when I was out with a posse. I've not seen hide nor hair of any of them since. That was twenty years ago. Don't know where they are. You, Frank?"

"A long time ago. Right after the war. We weren't married long. It didn't work out. I've been drifting ever since."

"Yeah, me too, but I don't blame that on her. I reckon I'm just meant to wander, that's all." Jerry stood up. "I need to go back to the roomin' house and get my things, Frank. OK with you?"

"Sure. Go ahead. I've got an appointment to see

Mrs. Browning this morning. I'll probably be gone time you get back."

"That's a nice lady."

"Yes, she certainly is."

Jerry left and Frank looked in on Doc Bracken and his assistant. "You going to be much longer, Doc?"

"'Bout ten more minutes. I've got all the shot out of this man's butt that I can. The rest will have to stay. Some will work out in time, but he'll be sitting on a lot of bird shot for the rest of his life."

"I'll kill that son of a bitch who shot me," the butt-shot Bud groaned through his laudanum-induced haze.

"Shut up," Doc Bracken told him. "You'll have lots of time to think up threats while you're in prison. You'd better be thankful it wasn't buckshot that hit you, fellow. You wouldn't have any ass left."

"Gimmie some more laudanum," Bud mumbled.

"You've had enough," the doctor told him.

Frank closed the door and sat down at his desk, bringing his jail book up to date. He checked all his dodgers for one on Bud Chase. There were no wanted fliers on Bud, but he did find the dodger on Lou Manning. He wrote out a wire to send to the Texas Rangers.

He glanced at the wall clock. He still had a few minutes before he was due to meet Viv. Frank leaned back in the wooden swivel chair. He did not delude himself about the likelihood of getting back with Viv. His chances were slim to none. Their worlds were too far apart now, and Frank was man enough to admit that. But they would enjoy each other's company while they had the opportunity. After that? Well, only time would tell.

Frank looked in on the prisoners, giving them a cup of coffee if they wanted it, then closed and locked the door to the cell block. He had given Jerry a set of keys to all doors, so he locked the front door upon leaving, too.

He strolled down the boardwalk, taking his time and looking over the town in broad daylight. A few of the stores that had been boarded up were already in the process of being reopened, getting ready to rent. He had been told the bank owned them. Mayor Jenkins didn't miss a bet. If there was a dollar to be made, as banker he was going to get a part of it.

Already new people were coming in from tiny communities that were close by, all of the newcomers riding in. Soon the wagons would be rolling in, and when the permanent structures were all taken—which wouldn't be long—wooden frames would be erected, and canvas fastened in place, forming roofs and sides. There would be a dozen makeshift saloons and eating places and what have you thrown up in less than a week. Hurdy-gurdy girls would be working around the clock, and so would the gamblers, and both spelled trouble with a capital T.

Frank walked into the Henson Enterprises building and past the workers in the front office just as Viv was coming out of her rear office. She saw him and smiled.

"Be with you in a moment, Marshal," she called.

All very proper and correct, Frank thought. He looked behind him. Hal was standing in the outer office. They nodded at each other. Jimmy would be working the outside, Frank figured. Every hour or so the men would swap up.

Viv motioned for Frank to come into her office. She closed the door and stood facing him. "Are you all right, Frank?"

"I'm fine."

"Conrad told me about the shooting incident."

Frank shrugged that off. "Where is Conrad?"

"At the mine. For his age, he's really a very responsible young man. He knows the business."

"I'm sure he is, Viv, and I'm sure he's a big help. He just doesn't much care for me, that's all."

"Give him time. Maybe things will change."

"Maybe they will. We'll see. Ready to take a stroll through town?"

"That will set some tongues wagging."

"That bother you?"

"Not in the least. I'll get my parasol."

With Hal and Jimmy hanging back a respectable distance, the two began their leisurely walk. *The gunfighter and the lady,* Frank thought with a smile. *That would make a good title for a dime novel.*

Heads did turn as the two walked slowly toward the Silver Spoon Café. Vivian was dressed in the height of Eastern fashion, and was a beautiful woman. Frank wondered why women toted around little parasols and didn't open them. What the hell was the point, anyway? The sky was a dazzling, clear blue, and it sure wasn't raining. Besides, he didn't figure the dainty little thing would even do much to keep off rain.

He concluded that he would never understand women.

"Town's being reborn," Viv remarked.

"Sure is. This your first boom town, Viv?"

"Yes."

"You ain't seen nothing yet. If this strike turns out to be as big as people are saying, there'll be a thousand more people packed in here before it's all over. Maybe more than that. It'll be a great big, sometimes uncontrollable, mess."

"You've worn a badge in other boom towns, Frank?"

"Yes. Several of them."

"I've tried to keep track of you over the years. But it hasn't been easy."

"I'm sure. I did move around a lot."

"And often disappeared for months at a time. Where did you go, and what did you do during those times?"

"Sometimes I worked on a ranch, under a false name."

"For thirty dollars a month?"

"Less than that a few times."

"But somebody would always come along who recognized you." It was not posed as a question.

"Yes. Or someone would get their hands on one of those damn books . . . all of them nothing but a pack of lies."

"I've read all of them."

Frank cut his eyes to the woman walking by his side. "You're joking, of course?"

"No. I swear it's the truth. I had to hide them from my husband, and from Conrad." She smiled. "It was a deliciously naughty feeling."

"Oh? Reading the books about me, or hiding them from your family?"

She poked him in the ribs and giggled. "Did you really take up with a soiled dove named Hannah?"

"Oh, hell, no!" Frank chuckled. A few seconds later he said with a straight face, "Her name was Agnes."

This time Viv laughed aloud and grabbed Frank's arm. "And she died in your arms after stepping in front of a bullet that was meant for you?"

"Slowest bullet since the invention of guns, I reckon. Took that writer a whole page to get that bullet from one side of the room to the other."

"You read them, Frank?"

"Parts of some of them. I haven't read any of the newer ones."

"I have a confession to make."

"Oh?"

"The man who writes those novels was a good friend of my husband. He lives in Boston. He used to come over to the house quite often for croquet and dinner."

"Ummm. Is that so? How difficult was it for you to keep a straight face?"

"Terribly difficult."

Their conversation ground to an abrupt halt when they

met a gaggle of ladies coming out of Willis's General Store. The ladies had to stop and chat for a few minutes with Vivian and oohh and aahh about her dress and hat. Frank stepped over to one side, rolled a cigarette, and smoked and waited for the impromptu hen party to end.

When the gossiping was over and the town's ladies had sashayed on their way, Viv smiled at Frank. "Sorry about that, Frank."

"It's all right. What in the world did you ladies talk about?"

"You, mostly."

"Me!"

"Yes. They wanted to know how I knew you."

"And what did you tell them?"

"The same thing I told Conrad: that I knew you years ago when you were a young cowboy."

"Conrad doesn't believe that."

"You know something?"

"What?"

"Those ladies didn't, either."

By nightfall, thanks in no small part to the ladies who had chatted with Viv earlier, it was the talk of the town that Mrs. Vivian L. Browning, president of Henson Enterprises, was seeing the town marshal, Frank Morgan. Tongues were wagging in every store, home, saloon, and bawdy house.

Frank and Jerry saw that the prisoners were fed and locked down, and then made their early evening rounds. "There is the first wagon coming in," Jerry said, looking up the street. "They must have traveled all night after hearing the news off the wire."

"There'll be a hundred more by week's end," Frank opined. "We're going to have our hands full."

The sign on the side of the gaily painted wagon read:

DR. RUFUS J. MARTIN
DENTIST EXTRAORDINAIRE

"What the hell does 'extraordinaire' mean?" Jerry asked.

"Extra special, I suppose, would be one definition."

"What's so special about gettin' a tooth pulled?"

Frank did not reply to the question. His gaze was on a man riding slowly up the street. His duster was caked with trail dirt, and his horse plodded wearily. Rider and horse had come a long way.

Jerry had followed Frank's eyes. "You know that man, Frank?"

"Yes. That's Robert Mallory. Big Bob. From out of the Cherokee Strip."

"I've heard of him. He's a bad one, isn't he?"

"One of the worst. He's an ambusher; a paid assassin. He's probably got three dozen kills on his tally sheet . . . at least. From California to Missouri. Most of them backshot. He rides into an area, someone is found dead, he rides out."

"He's never been charged?"

"No proof that he ever did anything. Dead men don't talk, Jerry."

"But I've heard he's a gunfighter."

"He is. He's quick as a snake if you push him. Big Bob is no coward. Believe that. But he'd rather shoot his victim in the back."

"Frank, no one just rides into this town by accident. It's too far off the path."

"I know."

"You think he's after Mrs. Browning?"

"Only God, Big Bob, and the man who is paying him knows the answer to that. But you can bet your best pair of boots he's after somebody."

"Let's see where he lands for the night."

"The best hotel in town—that's where. Bob goes first-class all the way. That's his style."

"Frank . . . he might be after you."

"That thought crossed my mind."

"You two know each other?"

"Oh, yes. For many years. And he dislikes me as much as I do him."

"Why?"

"The dislike?"

"Yes."

"We're opposites, Jerry. He'll kill anyone for money. Man, woman, or child. And has. He doesn't have a conscience. There isn't the thinnest thread of morality in the man. And he doesn't just kill with a bullet. He'll throw a victim down a deep well and stand and listen to them scream for help until they drown. He'll set fire to a house and burn his victims to death. He'll do anything for money."

"Sounds like a real charmin' fellow."

"Oh, he is. He swore to someday kill me. Swore that years ago."

"Why?"

"I whipped him in a fight. With my fists. Beat him bloody after he set a little dog on fire one night up in Wyoming. He still carries the scars of that fight on his face, and will until the day he dies. And I hope I'm the person responsible for putting him in the grave."

"Why did he do that? That's sick, Frank. Decent people wouldn't even think of doing that."

"Because he wanted to do it—that's why. He's filth, and that's all he'll ever be. Besides, I like dogs. If I ever settle down somewhere I'll have a dozen mutts."

"I've had a couple of dogs over the years. Last one died about five years ago. You know, it's funny, but I still miss that silly animal."

"I know the feeling. What was his name?"

Jerry laughed. "Digger. That was the durnedest dog for diggin' holes I ever did see." Jerry was silent for a moment. "Let's take a walk over to the hotel and see what name Mallory registers under," he suggested.

"His own. He always does. He's an arrogant bastard. He

knows there are no dodgers out on him. He likes to throw his name up into the face of the law."

"If he isn't after you, Frank, I'm surprised he came here, knowing you're the marshal."

"I doubt if he knows."

A man came running up. "Trouble about to happen at the Red Horse, Marshal," he panted. "Gun trouble."

"Go home," Frank told him. "We'll handle it."

"I'm gone. I don't like to be around no shootin'."

The man hurried away.

"Let's go earn our pay, Jerry," Frank said.

No sooner had the words left his mouth than a single shot rang out from the direction of the Red Horse Saloon.

"Damn!" Jerry said, and both men took off running.

CHAPTER 12

Frank and Jerry pushed open the batwings and stepped into the smoke-filled saloon. A man lay dead on the dirty floor. Another man stood at the end of the bar, a pistol in his hand. Frank noted that the six-gun was not cocked. The crowded saloon was silent. The piano player had stopped his playing, and the soiled doves were standing or sitting quietly.

"Put the gun down, mister," Frank ordered.

"You go to hell, Morgan!" the man told him.

"All in due time. Right now, though, I'm ordering you to put that gun away."

"And if I don't?" The man threw the taunting challenge at Frank.

"I'll kill you," Frank said softly.

"Your gun's in leather. I'm holdin' mine in my hand, Morgan."

"You'll still die. Don't be a fool, man. If I don't get you, my deputy will."

Jerry had moved about fifteen feet to Frank's right.

"What caused all this?" Frank asked the shooter.

"He called me a liar, and then threatened to kill me. I don't see I had no choice."

"He's right, Marshal," a customer said. "I heard and seen it all."

"All right," Frank replied. "If it was self-defense, you've got no problem. Why are you looking for trouble with me?"

" 'Cause you ain't takin' me to jail—that's why."

"I didn't say anything about jail, partner. I just asked you to put your gun away."

"You ain't gonna try to haul me off to jail?"

"No. Not if you shot in self-defense. Now put that pistol back in your holster."

"All right, Marshal," the shooter said. "I'm doin' it real easy like."

The man slipped his pistol back into leather and leaned against the bar. Frank walked over to the dead man on the floor and knelt down. The dead man's gun was about a foot from the body, and it was cocked. Obviously he had cleared leather when he was hit. Frank stood up. "I need some names."

"My name's Ed Clancy," the shooter said. "I don't know the name of the guy who was trouble-huntin'."

"Anybody know who he is?" Frank asked. "Or where he's from?"

No one did.

"Get the undertaker, Jerry," Frank said.

Jerry left the saloon, and Frank walked over to the shooter by the bar. "Where are you from, Ed?"

"Colorado. I come down here to look for gold."

"Gold?"

"Yeah. But there ain't none. Not enough of it to mess with, anyways."

The bartender was standing close by, and Frank ordered coffee. "You have a permanent address, Ed?"

"Not no more. You want me to stick around town for a day or so?"

"If you don't mind."

"I'll stay. I don't mind. Reason I got my back up was I figured you was gonna kill me, Morgan. I'm sorry I crowded you."

"That's all right, Ed. I understand. Where are you staying in town?"

"Over at Mrs. Miller's boardin ' house."

"Thanks, Ed. I'll probably have all the paperwork done by tomorrow, and you can pull out after that if you've a mind to."

"Thanks, Marshal. You're all right in my book."

Undertaker Malone came in, and Frank and Jerry watched as he went through the dead man's pockets looking for some identification. There was nothing.

Malone stood up. "He's got enough money to bury him proper, Marshal. But no name."

Jerry had circulated through the crowd in the Red Horse, asking about the dead man. No one knew who he was.

"Put his gun and everything you found in his pockets on the bar, Malone," Frank said. "I'll hold it at the office."

"How 'bout his boots?" Malone asked. "They're near brand-new."

"Bury him with them on."

"That seems a shame and a waste to me, Marshal."

"Did I ask you?"

"No, sir."

"Then get him out of here. Jerry, start poking around and see if you can locate the man's horse. I'll be here for a few more minutes."

Frank drank his coffee and watched while the body was carried out. The saloon swamper came over and mopped up the blood, then sprinkled sawdust over the wet spot. Frank waited by the bar until Jerry returned.

"Man's horse was over at the livery, Frank. But no saddlebags, and no rifle in the boot."

"All right. We'll check the hotel and the rooming houses

tonight. If we don't have any luck there, we'll start checking the empty houses and tents in the morning."

"Might not ever know who he is," Jerry opined.

"That might very well be true, Jerry. The West is full of unmarked graves." *I've put a few men in those unmarked graves myself,* Frank added silently.

Frank and Jerry drew a blank at the hotel and the town's several rooming houses. At the hotel, Frank pointed out a name on the register: Robert Mallory.

"Big as brass," Jerry said.

"He's proud of his name, for sure. Loves to flaunt it in the face of the law. Let's call it a night, Jerry. We'll start checking the town tomorrow."

"OK, Frank. You off to bed?"

"In a little while."

"You want me to make the late rounds? I'll be glad to do it."

"No. I'll do it. Thanks for the help tonight, Jer. See you in the morning."

Frank stepped into the Silver Slipper Saloon and ordered coffee. He stood at the far end of the bar and drank his coffee, looking over the now thinning-out crowd—a quiet crowd, as many had gone home for the night. A few people spoke to Frank; most gave him a wide berth, accompanied by curious glances. By now everyone in town, newcomer and resident alike, knew that one of the last of the West's most famous, or infamous, gunfighters was marshal of the town.

Frank stayed only a few minutes, and when he left he used the back door, stepping out into the broken bottle and trash-littered rear of the saloon. He stood for a moment in the darkness, further deepened by the shadow of the building.

He heard the outhouse door creak open and saw a man step out, buttoning up his pants. Frank knew who it was, for few men were as tall as Big Bob Mallory.

"Big Bob." Frank spoke softly.

Bob paused for just a couple of seconds, then chuckled. "I know that voice for sure. Heard you was law doggin' here at the Crossin', Morgan."

"You heard right, Bob. What are you doing in town?"

"None of your goddamn business, Morgan—that's what!"

"I'm making it my business. Now answer the question."

"Takin' a vacation, Morgan. Just relaxin'."

"A vacation from what? All you do is back-shoot folks a couple of times a year. Doesn't take much effort to pull a trigger. I don't think you've ever had a real job."

"Ain't nobody ever proved I shot anyone, Morgan. And you damn sure can't do it. And I do work now and then, and can prove it. I do odd jobs here and there to get by. Doesn't take much for me to live on."

"Don't screw up in my town, Bob. You do, and I'll be on you quicker than a striking snake."

"You go to hell, Morgan!"

"If you've a mind to, we can sure settle it right now."

"You must be tired of livin', Morgan."

"Anytime you're ready to hook and draw."

"I think I'll let you worry and stew for a while longer."

"What's the matter, Bob? Would it help you reach a decision if I turned my back?"

Frank watched the big man tense at that. For a few seconds, he thought Bob was going to draw on him. Then Mallory slowly began to relax.

"Good try, Morgan," Bob said. "You almost had me goin' then."

"What stopped you?"

Bob refused to reply. He stood there, silent.

"Don't cause trouble in this town, Bob. Any bodies show up without explanation, I'll come looking for you and I'll kill you on sight."

"That's plain enough."

"I hope so."

"Mind if I go back in the saloon?"

"I can't legally stop you, Bob. I could order you out of town. But"—Frank paused—"I won't do that. Not yet."

"Getting soft in your old age?"

"You want to keep running that mouth and find out?"

Bob laughed. "I don't think so. Maybe later."

"Anytime. Face-to-face, that is."

"It'll be face-to-face, Frank. When the time comes. You can count on that." Bob walked up to and then past Frank without another word. He opened the back door of the saloon and stepped inside, closing the door behind him. The night once more enveloped Frank.

"Getting real interesting around town," Frank muttered. "Hope I can stay alive long enough to see how it all turns out."

CHAPTER 13

Frank slept well that night, and no one came prowling around his house in the quiet of darkness. Jerry had fed the prisoners when Frank reached the jail the next morning. There had been no new additions to the cell block during the night. The two men walked over to the Silver Spoon to have breakfast.

"Any luck on finding out the dead man's name?" Angie asked, filling their coffee cups.

"Not yet," Frank told her. "We're going to try again after breakfast. But I have my doubts about whether his rifle and saddlebags will ever show up."

"Another unmarked grave," Angie said before moving off to take the order from another customer. "People ought to carry something on them in the way of identification."

"She's right about that," Jerry said.

"I reckon so," Frank replied, sugaring and stirring his coffee. "There might even be a law about that someday."

The men ate their breakfasts and watched as the town's population grew by about fifty people in just the time it took them to eat their food.

Several men, their clothing caked with the dirt of hard traveling, stepped into the café. "Where's the gold strike?" one of them demanded in a very loud and irritating tone.

"What gold strike?" Angie asked.

"Lady, don't act stupid," the second man said. "We've come a long way for this."

"There is no gold here," Frank said in a low voice. "Silver, not gold."

"Who the hell asked you?" the man asked.

"And this is only a small sample of what we'll be facing in the weeks ahead," Frank whispered to his deputy. He pushed his chair back and stood up, facing the two men. Their eyes flicked briefly to the star on Frank's vest. "I didn't know I needed an invitation to speak."

"That two-bit star don't mean a damn thing to me," the man said.

"Yeah," his partner said. "Why don't you sit down and be quiet, Marshal?"

"I don't believe this," Jerry muttered, pushing back his chair and standing up.

"Back off, mister," a customer said softly. "That's Frank Morgan."

Both miners went suddenly slack-jawed and bug-eyed for a few seconds. They exchanged worried glances. The bigger of the pair finally found his voice. "Sorry, Marshal Morgan. I guess we stepped over the line there."

"It's all right, boys," Frank told them. "Sit down and have breakfast and cool down. The food is mighty good here."

"Good idea," the other miner said. "I am hungry as a hog. Ain't neither one of us et since noon yesterday. After we eat maybe we can talk about the big gold strike."

"Right," Frank agreed with a small smile. "The big gold strike."

Frank and Jerry sat back down and Jerry said, "We're really in for it if there is a rumor about gold here."

"More than you know, Jerry. I've been in towns after several hundred very angry miners learned strike rumors were false. It can get real ugly in a hurry."

"Look there," Jerry said, cutting his eyes to the street.

Frank turned his head and watched as a dozen or so riders, all leading packhorses, rode up the street. "Yeah. And it'll get worse."

"At least they're not gunslicks."

"Not yet," Frank said. "They'll come next, with the gamblers and con artists and whores."

"There's Mrs. Browning's son," Jerry said. "Sneakin' around like he's been doin' for the past couple of days. He seems to be watchin' you, Frank."

Frank looked and shook his head. "I thought I saw him yesterday snooping around. That boy is mighty curious about me."

"Any reason he should be?"

Before Frank could reply, the front door burst open. "It's the Pine gang!"

"Here?" Frank blurted, jumping to his feet.

"Well . . ." the man said. "One of them."

Frank relaxed just a bit. "One?"

"Who is it, Pete?" Angie called.

"That Moran kid. I seen him personal on the edge of town. He's just sittin' his horse and watchin'."

"Kid Moran?" Frank asked. "Here? Part of the Pine gang?"

"Yes," Jerry replied. "But that can't be proved. At least no one's ever come forward. I don't think there are any dodgers out on him, either."

"Why would he be comin' here?" a customer asked.

"Probably to try me," Frank said. "He's a gun-happy kid looking for a reputation.

"He's already killed five or six men," said the man who brought the news. "Maybe more than that."

"About that," Frank said. "Wounded two, three more. He's quick, so I hear."

Jerry had a worried look. "Moran is young and fast, Frank."

Frank smiled. "And I'm older and faster, Jerry. But maybe it won't come to that. We'll see." Frank picked up his coffee cup and drank the last couple of swallows. Then he walked toward the door.

"Frank," Angie called.

With his hand on the door handle, Frank cut his eyes.

"It might be a setup," she said.

"Might be, Angie. We'll see." Frank stepped out onto the boardwalk and looked up the street. The Kid was still there, sitting his horse. Frank leaned against a support post and waited for The Kid to make the first move.

Kid Moran spotted Frank and began slowly walking his horse toward the center of town. Frank got his first good look ever at the young man with the growing reputation as a gunslick. The Kid was of average height and weight, and slender built.

As he drew closer, Frank could see only two things that were menacing about the Kid: the matched pair of .45's belted around his waist. But Frank also knew that some people saw beauty in a scorpion, a tarantula, and a rattlesnake.

Kid Moran was as deadly as they came, Frank knew, and he also knew that The Kid was lightning fast.

The Kid rode slowly toward Frank. He touched the brim of his hat and smiled at Frank as he rode past. *More of a smirk than a smile,* Frank thought as he held up one hand in return greeting.

He watched The Kid rein in at a hitch rail in front of the general store and dismount. Frank decided against going over to the store . . . at least not yet. He did not want to provoke an incident with The Kid. Frank felt The Kid would try him, sooner or later.

Conrad Browning walked up the boardwalk—Frank had not seen him cross the street—and stopped just to Frank's left. "Good morning, Marshal Morgan."

"'Mornin', Conrad. You always up this early?"

"Always. I like to open up the office for Mother. It's just one less thing for her to do."

"Very conscientious of you."

"Marshal? May I ask you a question?"

"Sure."

"Sometimes you speak as if you had attended some sort of institution of higher education. Other times you don't. Why is that?"

Frank smiled at the question. "I read a lot, Conrad. I always have at least one book in my saddlebags. I enjoy reading."

"I see. Who is your favorite author?"

"I don't think I have one. A while back I did get interested in this fellow Plato. He has quite a way with words."

"Plato? Ummm. Yes, I would say he does."

Hal was across the street, watching Conrad as he chatted with Frank. Jimmy and Hal were taking no chances, figuring that if the outlaws couldn't grab Vivian they might try for her son. Kid Moran was still inside the general store.

"Who is that young man that just rode into town, Marshal?" Conrad asked. "He seems to be of great interest to you."

"A gunfighter. Calls himself Kid Moran."

"Kid Moran. How quaint. He appears to be still in his teen years."

"He's about twenty, I reckon. But he's shot more than his share of men."

"Why?"

"I beg your pardon?"

"Why did he shoot them?"

"I reckon 'cause he wanted to. Trying to build himself a reputation as a gunslick."

"And that's important out here?"

Again, Frank smiled. "Well . . . it is to some folks, Conrad."

"Sort of like being the town bully, I suppose."

Frank nodded his head. "Yes, that's a very good way of putting it."

"But with a gun."

"Yes."

"Thank you, Marshal. I believe I have a better understanding of the West now. You have a nice day." Conrad strolled off toward the Henson office building.

"Strange boy," Frank muttered. "In many ways, more man than boy."

Kid Moran stepped out of the general store and leaned against an awning post. He stared across the street at the marshal.

What's wrong with this? Frank thought. *Something isn't right, but I can't put my finger on it.*

Frank looked up at the buildings across the street. Was there a second shooter on a rooftop somewhere? If so, was it in front or behind him? Had Pine or Vanbergen sent The Kid in to check out things, or had The Kid come in on his own?

The café door opened behind him and Jerry asked, "What's wrong, Frank?"

"I don't know, Jer. Maybe nothing. But I've got a funny feeling about this thing."

"Far as I know, this is the first time The Kid has ever ridden in alone."

"He's been here before, then?"

"Oh, yes. But always with others. Never alone. Frank, I'm goin' to check out the back of this block of buildings. Don't step out until you get a signal from me."

Jerry exited the rear of the café while Frank waited on one side of the street, Kid Moran on the other. They leaned up against awning support posts and stared at each other without speaking.

As it nearly always happened in Western towns, the word spread fast and the main street became quiet—no riders, no one walking up and down.

"All clear back here, Frank," Jerry called from one end of the block.

"OK, Jer." *Then why am I so edgy?* Frank wondered. He wasn't afraid of facing The Kid in a hook and draw situation. Frank made it a point to find out all he could about any and all gunfighters, new and old, and he knew that while The Kid was very quick, it was reported that he almost always missed his first shot. Frank used to be the same, until he began spending countless hours practicing, making that all important first shot count.

Fear wasn't a factor in the edgy feelings Frank was experiencing.

Frank again searched the rooftops of the buildings across the street. As near as he could tell, there was no one up there. The Kid was still leaning against the post across the street, staring at him.

"All right," Frank muttered. "I've had enough of this. I'm going to find out what The Kid has on his mind." He stepped off the boardwalk and into the street.

The Kid immediately straightened up and began walking away from Frank, heading down toward the end of the street. Frank signaled Jerry to stay put, and began following The Kid. He didn't have a clue as to what was going on . . . but something was up—he was sure of that.

The Kid suddenly stopped and looked around him—everywhere but directly at Frank. Then he crossed the street.

Frank was now standing in the middle of the wide street.

"Well, damn!" Frank muttered.

Half a dozen fast shots blasted the early morning air, as near as Frank could tell, coming from near the Henson office building. He looked for The Kid, but Kid Moran had vanished.

"Goddamn it!" Frank yelled, and took off running.

CHAPTER 14

Frank rounded the corner of the street just as Hal went down in another roar of lead from several pistols in the hands of men standing in the middle of the street in front of the Henson building. The bodyguard spun around, hit several times, and slumped to the dirt. Frank shot the first assailant in the belly, and his second round knocked another down in the street, hip-shot. Frank was forced into an alley as several hidden gunmen opened fire, the bullets howling and whining all around him. The third gunman in the street jumped behind a water trough.

Frank had caught a quick glimpse of Conrad, huddled in the doorway of the office building. He didn't appear to be hurt, but was apparently too frightened to seek better cover. And Vivian was due to arrive at any moment.

Frank snapped a quick shot at a man standing in a doorway.

The bullet knocked a chunk out of the door stoop and sent splinters into the face of the man. Screaming in pain as one of the splinters stuck in his eye, he stepped out of cover.

Frank put a bullet in the man's guts that doubled him over and sent him stumbling into the street. He collapsed facedown in the dirt, and was still.

Jerry's six-gun cracked from the other end of the street, and a man yelled and went off the roof of a boarded-up building. Anyone within earshot could hear his neck break as he landed in the street.

"This ain't workin'!" a man yelled. "Let's get the hell outta here!"

Frank and Jerry waited.

"How?" another man shouted.

"Through the pass, you nitwit. Just like we planned."

There was silence for a moment, then the sounds of several horses being ridden hard away from the edge of town.

Jerry ran over to Frank, a pistol in each hand. "Are you hit?"

"No. Let's see about the boy. I don't think he's hurt, just scared."

Conrad was getting to his feet when Frank and Jerry reached him. His face was ashen, and he was trembling. "They were going to kidnap me!" Conrad blurted. "Hal pushed me down and stood in front of me." He looked at Hal, bloody and dead in the street. "Oh, my God!" Conrad started to move toward Hal, and Frank stopped him.

"Easy, boy. No point. He's beyond help."

"You don't know that!"

"I know, boy. I saw him take three rounds in the center of the chest."

"I liked that man. I didn't at first. But I really liked him. He saved my life."

"That's what he was paid to do, Conrad."

Jerry was checking the dead and the wounded. "Two alive, Frank. And one of them ain't gonna be for long."

"Good," Frank said. "The jail's gettin' full." A crowd had gathered at the mouth of the street. "One of you get Doc Bracken, and someone get the undertaker. Move!" He turned to Jerry. "See if you can locate Kid Moran. Don't brace him, Jerry. Just see if he's still in town."

"Will do."

Jimmy and Vivian walked up. Vivian was pale with shock, and Jimmy was killing mad. Frank could read it in his eyes. "Settle down, Jimmy. They're gone."

"Me and Hal been pards for a long time, Frank. I ain't likely to forget this."

"See to Mrs. Browning and her son, Jimmy. Right now!"

Jimmy nodded and took Viv's arm, leading her and Conrad toward the front door of the office building and inside. Jimmy stood in the doorway for a moment, looking at the bloody and still body of his longtime friend. The man touched the brim of his hat and walked inside the office, closing the door.

Someone called that the doctor had been roused out of bed and was on his way, as was Malone, the undertaker. Frank walked over to the hip-shot gunman. On closer investigation, he recognized him—Max Stoddard. He was wanted in several states for murder, and there was a hefty reward for his arrest.

"You boys are making me a princely sum of money, Max," Frank told him.

"Go to hell."

Frank smiled at the outlaw. "Time I get through here, I'll be near'bouts able to retire, I reckon."

"Damn you, Morgan!"

Frank reached down and slipped an over-and-under derringer from the outlaw's left boot. "Were you thinking I'd forget about this little banger, Max?"

"I was hopin' you would, you bastard."

Frank laughed at him and took a long-bladed knife from the sheath on the outlaw's belt. "Not likely, Max. I haven't stayed alive this long by being careless."

"Ned or Vic will get you, Morgan. You can count on that. They'll get you 'fore this is over."

Doc Bracken was pushing his way through the still gathering crowd, cussing loudly and ordering the gawkers to get the hell out of his way.

Mayor Jenkins was right behind him, both of them looking as though they had jumped into their clothes, unshaven and with disheveled hair.

"What the hell happened here?" the mayor shouted.

"These men tried to kidnap Conrad Browning," Frank said, pointing to the dead and wounded in the street. "Conrad's bodyguard was killed. Conrad and his mother are safe. They're in the office building."

"My God!" the mayor whispered. "Do you know any of these men, Marshal?"

"I know this one. Max Stoddard. He's wanted for murder in several states. All these men are part of the Pine and Vanbergen gangs."

The mayor patted Frank on the arm. "Wonderful job, Marshal. Superb."

The mayor wandered off into the crowd. Frank turned his attention to the doctor, watching him work on Stoddard for a moment.

"No permanent damage to the hip," the doctor said. "But he won't be walking for a while. Some of you men take this hombre over to the jail." Doc Bracken moved quickly to the other outlaws. "Dead," he said twice. "And this one won't last long. Some of you men make him as comfortable as possible. He'll be dead in a few minutes."

"Damn you to hell, Morgan!" the dying man said.

"Here, now," Dr. Bracken admonished him. "That's enough of that. You best be making your peace with God."

The outlaw started cussing, spewing out a stream of profanity. Suddenly he began coughing. He arched his back, and then relaxed in a pool of blood.

"He's gone," Doc Bracken said.

Frank went with the undertaker and searched the pockets

of the dead men. They had no identification on them. He took their guns and walked back to his office. Jerry met him on the way.

"Kid Moran left town when the shooting started, Frank. Half a dozen people seen him hightail out."

"All right. What about this pass the outlaws took to get out of town?"

"Cuts through the mountains yonder," he said, pointing. "But it's tricky, so I'm told. If you don't know the way, you can get all balled up and lost and find yourself dead-ended on a narrow trail."

"Can't go forward, and you have hell going back?"

"That's it."

"You been up there?"

"No. It's outlaw controlled on the other side of the mountains. Only the outlaws use it, and they don't use it very often. Men and horses have been killed up there, slippin' off the narrow trails."

"So the Pine and Vanbergen gangs are headquartered just over those mountains?"

"Yep. Not five miles away, as the crow flies. But they might as well be plumb over on the other side of the moon, if you know what I mean."

Frank nodded his head. "I do. Let's go see about our new prisoner and then arrange a nice service for Hal."

A week after the shoot-out in which Hal was killed, a deputy U.S. Marshal came by train to Denver and then took the spur line down to the border and went from there by horse to the Crossing and picked up two of the prisoners Frank was holding. Frank's bank account grew substantially. Ten days later another deputy U.S. Marshal rode in and promptly rode out with Max Stoddard. Stoddard had a two thousand dollar reward on his head, and so did one of the other dead men. Frank gave half of the money to Jerry, and Jerry almost pumped his arm off shaking his hand. Frank's bank account grew even larger.

Hal was buried in the local cemetery, and Vivian bought a nice headstone for the grave.

Barnwell's Crossing grew by almost a thousand people in two weeks. Most were coming in because of the rumor of a major gold strike, and nothing anyone could say would make them believe it wasn't true.

"Hell with them," Frank told Jerry one morning. "When they get tired of digging they'll leave."

The county now had a judge—Judge Walter Pelmutter—assigned to the town of Barnwell's Crossing, and that made the disposition of those arrested a lot faster. The marshal's office got two dollars out of every fine, and Frank split that with Jerry. Judge Pelmutter was a no-nonsense, by-the-book judge who cut no slack to anyone for anything. The jail was usually full at night and emptied out the next morning after court.

Frank checked the wall clock. Eleven o'clock. He had a lunch date with Vivian at her home in half an hour. After lunch they were to go riding and spend the afternoon together. Conrad would stay at the office. That would give Jimmy a much needed break. Frank had offered to hire another bodyguard, but Jimmy had said he didn't want to work with anyone else . . . not for a time yet. Jimmy was gradually working his way out of his grieving over the loss of his saddle pard, but he still had a ways to go.

"I'm going to go home and wash up some and change clothes, Jerry," he told his deputy. "Then I'm over to Mrs. Browning's house. We're going riding down in the valley."

"Don't worry about a thing, Frank. I'll take care of any problem that comes up. Y'all have fun and relax."

At his house, Frank cleaned up and changed clothes—black trousers with a narrow pinstripe, black shirt. He tied a red bandanna around his neck and slipped on a black leather vest. He combed his hair, put on his hat, and then inspected himself as best he could in the small mirror he'd bought at Willis's General Store.

"Well, Morgan," he said to the reflection. "You're not going to win any contests for handsome. But you don't look too bad, considering what you have to work with."

He buckled on his gunbelt and stepped out onto the small front porch. The day was sunny and cloudless, the sky a bright blue—a perfect day for a ride in the country.

He rode the short distance over to the Browning estate and talked with Jimmy for a few minutes before walking up to the porch and being admitted inside the grandest house in town.

"You look lovely," he told Vivian, as she opened the door and he stepped inside.

"You wouldn't be the least prejudiced, now would you, Frank?" she teased.

"Not at all. You're as pretty as the day we married."

"And you tell great big fibs, Frank Morgan. But do continue."

Lunch was fried chicken, hot biscuits, mashed potatoes and gravy.

"Did you fix this?" Frank asked.

"I certainly did. The servants have the afternoon off. And I told Jimmy to take off as soon as you got here."

"How about Conrad? Is Jimmy going to the office?"

"No. I asked a couple of my miners to look after him. Those men have been with me for years. Completely trustworthy."

After lunch, over coffee, Vivian said, "I' m going to change clothes, Frank. I hate to ride sidesaddle. Will you be shocked if I change into britches?"

Frank chuckled. "I knew you pretty well a long time ago, Viv. I think I'm past being shocked by anything you do."

She laughed. "Don't say I didn't warn you."

She came out of her bedroom a few moments later wearing very tight-fitting men's jeans and a checkered shirt, open at the collar. Frank almost choked on his coffee.

"Damn, Viv!" he managed to say, wiping a few drops of coffee off his chin.

"You don't approve, Frank?" she teased him.

"'Approve' is . . . not quite the word."

"Come on, let's get saddled up and get out of this town. I want to forget business for a few hours. I want us to be totally alone, and I want a good, hard ride."

Frank grinned and held his tongue on that one . . . but oh, what he was thinking.

She caught his smile. "You're naughty, Frank. But don't ever change."

"I'm too old to change now, Viv."

Five minutes later they were riding out of town, heading toward the mountains and a pretty little valley that lay in the shadows of the mountains.

Shortly after they rode out of town, four men dressed as miners rode out. They occasionally exchanged smiles as they followed the man and woman. They had traveled a long way to get to the town of Barnwell's Crossing. The five thousand dollars that Vivian's father had placed on Frank's head had grown to ten thousand over the years, and the man who was overseeing the bounty, controlling the purse strings—a close friend of the family, and legal advisor—had added ten thousand, plus a substantial bonus if the body was never found, for Vivian's death.

The four paid assassins had been lounging around town for a week, staying out of sight and waiting for the right moment . . . and this was it.

CHAPTER 15

The valley was an oasis of green surrounded by mountains, a profusion of multicolored wildflowers and gently waving grass in the slight breeze.

"It's lovely," Viv whispered as she and Frank rested their horses at the mouth of the valley. "So beautiful and peaceful."

Frank had carefully checked out the valley a few days before, and had been pleasantly surprised to find it as Vivian had just described it.

"A little creek is over yonder," Frank said, pointing. "Water is cold and pure. I had me a drink, and it numbed my tongue."

"Large enough to take a swim?"

"No. If you're brave you could stick your feet in it, though. But you won't leave them in there for long."

"I'm thirsty."

"We'll ride down and have us a drink. Fill up our canteens."

"I wrapped up some of that chicken and biscuits."

"I'm so full now I'm about to pop, Viv. But it'll sure taste good later."

Vivian took off her fashionable boots and put her feet into the fast-running creek . . . for about one second. She squealed, jerked her feet out, and immediately began rubbing them. "I have never felt water that cold!"

"I warned you," Frank said with a laugh. He quickly cut his eyes to the horses, grazing a dozen yards away. Their heads had come up quickly, and their ears were pricked. The nostrils on Frank's horse were flared, and his eyes were shining with a wary and suspicious light.

"Stay put, Viv. Don't move unless I tell you to. And if I tell you, get behind that clump of trees just to your left."

"What's wrong, Frank?"

"I don't know. But the animals suddenly got jumpy, and I've learned to trust that big horse of mine. He's saved my skin more than once."

Frank stayed low and worked his way over to his horse. Using the big animal for cover, he pulled his rifle from the boot. He opened a pocket on the side of the boot and took out a box of cartridges and slipped them in his back pocket. Frank preferred the rifle because it packed a hefty wallop and had excellent range.

He crawled back to Viv and motioned for her to head for the copse of trees he had pointed out.

In the trees, she looked at him through worried eyes. "What's wrong?" she repeated.

"I saw one man, maybe two, slipping around on that ridge over there, dead in front of us."

"The Pine and Vanbergen gangs?"

"Maybe. Can't be certain about that. But folks who slip around are damn sure up to no good."

"Conrad!"

"The boy will be all right, Viv. You've got people looking out for him, and Jimmy will be in town and so will Jerry. Don't worry about him."

She peered through the weeds at the ridge. Frank felt her stiffen beside him.

"What's wrong, Viv?"

"I just caught a glint of sunlight off of something."

"Where?"

"Way over there to our right. In those rocks."

"That's three men, then. At least."

"We're in deep trouble, aren't we, Frank?"

"Well . . . yes and no. To get behind us would take some doing. It's all nearly wide-open meadow for a long way on either side of us. An Indian could do it easy enough, but these men aren't Indians."

"The question is, who are they and what do they want?"

"You or me, or both of us."

"So we do . . . what?"

"We wait, Viv. By now they're sure to have figured out we've spotted them, so surprise is out of their plans. That's a plus for us."

"The minus is, there appears to be only one easy way into this valley, right?"

Frank smiled. "You're still a very observant lady, Viv. That's right. There are a half-dozen ways in and out, but only one easy way. And they've got it covered."

"And the other ways out?"

"Rough. Danger of slides, mostly. To the north is completely out of the question. That pass is controlled by the Pine and Vanbergen gangs."

"Well . . . we've got a little food and plenty of water. I can stand to lose a few pounds, anyway."

Frank chuckled. "You're a tough lady, Viv. Tougher now than when we first met."

"Dealing with male heads of business and shifty attorneys can do that."

"I 'spect you've had plenty of practice in dealing with both over the years."

"Running a conglomerate of businesses is tough enough for a man in a man's world, Frank. Being a woman makes it doubly tough."

The ugly whine of a bullet put an end to that conversation. The bullet slammed into a tree behind the pinned-down pair and tore off bits of bark.

"They sure know where we are," Viv remarked, raising her head and looking around.

Frank did not immediately reply. He was trying to determine where the bullet came from. He had a hunch it came from the location of a fourth man. Finally he said, "I'm sure there is another man behind the rocks near the entrance to the valley, Viv. That makes four."

"The odds just keep getting worse."

"We've got good cover, and that bullet came nowhere near us. I'm not even sure they know exactly where we are. They may be just trying to flush us."

"You will excuse me if I don't share your cool calmness, Frank. I'm a stranger to this type of thing."

"You're doing fine, Viv." He looked up at the sun. About five hours of good daylight left, maybe less. "If it comes to it, Viv, I can lead us out on foot come dark."

Another bullet bowled into the copse of trees; then several more came whistling in.

"I think they have guessed we're here, Frank."

"I think so, too. This was the logical place for us to take cover."

"I counted four rifles."

"Yes. Me, too. I think someone is using a .32-.20. Another sounds like a .45-.70."

"Is all that supposed to mean something to me?"

Frank grinned at her. "When we get out of this pickle I'll give you a short course in firearms."

"I can hardly wait. In more ways than one."

The gunmen on the ridges and in the rocks opened up again, and Frank and Vivian could do nothing but huddle behind cover, all thoughts of talk obliterated by the roar of gunfire and the bowling of bullets.

"This is beginning to make me mad," Frank muttered, when the gunfire ceased for a moment.

Viv looked at him in astonishment. She had taken off her hat, and her hair was just slightly disheveled. Her white blouse was spotted with dirt and grass stains. "You're just now getting angry, Frank?"

"Yeah. That bunch of yellow bastards over yonder is really annoying me now." He lifted his rifle to his shoulder and mentally figured the range before squeezing off a round. The bullet was low, and he compensated for that before squeezing off another round. This time the bullet must have come very close to the hidden sniper, for both Frank and Viv heard a yelp of surprise.

"You hit?" the question was shouted.

"Naw. But that bastard can shoot."

"We all knowed that startin' off, Dick."

There was more conversation between the snipers, but it was so faint neither Frank nor Viv could make out the words.

Then one of the gunmen called, "This ain't workin' out, boys."

Frank and Viv looked at each other.

"What do you mean, Rob? We got 'em cold. All we got to do is wait 'em out."

Another voice was added. "Yeah? But for how long?"

"That's right. Them two got good cover, and we can't get to them to finish this."

"He's right 'bout that," another called. "It's all open twixt us and them."

"Goddamn it, no names, you idgits!"

"Rob and Dick," Frank muttered. "Remember those names, Viv."

"Forever," she whispered.

There was more murmuring of words between the gunmen, again so faint that Frank and Viv could not make them out. They waited in the copse of trees.

Then there was nothing but the gentle sighing of the wind in the valley.

"Have they gone?" Viv asked.

"I don't know, honey. It may be they just want us to think they've left."

"If wishes were horses . . ."

"What?"

"Nothing," she said with a quiet laugh. "Don't pay any attention to me. I'm babbling."

"Babble on, Viv. I'm going to ease out of here and take a look around."

She cut her suddenly alarm-filled eyes to him. "Frank—"

"Relax. I'm not going far, and I'm not going to take any chances. Take it easy, Viv. I'll be right back."

"Promise?"

"Cross my heart. You want to spit in my palm?"

She smiled, and Frank could see her tension ease. "Get out of here, you nut!"

Frank eased out of the trees and wormed his way down to and over the creekbank, then worked his way about fifty feet. Easing up behind a clump of weeds, he gave the rocks and ridges a good visual going-over. He could see nothing moving. His and Viv's horses had moved a few yards during the gunfire, but were now grazing calmly. His big horse was showing no signs of being alarmed.

Frank crawled over the creekbank and quickly got to his feet, running toward the horses. No shots boomed; no lead came howling in his direction. He led the horses over to the thick copse of trees.

"They're gone, Viv. Come on. I want to take a look at the ridges. I might find some sign that I can use."

Frank found some brass from a .45-.70 and a .32-.20. But it was the butt-plate markings that caught and held his attention. They were strange looking.

"What's wrong, Frank?"

"The butt-plate on this rifle. It's the strangest I've ever

seen." He snapped his fingers. "I know what it is. It loads through the buttstock. I'll bet you it's a bolt-action military rifle."

"Are they rare?"

"They are out here."

"And if you find a man in town who has one, it's a good bet he's one of the men who attacked us."

"That's it, Viv. Come on, let's ride. It's a good hour back to town, and we're not taking the same trail back we used to get up here."

Frank found the tracks of the men who'd attempted to kill them, and there were four horses. The hoofprints led straight toward town. Frank cut across country, and they made it back to town in just over an hour. Frank saw Vivian back to her house, where Jimmy was waiting on the porch.

Jimmy saw the dirt and grass stains on their clothing and asked, "Trouble?"

Frank explained what had happened.

"I bet that's one of those Winchester-Hotchkiss so-called sportin' rifles," Jimmy said. "The army has some of them, but they're rare out here."

"Keep your eyes open for one, Jimmy."

"Will do."

At the office, while Jerry made a fresh pot of coffee, Frank told him about the events of that afternoon.

"You think they were after you, or Mrs. Browning?"

"Both of us. And I'm getting damn tired of it."

"You think the Pine and Vanbergen gangs were behind the ambush?"

Frank shook his head. "I don't think so, Jerry. They want to kill me, yes. But I believe there are other forces working to kill both of us."

"Who?"

Frank explained in as much depth as he knew about Viv's father and his deathbed desire to have him killed. He ended with, "This attorney, whoever he is—and Viv told me they have a couple of dozen lawyers, maybe more than that, working for the company—has some big ideas, I think. Ideas about controlling the various companies that make up Henson Enterprises. But first he has to get rid of Vivian."

Jerry slowly nodded his head. "OK. But that still leaves the son."

"Who is not twenty-one years old, and legally can't do a damn thing until he is."

"Ah! Yeah. I'm getting the picture now. But you have no proof of any of this."

"Not a bit. It's all speculation on my part."

"Now what?"

"Now I go visit the saloons."

"You saw the men who attacked you?"

"No. But if I show up where they are, one of them just might get nervous and tip his hand."

"Could be. Want me to tag along?"

"No. You do the early business check on Main Street. I'll handle this on my own."

The men sat for few minutes and drank a cup of coffee. The cell block area of the jail, for the first time in a long time, was empty. Frank finished his coffee and stood up to leave. He really wanted another cup, for Jerry made good coffee, but he had a lot to do, and wanted to get started. He could get a cup in one of the saloons, although theirs usually tasted the way horse liniment smelled.

Frank tucked the short-barreled Peacemaker behind his gunbelt, butt forward on the left side, and headed out. He had filed the sight off so it would not hang up.

His first stop was the Silver Slipper Saloon, and it was doing a booming business. He walked through the saloon, speaking to a few of the patrons. Just as he was about to exit out the back way, he cut his eyes over to a far corner table and stopped. Big Bob Mallory was sitting alone. Frank had thought Big Bob was long gone, for he hadn't seen him in a couple of weeks. He walked over and sat down.

"Make yourself right at home, Frank," Bob said. "Uninvited, of course."

"I was hoping I'd seen the last of you, Bob. I thought you'd long rattled your hocks."

"I been here and there, Frank. But I'll leave when I get damn good and ready."

"Where were you this afternoon?"

"Not that it's any of your damn business, but I was playin' poker over at the Red Horse. All afternoon. Check it out if you don't be-lieve me."

"I will, and I don't believe you. I wouldn 't believe anything you had to say even if you were standing in the presence of God."

Bob smiled at him. "You're not goin' to rile me into pullin' on you, Morgan. Not now. I'm tellin' you the truth 'bout this afternoon. You'll see."

"Don't screw up in this town, Bob. I told you before, and I'm telling you now."

Bob smiled at him and said nothing.

Frank pushed back his chair and walked away, exiting out the back door, stepping into the night. The darkness was broken only by the faint glint off the many empty whiskey bottles that littered the ground. Someone was grunting in the outhouse. Frank ignored that and walked on, up the alley and back onto the street. He stood in the mouth of the alley for a moment.

The foot traffic was heavy early in the evening—mostly miners wandering from saloon to saloon to whorehouses located at each end of the town, just past the town limits.

Frank stepped out of the alley and started walking toward the Red Horse Saloon. He hadn't gone a dozen steps before three shots blasted the air. The sound was muffied, and Frank knew they came from inside a building. Probably the Red Horse.

"Here we go again," Frank said, and began running toward trouble.

CHAPTER 16

Just before Frank reached the entrance to the Red Horse, a man staggered out, both hands holding his bloody stomach and chest. The gut-shot man fell off the boardwalk and collapsed on the edge of the street. He groaned in pain and tried to rise. He didn't make it. He died in the dirt before Frank could reach him.

Frank pushed open the batwings and stepped inside the smoky saloon. The large crowd had shifted away from the bar, leaving the long bar empty except for two young men dressed in black, each of them wearing two guns, tied down low. Frank guessed them to be in their early twenties. The music and singing had ceased; the crowd was still, and gunsmoke hung in the air.

Trouble-hunting punks, Frank thought. *Well, they've damn sure found it.* "What happened here?" Frank said.

"Who the hell are you?" one of the young men at the bar asked belligerently.

"The marshal. I asked what happened here."

"He got lippy and wanted trouble—that's what. We gave it to him."

"Both of you shot him?"

"Yeah," the other young trouble-hunter mouthed off. "What's it to you, Mr. Marshal?"

"Sonny boy," Frank said, taking a step closer to the young men. "I've had all the mouth I'm going to take from either of you. I'll ask the questions, you answer them. Without the smart-aleck comments. Is that understood?" Frank took a couple more steps toward the pair.

One of the punks feigned great consternation at Frank's words. "Oh, my! I'm so frightened I might pee my drawers! How about you, Tom?"

"Oh, me, too, Carl. The old-timer's words is really makin' me nervous."

Both of them burst out laughing.

Frank took several more steps while the pair were braying like jackasses and hit Tom in the mouth with a hard straight left. The punch knocked the punk clean off his boots and deposited him on the floor. Frank turned slightly and drove his right fist into the belly of Carl. Carl doubled over and went to his knees, gagging and gasping for air.

Frank reached down and snatched the guns from Tom, tossed them on a table, and then pulled Carl's Colts from leather. He backed up, holding the punk's twin pistols, and waited.

Tom got to his feet first, his mouth leaking blood. He stood glaring at Frank.

Someone out on the boardwalk yelled, "Here comes Doc Bracken. Get out of the way, boys!"

"Get your friend on his feet," Frank told Tom. "Right now!"

Jerry pushed open the batwings just as both young trouble-hunters were on their feet, wobbly, but standing.

"Jerry," Frank said, "I want you to get statements from as many people as you can about this shooting. Get their names and tell them to drop by the office in the morning to verify and sign all they told you."

"Will do, Frank."

Frank motioned with the muzzle of the right-hand Colt. "Move, boys. To the jail."

"It was self-defense, Marshal!" Tom shouted. "He was pesterin' us."

"That's a damn lie," a miner said. "It was them pesterin' the other guy. They goaded him into a gunfight. They pushed him real hard. I wouldn't have tooken near'bouts as much as that other feller took. He had to fight. That's all there was to it. They didn't give him no choice in the matter. None a'tall."

"Yore a damn liar, mister!" Carl said.

"Give your story to my deputy," Frank told the man. "Move, boys."

"You're makin' a mistake, Marshal," Carl said.

"Shut up and move. If the other man started the trouble, you can ride on out of town."

"You son of a bitch!" Tom cussed him.

"Be careful, boy," Frank warned him. "Don't let your ass overload your mouth."

Frank locked the pair up and once more hit the streets. He began prowling the new makeshift saloons, and there were about a dozen wood-frame, canvas-covered drinking spots that had sprung up since the new silver strike and the rumors of a major gold strike.

The evening's rambling and searching produced nothing. Frank could flush no one. He finally gave it up and returned to the office.

"Any luck?" Jerry asked.

Frank shook his head as he poured a mug of coffee. "If I did see them, they're mighty cool ole boys. I didn't produce a single bobble."

"I might be on to something," Jerry said.

"Oh?"

"Four men are living in a tent 'bout a mile out of town." He pointed. "That way. Off the west trail. They staked a claim, but no one's ever seen them working it. Man I've known since I come to town told me about them. Only reason he brought it up was 'cause those ole boys is real unfriendly and surly like. I questioned him some and he said he seen them ride out 'bout noon today, and they didn't come back 'til late afternoon."

"You did good, Jerry. I appreciate it."

"There's more, Frank. My friend thinks one of them has a bolt-action rifle."

Frank sugared his coffee and stirred slowly. "I'll pay those ole boys a visit first thing in the morning. Going up there tonight would be asking for trouble."

"It sure would. And it isn't against the law to be unfriendly."

Frank smiled. "You're right about that. If it was, half the population would be in jail. How did the questioning over at the saloon go?"

"Those two trouble-hunters we have locked up started the whole thing. They needled the other fellow into pulling on them. But the other guy did go for his gun first."

"They'll probably get off, then. If the other man drew first, I don't know of any major charges that could be brought against them. But we'll keep them locked up until the judge opens court. It's his mess to deal with now. You go on to bed, Jerry. I'll make the late rounds."

"You sure, Frank?"

"Oh, yeah. I'm not a bit sleepy. Besides, I need to go over to the funeral parlor and find out what I can about the dead man."

"See you in the morning, Frank."

"'Night, Jer."

At the funeral parlor, Frank walked into the back, where the nude body of the stranger was on a narrow table. Malone was preparing the body for burial. He looked up as Frank strolled in.

"No identification on the body, Marshal. He had fifty

dollars on him. Ten dollars in silver, the rest in paper. His gun and clothes and boots are over there on that table next to the wall."

Frank carefully inspected the dead man's boots and gunbelt for a hidden compartment. There was nothing. "I'll pick up the gun and rig in the morning," he told Malone.

Malone nodded his head and kept working on the body. Frank got out of there. He walked over to the livery and asked if anyone fitting the dead man's description had stabled his horse there. The night holster nodded and pointed to a roan in a stall.

"Where's his saddle?" Frank asked.

"In the storeroom. Saddle, saddlebags, and rifle in a boot. Far right-hand corner."

Frank carried the gear over to the office and stored it as quietly as possible. Jerry was already in his room, in his bunk, snoring softly. Frank would go through the saddlebags in the morning, but he didn't expect to find anything in the way of identification. The grave would be just another unmarked one in a lonely cemetery. The West had hundreds of such graves. On the Oregon Trail, it was said, there were two or three graves for every mile of the pioneer trek westward. And still the people came, hundreds every week.

During his wanderings, Frank had seen countless abandoned cabins. He wondered how many of the pioneers gave up after a few years and went back east.

Frank locked up the office and walked over to the Silver Spoon for a cup of coffee. The place was dark, closed for the night.

He began making his rounds of the town, checking the doors of the businesses. He cut up the alley and came out near the Henson Enterprises building. He watched the building for a moment, then decided to check the windows and back door. The back door was unlocked.

Frank pushed open the door and saw the faint glint of

lamplight under the door, coming from Viv's office. Frank put his hand on the butt of his .45.

Then the door opened and Conrad stepped out. He spotted the dark shape of Frank and gasped, "Oh, my God! Don't shoot!"

"Damn, boy!" Frank said. "What the hell are you doing down here this time of night?"

"Marshal! Well . . . doing some necessary paperwork. Mother neglected her duties this afternoon. Mr. Dutton arrived on the stage, and was displeased to find Mother gone gallivanting about the countryside while so much work was left unattended here."

"Who the hell is Dutton?"

"Our company's chief attorney."

"What business is it of his what the president of Henson Enterprises does in her spare time?"

"I resent your tone, Marshal!"

"I don't give a damn what you resent. Your mother and I are old friends—a friendship that goes back twenty years. If she wants to go riding and relax, that's her business—none of yours, and sure as hell none of this Dutton fellow's. Is that clear, Conrad?"

"If you're such 'old friends' "—the young man put a lot of grease on the last two words—"why weren't you mentioned before now? Personally, I think you're both lying. What is it between you and my mother?"

"We're friends, Conrad. That's all. As to why I wasn't mentioned years back . . . well, after all, I do have something of an unsavory reputation. In very polite Boston society it just wouldn't do for your mother to let people know she was friends with a gunfighter."

"Ummm. Well, you're certainly correct in that assumption. But I still believe there is more . . . a lot more than either of you are willing to tell. And I shall make it my business to find out what."

Frank sighed. The young man was a bulldog, no doubt about that. "Whatever, Conrad. Where is this Dutton fellow?"

"At the hotel."

"Come on, then. Close up the place, and I'll escort you back to the house."

"I am perfectly capable of seeing myself home, Marshal. I bought a pistol today."

"God help us all," Frank muttered.

"Beg pardon?"

"Nothing, Conrad. What kind of pistol?"

"This one," Conrad said, reaching inside his coat and hauling out a Colt Frontier double action revolver. He pointed it at Frank, and Frank quickly pushed the muzzle to one side and took the weapon.

Frank stepped closer to the light streaming through the open door and inspected the pistol. A .45 caliber. "It's a good pistol, Conrad. Have you fired it yet?"

"Certainly not! And I won't until it becomes necessary."

"I . . . see. I think."

"It shouldn't take too much expertise to discharge a firearm. One simply points the weapon and pulls the trigger. Right, Marshal?"

"Well—"

"So, considering this recent firearm purchase, I shall now take over the job of protecting my mother. Your services will no longer be needed. If indeed they ever were."

"Is that right?"

"Quite."

Resisting a sudden urge to jerk a knot in the boy/man's butt, Frank instead suggested, "Why don't we let your mother decide that, Conrad?"

Conrad didn't speak for several seconds, then said, "Oh, very well, Marshal. Let's don't go into a lot of folderol about it. Now I have to lock up."

"I'll wait for you, Conrad."

"Very well, Marshal. If you insist."

Conrad blew out the lamps and locked the back door. Frank waited in the darkness of the alley. When Conrad turned around, Frank said, "Have you eaten, Conrad?"

The young man looked at Frank. Even in the darkness, Frank could feel Conrad's attitude toward him soften. "Why . . . yes, I have, Marshal. Thank you for asking."

"Come on, let's get out of this alley."

On the boardwalk, in a bit more light from newly installed oil lamps along the way, Conrad asked, "Who were those gunmen after today, Marshal—you or my mother?"

"I don't know, Conrad." Frank knew very little about the why of those wanting Vivian out of the way, but he did know he was not going to discuss it with Conrad. "Has your mother said anything?"

"Precious little. But something is weighing very heavily on her mind. I can tell that. She just won't open up to me. Perhaps she will, in time."

"I'm sure she will, Conrad."

They walked on for a half block. Frank felt his guts tighten as four men stepped out of an alley. They were lurching along as if they were drunk, but Frank wasn't sure about that. When they began singing, he was certain they were pretending.

"When I tell you to run, Conrad, don't argue with me, and for God's sake don't hesitate. Just run like the devil is after you. You understand?"

"Yes, sir. Those men up ahead of us?"

"Yes. I'm sure they're going to pull something. Get ready to flee, boy."

The four men began to separate until they were covering the whole boardwalk. Frank watched as one slipped his hand under his coat. When the hand came out holding a six-gun, Frank yelled, "Go, boy! Run!"

Conrad took off, and Frank snaked his Colt out of leather.

CHAPTER 17

Frank dived behind a water trough just as the quartet opened up, the lead howling all around him. He managed to snap off one shot that brought a yelp of either pain or surprise from one of the gunmen—Frank wasn't sure.

He was astonished when a shout came from the other side of the street.

"You filthy savages!" Conrad shouted. "Damn you all!" Conrad pointed his big .45 in the general direction of the quartet of gunmen and pulled the trigger.

The bullet tore the hat off one of the men and sent him hollering and scampering toward a doorway stoop. "Jesus Christ!" he yelled.

Conrad's next shot knocked the heel off the left boot of another man and sent him sprawling to the boardwalk. "My leg!" he squalled. "I'm hit, boys!"

Jiggs from the apothecary shop came running up the boardwalk, a shotgun in his hand, just as Conrad cut loose again. The bullet whined past Jiggs's head, missing his nose by about one hot half-inch.

"Oh, shit!" the druggist whooped, and he ran for cover

into the general store . . . right through the closed and locked front door. Jiggs took the door with him.

"Get that punk!" one of the gunmen yelled.

Conrad pointed the .45 at the man and triggered off another round. The bullet took off a tiny piece of the man's ear, and the assassin started jumping up and down and yelling as if he'd been touched by a hot branding iron.

"I been shot in the head, boys. Oh, Lordy, I'm done for, I reckon."

Conrad shot him again . . . or at least came really close to upsetting the man's evenings for a long time to come. The bullet nicked the gunman's inner thigh, just a microscopic distance from his privates.

"Oh, good God!" the man screamed. "I'm ruint, boys. He's done shot me in the balls!"

Conrad took that time to reload with a handful of cartridges from his coat pocket. Fully loaded, he continued his cussing, shouting insults, and firing.

"You rotten scalawags!" Conrad shouted. "You all belong in a cage!"

"Then put me in a cage!" yelled the man who thought he'd been shot in the doo-das. He had both hands between his legs, holding onto his precious parts . . . what he thought was left of them. "Anywhere! Just get me away from that crazy kid!"

"I'm out of here," the fourth outlaw yelled, running up to where Frank lay crouched behind the water trough.

Frank reached out and grabbed the man's ankle, spilling him onto the boardwalk. The man lost his pistol on his way down, banged his head on the rough boards, and knocked himself goofy for a few minutes.

Conrad fired again, the bullet knocking splinters into the face of the man who had lost his hat to Conrad's first shot.

"I yield!" the man yelled, throwing down his gun. "Don't shoot no more."

"Somebody get me a doctor!" shouted the man who thought he'd been violently deprived of his private parts as hot blood from the nick on his thigh ran down his leg. "Oh, Lord, get me to a doctor."

Frank then realized what the man was so upset about. He got to his boots, trying to keep from laughing at the total absurdity of the entire situation, and told the man who thought he'd been shot in the gonads, "What do you think the doctor's going to do, you idiot, sew the sac back on?"

That really set the man off. He began wailing and moaning so loudly windows began glowing with lamplight all up and down the street.

Jiggs stepped out of the general store, his shotgun covering the two would-be kidnappers who were still standing and in one piece, more or less.

Jerry had showed up, and had talked Conrad into giving him his .45.

"Thank God," Frank muttered.

Doc Bracken walked up. "What in the world is going on here?"

"Here's the doctor, buddy," Frank told the man who was making moaning sounds . . . sort of like a train whistle with a stopped-up valve.

"What's his problem?" Doc asked.

"He thinks his balls have been shot off."

"Good Lord! That's terrible. Did you find them?" Doc asked, after glancing at the man's bloody britches. He began looking all around him on the boardwalk and in the street. "I might be able to sew them back on. I've heard it's been done."

"Do they stay on?" Frank asked.

"Not so far. Infection always sets in, and they rot off." That really got the mournful sounds cranked up from the would-be kidnapper who thought his cojones were gone forever, and they echoed around the mountain town. A dozen bound dogs joined in from various parts of town, and the noise brought a hundred or more people out of their homes and into the street.

Conrad was shaking so much Jerry had to lead him over to the boardwalk on the opposite side of the street and sit him down.

"Oh, my God," Conrad said, his voice shrill from nervousness. "Did I actually hit somebody?"

"Way I heard it, you shot a feller's balls off," Jerry told him.

"Oh, my goodness!"

"That's him over yonder, wailing like a train whistle. I reckon he's a mite upset." Jerry paused and reflected for a few seconds. "I damn sure would be."

"I think I'm going to be sick," Conrad said, putting a hand to his mouth.

"Let me back up 'fore you puke," Jerry said quickly. "These are brand-new boots."

Frank was trying to get matters settled. He finally told everyone not involved in the shooting to go home, clear the street. After a few minutes the crowd began to disperse.

Jerry told Conrad, "You stay right here, boy, until you get to feelin' better. Then you come over and join Frank and me, OK?"

"Yes, sir," Conrad said softly. "This has really been a very traumatic experience for me."

"I'm sure it has, son. Whatever that means. You stay put, now." Jerry walked across the street and handed Conrad's gun to Frank, butt first. "The boy's cannon. That's a hell of a pistol, Frank. Where'd he get it?"

"Bought it today, I think." Frank smiled. "But he sure played hell with these four rounders, didn't he?"

Jerry grinned. "That he did. How about the feller with no balls? He quieted down in a hurry."

"He's all right. The bullet nicked the fleshy part of his inner thigh just below his privates. Gave him a good scare, that's all."

The four assailants were sitting on the edge of the boardwalk, guarded by several citizens with shotguns, while Doctor Bracken worked on them. All their wounds were very minor ones.

"These the four men who attacked you and Mrs. Browning?" Jerry asked.

"No. These men heard about the attempted kidnapping, and tried a copycat attempt. All they'll be getting out of it is long prison terms."

Jerry took off his hat and wiped his brow with a bandanna. "Stupid of them."

"Very stupid. I'll send some wires in the morning, see if they're wanted anywhere else. But I doubt they are. How's Conrad?"

"Scared, shook up some, and sort of sick to his stomach. But he's not hurt. I told him to stay put over yonder until he got to feeling better."

"Here come Vivian and Jimmy," Frank said, looking up the street as a carriage came rolling up. A servant was handling the reins, and Jimmy was sitting in the back with Viv.

Frank walked out into the street as the carriage came to a halt. "Conrad's all right, Vivian. He didn't get a scratch. Actually, he was the hero this night. Did you know he had bought a pistol?"

"Conrad?" she asked, her eyes wide. "My God. Conrad bought a pistol?"

"Yes."

"I had no idea. He's never fired a gun in his life."

"Well, he sure busted a few caps this night. He didn't kill anyone, but he sure gave a couple of those ole boys sitting over there on the boardwalk a fright." Frank couldn't help himself. He started laughing, and Vivian gave him a strange look.

"You find this funny, Frank?"

"Well, Viv," Frank said, wiping his eyes. "Yes, I do. If

you'll pardon the crudeness, one of those attackers thought Conrad shot his . . . well, privates off."

Jimmy almost swallowed his chewing tobacco.

Vivian tried to look stern, but just couldn't pull it off. She fought back laughter. "Well," she finally managed to say, having a terrible time attempting to control her mirth. *"Did* he shoot the man's balls off?"

That did it for Jimmy. He swallowed his chew. "Mrs. Browning!" he gasped.

"No," Frank said. "But I have to say the man had a few anxious moments."

Jimmy got out of the carriage and was coughing and hacking and spitting.

"What's the matter with you, Jimmy?" Viv asked.

"Swallered my chew," Jimmy gasped.

"I'll get Conrad for you, ma'am," Jerry said. "And you can take him home. He's some shaky."

"Thank you, Deputy." Vivian looked at Frank in the flickering streetlamps. It was past time for them to be snuffed out. "I believe I've had quite enough excitement for one day, Frank."

"I agree, and I'm pretty sure Conrad will say the same."

"Quite. And another thing: I shall make sure he puts away that pistol."

Frank smiled. "That's wise, Vivian. At least until he puts in some long practice hours. Although I have to say it was his shooting that broke up the assault tonight."

"No, Frank. His days as a pistol shooter are over. He starts his second year at Harvard this fall. I'm tempted to send him back right now."

"That also might be wise. Viv, what about this Charles Dutton?"

"Here's Conrad. I'll talk to you about Charles tomorrow, Frank. And we must talk."

"All right. There are some things I want to tell you, Viv. No proof, just pure suspicion."

Frank watched the carriage until it was out of sight and then turned to Jerry. "Is Doc Bracken about through with those boys?"

"I think so. None of them was hurt bad."

"Let's lock them down and hit the sack."

"If I can get back to sleep," Jerry said with a smile.

"The way you saw logs, Jer, I don't think you'll have all that much trouble."

"Are you tellin' me I snore, Frank?"

"Either that, or there's a railroad runnin' through the office."

"Maybe it's my snorin' that wakes me up sometimes. You reckon?"

"Could be."

"Doc!" The voice carried to the men across the street. "Are you sure I ain't been shot in the precious parts? It's all numb down there."

"On second thought," Frank said, "if he keeps that up, maybe you won't get much sleep."

"No, damn it, you haven't been shot in your parts. Good God, man. I've told you ten times. Why don't you look for yourself, you ninny?"

"I'm afeared to. Are you real sure, Doc?" the man persisted. "You won't lie to me about that now, would you?"

"If you don't shut up about it," Doc Bracken said, clearly irritated, "I can fix it so you won't have to worry about your precious parts ever again."

"How would you do that, Doc?"

"I'll cut the damn things off!"

The man started howling again, and that started the dogs in town answering him.

"Oh, Lord!" Jerry said. "It's gonna be a long night."

CHAPTER 18

Just as dawn was coloring the skies over the mining town, Frank approached the tent where the four men were reported to be living. A man stepped out of a ramshackle building across the rutted trail and waved to Frank.

"Those ale boys pulled out late yesterday, Marshal. Packed up ever'thing and rode out. I'm glad to see them go, personal. Unfriendly bunch, they was."

"Did one of them have a bolt-action rifle?"

"A what?"

"A rifle with a piece of metal sticking out of the top of one side."

"Oh. Come to think of it, yeah, one did. That rifle had a telescope on it, too."

"They left their tent."

"Naw. That tent belongs to whoever claims it. It's been there for a long time. Ain't worth a damn. Leaks."

Frank pulled back the flap and looked inside the tent. The ill-fitting board floor was dirty and littered with bits of trash. The interior smelled foul. Frank backed out, wondering how anyone could live that way.

"Did any of them ever talk to you?" Frank asked the miner.

"Nope. Never said nothin' to nobody 'ceptin' themselves. They was a surly pack of yahoos. And I don't think they was up to no good, neither. Had a evil look about 'em. If you know what I mean."

Frank rode back into town and went into the Silver Spoon for breakfast. Jerry had already been in, getting breakfast for the prisoners—biscuits and gravy. Frank did not wish any conversation that morning, and took a table away from the other diners. He was edgy; in the back of his mind was the feeling that major trouble was looming just around the next bend in the road. And Frank had learned years back to pay close attention to his hunches.

He lingered over coffee, watching the town come alive. The smelter kicked into life, along with the steam whistle telling the workmen it was time for another day's labors to begin. Frank watched as two men rode into town. It wasn't the men who caught and held Frank's attention; it was their beautiful and rugged horses, bred for staying power. A few minutes later, two more men rode in, on the same type of horses.

Frank had wandered across the line onto the hoot owl trail several times in his life, and he knew what kind of horseflesh outlaws preferred: the type of horses he'd just seen, with plenty of bottom to them. Outlaws often rode for their very lives, and their horses had to be the best they could buy or steal.

Frank sipped his coffee and watched as two more men rode in on the same type of horses.

The Pine and Vanbergen gangs, he thought. *Part of them, at least. Coming in a few at a time. Getting ready to make their move . . . but what kind of move?*

Frank knew how Ned Pine and Vic Vanbergen operated. Neither one would risk coming into a town this size—now that there were more than a thousand people in and around it—and pulling anything. At least, he didn't think they would. But then, time marched on, and people changed. Lawmen around the country were getting better organized, telegraph wires were damn near everywhere, and if a bank was robbed in Springfield, Missouri, people in Dodge City, Kansas, and Louisville, Kentucky, would know about it within seconds.

So was this a breakaway part of the gangs, or some new gang that had just heard about the rumored gold strike and decided to pull a holdup . . . of what?

Frank sat straight up in his chair, his coffee forgotten and cooling.

The bank, of course.

"Damn," he whispered.

Frank pushed back his chair and stood up, reaching for his hat. He paid his tab and headed for the jail. He told Jerry, "Keep the rifles and the shotguns loaded up and within reach. Maybe stick another short gun behind your gunbelt. I think we've got some trouble riding in."

"I saw those men on the fine horses, Frank. The animals were a dead giveaway."

"Six of them so far. Might be more coming in. We'll keep our eyes open."

"I'll check the livery and hotel and the roomin' houses, try to pick up some names. Not that it will do much good."

"For a fact, they'll probably all be false." He glanced at the wall clock. "I've got to meet Mrs. Browning, Jer. I'll be over at her office if you need me."

"See you later."

Walking over to Viv's office, Frank noticed that the six men had all stabled their horses at the livery. *That means they're not going to pull anything immediately,* he decided. *They'll check on the town first. And maybe won't,* he amended.

Frank glanced at the bank building. He wondered how much cash Jenkins had in his bank. Thousands and thousands of dollars, for sure. It would be a tempting target for any outlaw gang. Jenkins had a bank guard, but the old man was more for show than effect. Frank doubted the man would be very effective against a well-planned bank holdup.

He couldn't go to Jenkins with a warning, for he had no proof. The six newcorners might well be looking to invest in mining property or some other business . . . but Frank felt in his guts they were outlaws.

Vivian was not in her office. The office manager said she had sent word she was not feeling well, and was staying home that morning. Conrad was staying home with her. He added that Conrad was still very shaken from the events of the past night.

Frank walked over to the livery and took a look at the horses the six men had ridden in. Fine horseflesh. Big and rangy, and bred for speed and endurance. The saddles were expensive. The men had, of course, taken their rifles and saddlebags with them. There was nothing else Frank could do, so he returned to the jail.

"Judge Pelmutter was called out of town," Jerry said. "He left on the stage about ten minutes ago . . . some sort of family emergency. Said he'd be back next week . . . on the Friday stage. Said unless you want to file charges against those two young punks who killed that man, cut them loose."

"I figured that much. How about the four we arrested last night?"

"Said to hold them."

"All right. Turn the two young hellions loose and tell them to hit the trail and don't come back here."

"Will do."

Frank looked out the front window of the jail office. Big Bob Mallory was sitting on a bench under a store awning across the street, staring at the jail.

"What the hell does he want?" Jerry asked, walking over to stand beside Frank.

"Me. I'm sure of that. And maybe Mrs. Browning. But

he's got enough sense to know he'd better get rid of me first. He knows if he harmed Viv, I'd track him up to and through the gates of hell."

"Those six got rooms at Mrs. Harris's boardinghouse. Hotel is full up. She said they told her their names were Jones and Smith and Johnson, and so forth."

"Something is up, Jer. I just don't know what. All we can do is keep our eyes open and stay ready."

Frank left the office and began walking the town. After a while he walked over to the second livery that had just opened a week before. There were half a dozen fine-looking horses there he wanted to take another look at. They were beautiful animals that the owner had brought in with him. Several people had tried to buy them, but the livery owner had told each prospective buyer he was not yet ready to sell them.

Frank looked for the horses in the corral, but they were gone. He went inside the old barn and looked around for the owner. He was nowhere to be seen. The six horses were in stalls, all saddled up and ready to ride.

"What the hell?" Frank muttered.

Then it dawned on him. Six men ride into town on fine horses. They register at a rooming house under obviously false names. A livery man comes into town a week before, and brings six fine horses with him and opens for business, but won't sell the horses. Now those six animals are saddled up and ready to ride.

"Real good plan, boys," Frank whispered. "It almost worked out exactly as planned."

Frank walked swiftly back to the office. Jerry was out doing something. Frank paced the floor, thinking. He had no firm proof the six men were guilty of anything. Everything he had was suspicion, nothing more. He didn't want to alarm the bank personnel and have his suspicions turn out to be nothing. One of the six men was surely watching the bank, and if he spotted any panic, the robbery—if one was planned—would just be put off for another time . . . or if it went ahead, a lot of innocent people would be killed.

"Damn!" Frank muttered, gazing out the window. The town was already getting busy, even though it was still very early. Kids were playing, and women were shopping and standing on the boardwalk talking.

"All I can do is wait," he said. "Right now I'm between a rock and a hard place."

Frank walked over to the gun rack and put his hand on a rifle. Then he pulled it back. He shook his head. If the outlaw lookout spotted him carrying a rifle around town on this beautiful peaceful day, he would alert the others, and they would immediately suspect their plans had been queered.

Frank loaded up his pistols full, slipping a cartridge into the sixth chamber, which he usually kept empty; the hammer rested on that chamber. He walked out of the office and sat down on the bench on the boardwalk. All he could do was wait. He wondered where Jerry had gotten off to.

Ladies passed by, and Frank smiled and touched his hat in greeting. Most of them spoke; some did not. Frank did not take umbrage at being snubbed. He was a notorious gunfighter and a few residents of the town still felt a man of his dubious reputation should not be wearing a badge.

Jerry came strolling up and sat down beside Frank. "Anything happening, Frank?"

Frank explained briefly what he had found and what he suspected.

Jerry didn't question Frank's suspicions. "I'll get my other pistol," was all he said. When Jerry returned a moment later, he asked, "Do we alert some other men?"

"And tell them what, Jer? We don't have a shred of hard evidence to back up my suspicions. Way I see it, all we can do is wait."

Jerry was silent for a moment. "Frank, one of those six

men just sat down across the street. Just to the right of the ladies' shop."

Frank cut his eyes without moving his head. "I see him. And yonder comes the livery man with one of those fine horses he's been stabling."

"The seventh man?"

"Has to be, Jer."

They watched as the stable owner looped the reins over a hitch rail just few yards from the bank's front door and walked slowly back toward his livery.

"Two or three of the horses will probably be led around to the alley behind the bank."

"I'll take me a stroll up the street to the end of the block, howdy doin' and chattin' along the way," Jerry said. "Then I'll cut across to the other side, go into the general store, and take me a look-see out the back door."

"OK. Stay over there. I think we're going to see some action in a few minutes."

"Bank's goin' to be crowded, Frank."

"Yes. Full of people. Let's don't get any innocent person hurt or killed."

Jerry paused in his rolling of a smoke. "That might be just wishful thinkin', Frank."

"I know. But we can try."

"Here comes one of those men ridin' up to the bank big as brass."

"And not a head on the street is turning in curiosity," Frank observed. "These ole boys are pretty damn sharp in their planning."

"It's goin' to happen soon, Frank."

"Yeah. Get going. Jer? Good luck."

Jerry smiled. "All in a day's work, Frank."

"Let's hope there aren't many days like this one."

Jerry walked off up the street, speaking to the ladies as he slowly strolled along.

Frank watched as the livery man rode another of the fine horses up the street and hitched him to a rail on the other side of the bank. Then Frank watched as two of the newcomers in question came strolling up, paused for a moment, then entered the bank.

OK, boys, Frank thought as he spotted another of the six men come riding up. *Let's do it and get it over with.*

CHAPTER 19

Frank walked up the block to the corner before turning and crossing the street. He had already spotted the lookout, and kept on walking past the street intersection. He quickly cut into a very narrow alley and then surprised a couple of ladies who were shopping for bustles or corsets or dainties or something along that line.

"Pardon me, ladies," Frank said, quickly walking through the store. "There is apt to be a little trouble on the street in a few minutes, so please stay inside. Thank you." He exited the store as fast as possible. Being around a gaggle of women shopping for unmentionables always made Frank nervous.

Just as Frank closed the door behind him, he heard one woman say, "I think he's so *rugged,* don't you, Ophelia?"

"And so *capable,* too."

"Oh, Lord!" Frank muttered.

Frank eased up behind the lookout man and stuck the muzzle of a .45 in the man's back. "Take a hard right, hombre, and step into this store. That's a good boy. You try to give any type of signal and I'll blow your spine around your guts."

Frank stepped out of the store just in time to see three more of the outlaws enter the bank. That left the livery owner still out somewhere. Frank and Jerry would have to worry about him later.

"What the hell is going on here, Marshal?" the man blustered as soon as Frank had him inside the store.

Frank relieved the outlaw of his guns, holstering his own .45. "Mr. Harvey!" Frank called, ignoring the outlaw's question.

"Marshal," the store owner replied.

"You have a gun?"

"I sure do."

"This man is part of a gang that is right now in the process of robbing the bank. If he tries to move or yell, shoot him. Will you do that for me?"

Harvey reached under the counter and came up with a Greener—a sawed-off, double-barreled shotgun. "Rob our bank? Why that sorry son of a bitch! You bet I'll keep him here and quiet. This here is loaded with nails and screws and bits of metal from the smithy's shop, Marshal. If that man tries to move, I'll spread him all over the store." Harvey jacked both hammers back with an ominous sound.

The outlaw paled. He wanted no trouble with a Greener. He cut his eyes to Frank. "How'd you make us, Marshal?"

"Just luck, hombre. Now you be very still and very quiet."

"I ain't movin' nothin'."

"Not if you're smart," Harvey warned. "I've fought Injuns and outlaws, and killed my share of both. One more wouldn't bother me one whit."

"I believe you, mister," the outlaw said. "I do believe you."

"Where is the man from the livery?" Frank asked.

The outlaw smiled. "He's out yonder somewheres. Chances are, he'll find you."

"Play it your way, hombre. See you in a little bit, Mr. Harvey."

"I'll sure be here, Marshal. And so will this one. Either standin' up or in pieces all over the store."

"Sit down on the floor and put your hands under your butt," Frank told the outlaw. "That's good. Now stay that way."

Stepping out of the store but staying on the stoop, Frank peeked around the corner of the stoop. He smiled when he saw the livery man standing in front of the bank, his thumbs hooked in his gunbelt. Frank stepped out and began walking toward the man, whistling a tune as he walked.

The livery man suddenly got really nervous as he saw Frank and no sign at all of his buddy, who was supposed to be standing in front of the store.

"Howdy, there, partner," Frank called cheerfully as he drew closer to the man. "Say, you don't have the time, do you?"

"Don't own no timepiece," the so-called livery man grumbled.

"Oh. Well. Too bad. Sure is a nice mornin', ain't it?"

"It'll do." The man cut his eyes to the bank.

"Bank's open if you're interested in opening an account," Frank told him. "Or maybe you're more interested in a withdrawal?"

"Huh? Naw. I'm just waitin' on a friend."

"Fine-looking animals there. All saddled up and ready to go, too. Got saddlebags all filled up with stuff, and bedrolls tied in place. But you have one too many horses."

"Huh? What are you talkin' 'bout, Marshal?"

"You have seven horses hitched up. There's only six of you."

Frank watched the man's eyes flick up the street toward the store where the lookout was supposed to be.

"He's not there, livery man," Frank told him.

"Huh? Who you talkin' ' bout?"

"Your friend. The rider of the seventh horse. He is, well, sort of occupied at this time."

The so-called livery man was even more nervous. Then he made the mistake of brushing back his coat and touching the butt of his pistol. Frank drove his left fist into the man's belly, knocking the air from him and doubling him over. Frank pushed him off the boardwalk, which was about two feet off the ground at this part of the street. The man bit the ground on his belly, which further knocked the wind from him.

Jerry ran up and jerked the man's pistol out of leather just as one of the bank robbers stepped into the doorway of the bank and looked out, a pistol in his hand. He leveled the pistol, taking a dead bead at Jerry.

Frank shot him, drilling the man in the center of his chest. The slug drove the man backward and knocked him into another bank robber. Both of them staggered back and fell to the floor.

Frank jumped into the bank, both hands filled with .45's. "That's all!" he shouted. "Give it up. You can't get out of town."

One of the outlaws cussed him and swung his pistol in Frank's direction. Frank shot the man between the eyes. The bank robber died with a very peculiar expression on his face. He slumped to the floor and remained on his knees for a few seconds before toppling over on his face.

The others gave it up. They dropped their pistols and stood with their hands in the air. A short, stocky outlaw said, "Don't shoot, Marshal. We yield."

"Good God!" another bank robber whispered. "That's Frank Morgan!"

Jenkins and two of his tellers now had pistols in their hands, as did three men who were in the bank doing some early-morning transactions, and all were damn sure ready to use them.

"Outside," Frank told the outlaws. "And keep your hands in the air."

"Wonderful work, Marshal!" said Mayor Jenkins, the banker. "By God, it certainly was!"

What was left of the outlaw gang was marched over to the jail through a gathering crowd of citizens, a few of whom had ropes in their hands and were making crude suggestions as to what should be done with the would-be bank robbers . . . immediately.

"There'll be none of that!" Frank shouted, momentarily stilling the demands of the crowd. "These men are in my custody, and I'll see they'll get a fair trial. Now break this up and go on about your business."

"The marshal's right, folks," Mayor Jenkins shouted. "The excitement's over. Let's all settle down now."

Doc Bracken pushed through the crowd. "Anyone hurt over at the bank?"

"Two dead," Frank told him. "Somebody go fetch Mr. Malone and tell him he's got some business."

"I'm right here, Marshal," the undertaker called from the rear of the crowd. "I'll see to the departed immediately."

Two well-dressed men stood on the boardwalk on opposite sides of the street. One was watching through very cold and cunning eyes. The other one was scribbling furiously in a notebook.

"Very impressive," said the man with the cold eyes. "Very impressive, indeed."

"What a story this will make," said the other man. "Where is the telegraph office, friend?" he asked a citizen standing next to him.

Frank and Jerry locked up the survivors of the attempted bank robbery and Jerry set about making a fresh pot of coffee while Frank logged the events of the morning in the jail book. The coffee was ready just about the time Frank finished his report, and the men settled down to enjoy a cup.

The door to the jail office opened and a short, stocky

man wearing a suit stepped in. "Gentlemen," he said. "I'm Louis Pettigrew. Marshal Morgan, it is indeed a pleasure to meet you . . . finally."

"Finally?" Frank asked.

"I'm the author of the books about you, sir."

"Wonderful," Frank muttered.

Frank finally got rid of the writer after assuring him that he would give some thought to helping the man write the story of his life . . . something that Frank had absolutely no intention of doing.

"I've seen those books from time to time, Frank," Jerry said with a smile.

"Don't start, Jer."

Jerry laughed at him and got to his boots. "Maybe this writer fellow could arrange for you to go back east on a tour. You could do some trick shootin' and twirl your guns. That ought to give the folks back there a real thrill."

Frank picked up an inkwell and moved as if to throw it at Jerry. Laughing, Jerry left the office. Luckily for Frank, the inkwell was empty.

Frank locked up the office and walked over to the Henson Office building. He walked in just in time to see and hear a well-dressed man really browbeating one of the office workers. Frank listened for as long as he could take it and then walked up and deliberately bumped into the man, almost knocking him down.

The man caught his balance and turned on Frank. "You damned clumsy oaf!" he raged.

"Back off, mister," Frank warned him, "before you step into something you can't scrape off." He looked at the employee who had been the brunt of the Eastern man's rage. "You go get a cup of coffee and relax, partner."

"You stay right where you are, Leon!" the dude told the employee. "Now you see here, Marshal!" the man said, turning to Frank. "I am Charles Dutton, Mrs. Browning's attorney. And I resent your interference in a company matter."

Frank smiled and pulled out his second pistol. "You ever fired a pistol, Leon?"

"Yes, sir. During the war. I was a sergeant in a New York regiment."

"Take this pistol."

Leon took the pistol and held it gingerly.

"Now you go get a six-gun," Frank told Dutton.

"I beg your pardon?" the lawyer questioned.

"You speak to this man like he's some sort of poor cowed dog, mister, and you expect him to take it without him biting back or even showing his teeth in a snarl. That ain't the way it works out here. Now you go get a six-gun and meet this man in the street out front."

"I will not! Are you insane?"

Vivian's entrance into the building probably prevented Frank from knocking the Boston lawyer on his butt. Frank could not take an employer berating an employee in public. It was something that set him off like a firecracker.

Leon handed Frank's short-barreled .45 back to him, and Frank tucked it behind his gunbelt and turned to greet Vivian. The look that she gave Dutton was a combination of ice and fire.

"This is your friend, Vivian?" Dutton asked, referring to Frank. "This . . . bully with a badge?"

Vivian ignored that. When she spoke, it was to Leon. "What is the problem, Leon? Speak freely, please. Charles Dutton has no authority here."

"It, ah, concerned the weekly reports on the grade of silver being taken from mine number three, Mrs. Browning," Leon told her.

"The analysis of the purity of the silver?"

"Yes, ma'am."

"Give the reports to Mr. Dutton, Leon."

Leon held out the laboratory reports.

Dutton looked at the papers without taking them. "What is the meaning of this, Vivian?"

"The lab is about one mile out of town, Charles," Vivian told him. "Anyone can point the way. Why don't you go up there and tell the engineer in charge that you are taking over, and will personally run the tests? Can you do that, Charles?"

"I am your attorney, Vivian, not a chemist or an engineer."

"Can you do it, Charles?" Viv persisted.

"No. I cannot, Vivian."

"Then why don't you shut up and tend to your business? Stay in your area of expertise, and stay out of areas in which you have no knowledge."

For a moment, Frank thought Charles was going to pop his cork. He turned red in the face, and his eyes bugged out. He struggled to speak and then, with a very visible effort, calmed down. "As you wish, madam," he said, very slowly. "However, I was only trying to help."

"And any constructive help you might offer is certainly welcome, Charles. But I personally do not believe in berating employees in private, much less publicly."

"I shall certainly bear that in mind."

"Thank you, Charles."

"If by chance you should need me this afternoon, I will be at the hotel."

"I thought the hotel was full," said Viv.

"Not the luxury suites at the end of the hall. They have private baths. I insisted upon that."

Frank rolled his eyes and looked heavenward.

Viv caught his eye movement and fought back a smile. "Of course you did, Charles."

"It's so primitive out here," Dutton complained. "I don't understand how you tolerate these barbaric conditions, Vivian." He plopped his hat on his head and walked toward the front door without another word.

"Nice fellow," Frank remarked.

Leon muttered something under his breath that sounded suspiciously like "He's a turdface!" *But surely not,* Frank thought.

"Frank," Vivian said. She had dropped the "Marshal Morgan" when addressing him. There was no point in any further pretense. The whole town knew they were seeing each other socially. "Could I see you in my office, please?"

Seated in Viv's office, Frank asked, "How's Conrad?"

"He's all right, but I insisted that he stay home today. I've just about convinced him that he should return east as soon as possible."

"I'm not sure about that now, Viv. As long as he stays here, there are plenty of us to keep an eye on him. Back there, he would have little if any protection."

Viv frowned, then slowly nodded her head in agreement. "You're right, Frank. I hadn't thought about that."

"Might be a good thing to keep him here until we get this situation straightened out and decide who's trying to kill us both. As if we didn't already know."

Before Viv could reply, they heard the sound of running boots in the outer offices. Jerry burst into the room. "Frank! Outlaws just hit the Lucky Seven. Got the payroll and killed the owner and his foreman."

Frank was on his boots instantly. "That's the mine about four miles from town, right?"

"That's it."

"Get a posse together. I'll get my horse and meet you at the office."

"Will do." Jerry left the office in a run.

"Be careful, Frank," Viv cautioned.

Frank winked at her. "Long as I got you to come back to, Viv."

"I'll be here."

CHAPTER 20

Frank looked at the bodies of the mine owner and his foreman and shook his head in disgust. The men had been shot to ribbons, each one more than a dozen times. Their faces had been deliberately shot away. He ordered the bodies taken back to town in a wagon.

"Marshal," said one of the men in the posse. "Those robbers used them men for target practice. They made a game of it."

"I know," Frank replied. "They shot them in the knees, then the arms, then in the belly. They tortured them for the fun of it." Jerry walked up and Frank asked him, "How about the workers—did any of them see anything?"

"One did," Jerry said. "The other three were in a secondary shaft of the mine . . . looking for gold," he added. "It was part of the Pine and Vanbergen gangs. The man is sure of that."

"How can he be sure?"

"He knows a couple of them. Was in jail with them once. They broke out, or was broke out. One or the other. He done his time for drunk and fighting, and hasn't been in trouble since."

"Those two gangs just keep getting more and more vicious," Frank said. "This is not the first time they've done something like this. It's fortunate that no women were out here. We all know what happens to women they take captive. Which way did they head out of here?"

"Straight into the mountains, Marshal," a posse member said. "They're long gone through the pass now. And I ain't goin' into the pass."

Frank did not have to question any of the others about that. He knew without asking none of the men would be willing to enter the outlaw-controlled pass through the mountains. And he really didn't blame them one bit.

"Take the posse back to town, Jerry, and look after things until I get back. I'm going to prowl around some."

"You goin' to the pass, Frank?"

"I'm going to look it over, yes. I might not be back tonight. If that's the case, I'll see you late tomorrow."

After the posse was gone, Frank made sure his canteen was full of fresh water. Then he looped an ammo belt over his shoulder and across his chest. The belt was filled with .44-.40 rounds. Every loop in his gunbelt was full of .45 cartridges, and he had more rounds for the rifle and pistols in his saddlebags.

He began slowly tracking the outlaw gang through the rocky terrain. It wasn't that difficult, for the outlaws had made no effort to hide their tracks.

It took Frank a couple of slow-riding and very cautious hours to reach a good vantage spot about a hundred yards from the mouth of the pass. There he dismounted in a small patch of grass, eased the cinch strap, and let his horse blow and then graze. Frank took a pair of binoculars from his saddlebags, looped them around his neck, then slipped his .44-.40 from the boot. He climbed up the rocky ridge for about a hundred feet or so and settled himself in for a long, careful look-see.

What he saw was the nearly impassable entrance to the pass, and he had no doubts about it being guarded by at least two men around the clock. It was as he had been told: if you didn't know your way through, you would be in deep trouble. Even if you did know the tricky route, one of the Pine and Vanbergen guards would surely nail you if you tried.

The ways around the range were about forty miles east or west, and by the time a posse reached the outlaw stronghold they would be long gone.

"Damn," Frank muttered. He knew that north of the pass and the outlaw stronghold the terrain was badlands for miles and miles. A railroad spur line came down to a small town just north of the badlands, and that is where the mines in Barnwell's Crossing took their silver to be shipped out . . . providing they could get it to the spur line by wagons, which meant rolling right through outlaw territory on the single road that led to the tracks. Only about half of the silver-laden wagons had made it through thus far.

Frank watched the pass for half an hour before deciding he was accomplishing nothing by staying there. The only way the outlaw stronghold could be taken was with an army, and that would still mean a terrible loss of life.

Frank climbed down to his horse, tightened the cinch strap, and swung into the saddle, holding his rifle in his right hand, across the saddle horn. He headed back to town, feeling that he had accomplished very little with his long ride to the pass.

He rode into town just after dark, stabled his horse, and walked over to the jail. Jerry had fed the prisoners after Doc Bracken had made his daily visit to check on the wounded, and he had just made a fresh pot of coffee.

"Didn't expect to see you back this early, Frank."

"I looked over the entrance to the pass and decided this

was not a good day to die," Frank said, pouring a mug of coffee. "The place is a death trap."

"The south entrance sure is. The best way in is from the north."

"But we don't have any authority up there," Frank told him. "I wonder why Colorado won't deal into this game with us?"

"I don't know if they've even been asked."

"I know there's a few small towns just north of the border with us. On the edge of the badlands. But Pine and Vanbergen are smart in that they don't pull anything up there, so they're not wanted in those areas."

It was a policy that was slowly dying out in the West, but for many years if a man was not wanted in a specific area or community, the local lawman would, in many instances, leave him alone as long as he did not cause trouble within that lawman's jurisdiction.

"Was either the mine owner or the foreman married?" Frank asked.

"Yes. Both of them. Wives are here. But neither of them had kids."

"That's good . . . that is, if anything about this mess can be called good."

"What about this Charles Dutton fellow, Frank? I just don't like that uppity bastard."

"Neither do I, Jer. I think something is going to break loose here in town very quickly now."

"Because this Dutton dude is here?"

"Yes. And Big Bob Mallory and Kid Moran, and those four assassins who came after Viv and me, and all the rest of it. Dutton is tied in with it all. I'm sure of it. I just don't know the big picture yet."

"This is gettin' mighty complicated, Frank."

"A fellow named Sir Walter Scott wrote some verse once that went something like: 'O, what a tangled web we weave.' I don't remember the rest of it. But that much did stick in my mind."

"This mess is sure all tangled up, for a fact."

A citizen stuck his head in the office. "Marshal, sorry to disturb, but I thought you ought to know that Kid Moran is back in town. I was usin' the privy—just steppin' out, that is, after I—finished my business—when I seen him coming down the back way of the hotel. Usin' them steps that lead up to the fancy rooms. He was sort of slippin' down them, real quiet like, if you know what I mean."

"Thank you," Frank said. "I appreciate it."

"It's my pleasure, Marshal, for shore. If I see anything else suspicious like I think you should know about, I'll get right over to you with it."

"Thanks."

After the citizen had closed the door and walked on, Jerry asked, "What was that all about?"

"Charles Dutton has the most expensive suite in the hotel rented for his stay here."

"You think he's tied in with Kid Moran? A fancy Dan rich man like that?"

"It wouldn't surprise me any. Way this situation is shaping up here in town nothing would surprise me anymore."

"What was the line you recited? 'What a tangled web we weave?' I knew several families name of Scott back home when I was a kid. One of them was always quotin' that fellow Shakespeare. Like to have drove the rest of us goofy. You reckon they might be related to that poet?"

The next morning, Frank took a good bath and then carefully shaved. He blacked his boots and dressed in a new suit he'd bought just recently. No special occasion—he just felt like putting on some fancy duds.

He stepped out into a beautiful day in the high country: a blue, cloudless sky and warm temperature. He walked up to the Silver Spoon and took a seat, ordering a pot of coffee and breakfast. Kid Moran was seated across the room, staring at him, smiling at him. The Kid had taken no part in the attempted kidnapping of Conrad and the killing of Hal . . . at least, no part that could be proved. Kid Moran could come and go as he pleased.

Frank ate his breakfast and drank his coffee, ignoring The Kid. The Kid left the café before Frank, walking across the street and sitting down on a bench.

Angie came to Frank's table to clear off the breakfast dishes and said, "Be careful, Frank. There's something in the wind this morning."

Frank smiled up at her as he smoked his cigarette. "What do you think it is, Angie?"

"Killing you."

"You a fortune-teller? Maybe you can see the future?"

"Joke if you want to, Frank. But I've served half a dozen hard cases breakfast this morning."

"Sometimes it's difficult to tell a hired gun from a drifting cowboy, Angie."

"And sometimes it isn't." She refilled his coffee cup and said, "You watch yourself today. This town's become a powder keg, and the fuse is lit."

She turned to leave, and Frank put out a hand. "Angie, what is it you're not telling me?"

"Nothing that I can prove. It's just a feeling I get every now and then. But over the years I've seen the best and the worst out here. I saw Jamie MacCallister go into action once. I've seen his son, Falcon, hook and draw. I personally know Smoke Jensen and Louis Longmont. I've been working in Western cafés since I was ten years old." She smiled. "And I'm no kid, Frank. I've got more than a few years behind me. You just be careful today, all right?"

"All right, Angie."

Frank looked out the window. The Kid was still sitting on the bench across the street, staring at the café.

Frank paid his tab and stepped out onto the boardwalk. None of his mental warning alarms had been silently clanging that morning, so what did Angie feel that he didn't? And why? The Kid was in town, probably to try to provoke a showdown with him. That was something that Frank had felt all along was bound to happen—no surprise there. And it might well come to a head on this day. If so, so be it.

The hard cases she had mentioned? Did she personally know those bad ole boys, or had she just recognized the hard case look? *Probably the latter,* Frank concluded. And Frank knew that many toughs wore the same look, or demeanor.

Frank walked one side of the main street looking at the horses at the hitch rails. There were some fine-looking animals there, and none of them wore the same brand. But what did that prove conclusively? Nothing. Nothing at all.

Frank cut his eyes. Kid Moran was pacing him on the other side of the street. Maybe it was time for Frank to settle this thing. He hated to push it, but damned if he was going to put up with being shadowed indefinitely. It was already beginning to get on his nerves.

He looked up the street. Damned if more newcomers weren't pulling into town. Two wagons coming in, four outriders per wagon. And Frank felt that was odd. Most Indian trouble was over, so what could the newcomers be hauling to warrant eight guards? The wagons weren't riding that heavy.

Frank paused for a moment to watch the wagons as they rolled slowly into town. One wagon stopped at one end of the street; the other one rolled on and stopped at the far end of the main street.

"What the hell?" Frank muttered. He looked over at the bank building. The guard was just unlocking the front door, getting ready for another business day.

"'Mornin, Marshal," a citizen greeted Frank.

"'Morning," Frank responded.

The citizen strolled on, whistling a tune.

Frank looked at Kid Moran. The Kid was standing on the boardwalk, directly across the street, staring at Frank, smiling at him. Even at that distance, Frank could tell the smile was taunting, challenging.

"What the hell is with you, boy?" Frank whispered. "What's going on here?"

Jerry walked up, smelling of bath soap and Bay Rum aftershave.

"Jerry," Frank greeted him.

"Frank," Jerry replied. "You're lookin' spiffy this mornin'. You're duded up mighty fancy."

"And you smell like you're goin' on a date," Frank said with a smile. "You got you a lady friend?"

Jerry laughed. "Well . . . me and Miss Angie might go for a walk this mornin'. We both been makin' goo-goo eyes at each other here of late. She's a nice lady."

"Yes, she is. And a damn good cook, too."

Jerry patted his belly. "I know!"

"Going to get serious, Jer?"

"I don't know. Maybe. Luckily we're both adults, and have been up and down the road a time or two. It isn't something new to either of us. So we're cautious." Jerry paused and looked at the wagons that had just rolled into town. "What the devil are those wagons doing, Frank? Looks to me like they're going to block both ends of Main Street. My God, they *are* blocking both ends."

Frank looked first at one end of the street, then the other. The wagons were not long enough to completely block off the wide streets, even with the teams, but it looked as if they were sure going to cause some major problems for other wagons trying to get past.

"Frank, they're folding back the canvas on both wagons. Heck, maybe it's some sort of circus come to town, or some minstrel show. You reckon?"

"I don't know what's going on, Jer. But I damn sure intend to find out."

"I'll take this end," Jerry said, pointing. "You take the other."

"Marshal Morgan," Jiggs said, walking up. "What in the world is happening? Those wagons are blocking the street. That can't be allowed."

"We were just about to straighten out this mess, Jiggs."

"I swear, Marshal, some people have no consideration for others, do they?"

Before Frank could reply, Jerry said, "Frank, what is that machinery those guys are uncovering? I never seen no minin' equipment that looked like that."

Frank looked and felt cold sweat break out on his face. He blinked, thinking he was surely mistaken. He stared. No doubt about it: his first look was correct. "Those are Gatling guns, Jer!"

"Gatling guns?" Jiggs blurted. "Good God! Are you joking?" He stared at first one wagon, then another. "By the Lord, you're right, Marshal. What are those people going to do? Put on some sort of a demonstration?"

A couple of seconds after Jiggs asked his question, a tremendous explosion rocked the town. A huge cloud of dust enveloped the road leading out of the main street and up to the mines. The immense explosion was so powerful it cracked windows and sent some people stumbling off the boardwalk and into the street.

"The road's blocked!" an excited man yelled from the other end of the street a few seconds after the explosion. Then he started coughing when the enormous cloud of dust began settling over the main part of town, covering everything.

The men in the wagons began cranking the Gatling guns, and lead started flying all up and down Main Street. Several men and women were hit and knocked spinning by the gunfire.

Pistol fire joined the rapid fire from the Gatling guns.

On his belly on the boardwalk, Frank watched as half a dozen men, all carrying guns and cloth bags, entered the bank.

"Bank robbery!" Frank yelled, and rolled off the boardwalk and into the street just as the carriage from the Browning estate turned onto the main street from a side street. Frank could do nothing except stare in horror as a dozen rounds of lead raked the carriage. Vivian was knocked out of the carriage to lie still and bloody in the dirt.

CHAPTER 21

Frank snapped off a lucky shot that hit the gunner in one of the wagons in the shoulder, knocking him back. But in a heartbeat another man had taken his place and was cranking out the lead, spraying death in all directions. Frank tried to get up and make his way to Vivian, but the intense fire from the Gatling guns forced him back. He crawled behind a water trough as the bullets howled and whistled all around him.

Frank glanced over to where he'd last seen Jerry. The deputy was apparently all right, and had taken shelter in a store, returning the gunfire as best he could whenever the hail of bullets ceased for a few seconds. All the stores up and down the street, on both sides, were missing windows. The wounded were moaning, and many were crying out for help. There were men and women and a few children among them.

One of the bank clerks staggered out of the bank, his chest bloody, and fell facedown on the boardwalk. A young child, a girl, sat in the dirt beside her fallen mother and cried. Many of the horses that had been tied at hitch rails in front of various stores had broken loose and bolted. Others were badly wounded, screaming and thrashing on the ground, unable to get up because of their grievous wounds.

While the gunners were changing magazines on the Gatlings, Frank dropped one of the outlaws, who was exiting the bank with a bagful of money. Frank shot him twice, once in the belly, once in the chest, ending the man's outlawing days forever.

Jerry shot another one leaving the bank, shot him in the throat with a hurry-up shot. The .45 round almost took the man's head off. He fell back against the front of the bank building and lay kicking and jerking and trying to push words out of his ruined throat, the bag of money beside him forgotten in his horrible agony.

Frank rolled away from the trough and under the raised boardwalk, squirming his way a few yards closer to one of the death wagons. He shot the gunner in the head just as another charge of dynamite was lit and tossed. The barber shop exploded in a mass of splintered wood and broken glass. The peppermint-painted barber pole was blown a hundred feet into the air. It came down in the alley behind the barber shop and landed on the slant roof of a privy, crashing through and almost conking a man on the head who had taken refuge in there. He jumped out of the privy and took off, running toward the edge of town.

The main street was once more covered in dust and smoke and confusion. The Gatling guns resumed their spitting out of misery and destruction. Frank nailed another outlaw coming out of the bank, his shots turning the robber around and around in a macabre dance on the boardwalk. He dropped his bulging sack of money just before he slumped to the street and died beside the bag of money that cost him his life.

Frank heard a shotgun boom inside the bank, and an outlaw was knocked through the big front window, dead from the shotgun blast before he hit the boardwalk.

Frank took that time to jump up and make a run closer to one of the wagons. He made it to a dead horse and jerked the .44-.40 rifle from the saddle boot. Before he went belly down on the ground, he chanced a look toward Vivian. She had not moved. Frank was suddenly filled with a terrible rage. He levered a round into the chamber of the rifle and sighted in the new gunner cranking the Gatling gun. Frank shot him in the chest and knocked the man out of the wagon. No new gunner came forward to take his place. The bank robbers were running out of men.

Frank ran toward the wagon and jumped in. He swiveled the Gatling and began cranking, the rounds literally tearing the wagon at the end of the block to splinters, all mixed in with the blood and shattered bone of the two outlaws who were inside the wagon.

The outlaws who were not dead or wounded, or being held prisoner by various townspeople, were in the saddle and riding hell-for-leather out of town, toward the pass.

Doc Bracken was busy working on the wounded citizens, pointedly ignoring the calls for help from the wounded outlaws.

"Help me, Doc!" one called.

"Go to hell, you bastard," Doc Bracken told him without looking up from the bloody little girl he was working on in the middle of the street.

"I'm hard hit, Doc," the outlaw pleaded.

"Good," Bracken replied. "Go ahead and die. Rot in hell."

Frank hurried over to Vivian and knelt down. She had taken two rounds in the chest from the big-bore Gatlings, but she was still breathing.

"Hang on, Viv," Frank said. "Doc Bracken's coming over soon as he can."

"Tell him not to waste his time, love. I'm all torn up inside."

"Hush, now, Viv. Don't talk like that."

"Talk while I have time to talk. I'm in no pain, Frank. It's all numb inside of me, but it's difficult to breathe. I've been lung shot, haven't I?"

Frank had seen the pinkish-looking fluid she'd coughed up. "I don't know for sure, Viv."

"I think I am. Let me talk while I still can, Frank. Don't interrupt, please?"

"I won't, Viv."

"You own five percent of Henson Enterprises, Frank. I saw to that just last week. The papers are filed, and it's all legal. Dutton can't do a thing about it except gripe. Money will be deposited in your name in a bank in Denver every month. It's all spelled out in the papers. Mayor Jenkins has them. He's a good, trustworthy man."

Frank waited while Vivian coughed up more fluid. It was pinkish in color. Holding her, he felt his hand at her back grow wet. He lifted one side of her jacket and found another bullet hole. He knew that unless the slug had veered off, it had probably blown right through a kidney.

"Is the sun going behind a cloud, Frank?" she asked. "It's getting darker."

"Yes, love. Clouds are moving in. It's going to rain, I reckon."

There was not a cloud in the sky.

Doc Bracken came over and looked at Vivian for a few seconds. He lifted his gaze to Frank and shook his head. The doctor's eyes were filled with sorrow.

Frank felt as though an anvil had fallen on him.

"Look after Conrad, Frank," Vivian told him. "Promise me you'll do that."

"I will, Viv. I promise."

"He's home right now. I gave him a sedative. He probably slept right through the shooting."

"I'll do my best to take care of him, Viv."

"Let's get her to my office, Frank." Bracken had placed a

cloth over Viv's major chest wound. "Stops the sucking, Frank. She might have a chance."

Bracken waved some men over and they gently picked Viv up and carried her away. Frank stood up and looked around him. The main street of town resembled a war zone. There were at least two dozen men, women, and children dead or wounded. There wasn't a window left intact. The barber shop was gone, and the buildings on either side of it were heavily damaged.

Jerry walked up, a bandage on his head. "You hurt bad?" Frank asked.

"Naw. I just got conked on the head by a flying board, that's all. Bled like crazy for a few seconds. Angie thought I was bad hurt. How's Mrs. Browning?"

Frank shook his head. "Real bad," he said softly. "She caught three bullets in the chest."

"I'm sorry, Frank. Jimmy?"

"Dead. That's him between the seats in the carriage."

"The driver is dead, too. He's on the other side of the carriage."

"Let's go see what we can do to help and get the prisoners over to the jail."

"We might have some trouble keeping a lynch mob from taking the prisoners."

"I couldn't blame them for trying," Frank replied. "But that's not going to happen in my town."

Frank and Jerry rounded up the surviving outlaws and marched them over to the jail and locked them down. "Stay here," he told Jerry. He left the office and walked up to a group of businessmen. "You're all deputized," he informed them. "Your job is to stay at the jail and guard the prisoners. You will prevent a lynching. Is that understood?"

It was, and the men agreed, although quite reluctantly.

"Fine. Get over to the jail and relieve Jerry. Tell him I need him out here, now. Move!"

Jerry joined him in the street and Frank said, "Let's get a

tally of the dead and wounded. You start that while I find Jenkins and see how hard the bank was hit."

"Will do, Frank."

Men were shooting badly injured horses, putting them out of their misery.

"They didn't get away with a nickel," Jenkins told Frank. "We recovered every dollar. How many dead do we have?"

"I don't know yet. Jerry's checking on that now. But it's going to be high."

"Mrs. Browning?"

"Doc Bracken said she was still alive, but unconscious. She's hard hit."

"Was it the Pine and Vanbergen gangs that hit us, Frank?"

"Yes. Selected members. The rest of the gang was scheduled to pull something else."

"For God's sake, what? And where?"

"The one doing all the talking didn't know. Or said he didn't."

"You believe him?"

"He's pretty damned scared, Mayor. There's a chance he's telling the truth."

A citizen ran up to the men, nearly out of breath. "We've got over twenty dead so far, Mayor, Marshal," he gasped. "About that many wounded."

"Dear God!" Mayor Jenkins breathed. "How many of the wounded are critical?"

"Near'bouts all of them."

"All right, mister. Thanks," Frank told him. "Go sit down over yonder and catch your breath."

"No time," the citizen said. "One of the dynamite charges was tossed into Miss Rosie's place up on the hill. Some of her girls is still buried under the rubble. Maybe eight or ten of them. And Miss Rosie's missin', too."

"My wife's been griping and raising hell about that whorehouse for months," Jenkins said. "She wanted it gone, but not this way."

Frank swung into the saddle of the first horse he came to and rode up to Rosie's House of Delights, or what was left of the place, picking his way around the blocked road. There were dead and badly injured soiled doves on both sides and in front of the ruined old two-story home. There were plenty of men helping to search for and dig out those trapped, so Frank rode on.

No one had thought to look for dead or wounded at the small—mining claims that dotted the area around the town, and Frank had a hunch that had also been part of the gang's plan. Many of the men working the smaller mines had found pockets of gold, and did not trust the bank to hold it for them. They kept it in hidden places around their shacks. Ned Pine and Vic Vanbergen would have had spies working the town, buying drinks for thirsty miners, and would know some of the claims that were producing.

Frank's worst hunch paid off. The roar of the Gatling guns, the booming of the dynamite, and the screaming of the wounded had managed to cover the sound of the attack on a number of the small mines . . . and the attacks had been especially vicious. There were dead men and women nearly everywhere Frank looked.

Frank found one dazed but unhurt young man. "You have a horse, boy?"

"Yes, sir."

"Get on it and ride into town. Tell my deputy what's happened up here." Frank stared at the confused-looking teenager. "Do you understand what I just told you?"

The young man blinked a couple of times. "Ah . . . yes, sir."

"Move, boy!"

Frank did what he could for the wounded and waited for help from the town to arrive.

Soon Jerry rode up with about a dozen men, and for a moment they sat their horses and stared in disbelief at the carnage.

"A couple of you check out those mines up ahead for dead and wounded," Frank said. "Rest of you get down and help me identify these bodies."

"The telegraph is out, too, Frank," Jerry told him. "I guess the gangs pulled down the wires just as they were hitting the town."

"It was sure a well-thought-out plan, Jer, no doubt about that."

"They didn't care who they killed. I've never seen anything so vicious."

"The death count still rising?"

"Yes. By the minute, it seems like. A lot of women and kids were killed." Jerry shook his head. "Most of the stores on Main Street were damaged. Several of them will be closed for a long time while repairs are made."

"Some of them probably won't ever reopen. God!" Frank exclaimed. "Look at the bodies."

"We're going to have to match up the names of some of these people with records from the assayer's office."

Frank nodded his head. "We'll be lucky to match up half of them. Jerry, did you see Kid Moran do anything to aid the outlaws?"

"No. Not a thing. And he's gone. So is Big Bob Mallory."

"Figures. How about Charles Dutton?"

"I guess he's still in town. I haven't seen him."

"Any chance of getting Doc Bracken up here?"

"Not a chance, Frank. He's operating fast as he can, and the wounded keep piling up. He's moved his operatin' to the church buildin' on Willow Street."

"All right. See if you can get a couple of wagons. We'll move the wounded into town."

"How about the bodies?"

Frank sighed. "I guess we'll leave them where they fell for the time being. Let's see to the living first."

"Frank, I haven't seen Conrad Browning."

"Vivian told me she gave him a sedative this morning.

He slept through the attack. I'd better go check on him and get him up and moving. He might not get another chance to see his mother alive."

"Don't give up on her, Frank. She's a strong woman with a powerful will to live."

"She took three rounds in the chest, Jer. Looks like one went through a lung and another punched through a kidney."

"But she's still alive."

"Yeah. Take over here, Jer. I'll be in town."

Frank rode into town and checked on Vivian. She was still clinging to life. He went to the Browning estate and got Conrad up and moving. He made coffee while Conrad washed his face and dressed. Then he told him what had happened.

The young man went white in the face with shock. "Mother?"

"She's still alive."

"Take me to her, Marshal."

"Of course."

Frank took Conrad to the doctor's office, where a local woman who was Bracken's nurse was sitting with Vivian. A very subdued Conrad took a chair by his mother's bed and reached out, touching her and finally taking her hand into his.

Frank slipped outside, leaving the mother and son together. He stood alone for a few moments, then carefully rolled a cigarette and smoked it, but he got no pleasure from it. The tobacco was bitter tasting on his tongue, all mixed up with the lonely feelings of sorrow and regret, for himself, for Conrad, and especially for Vivian. *And,* he thought with a sigh, forcing himself to admit it, *for all the things that might have been and now can never be. Never, ever be.*

Jerry rode up and dismounted, walking over to Frank. "How is she, Frank?"

"Doc Bracken says there is no hope, Jer. Conrad is in there with her now."

"How is he holdin' up?"

"Being a very strong and brave young man. But I don't think that's going to last for any length of time."

"They were real close, weren't they?"

"Yes."

"Frank, I hate to bring this up now, but I've got to. We've got forty-two people dead and seventy wounded, some of them real serious. We can't get word out, the telegraph is down, and the road is blocked by the outlaws about three miles out of town."

"What?"

"They want the money in the bank, Frank. All of it. We just got that word. And they know to a penny how much Jenkins had in his bank."

"How the hell could they know that?"

"One of the tellers was involved. Young man name of Dean Hill. His girlfriend came to the office and told me about him. She's over there now. Wants to talk to you."

"All right. Where is this Dean Hill now?"

"He rode out with the survivors of the holdup."

"I'll make you a wager. If he isn't dead by now, he will be very shortly."

"No bet. The young man has served his purpose. No point in keepin' him around. Those outlaws damn sure aren't goin' to share with him."

"Let's go see this girlfriend. Not that she'll be able to tell us much. How long do the outlaws think they'll be able to keep the pass closed?"

"Forever, Frank. She told me they plan on warning anyone wanting in that there is a smallpox epidemic in town. No one is allowed into town."

"Pretty good plan Vic and Ned worked out."

"Yeah. What are you goin' to do, Frank?"

"See this girl. Then I'm going to open the road . . . or die trying."

CHAPTER 22

Frank talked briefly with the frightened young lady in his office. She told him basically what she had told Jerry. She ended with, "What do you suppose will happen to Dean?"

Frank didn't want to tell her that her beau was probably already dead. "He'll have to stand trial, miss. I don't know what the judge will do." *If he is alive he'll spend the rest of his life in prison,* he thought.

After the young woman had left, Frank told Jerry, "Have a wagon hitched up. Transfer one of those Gatling guns over to it, and fill all the magazines."

Jerry looked at him.

"And some dynamite and caps, too," Frank added.

"Sounds like you're about to declare war, Frank."

"I am, Jer. For a fact."

Jerry left the office at a run, and Frank began putting together some gear. He was filling the empty loops in his ammo belt with .44-.40 cartridges when Mayor Jenkins came in.

"Coffee over there on the stove, Mayor," Frank told him. "It's fresh and hot. Help yourself."

"Good." Jenkins reached into his suit coat and pulled out

some papers. "While I'm doing that, you sign these where I've put an X."

"What am I signing?"

"Some very important papers." He pushed a pen and ink-well across the desk. "Sign them and date them."

Frank scrawled his name, looked at the calendar and printed in the date, then pushed the papers away.

"I just spoke with Dr. Bracken, Frank. There is no change in Mrs. Browning's condition."

"I know."

"Doc Bracken is worried about Conrad. The boy is very shaky."

"He's learning that death is a part of living, Mayor. The kid is tougher than most people think. He'll be all right."

"I know you're about to do something. You want me to put a posse together, Frank?"

"No. This is something I have to handle myself. There has been enough loss of innocent life this day."

"One man against two large gangs?"

"If I decide I need help, Mayor, I'll send word back. What I would like for you to do is officially deputize some of those men I had guarding the prisoners earlier. They can take care of the town. I want Jerry with me at the blockade."

"I'll do that immediately."

"Thank you."

"Be careful, Frank."

"I won't promise that, Mayor."

Jenkins smiled his understanding, nodded his head, and picked up the papers. "I'll send over your copies in a few days. I want to have these recorded."

Frank finished filling the loops in both gunbelts, .44-.40 and .45, then filled up a large canteen with fresh water. Jerry walked in about the time he was finished.

"Got the Gatlin' gun loaded, Frank. Several cases of filled-up magazines."

"Dynamite?"

"Enough to blow up a mountain. You ever handled dynamite?"

"Plenty of times. One more thing: go over to Angie's and tell her to fix us some sandwiches to take with us."

"On my way."

Frank stowed his rifle and canteen in the wagon outside the office and looked over the team: good, powerfully built horses. Doc Bracken walked up. Frank guessed the doctor was taking a much needed break from his patients.

"Mrs. Browning is drifting in and out of consciousness, Marshal. She wants to see you. You'd better come now. I don't believe she can last much longer."

Frank walked over to the doctor's office and pushed open the door leading to the tiny clinic. Conrad was sitting by his mother's bed. He looked up at Frank.

"I'll leave you alone for a few minutes, Marshal," the young man said, standing up. "Then I'll be back. I have something to say to you."

"All right, son."

"I am not your son!"

"Yes, you are," Vivian whispered.

Conrad whirled around. "What did you say, Mother?"

"Frank Morgan is your father."

"Mother! You don't know what you're saying."

"Mr. Browning knew you weren't his own son, but he raised you as if you were. Frank and I were married in Colorado right after the war. I was pregnant with you when your grandfather drove him away."

Conrad stared at Frank for a moment, then charged out of the office.

Frank sat down in the chair beside Viv's bed and took her hand. "I guess he had to know, Viv."

"It was past time."

"You're going to pull through this, Viv."

"No, I'm not, Frank, and you know it. I can read that in Dr. Bracken's eyes, and yours."

Frank didn't know what to say. He held her hand.

"Listen to me, Frank. Please. I don't know how long I'm going to stay conscious. I don't want you to see me . . . die. I don't want that to be the last memory you have of me. I don't want that image to be the one you carry in your mind for the rest of your life. Do you understand that?"

"Of course I do, Viv."

"Promise me you'll take care of Conrad. Promise me you'll try to see him into manhood."

"I'll try, Viv. I'll do my best, if he'll let me. But if he won't . . . what can I do?"

"Nothing. If you'll try, that's all I ask."

Vivian closed her eyes, and Frank thought for a few seconds he had lost her. Then she took several ragged breaths and once again opened her eyes.

"Did you sign the papers Jenkins brought over to you?" she asked.

"What? Oh. Yes. I signed something this morning. He said it was important."

She tried a small smile. "They were very important, Frank. Thank you. How is Jimmy?"

"He's dead, Viv. And so is the servant."

"I'm so sorry. What a mess. It was a bank robbery, wasn't it?"

"Yes. They tried to rob the bank. They didn't get away with a nickel of the bank's money."

She stared at Frank for a moment. "You're going after them, aren't you?"

"It's my job, Viv."

"Frank?"

"I'm right here."

"I never stopped loving you. I want you to know that."

"Nor did I stop loving you, Viv."

"That makes dying so much easier, Frank."

"Now you stop that kind of talk. You hear me? You're

going to pull through this, Viv. You are. You've got to try, honey. Try!"

"I'm awfully tired, Frank. And I'm suddenly at peace. I . . . really can't describe it."

"Viv!"

"Try to look after Conrad, Frank. Will you? Remember, you promised."

"I'll do my best, Viv."

Vivian closed her eyes.

"Viv! Viv!"

Conrad burst into the room, the nurse right behind him.

"Both of you get out!" the nurse commanded. "Right now! Move."

Conrad confronted Frank in the outer office. "I don't care what mother says. You're not my father!"

"But I am, boy. She spoke the truth. Let me tell you what happened."

"I don't want to hear anything you have to say. It's all a pack of lies!"

Frank checked himself before he could strike the young man. "Your mother is not a liar, boy."

"Of course she is!" Conrad came right back at him. "If what you say is true, she's lied to me for years. Now let me hear you deny that."

Before Frank could reply, Conrad said, "You can't, can you? No, because it's the truth."

"If you will just let me try to explain, Conrad—"

"I hope to God I never see you again," Conrad blurted. "All this tragedy is your fault. It never would have happened if you hadn't showed up here."

Frank struggled to grasp the logic behind the young man's words. What did his coming to town weeks back have to do with an attempted bank robbery? He shook his head. "Conrad, you're not thinking straight. I—"

"I don't want to hear anything you have to say. I just want you to leave. I don't wish to ever see you again."

"Boy, I made a promise to your mother that I would take care of you. I—"

"You!" Conrad hissed at him. *"You* take care of me? Oh, I think not. Get out and leave me alone."

Frank stared at his son for a few seconds. "All right, boy. But I'll be back. You can count on that. Then we'll talk more."

"Not if I have anything to say about it."

The nurse walked into the room, dabbing at her eyes. "One of you go get Dr. Bracken. Hurry."

"Mother?" Conrad blurted.

"Fading very fast. Hurry, boy."

Conrad ran out of the office. "Is she conscious?" Frank asked.

"No. My God, this has been a horrible day."

Frank recalled Viv's words: *I don't want you to see me die. I don't want that to be the last memory you have of me.*

"Yes, it certainly has been that."

The nurse gripped Frank's arm. "Kill those outlaws, Marshal. Kill every one of them. Avenge this town."

"I plan on bringing them to justice, ma'am."

The nurse looked at him for a moment and then turned away, walking back into the tiny clinic of Dr. Bracken without another word.

Frank touched the butt of his pistol. "Yes, I certainly plan on delivering justice, ma'am."

Frank headed for his office. Jerry was waiting on the boardwalk. "Is Mrs. Browning—" He could not bring himself to finish the question.

"It won't be long, Jer. You ready to go?"

"Ready. I put the sandwiches in the wagon."

"All right. You drive the team. I'll follow with our horses. What's the latest on the death count?"

"Still climbing."

"Let's go even the score."

CHAPTER 23

About half a mile from the blockade, Frank left Jerry with the wagon and rode up to take a very cautious look-see, walking the last hundred yards and peeping around the sheer rock wall on the left side of the road. The Pine and Vanbergen gangs had blocked the road with a heavy chain stretched across it and then stationed two wagons, tongue to rear, in back of that. They had two red flags on poles in front of the chain, signifying danger, and four men with rifles were on guard.

"Slick," Frank muttered. "Very slick." He looked up and shook his head. No way to get above the blockade, for the sheer rock face was several hundred feet high. Any assault would have to be a frontal one. And Frank guessed that the main body of the gangs was camped not too far off, so they would come running at the first sounds of trouble.

It had been suggested to Frank that a rider from town try to make it through the outlaw pass. He had smiled at that and asked for volunteers. When no one stepped forward that suggestion was dropped.

Frank rode back to Jerry now, and swung down from the saddle. "One way through, Jer."

"Straight ahead, right?"

"That's it."

"They're going to hear the wagon when we move it into place, for a fact," Jerry said. "But what the hell? Surely they know we're here."

"Oh, they know, all right. This is how we'll play it: I'll handle the Gatling, and you get the wagon in place, as close as you can without exposing yourself. There's a place to turn the team just before the curve."

"And then what?"

"Then I start cranking and clear the roadblock."

"And the gangs come on the run."

"Probably. But they're going to run right into our fire. You have a better idea?"

Jerry smiled and shook his bandaged head. "Can't say as I do. I'll get the wagon in place."

"I'll be at the curve with a rifle. As soon as they hear you they'll get ready to open fire. Just as soon as I get a target, I'll drop him."

"Sounds good to me."

"Good luck, Jer."

Jerry nodded his head and climbed into the wagon. Frank walked back to the curve and got into position. The guards had probably been warned by a lookout high above the road, for there was no one in sight.

As he waited for Jerry to get into place, Frank wondered if the four men who had ambushed him and Viv that sunny afternoon had been part of the two gangs. He didn't think they were. Dutton's men, he was sure.

Another man he damn sure had to deal with as soon as he got the road opened. And he would get the road open. Frank didn't have any doubts about that. Doubts about his ability to deal with any given situation were not something that plagued him. He just bulled ahead and got it done.

Jerry got the wagon into position and unhitched the team, leading them to safety, then came back and removed the cases of dynamite and caps, stashing them behind some rocks, well out of the line of fire. He returned to crouch beside the wagon, rifle in his hand.

"Ready for the dance?" Frank called.

"Play the fiddle, Frank. It's your tune."

Frank started cranking, the lead flying from the hand cranked machine gun. The heavy slugs tore into the wagons, knocking great chunks from the sideboards.

"I thought you said both them Gatlin's had been ruint?" someone called from the outlaw side.

"Yeah," another man yelled. "Damn shore don't sound like it to me."

Frank gave the outlaws another half a magazine and got lucky this time: a man staggered out, both hands holding his torn-up belly. He collapsed on the rocky road and died.

"Jess is dead!" a man called.

"I see him, you idgit! I ain't blind."

"No, yore just stupid! That there is Frank Morgan, and I told you he wasn't gonna take this lyin' down."

"If you want your share of that money in the bank you'll shet your mouth and hold this here road."

"I want me some of them women in the town," another man said, his voice carrying clearly in the thin mountain air. "I got me a real powerful yearnin.'"

Frank gave the outlaws another half a magazine, and that ended conversation on their side for a few minutes.

While Frank was changing out the magazine, Jerry's rifle cracked and an outlaw screamed and fell to the hard road, one leg broken. The .44-.40 slug had busted his knee. Moaning in pain, the man dragged himself out of sight, behind some rocks on the side of the road.

Hundreds of feet above the road, some of the outlaw gang began hurling large rocks down at the road. But the top of the ridge angled outward, and rocks hit nowhere near the wagon. The outlaws gave up their rock throwing very quickly.

For a few moments, the siege became quiet, both sides apparently at an impasse.

Jerry edged closer to Frank. "How are we goin' to get the dynamite down to the blockade? We sure can't toss it down there. It's too far."

"I've been studying on that, Jer. I think we'll use the spare wheel off the wagon."

"A wheel?"

"Yes. It's a gentle slope down to the blockade, and the road is fairly smooth. We'll tie the charge to the wheel, light it, and roll it down there."

"And if it falls over, or rolls off the edge before it gets there?"

"There are four more wheels on the wagon. And we've got lots of dynamite. The trick is going to be cutting the fuse the right length."

"I'll get the wheel. You handle the charges. Me and dynamite made a bargain a long time back: it leaves me alone, and I do the same for it."

Frank smiled. He was an experienced hand with dynamite, and knew that it wasn't just the charges one should be cautious with, but the caps. He'd seen men lose fingers, hands, and entire arms after getting careless while capping dynamite.

Frank tied together a dozen sticks of explosives and carefully capped the lethal bundle. Jerry rolled the big wheel up and squatted down, watching while Frank cut and inserted the fuse. Then Frank secured the charge to the wheel with a cord and looked at his deputy.

"You ready?"

"If that's a fast-burnin' fuse, we're in trouble," Jerry said.

Frank chuckled. "We'll soon know, won't we?"

"You don't know?"

"Nope. You got the dynamite and fuses. Didn't you ask?"

"'Fraid not."

Frank struck a match and lit the fuse. "Roll it, Jer!"

Jerry was only too happy to start the wheel rolling. He breathed a sigh of relief when the wheel was on the road. The heavy wheel bounced and wobbled down the gently sloping road, the fuse sputtering and sparking as it rolled.

"Get the hell out of here!" an outlaw yelled. "That's dynamite comin' our way."

"Shoot the wheel and stop it!" another gang member shouted.

"You shoot the goddamn thing, Luke. I'm outta here."

For a few seconds it looked as though the wheel was going to topple over before it reached the blockade. Then it straightened up and picked up speed, rolling true.

At the blockade, outlaws were scrambling to get clear. They were running and cussing and slipping and sliding.

The wheel ran into a wagon and lodged under the wagon bed for a few seconds before exploding. It went off with a fury, sending bits and pieces of the wagon flying in all directions. The explosion lifted the second wagon up and over the edge of the road. The chain that had been stretched across the road was blown loose, and fell to the road. A huge dust cloud covered and obscured the area where the blockade had been. When the dust settled, the road was clear.

Several of the outlaws had not gotten clear: there were three men sprawled unconscious on the road. One of them was clearly dead, his neck twisted at an impossible angle. He had been picked up by the concussion and thrown against the cliff.

"Jesus!" Jerry said, his voice hushed. "How many sticks did you lash together, Frank?"

"Twelve."

Jerry cut his eyes to Frank and shook his head in awe. "Warn me next time, will you?"

"I hope there won't be a next time," Frank replied.

"It ain't over, Frank!" the shout came from high above the road. "You son of a bitch!"

"Vic Vanbergen," Frank said. "I recognize the voice."

"We'll meet again, you sorry son!" Vic yelled. "You can count on that."

"And that goes double in spades for me, Morgan!"

"Ned Pine," Frank said. "It's over here, Jer. They're making their brags and threats now."

"Watch your ass in town, Morgan," Vic yelled. "It ain't over by a long shot."

"He's tellin' you they've got men in town waitin' for you, Frank," Jerry said.

"Sure," Frank said calmly. "Big Bob Mallory will be back, and Kid Moran. Several others, I'm sure."

The lawmen waited on the road for several minutes more, but there was no more yelling from the top of the ridge. The Vanbergen and Pine gangs had pulled out.

Frank and Jerry made their way cautiously down to the now wrecked blockade. Two of the outlaws who had not cleared the blast were dead, one with a clearly broken neck, the other with a massive head wound caused by the fallen debris. The others were gone.

"I'll hook up the team," Jerry said. "Bring the wagon down and we'll tote the dead back." He smiled. "Might be a reward on them."

"You're learning. I'll start clearing away some of this junk."

"Frank?"

"Yes?"

"Pine and Vanbergen knew they couldn't keep this road closed. Why did they even try?"

"I think they were counting on us being dead. Our coming out alive put a kink in their plans."

"You're really gonna have to watch your back careful in town, Frank."

"I've been doing that for many years. It's as automatic for me as breathing. Come on, let's get these bodies loaded up and get back to town."

* * *

Vivian was in a coma. Dr. Bracken told Frank that she might linger that way for hours, or even days. There was just no way to tell.

The two dead outlaws were both wanted and had a price on their heads. And they both carried some identification on them, which was a lucky break for the lawmen. Frank would wire the states where they were wanted as soon as the telegraph wires were repaired.

Frank filled out his daily report in the jail journal and then went on a walking inspection of the town. The main street was still a mess. The bodies of the dead had long been carried off, and the wounded were in makeshift hospitals. The undertaker had bodies stacked all over the place, overflowing out into the alley behind his parlor. There was just no time to embalm them all, nor did Malone have enough supplies to do so. The funerals were starting as soon as carpenters could knock together caskets.

Some of the caskets were tiny, and that was heartbreaking for anyone with a modicum of feeling.

Frank tried to talk with Conrad, but he refused to see him. After Frank tried twice and was rebuffed both times, he decided to leave his son alone. Frank would be in town and available when or if the young man wanted to talk.

Kid Moran and Big Bob Mallory were back in town. They were doing nothing to help out, just sitting and watching as the town struggled to pull itself out of the wreckage and cope with the heavy loss of life.

Frank didn't push the pair. There had been quite enough killing. But he knew they were there for a showdown. It was just a matter of time. With The Kid it was an ego thing. Kid Moran wanted a reputation. Frank still wasn't certain who was paying Big Bob, but Charles Dutton was at the top of his list.

Dutton was Conrad's shadow that day, all concern and sorrow and sympathy, and the young man was certainly receptive. Frank didn't, couldn't, blame the boy. Conrad didn't have any idea what was going on; apparently Vivian had never gotten around to talking with her son about her deep and dark feelings concerning Dutton.

And now it's too late, Frank thought with a silent sigh. *Too late for a lot of things.*

He was tired and taking a break, sitting on the bench outside the marshal's office, having a cup of coffee. Late afternoon shadows were creeping about the streets of the mountain town, creating little pockets of darkness in hidden corners. This had always been one of Frank's favorite times of the day, when dusk was reaching out to slowly melt and mingle with sunlight. But on this day of tragedy he was filled with various emotions: a hard sense of loss, a feeling of impending doom, a sense that his time in the mining town was nearly over; other emotions that were strong but not yet identifiable. Well . . . one of the emotions was certainly familiar—the feeling that he had screwed up his life beyond salvaging.

Frank was a middle-aged man with a very dubious past, and not much of a future.

And damned if he knew how he could change it.

The voice of Dr. Bracken broke into his thoughts. "You mind some company, Marshal?"

Frank looked up. "Not at all, Doc. Glad to have some company." He scooted over on the bench. "Might improve my disposition."

Bracken looked at the cup in Frank's hand. "That coffee drinkable?"

"You bet. Hot and fresh." Frank started to rise. "I'll get you a cup."

Doc Bracken put a hand on his shoulder. "Sit still. I'll get it." He walked into the office. A moment later, a mug of coffee in his hand, Bracken sat down on the bench. "You were deep in thought, Marshal, your face a study in emotion. Anything you want to talk about?"

"Oh, not really, Doc. I guess I was just sitting here sort of feeling sorry for myself."

"You do that often?"

Frank smiled. "Not very often, Doc. Looking over the wreckage of this town brought it on, I suppose."

"That and Mrs. Browning," the doctor said softly.

"Yes. That, too."

"Frank, the West is still a small place, speaking in terms of population. Hell, man, half the town knew that you and Vivian Browning . . . ah, Henson . . . were once married. Many of those knew that old man Henson trumped up some false charges against you, and you had to leave. The story was all over the West back then. Newcomers, Johnny-come-latelies, don't know it, but we old-timers do. I've had people today, in the midst of all this tragedy, tell me that it's admirable how well you're holding up. Most of the people here in town, the regulars, the permanent residents . . . why, they like you, Frank. They've found that all your dark reputation is pure bunk. For whatever it's worth, the town is behind you."

"Doc, I'm going to hunt down that gang—every member—and I'm going to kill them, all of them. My reputation is about to get a lot darker."

"Only one man was cranking that Gatling gun, Frank."

"But they were all involved. And no one tried to stop that one man."

"I can't argue that point.

"Viv and me, Doc, we were picking up the pieces. We were going to start all over. Move to California, maybe, where very few people have even heard of me . . ."

That got Frank a quick, sharp look from Doc Bracken. Frank Morgan still didn't realize that most people over the age of eight had heard of him. He didn't know that there had been dozens and dozens of newspaper articles written about him. People knew about Frank Morgan's exploits from coast-to-coast and border-to-border. Now many in the press were beginning to call him the last gunfighter—Frank Morgan, the Last Gunfighter.

"All that's gone up in a few minutes of gunsmoke. Vivian is lying in a coma, dying. My"—Frank caught himself, but not before Dr. Bracken picked up on the hesitation—"her son won't speak to me. He blames me for all that's happened. Hell, maybe he's right. Not entirely, but partly. I accept it. What choice do I have?"

"That's nonsense, Frank. She got caught in the line of fire—that's what happened."

Frank sighed. "You don't know the whole story, Doc. And it's best you never do."

"If you say so, Frank." He took another sip of coffee. "Good. I needed that. It's been a long day, and it's going to be an even longer night."

"I'm sure."

Jerry walked up, a toothpick in his mouth. "Doc," he greeted Bracken. "You better go put on the feedbag, Frank. Angie's laid out quite a spread at the café."

"Yeah, that's a good idea. I am kinda hungry. Doc, how about you?"

"In a little while. I want to check on a couple of patients first."

When the doctor had gone, Jerry said, "Big Bob Mallory was seen leavin' the hotel about fifteen minutes ago, totin' his rifle."

"It's about time for the showdown, then. I've been feeling it coming for several hours. Where is Kid Moran?"

"Disappeared. I looked around and he was nowhere to be seen. Come on, I'll have coffee while you eat."

"Not looking a gunfight in the eyes, Jer. I changed my mind. A big meal slows you down. I'll eat later." Frank smiled. "Providing I still can eat, that is."

CHAPTER 24

With Jerry walking a dozen yards behind him, carrying a rifle and covering his back, Frank strolled down to the café. The front windows had been knocked out, and were now boarded up, but the horrible events of that day had not affected the quality of food. The delicious odors drifting out into the street made Frank's mouth water, bringing home the fact that he had not eaten all day. But he did not want to eat a large meal and then have to face a very fast gunslick. And Kid Moran was very fast.

Frank settled for a piece of pie with his cup of coffee. Then he had a cigarette with his second cup in the Silver Spoon Café. He was stubbing out the cigarette butt when Jerry came in and took a seat.

"Kid Moran's waiting for you, Frank. He's standing on the corner. He's got a third pistol shoved in his gunbelt."

"He must be figuring I'm going to be hard to put down," Frank said as he rolled another smoke.

"Don't forget he usually misses his first shot," Jerry reminded him.

"Yeah. And sometimes he doesn't. Always expect the unexpected in these things, Jerry. I've learned that the hard way over the years."

"I'll never have a stand up and hook and draw fight, Frank. I know better. I'm as slow as cold molasses."

"I hope you never do, Jer."

"Frank, let's you and me take him alive," Jerry suggested. "We'll get a couple of Greeners from the office and take him that way. How about it?"

"It wouldn't work."

"Why?"

"He'd fight, and we'd both run the risk of getting plugged. What he's calling for right now is still legal out here, and probably will be for some years to come. Have you seen Big Bob anywhere?"

"No. This smells like a setup to me, Frank."

"The Kid drawing me out, and Big Bob shooting me in the back?" Frank shook his head. "No. No, I don't think so. Bob Mallory works alone. Always has."

"There's always the first time."

Again, Frank shook his head. "No. The Kid's looking for a reputation, and Bob is getting paid by somebody—probably Dutton—to kill me." Frank paused in his lifting of his coffee cup. "Or maybe it's Conrad he's after. Jer, go check on Conrad. Keep an eye on him for me, will you?"

"If you order me to do so, Frank, I will."

"Do I have to order it done?"

"No. Of course not. I'm gone."

Frank finished his coffee and stood up, slipping the hammer thong off his .45. Angie was watching, and frowned.

"Frank, isn't there another way?"

"No, Angie. There isn't. Not with The Kid. He wants a reputation."

"He's lightning fast."

Frank smiled. "I'm no tenderfoot, Angie."

She returned the smile. "Of course, you're not. I didn't mean to imply—"

Frank held up a hand. "I know what you meant, Angie. Keep the coffee hot, will you?"

"Just for you and Jerry. And I'll have some supper for you, too."

Frank picked up his hat, settled it on his head, and stepped out of the café. He looked to his left. There was The Kid, waiting at the end of the block.

"Might as well get this over with," Frank said, thinking: *One way or the other.* He touched the brim of his hat in a salute to The Kid, a signal that he was ready, and stepped off the boardwalk and into the street.

Kid Moran did the same.

The word had spread about the pending gunfight. The main street was deserted of carpenters and other workmen. In only a few more years, stand up, hook and draw showdowns such as this would be mostly a thing of the past, but for now, it was still legal in most small towns in the West. If not legal, at least accepted by many.

Louis Pettigrew, the book writer from the East, was standing in the lobby of the hotel, watching it all and scribbling furiously in his notebook. He had written about dozens of shoot-outs, but this was the first actual gunfight he had ever witnessed. It was enthralling and exciting. What a book this would make: the aging king of gunfighters meeting a young, but fast, upstart prince in the dusty street for the title of the best of the fast guns. Wonderful!

Conrad was not watching the slow walk toward death in the street. He was sitting quietly beside his mother's bed.

Charles Dutton was watching from the hotel, a faint smile on his lips.

"Ride out of here, Kid," Frank called. "Don't throw your life away for nothing."

"It ain't nothin' to me, Morgan," The Kid called.

"Boy, the day of the gunfighter is nearly over. And as far as I'm concerned, it's past time."

"What's the matter, Morgan?" The Kid taunted. "You gettin' old and yeller?"

Getting old, for sure, Frank thought. *He's damn sure right on one count.* "Don't be a fool, boy. You know better than that."

"Frank Morgan done lost his nerve," The Kid yelled. "By God, it's true. You beg me to let you leave and you can ride out of here, Morgan. Beg for your life, old man."

The Kid's been drinking, Frank thought. *Where else would he get such a silly idea?* "Forget it, boy," Frank called. "That won't happen."

The distance between them was slowly closing. Little pockets of dust were popping up under their boots as they walked toward sudden death and destiny.

"Why don't you draw, old man?" The Kid yelled. "Come on, damn you. Pull on me!"

"It's your play, Kid," Frank said calmly. "You're the one challenging the law here in town. I'm ordering you to give this up and ride on out."

The Kid suddenly stopped in the middle of the street. Frank stopped his walking. There were maybe fifty or so feet between them. Plenty close enough.

"Suspenseful," Louis Pettigrew muttered. "I never knew it could be like this."

"Insane," Mayor Jenkins muttered, watching from inside his bank. "When is this going to stop?"

Angie stood in the doorway of her café, a just poured cup of coffee forgotten in her hand.

Undertaker Malone was watching from an alley. He was taking a much needed break from his work. The bodies of that day's tragic events were still stacked up inside his parlor and outside behind his establishment. Many had already been buried without benefit of Malone's services.

Willis was watching from his general store. He had sent his wife and kids into the rear of the store, safe from any stray bullets.

"Draw on me, you old bastard," Kid Moran yelled, "so's I can kill you and have done with this."

"Drag iron, son," Frank replied. "I told you this is your play."

The Kid stared at Frank, then shook his head. "You yeller son of a bitch!" The Kid hollered. "You're afeared of me. I knowed you had a yeller streak up your back."

Frank waited, silent and steady—a man alone in the middle of the street, the tin star on his coat twinkling faintly in the last rays of late-afternoon sun. Frank sensed The Kid was getting nervous, and that emotion would be a plus for him.

"What's the matter, boy?" Frank called. "You sound real edgy."

"Ain't nothin' the matter with me, you old fart! Are you gonna draw, or rattle that jaw of yourn?"

"I keep telling you, boy, it's your play. Are you deaf, or just plain stupid?"

"Goddamn you!"

Frank waited patiently.

Someone standing in the doorway of the saloon laughed.

The Kid cut his eyes away from Frank for just a split second. "Are you laughin' at me?"

Frank could have drawn and fired during the half second The Kid had averted his eyes. But he didn't. Frank really didn't want to kill The Kid. He knew, though, that The Kid wasn't about to give him any other option.

The Kid settled that quickly. "You damned yeller belly. I'm countin' to three. You better draw on me, Morgan. Sometime durin' the count. If you don't, that's your hard luck. It don't make no difference to me nohow. I'm gonna kill you anyways. I'm tared of all this jibber jabber."

"You're under arrest, Kid Moran," Frank called, making what he knew he had to do legal.

"Huh? I'm whut?"

"You're under arrest."

"Whut charge?"

"Threatening the life of a peace officer. Now come along peacefully or suffer the consequences."

"You go to hell, Morgan!"

"That's the last chance I'm giving you, boy."

Kid Moran cursed and grabbed iron. He just thought he was quick on the shoot. Frank beat him to the draw and shot him in the belly.

"Damn!" The Kid gasped, doubling over. But he held on to his gun.

"Drop your gun, boy!" Frank called.

"Hell with you, Morgan." The Kid lifted his .45 and jacked back the hammer.

Frank shot him again. The impact turned The Kid around in the street. He stumbled a couple of times, but he just wouldn't go down.

Kid Moran straightened up and grinned at Morgan. "Now you're dead, Morgan," he gasped. "Now it's my turn."

The Kid lifted his pistol and Frank drilled him again. This time The Kid went to his knees, but didn't stay down long. He dropped his pistol and, bracing himself with that hand, struggled to his feet, drawing his second pistol.

"Damn you to hell, Morgan!" The Kid managed to spit out the words. Then he turned to one side and lifted and cocked his left-hand gun.

Frank dusted him with his fourth round, the bullet slamming into The Kid and blowing out the other side. This time Kid Moran went down and stayed down. He tried to rise, but just couldn't make it. His pistol slipped from his hand to lie in the dust.

Frank unconsciously twirled his pistol before holstering it. He walked over and looked down at the bullet-riddled young man. "Sorry about this, Kid. I really am."

"You really are . . . fast, Morgan. I never . . . seen nobody fast as you."

Frank knelt down beside The Kid.

Kid Moran struggled to speak, then gave it up, gasping for breath. "I'll get the doc, boy." Frank looked around. Dr. Bracken was walking toward the fallen Kid, his black bag in his hand.

Frank stood up and met the doc halfway. "I put four rounds in him, Doc. I don't see how he's still alive."

"I saw and heard it all, Frank. You gave him every opportunity to surrender. You only did what you had to do."

The men walked over to where The Kid lay. "Let me take a look at him," Bracken said.

"Forget it," The Kid gasped. "I'm done for and I know it. I'm fillin' up with blood. I feel it. Don't move me."

"All right, boy," Doc Bracken said.

"You got any kin, Kid?" Frank asked.

"Nobody that gives a damn."

"Your mother and father?"

"Wherever they are"—The Kid coughed up blood—"they can both go to hell!"

"You want some laudanum?" Doc Bracken asked.

The Kid didn't reply. His eyes were wide and staring in death.

Malone walked up. "I know The Kid had money," the undertaker said. "What do you want on his tombstone?"

Frank thought for a moment. Then he said, "Put on it: He died game."

CHAPTER 25

The bloody, bullet-riddled body of Kid Moran was carried off and stored with other bodies behind Malone's funeral parlor. The undertaker would get to Moran when time permitted.

Big Bob Mallory had been spotted leaving town. Frank checked his room at the hotel and found it bare. Big Bob was indeed gone, but where and for how long remained unanswered.

"Maybe he decided not to take the job," Jerry opined. He and Frank were sitting in the jail office, the day after the attack on the town.

"Don't count on that," Frank replied. "Big Bob demands money up front. If he takes the money, he'll finish the job."

"Wishful thinking on my part."

"You ready to take over the marshal's job, Jer?" Frank abruptly tossed the question at his deputy.

Jerry almost spilled his coffee down the front of his shirt. He stared at Frank, his mouth open; then he shook his head and said, "You goin' somewhere for a while, Frank?"

"As soon as it's . . . over for Mrs. Browning, I'm pulling

out. I think you'll make a fine marshal, Jer." He smiled. "You and Angie will be assets to this community, for sure."

"You goin' after the Pine and Vanbergen gangs, Frank?"

"Yes."

"Alone?"

"Yes."

Jerry was silent for a moment, staring at the floor. He lifted his head and looked at Frank. "That's crazy, Frank. That's suicide."

"My mind is made up. You want the job, or not?"

"Well . . . sure, I do. If you leave, and the town council approves it."

"They'll approve it. You're a good, solid, steady man, Jerry. Both you and Angie are respected by the townspeople. You'll both do just fine."

"Maybe Mrs. Browning will pull through."

"I don't believe in miracles. Doc Bracken told me this morning her coma has deepened. She'll starve to death if she doesn't come out of it."

"What about the outlaws?"

"They're gone. Packed up, saddled up, and gone. Very doubtful they'll ever be back."

"Your mind's made up, isn't it?"

"All the way, Jer."

"Maybe something will happen that will change your mind. I'd like to see you stay."

Frank nodded his head in understanding and stood up. "I don't know what that would be, but thanks for saying it. The prisoners are all settled down. It's all quiet. Let's go walk the town."

"They put The Kid in the ground yet?"

"I don't think so. I don't think Malone's had time to fix him up yet."

"To be no bigger than he was, The Kid could sure soak up some lead."

"He did, for a fact. The Kid was as game as any man I ever faced."

The two lawmen walked the town, the sounds of sawing and hammering all around them, the smell of fresh-cut lumber strong in the air.

"This town might be here even when the mines play out," Jerry remarked.

"Could be. It sure wouldn't surprise me at all. Some cattlemen are gonna have to come in here. Maybe a few people raising horses. When the mines play out, the town will shrink down. But you've got a telegraph office and a bank, and some determined people. That's what it takes."

"Oh, hell!" Jerry said. "Here comes that writer fellow."

"Damn!" Frank muttered.

"Marshal Morgan," Louis Pettigrew called. "Might I have a word with you, sir?"

"Do I have a choice?" Frank whispered.

Jerry laughed. "I'll make the rounds. You two have a good time."

"Thanks, Jer. You're a real pal."

Jerry waved and walked on, leaving Frank with Pettigrew. Frank noticed Conrad and Charles Dutton walking up the boardwalk on the other side of the street. Even from that distance Frank could tell that Conrad appeared very pale. *Boys under a hell of a strain,* Frank thought. *Dutton probably got him away from his mother's side to get him out for a walk and some fresh air. Or,* Frank amended, *maybe the bastard has something else up his sleeve, like setting the boy up for a kill.*

"Ah, Marshal . . ." Pettigrew said. "I would like to talk with you about doing your life's story. Would you be willing to discuss that?"

Frank looked at the Boston writer. "I beg your pardon? What did you say?"

Pettigrew looked pained. He sighed and said, "I wish to

write your life story. There are a great many people back east who are clamoring for more information about Frank Morgan."

"Is that a fact?"

"Absolutely, Marshal. And it would be a very lucrative venture for you, I must say."

"I'll sure give it some thought, Mr. Pettigrew."

"Wonderful, Marshal. And let me say that the, ah, gunfight I witnessed yesterday out there in the street was a magnificent sight. Very dramatic."

Frank was watching Conrad and Dutton. They had stopped on the corner and were chatting. Conrad had his back to the street. "Dramatic, Mr. Pettigrew?"

"It certainly was. I can truthfully say I have never seen anything like it."

"You ever witnessed a hanging, Mr. Pettigrew?"

"Good heavens, no."

The morning stage was rumbling up the street, a day late due to the road being blocked the day before. The telegraph wires had been fixed, messages had been sent out that the reports of plague in the town were false, and the road had been reopened.

"A hanging can be very dramatic, Mr. Pettigrew. Especially when the neck isn't broken and the victim jerks around for several minutes, slowly choking to death. It's quite a sight." Frank said this with a very straight face.

Pettigrew was turning a bit green around the mouth. "I'll take your word for that, Marshal."

"I can probably arrange for you to witness an execution. If you would like that."

"Ah . . . thank you, Marshal, but no. Your description of the event is graphic enough."

Frank watched Dutton put his hands on the young man's shoulders and reposition him, fully presenting Conrad's back to the street, while Dutton was partly shielded by a post holding an oil-fueled streetlamp.

What the hell? Frank thought. *What's going on here? Very strange behavior on Dutton's part.*

"When would be a good time for us to get together for a long talk?" Pettigrew asked.

"Oh, sometime within the next couple of days, for sure," Frank responded.

"Wonderful. That will give me ample time to jot down pertinent questions. At your office, perhaps?"

"That will be fine."

"I'm so looking forward to it."

"Yeah, me, too," Frank replied with as much enthusiasm as possible, which was precious little. He had no intention of meeting with the writer. "I'll see you, Mr. Pettigrew. You have a nice day."

"Oh, I shall, Marshal. Thank you."

"You're welcome," Frank mumbled, as he began walking toward the corner. He stepped off the boardwalk and started crossing the street, his eyes on Conrad and Dutton.

"Hi, Marshal," a citizen yelled, catching Frank in the middle of the street.

Conrad spun around at the shouted greeting just as a rifle cracked somewhere behind Frank. Frank dropped into a crouch and turned around, snaking his .45 into his hand with a blurringly fast motion.

The rifle slug burned past Conrad, missing him by just a few inches. Had he not turned, the rifle bullet would have split his spinal cord. The slug slammed into a passerby who had just exited the newly arrived stage and was carrying his heavy traveling bag. The bullet meant for Conrad knocked the man off his boots and dropped him to the boardwalk, dead on impact with the dusty boards.

Frank triggered off a shot at a man in an upstairs window over a boarded-up shop, a man standing with a rifle in his hand, a faint finger of smoke leaking from the muzzle. The .45 round hit the man in his chest, just below his throat, and slammed him backward in the room.

"Conrad!" Frank yelled as rifle barrels began poking out of several second-story windows. "Get out of here, boy. Someone is trying to kill you!"

Frank ran for the protection of the stage, but the driver was no stranger to gunfire, having experienced it many times in the past, and he wanted no more of it. He yelled at his team, and the six big horses took off.

Frank sprinted for the dubious protection of an open carriage in front of a shop, running and twisting to afford the snipers less of a target. Bullets howled all around him. Out of the corner of his eye he caught a glimpse of Dutton hightailing it alone around a corner. The fancy lawyer and so-called friend of the family was leaving Conrad to deal with the problem on his own. The young man seemed frozen in place on the boardwalk until Jerry came charging around the corner and grabbed him up and off his feet. Jerry turned, and a slug tore into his left leg, knocking him down. Just before he fell heavily, Jerry shoved Conrad to safety inside a corner shop.

Frank slid on his belly in the dirt and reached the rear of the carriage in time to see Jerry crawl into the shop, dragging his bloody leg, leaving a trail on the boardwalk. At least he was still alive, and Conrad was safe.

Frank knelt behind the boot of the carriage and began throwing lead at the upstairs windows. It was returned as fast as it was received. One rifle slug knocked Frank's hat off and sent it flying somewhere behind him. Another rifle slug burned a hot crease on his shoulder. The crease turned wet and sticky as the blood began to flow. Frank ignored the burning pain and jerked his second gun from behind his gunbelt.

Jerry opened up from the doorway of the shop, and at that point the hidden gunmen above the street decided they'd had enough. The gunfire ceased, and the street fell silent.

Horses tied at hitch rails had bolted in panic when the rifle fire began, running in all directions. One horse ran into

Nannette's Boutique for the Discriminating Woman, and one lady (who was nearly the same size as the horse) ran out into the street dressed only in her bloomers, shrieking to high heaven. The sight of her stopped one man cold in his tracks.

"My Lord!" he hollered.

The panicked woman ran right over the man, knocking him into a horse trough. She kept right on running, and disappeared into the Silver Slipper Saloon. Men began exiting the saloon through all available avenues, preferring to face gunfire rather than confront the ominous presence of Mrs. Bertha Longthrower, wife of Reverend Otis Longthrower, pastor of Heaven's Grace Baptist Church . . . in her bloomers.

Bertha took one long look at her surroundings, her eyes lingering on the rather risqué painting on the wall behind the bar (which featured three naked ladies and a midget . . . in height only) and let out a whoop that would have shamed a Comanche Dog Soldier. She headed for the rear of the saloon, ran out the back door, and collided with a man just stepping out of the privy. Both of them were propelled back into the privy, which promptly turned over, trapping the scantily clad woman and the terrified man (who was certain he had been attacked by an enraged albino grizzly bear) in the narrow confines of the outhouse.

Back on the main street, Frank ran across the street and into an alley that led behind the line of shops, hurriedly reloading his guns. He caught a glimpse of a man with a rifle charging out of a back door, and yelled at him to halt. The man turned and fired at Frank, the bullet just missing his head. Frank drilled the man, the .45 slug striking the assassin in the chest, killing him instantly.

Frank cautiously made his way up to the downed and dead sniper. The rifle beside the body was a bolt-action Winchester-Hotchkiss. He had found one of the men who had ambushed him and Viv in the valley.

Two more of the men were still at large, but Frank suspected they were gone, having left ahead of the man on the ground. He picked up the rifle and walked back to the street. He wanted to have a long talk with Charles Dutton, but had no physical evidence at all with which to confront the man. Dutton was, so far, still in the clear.

Conrad was unhurt, and Jerry's wound, while painful, was not serious. The deputy would be off his feet for a few days, but was not in danger.

The passerby who had taken the bullet meant for Conrad was dead.

The horse who had invaded Nannette's had been led out and away, and the search was on for Mrs. Bertha Longthrower.

"Where is my wife?" Reverend Longthrower demanded.

"I think she's in the saloon," a citizen told him. "I seen her goin' in there . . . in her bloomers."

"In her what?" Reverend Longthrower thundered.

"Her drawers."

"Never!" the reverend roared.

"Hey, ever'body!" a man yelled from the saloon. "Otis is in the privy yellin' that he's bein' attacked by an albino bear. Come on."

Frank had a pretty good idea that the "bear" would turn out to be Mrs. Longthrower . . . in her drawers. That was not a sight he wished to see again. He told some men to get the body of the outlaw on the second floor and then went to check on Conrad and Jerry over at the doctor's makeshift hospital. Before he could cross the street Reverend Longthrower started hollering for his wife to get off of Otis.

"I imagine Otis would like that, too," Frank muttered.

Conrad had refused to lie down and rest for a while, choosing to go to the office. Frank sat down on the edge of the bunk and talked with Jerry for a few minutes.

"Doc says the bullet didn't hit nothin' vital," Jerry said. "He says I just have to stay off my feet for a couple of days and rest."

"You take as long as you need, Jer." He smiled. "I imagine Angie will see that you're well fed."

Jerry blushed under his tan. "Yeah. I 'spect she will." He looked closer at Frank. "You been hit, Frank! Your shoulder's bleedin.' "

"It's just a scratch. I'm heading over to the office now to clean it up."

"Take off your shirt, Frank," Dr. Bracken said from behind him. "Let me take a look at that wound."

"It's nothing, Doc."

"Take off your shirt. That's an order. You get blood poisoning, you won't think nothing."

Doc Bracken cleaned and bandaged the wound, told Frank to take it easy for the rest of the day, and sent him on his way. Frank didn't want to tell the doctor he'd hurt himself worse than that peeling potatoes.

On his way back to the office, Frank ran into Louis Pettigrew. "Marshal," the writer said, "I have made up my mind."

"Oh?" Frank was staring at the man's bowler hat.

"Yes. I am going to write a series of books about you. Not just one, but perhaps a dozen."

Frank did not reply, just stared at the man in stunned disbelief. He couldn't keep his eyes off the man's dude hat.

"I have wired my publisher, and am now awaiting his reply. I shall make it my life's work."

"Your life's work?" Frank managed to say.

"Yes, sir. I shall outfit myself and follow you no matter where in the wilds you might decide to go. I shall chronicle the day to day living of the West's most celebrated but least known gunfighter. Won't that be grand?"

"Words fail me, Mr. Pettigrew." *I gotta get out of here, and do it quickly,* Frank thought.

"As soon as I receive word from my publisher I shall make preparations," Pettigrew said.

"To do what?" Frank asked.

"To make the West my home! I must say, this is very exciting."

I'll leave in the dead of night, Frank thought. *Slip away like a thief.*

"I just thought you would like to know about my decision, Marshal. And I hope you're as excited as I am."

"Oh, I am, Mr. Pettigrew. I can't begin to tell you how your decision has affected me."

Pettigrew patted Frank on the arm. "I'm so pleased, Marshal. I really didn't know how you would react to the news."

"I'm, ah, still trying to get used to the idea of you becoming a citizen of the West, Mr. Pettigrew."

"I'm really excited about it."

"I'm sure you are."

"Well, then, I'll see you later on. We'll make an appointment to meet and start work on the first installment. Ta ta, Marshal."

"Yeah," Frank mumbled. "Ta-ta to you, too."

"What is the writer so happy about?" Mayor Jenkins asked, walking up just as Pettigrew was leaving.

"He's going to become a permanent resident of the West."

"Really?"

"That's what he told me."

"Well, he's certainly welcome. I just hope he gets rid of that damn silly hat," the banker said, "before someone shoots it off his head."

CHAPTER 26

Frank had just finished a fresh cup of coffee and a smoke and had his feet propped up on the edge of the desk when a man walked into his office. "Sorry to bother you, Marshal, but I found me a body on the way into town."

Frank's boots hit the floor. "Where?"

"Just the other side of where them outlaws had the road blocked. I seen the buzzards circlin' and went to take a look. It's kind of bad, Marshal. The body's shore enough tore up somethin' awful. The ants has been workin' on it, as well as them damn buzzards."

"I'll head on out there. Thanks, mister."

"No problem."

Frank picked up a spare horse at the livery and headed out. He was not looking forward to bringing the body back. Several days in the hot sun would have the body bloated and stinking. The ants and buzzards, and probably coyotes and other animals, had been working on it and would have left it in a real mess.

Frank saw the buzzards long before he reached the body,

about a hundred yards off the road, and up a natural game trail. Frank could tell by what was left of the clothing that it was more than likely the body of the young bank teller, Dean Hall, or Hill, or whatever his name was.

The body was a mess, not at all pleasant to look at, or smell. Buzzards and ants had been at the face and the eyes, and facial identification would be impossible. Buzzards, more than likely, had torn the stomach open, and intestines were stretched out for yards.

"Damn!" Frank said, trying to breathe through his mouth and not his nose. The stench was awful.

He found a big stick and beat off the buzzards, some of them so bloated from eating the putrid meat they could not fly. They waddled off and stared at Frank, giving him baleful looks, no fear in them.

He got the body on the tarp and rolled it up, securing it tightly with rope, closing both ends. That helped with the stench. It was going to be a real job getting the body tied down on the horse, for the animal was not liking the smell at all, and was trying to break loose and back off.

Frank didn't blame the horse at all.

Frank was securing a loose end of the tarp, one foot of the body sticking out, when he saw his own horse's head jerk up, the ears laid back, nostrils flared. Frank quickly jerked his rifle from the boot and grabbed the ammo belt he had looped over the horn. The tarpwrapped body forgotten, Frank jumped for cover, thinking, *Setup!*

Someone, maybe Ned Pine and Vic Vanbergen, maybe Dutton, *somebody,* had set him up for sure. And the setup had worked to perfection. He was damn sure set up, and boxed in.

Frank had just bellied down behind the rocks when the bullets started flying all around him. All he could do for several minutes was keep his head down and hope that no bullet flattened out against the rocks and ricocheted into him.

He wriggled into better cover during a few seconds

respite in the firing. He hadn't made any attempt to return the fire, for as yet he didn't have any idea where the gunmen were. He didn't know if there were two or ten of them. He knew only that if it lasted for very long he was in for one hell of a mighty dry fight. His canteen was on his horse, and the animal had wandered several dozen yards away—no way he could get to it. And there was little chance he could expect any help.

The firing began again, and this time Frank could pretty well add up the number of shooters he was facing, for not all of them were using the same caliber rifles. Five shooters, Frank figured. And several of them were slightly above him.

Two of the four assassins from the ambush in the valley and town were still alive; could they be a part of this?

Frank didn't believe so. But they could also very well be a part of a much larger picture. Maybe Dutton had hired an entire gang to rid himself of Vivian and Conrad. But why so much emphasis on him? Had Dutton found out that he was now a minor stockholder in the Henson Company?

"Damn," Frank muttered. "This is getting too complicated for a country boy."

Frank got lucky. He caught a quick glimpse of what looked like part of a man's arm sticking out from behind cover and snapped off a fast shot.

"Goddamn it!" he heard the man holler. "I'm hit. Oh, damn. I'm hit hard."

"Where you hit, Pat?"

"My elbow. It's busted. Can't use my arm at all."

"Hang on. I'm comin'."

The man who was heading to help his friend jumped up, and Frank dusted him, the .44-.40 round entering the man's body high up on one side and blowing out through his shoulder. The second shooter never made a sound. He folded like a house of cards and went down, his rifle clattering on the rocks.

Another voice was added. "Nick?"

Nick would never make another sound on this side of the misty vail.

"That bastard's got more luck than any man I ever seen," a third voice called.

"Yeah," a fourth voice shouted from off to Frank's left. "Let's get out of here, Mack. Let that damn lawyer fight his own battles. I'm done."

Frank waited for a few minutes, trying to pick up the sound of horses' hooves, but could hear nothing. They must have left their horses some distance away. Frank edged out of the rocks and ran a short distance to more cover. No shots came his way. He worked his way toward the higher ground cautiously. He found a blood trail that led off toward a clearing, but did not pursue it.

Working his way through the rocks, he found the dead man. He rolled the body over and went through the clothing, looking for some identification. He did find a wad of paper money . . . several hundred dollars. He shoved that in his back jeans pocket and dragged the man out of the rocks, then went back for the shooter's rifle. He began looking around for the man's horse, and after a few minutes found it. He led the animal back and hoisted the body belly down across the saddle, tying him securely with rope.

Frank managed to get the bank teller's tarp-wrapped body roped down in the pack frame, then headed back to town.

Townspeople paused on the boardwalk, watching Frank ride slowly up the main street. Doc Bracken came out of his office to meet Frank in front of the jail.

"The bank teller fellow's in the tarp," Frank told him. "I think it is, anyways. The other one is part of a gang that tried to ambush me. It was a setup to get me out of town. You seen that damn Charles Dutton fellow?"

"The Boston lawyer?"

"Yes."

"Not lately. Not since the shoot-out, I'm sure."

"I'll find him. How is Vivian?"

"Weaker, Frank. It's down to hours now, I'm sure."

"Conrad?"

"Finally accepting the fact that his mother is not going to make it."

"I'll get those bodies over to Malone." Frank reached in his back pocket and pulled out the wad of bills. "The shooter had this money on him."

"I'd give Malone twenty-five dollars and keep the rest, I was you."

"I'll give it to Jerry." Frank grinned. "For a wedding present."

"He and Angie have sure been making cow's eyes at one another of late."

"He'll make her a good husband, and she'll make him a good wife. Doc, you think this town is going to last after the mines play out?"

"Yes, I do, Frank. I just heard that a big cattle outfit is going to come in. The town will lose about half its population when the mines go, maybe more than that, but the solid citizens will stay. Why do you ask?"

"I told you, Doc. I'm pulling out. Jerry will make a fine town marshal."

"We'll hate to see you go, Frank."

"I forget the name of the writer who wrote that line about all things coming to an end . . . something like that. It's almost time for me to move on."

Dr. Bracken's nurse came running out of his office and over to the men. "Doctor! Mrs. Browning just slipped away."

Doc Bracken looked at Frank.

"Correction, Doc," Frank said. "It's time to move on."

CHAPTER 27

"Mr. Dutton left several hours ago, Marshal," the clerk at the hotel told Frank. "He had to make a very hurried business trip to Denver."

"Oh? How did he leave? There was no stage scheduled."

"Well, he had some rather rough-looking men escorting him. I'd never seen any of them before today."

"Thanks."

So much for Dutton, Frank thought, standing outside the hotel. *I'll deal with him when I find him . . . if I ever find him.* Frank had a hunch the Boston lawyer would never again set foot west of the Mississippi River.

The man who had told Frank about the body of the bank teller had hauled his butt out of town. No one had seen him before, and no one knew where he had gone. Another dead end. Undertaker Malone had stopped all other work to prepare Vivian's body. She was to be taken to the railroad spur line just across the border in Colorado and then to Denver. From there she would be transported back east for burial.

Conrad was to escort the body all the way back to Boston.

Frank walked over to Malone's funeral parlor. Conrad

was sitting alone in the waiting room. He did not look up as Frank entered.

Frank took off his hat, hung it on a rack, and sat down beside his son. "Don't you think we'd better talk?"

"We have nothing to discuss, Marshal."

"I'm your father, Conrad."

"Biologically speaking, I suppose I have to accept that as fact. I don't have to like it. Mr. Browning was my father. He raised me."

"And he did a fine job. I didn't know I had a son until your mother told me just a short time ago." *Just a few weeks back,* Frank thought. *And now she's gone . . . forever.* "I want you to believe that."

"I believe it, Marshal. But it doesn't change anything. I want you to believe that."

It's too soon to be discussing this, Frank thought. *I made a mistake coming over here. The boy is too filled with grief.*

"I know that Mother left you a small percentage of the company, Marshal. I will honor her wishes. I won't contest it."

"I didn't ask her for any part of the company, Conrad."

"I believe that, too."

"You want me to leave you alone?"

"I don't care, Marshal. You have a right to be here."

"I loved her very much. I never stopped loving her." Conrad had nothing to say about that.

"Did Malone say when the"—Frank started to say "body" but he couldn't bring himself to form the word—"when people can stop by here to pay their respects?"

"In a few hours."

Frank stood up and snagged his hat off the rack. "I'll leave you alone for a time."

Conrad met Frank's eyes for the first time since Frank entered the waiting room. "I appreciate that, Marshal."

"Well, maybe I'll see you in a few hours."

"All right."

Frank was glad to leave the stuffy and strange-smelling

waiting room of the funeral parlor. He had never liked those places. He stood on the boardwalk and took several deep breaths of fresh air, then looked up and down the street.

Another town I'll soon put behind me, Frank thought. *In a few months they will have forgotten all about me, at least for the most part. The town's residents will settle back into a regular way of life . . . and I'll do what I do best—drift.*

No, Frank amended. *Not just drift. I have a big job to do. I'll find the men responsible for your death, Viv. I promise you that. If it takes the rest of whatever life I have left, I'll do it.*

The news of Vivian Browning's death spread quickly through the town. People spoke in hushed, sorrowful tones to Frank as he walked back to his office. At his desk he wrote out a letter of resignation, effective when Jerry was able to return to work . . . which, according to Doc Bracken, would be in a couple of days. He dated and signed the notice, then sealed it in an envelope.

He checked on the prisoners, then walked over to his house and began packing up his possessions, leaving out a clean shirt, britches, socks, and longhandles. He went over to the livery and checked on his packhorse. The animal was glad to see him, perhaps sensing they would soon be again on the trail.

Frank stored his packed up possessions in the livery storeroom and then walked over to the café for a cup of coffee and perhaps a bite to eat. Angie took one look at Frank's expression and brought two cups and the coffeepot over to his table and joined him.

She touched his hand. "I'm sorry, Frank."

"I have to think it was for the best, Angie. Better than her starving to death. It was just her time to follow the light."

"That's beautiful, Frank. Follow the light. Frank? How is her son taking it?"

"He's all right. He's tougher than he looks."

"And you?"

"Getting ready to pull out. Just as soon as Jerry is on his feet."

"That quick?"

"Yes. I have things to do."

"I don't have to ask what those things are. Is that what Mrs. Browning would want?"

"It's what I want."

She lowered her eyes from his cold stare. She struggled to suppress a shiver. Looking into his eyes that day was like looking into a cold, musty grave. Years back, Angie had surprised a big puma feasting on a fresh kill. The puma did not attack, but the eyes were the same as Frank's—cold and deadly. Angie backed away quickly and left the puma alone to eat.

Frank drank his coffee, declined the offer of food, and walked over to Willis's General Store. There he bought bacon, beans, flour, and coffee. He bought a new jacket for the trail, for his old one was patched and worn. He took everything back to the office. There, he sat and waited.

Frank did not return to the funeral parlor to view Vivian's body. He respected her wish that he not have that image in his brain.

The next morning, Jerry came limping into the office about ten o'clock.

"You supposed to be up, Jer?"

"Doc said it was all right long as I don't try to run any foot races. Mrs. Browning's body is being loaded into the wagon now, Frank, for transport to the rails."

"I know."

"You're not going over there?"

"No." Frank stood up. "You ready to be sworn in, Jer?"

"I reckon so, Frank. If that's what you want."

"Wait here." Frank walked over to the bank and got Mayor Jenkins. Ten minutes later, Frank had handed in his badge, and Jerry had been sworn in.

Frank shook hands with Jerry and the mayor and walked out of the office. He did not look back.

A half an hour later, he was on the trail. He didn't know where the Pine and Vanbergen gangs had gone, but he would find them. All of them. One at a time.

PART TWO
THE LONER

CHAPTER 1

The cantina had no name, only a reputation for vice and violence. It was a squat adobe building in a squalid, sun-blasted village in the Four Corners area. Most of the inhabitants were uncertain whether it lay in Arizona, New Mexico, Colorado, or Utah. Most of them didn't give a damn. Such designations were legal matters, and here the only law that mattered was the law of the gun.

Three fine horses were tied up at the hitch rail in front of the cantina. In a place such as this, where most people tried to scratch a meager living out of the arid soil, horses such as these could only belong to outsiders. The only outsiders who passed through the village were those who rode the lonely trails, men who had heard the owl hoot on dark, blood-soaked nights. In fact, it was known among the community of such men that they were welcome here. The cantina's proprietor, Gomez by name, could provide whiskey, tequila, beer, tortillas, beans, *cabrito,* a place to sleep, all for a reasonable price, *señor.*

And women, ah, yes, women, too, although at the moment Gomez had only a few to offer, ranging from his rather buxom wife to a half-breed Navajo girl barely old enough to be considered a woman. The men who patronized Gomez's place were, as a rule, not too picky about such things.

The three men who owned the fine horses were the cantina's only customers at the moment. All the villagers were drowsing in the midday heat except for Gomez, who was behind the bar, and the Navajo girl, who brought drinks to the men when they called for them. Each time when she set the tray on the table where the men were, they laughed and pawed at her and said things that she didn't understand. She didn't particularly want to understand them. Their rough hands made their intent clear enough.

The oldest of the three men was middle-aged, with a face to which time had not been kind. Gray hair stuck out from under a flat-crowned black hat with turquoise-studded conchos on its band. He wore a sour expression, along with a black vest over a shirt that had once been white, black whipcord trousers, and twin gunbelts that crossed as they went around his hips.

Across the table from him was a stocky, bearded Mexican whose sombrero was pushed back so that it hung behind his head by its chin strap. He carried only one gun, an old Colt Navy in a cross-draw holster. He had three knives of varying lengths and styles concealed around his body.

The third and final man was big and young, with a moon face under a high-crowned white hat and a gut that stretched his gray shirt. He had only one gun as well, a long-barreled Remington. Despite his youth, his face already showed the marks of cruelty and dissipation.

In an impatient, high-pitched voice, he said, "We're gonna have to come up with some money pretty soon, Buck. We're about to run out. Time we buy a few more drinks and a roll in the hay with that gal, we'll be broke."

"What do you expect me to do about it?" the oldest of the trio asked. "Did you see a bank when we rode in?"

"No. There ain't much to speak of in this town."

"Well, we can't very well rob a bank that don't exist, now can we?" Buck asked. He took a swallow from a mug of beer. "I swear, Carlson, if you didn't have me around to do your thinkin' for you, I think you'd forget to wake up in the mornin'."

"Carlson is right," the Mexican said. "What will we do when our money runs out?"

"You let me worry about that, Julio. We've done all right with me runnin' the show so far, haven't we?"

Julio shrugged. "I cannot argue with that, amigo."

"Well, I can," Carlson said. "I can argue with anything."

Buck grunted. "Tell me about it. I think you'd argue with a tree stump, boy."

"I'd win, too," Carlson said with a grin.

Buck picked up one of the shots of tequila sitting on the table and tossed it down his throat. He wiped the back of his hand across his mouth. A look of intense concentration had come over his face. He turned to gaze at the bar, where the Navajo girl stood talking quietly to Gomez, who spoke her native tongue.

After a moment, Buck said, "I'm thinkin' we ought to ride down to Gallup. That's where Baggott and Hooper said they were headed. Maybe we can hook up with them and find some job to pull down there. It's been long enough since that other business."

"They have banks in Gallup," Julio said.

"That they do," Buck agreed.

"Wait a minute," Carlson said. "What are we gonna do for money between here and there? I told you, time we settle up with Gomez, we ain't gonna have any more."

"That ain't a problem. We just won't settle up with Gomez."

He said it loudly enough, and the gloomy, low-ceilinged room was small enough, so that Gomez heard. He protested, "Señor, you must be joking."

"I never joke," Buck said. Casually, he drew his left-hand gun and shot Gomez.

The gun was loud in the close quarters, loud enough to make Julio and Carlson wince. The girl had thrown herself aside, out of the line of fire, when she saw Buck pulling iron. She fell to her knees on the hard-packed dirt floor in front of the bar and screamed as Gomez stumbled backward under the bullet's impact. His stubby-fingered hands pawed at his chest where a crimson stain spread slowly on the front of his dirty shirt. He opened his mouth and tried to talk, but nothing came out except a trickle of blood. With a gasp, Gomez fell forward, landing across the bar with his arms flung out in front of him. He stayed that way for a second before gravity took over and hauled his body down behind the bar. He slid off the hardwood and landed with a heavy thud.

The girl kept screaming. "Shut her up," Buck said.

Carlson grinned as he got to his feet and lumbered toward her. "I got just the thing."

Before he got there, a large figure burst through the beaded curtain that hung over the door leading to the living quarters in the rear of the cantina. "Carlson, look out," Julio snapped as he leaped up out of his chair. His hand went to a sheath at the back of his neck, under the hanging sombrero, and came out with a throwing knife. The blade flickered across the room and lodged in the throat of the woman who had come through the curtain, yelling curses in Spanish and brandishing a shotgun.

The curses turned into an agonized gurgle as blood flooded the woman's throat. She was Gomez's wife, and she had heard what was going on in the cantina as she rolled tortillas in the back room. Too late to prevent her husband's murder, she had snatched up the scattergun and rushed out to avenge his death. To be sure, he frequently sold her to the men who stopped here at the cantina, but he was still her husband after all.

Choking and drowning in her own blood, she managed to

pull both triggers on the shotgun, but the twin barrels had dropped so that all the double charge of buckshot did was blow a hole in the dirt floor. She leaned forward. The shotgun held her up for a second as its barrels struck the floor, but then she toppled to the side.

"You are a lucky man, amigo," Julio said. "If not for me, that cow would have blown your head off."

"Yeah, I owe you my life," Carlson said. "You want to go first with the girl?"

Julio started across the room to retrieve his knife. "No, you go ahead," he said. "I am in no hurry."

Carlson grinned. He was looking forward to this.

The girl had stopped screaming. She cringed away, scuttling across the dirt floor as Carlson reached for her. She had been with many men in the time she had been here at Gomez's place. Some of them had been bad men and treated her rough. But these three were different, she sensed. These three would not leave her alive when they rode away from here.

Julio pulled his knife out of the dead woman's throat and used her skirt to wipe the blood from the blade. "Do you think anyone will come to see what the shots were about?" he asked Buck.

"Not likely," Buck replied with a shake of his head. "Those villagers'll be too scared to come outta their holes, like the rabbits they are." He downed another shot of tequila. "Now, we don't have to settle up with Gomez. I'll bet there's even some money in his till that we can help ourselves to. We'll have enough to make it to Gallup."

"*Sí,* I believe you're right."

"Damn it, girl," Carlson said, "don't run away from me. You'll just make it worse for yourself." He chuckled. "Not that it could get a whole lot worse'n what I got in mind for you."

Like a giant cat pouncing on a mouse, the big man suddenly lunged forward. A hamlike hand at the end of a thick, heavy-muscled arm wrapped around the girl's slender arm. She cried out in horror as Carlson jerked her toward him.

From the door of the cantina, a voice said, "I'd let her go if I was you."

The three outlaws looked toward the door. They hadn't heard a horse come up, but the man who stood there had to have gotten to the village some way. He wasn't one of the villagers, that was for sure. With the brilliant sunlight behind him, they couldn't make out anything except his tall, broad-shouldered silhouette, topped by a flat-crowned hat. His accent was American. Not very Western maybe, but still American. His voice held hints of culture and education. Despite that, the hard menace it contained was also obvious.

"Mister, you are a damned fool," Buck drawled. Despite his casual tone, he was tense and ready for trouble now. Men on the run could never let their guard down for too long. "If you've got any sense, you'll turn around and walk away from here. Hell, if you're smart, you'll run."

The stranger laughed softly. "That's one thing nobody's ever accused me of," he said. "Being smart." His head turned slightly as he looked at Carlson again. "I said let her go, fatty."

Carlson shoved the girl against the bar and took a step toward the newcomer. "Why, you son of a bitch—"

"I think I'll kill you last," the stranger mused. "Those two bastards with you strike me as being more dangerous."

The voice was so smooth it took a heartbeat for the three hardcases to grasp the implication of the words. Then Buck yelled, "Get him!" as he exploded from his chair, clawing at both guns.

The stranger went for Julio first, and it was a good thing he did, because the Mexican was a lightning-fast knife man. As it was, he barely beat Julio's throw. The Colt that appeared in the stranger's fist seemingly by magic blasted out a shot just a hair before the knife left Julio's hand. That was enough to throw off the Mexican's aim. The knife thudded into the wall just inches to the right of the door, the handle quivering as the blade stuck in the adobe. Julio was already crumpling to the floor, the stranger's bullet in his belly.

Buck had both guns out, their barrels rising. The stranger shot him twice. The slugs drove him backward as they punched into his chest. He tripped over the chair that had overturned when he leaped to his feet. The guns in his hands roared as his fingers jerked involuntarily on the triggers. The shots went into the cantina's ceiling.

That left Carlson. He had succeeded in dragging out his Remington while the stranger was disposing of Julio and Buck. He even got a shot off that knocked chips of adobe from the edge of the door as the stranger crouched. The Colt spouted flame again. The bullet hit Carlson just between his nose and his upper lip, traveling at an upward angle that sent the deadly chunk of lead boring deep into his brain. Carlson's head jerked back, but he managed to stumble ahead a couple of steps as the knowledge that he was dead slowly penetrated his piggish brain. His knees hit the floor; then he pitched forward on his face.

The stranger didn't pouch his iron. He stalked into the cantina with a pantherish stride and held the gun ready as he checked the bodies to make sure they were dead. Buck and Carlson were, but breath still rasped in Julio's throat as he lay there with his arms crossed and pressed to his bleeding stomach. The stranger bent down and plucked the gun from Julio's holster, placed it on the table. He took the knives he could see, too. It was possible Julio had more hidden on him somewhere, but gut-shot as he was, it was also possible he would never regain consciousness.

He'd probably be lucky if that turned out to be the case. Dying from a bullet in the belly was a bad way to go.

The stranger moved to the bar, where the Navajo girl still cowered. "Are you all right?" he asked as he holstered his gun.

She stared up at him in disbelief. Like an angel, he had

swooped in to save her, drawing his gun and firing with a speed the likes of which she had never seen before—and she had witnessed several gunfights here in Gomez's cantina.

Although it wasn't Gomez's anymore, she thought. He was dead, and so was his wife. She didn't know what would happen to the place now, or to her.

"Are you hurt?" her angel asked.

No, not an angel, considering that he was dressed all in black from head to toe. Devil was more like it. He had the Devil's own skill with a gun. He would have been handsome, the girl thought, with that long, sandy hair and close-cropped beard, if not for the coldness in his eyes.

Yet despite that coldness, the chilly glint that said he cared for nothing and no one, he had risked his life to save her. Julio and Carlson had both come within a whisker of killing him. The fight could have turned out very differently.

But it hadn't. Struggling to form the words in English, she whispered, "Yes, I . . . not hurt."

He nodded. "Good." His eyes went to the woman. "Was she your mother?"

"No, she . . . Gomez's wife."

"Gomez?"

The girl pointed behind the bar. The stranger took a look, shook his head. "Sorry," he muttered. "You just worked here?"

The girl nodded.

"Well, I reckon it's your place now, unless Señor and Señora Gomez have any relatives who want to claim it."

Her place? The girl couldn't imagine owning anything other than the dress she wore, let alone having her own business. The idea was . . . interesting, though.

"I'll find someone to help get these bodies out of here." He turned toward the door.

The girl plucked at the sleeve of his shirt. "Señor? You leave? If you stay . . . I be . . . very good to you."

"Sorry," he replied with a shake of his head. "I had business with those three, and now it's done. I'm just sorry I didn't get here in time to save Señor and Señora Gomez."

"You knew . . . those bad men?"

He nodded. "I knew them."

"But they not act like . . . they knew you."

A hint of a smile played around his lips. "I've changed a mite since the last time they saw me."

"S-Señor . . ."

That hoarse voice came from Julio. He had regained consciousness in time to hear what the stranger said. As the man came over to him, Julio fought off the incredible pain in his belly and went on. "Who . . . who are you?"

"Morgan," the man said as he hunkered on his heels next to the gut-shot Mexican. "Some call me Kid Morgan."

"I never . . . heard of you."

"You knew me by another name. Remember when you were in Carson City a while back? You remember Black Rock Canyon?"

Julio's eyes widened. "No. *Dios mio, no!* We heard . . . you were dead."

"You heard wrong."

"You came . . . all this way . . . to find us . . ."

"You three were just the first. You won't be the last."

A wave of agony began in Julio's midsection and washed through the rest of his body. "Ah," he breathed through clenched teeth.

"Hurts like hell, doesn't it?"

"*Sí* . . . Señor, I have no right . . . to ask any favors of you . . ."

"You sure don't."

"But . . . I beg you . . . in the name of El Señor Dios, who will send me to Hell . . . end it now. Spare me . . . this pain."

"You didn't spare me any." The Kid straightened and drew his gun. "But I reckon I can give you what you want . . . if you give me what I want." He looked over his shoulder at the girl, who watched with wide, dark eyes. "Run along for right now. Go find somebody to help you. And tell the people in the village that it'll be all right. I'll be gone soon."

She hesitated, then started tentatively toward the door. She was running by the time she went through it. A moment later, a shot blasted behind her in the cantina.

Kid Morgan walked out, untied the reins of a buckskin horse from the hitch rail, and swung up into the saddle. He turned the horse and rode at an easy pace out of the village.

Although he was glad he had caught up to the three men in time to save the girl from whatever they had planned for her, their deaths didn't ease the pain inside him. He wasn't sure anything could do that unless he could figure out how to turn back time. To go back to a better place, a better time, to the world he used to know . . .

To the man he used to be.

CHAPTER 2

Six weeks earlier

Nevada was beautiful this time of year. But then, any setting would be beautiful as long as Rebel Callahan Browning was in it, Conrad Browning thought.

"Here's to you, my dear," he said as he raised a fine crystal champagne flute. "You make a lovely view even lovelier."

"Why, Conrad, what a sweet thing to say." His wife smiled at him. The sunlight filtered down through the branches of the pine tree under which Conrad had spread the blanket he'd taken from the buggy. The golden glow struck highlights from her blond hair where it fell in thick waves around her shoulders. Her face was flushed with happiness. Or maybe it was just the champagne, Conrad thought.

She clinked her glass against his, and they both drank. He didn't need alcohol to become intoxicated these days. His wife's beauty and the clear, high country air were more than enough to cause that.

The remains of a picnic lunch were spread out on the blanket in front of them. Conrad had packed the lunch in a wicker basket, placed it in the buggy along with the blanket, and then surprised Rebel with his suggestion that they take a drive up here into the hills overlooking Carson City, Nevada.

"What about work?" she had asked with a puzzled frown.

"I'm the boss, aren't I? I think I can take half a day, or even a whole day, off if I want to."

"Yes, of course," Rebel had said. "But it's just so . . . unlike you."

"I'm not myself since we moved out here."

It was true. Conrad had felt himself changing ever since they'd left Boston behind and come to Carson City. He wished they had made the move earlier. He slept better, breathed easier, and was coming to realize that even though he had been raised in the East, this was now home to him.

It was all Frank Morgan's fault. Or perhaps it was better to say that Frank deserved the credit, although for a long time Conrad had been unwilling to give his father the least bit of credit for anything. All he had done was blame him for his mother's death.

Conrad Browning was practically a grown man before he found out that his father was Frank Morgan, the notorious Western gunfighter known as The Drifter. Frank hadn't known he had a son either, because Conrad was the product of a brief marriage when he was a young man, a marriage that his beloved Vivian's father had ended abruptly. Vivian had gone on to marry again and to found a business empire that stretched across the continent. She and her second husband had raised Conrad, who had taken his stepfather's last name.

Several years earlier, during a trip West, outlaws had murdered Vivian. Those same outlaws had kidnapped and tortured Conrad. He had Frank Morgan to thank for saving his life. Conrad had been in no mood to thank the man, however. He had found out by then that Frank was his real father, and he didn't care for that news at all. He had been a bit of a prig in those days, he often thought now.

More than a bit actually.

Frank hadn't given up on him, though, and over the course of several adventures they had been drawn into, Conrad had come to respect his father, even to feel genuine affection for him. They worked well together.

It was during one of those adventures, in fact, that Conrad had met and fallen in love with Rebel. After their marriage, they had gone back to Boston, but circumstances kept pulling them westward. They had spent some time in Buckskin, a mining community in the mountains southeast of Carson City, where Frank had served as the marshal for a while. Seeing how Rebel thrived in the frontier atmosphere had convinced Conrad to move out here permanently. With telegraph wires and railroad lines stretching all across the country now, there was no reason why he couldn't manage the Browning business holdings just as effectively from Carson City as he did from Boston.

"Well, whoever you are these days, I like him," Rebel said. She finished her champagne, placed the glass in the basket, and lay down on the blanket, stretching her arms above her head so that her breasts rose enticingly.

Conrad couldn't resist the temptation. He set his glass down and moved alongside her, propping himself up on an elbow so that he could lean over her and press his lips to hers. The kiss was sweet and gentle at first, but it grew rapidly in intensity. Passionate urgency surged through Conrad's body. Rebel wrapped her arms around his neck and pulled him tighter against her. Their bodies molded together, her breasts flattening under the pressure of his muscular chest.

She was breathless with desire when he pulled back and broke the kiss. He slid his left hand between them to caress her right breast through her dress. "Conrad," she said in a husky voice, "it's broad daylight, and we're right out in the open . . ."

"And there's no one but us around for miles," he said. He

didn't know that for a fact, but he felt fairly certain it was true. He wanted it to be true. He kissed Rebel again.

Her hands clutched at him. He reached for the hem of her skirt and drew it up, exposing sleek, bare, beautiful legs. His fingers stroked the softness of her thighs.

Somewhere not far off, hoofbeats thudded on the ground.

Rebel gasped and started pushing Conrad away. He went willingly, but not happily. He didn't particularly want anybody riding up on them like this either. He rolled off Rebel and sat up. Beside him, she hastily tried to tug her skirt down. She didn't manage to cover herself completely before half a dozen men rode out of the trees and into sight. They had to have gotten at least a flash of her bare legs before she finally got her skirt over them.

As the men reined in, Conrad's eyes darted from them to the picnic basket. A short-barreled Colt .45 revolver was in the basket, within reach if he needed to grab it. When he and Rebel set out on this excursion, he certainly hadn't anticipated running into any trouble, but one of the things he had learned from being around his father was that it was best to be prepared.

The gun had only five rounds in its cylinder, though; the hammer rested on the empty sixth chamber. Something else he had learned from Frank. Five bullets, six men . . . that could present a challenge.

Stop jumping to conclusions, Conrad told himself. These men probably meant them no harm. He was sure they hadn't even known that he and Rebel were here.

He got to his feet, brushed off his trousers, and nodded to the strangers. "Gentlemen," he said. "It's a beautiful day, isn't it?"

"It sure is," one of the riders replied. He gestured with his left hand toward the blanket and the wicker basket. "We didn't mean to interrupt your picnic."

"That's quite all right. We were finished anyway." Conrad held a hand down to Rebel. "Weren't we, my dear?"

"That's right," she said as she grasped his hand and let him help her to her feet.

The man who had spoken before grinned and said, "Don't let us run you off, folks." He was a narrow-shouldered man with a ginger beard and a cuffed-back hat. The well-worn walnut grips of a revolver jutted up from the holster on his hip. The men with him were similar sorts, all dressed in range clothes. Some were bearded, some clean-shaven, but they all had hard-bitten faces. Conrad had seen plenty just like them, men who were no better and no more honest than they had to be. Just like the outlaws who had sliced off the top of his left ear to torture him while he was their prisoner. He wore his sandy hair long to cover up that disfigurement.

Conrad tried to ignore the cold ball of fear that had formed in his belly. He wasn't afraid for himself so much as he was for Rebel. Out-numbered as the two of them were, if the men decided to attack them, they could probably overpower him and do whatever they wanted to her.

Some of them would die in the process, though. He made that vow to himself, even as he tried to keep what he was feeling from showing on his face.

"That's all right," he said as he reached down to pick up the basket. "We were leaving anyway. Got to get back to town."

"Live in Carson City, do you?"

"That's right." Conrad felt a little better now that he had the basket in his left hand where his right could swoop into it and snatch out the Colt. There was a Winchester in the buggy. He wondered if Rebel could reach it while he gave her some covering fire. If she got her hands on the rifle, they could give a better account of themselves. Rebel was a better shot with a Winchester than he was, and she had the fighting spirit of a girl who had grown up on the frontier.

If those varmints started any trouble, they'd get a warmer reception than they likely expected, Conrad thought.

But then the spokesman surprised him by reaching up,

tugging on his hat brim, and nodding pleasantly. "Guess we'll be ridin' on then," he said. "You folks have a pleasant day." He turned his horse, hitched it into motion, and jerked his head at the other men to indicate that they should follow him.

Conrad slipped his right hand into the basket and closed it around the butt of the Colt, just in case this was some sort of trick. That didn't appear to be the case, though. The men rode on around the shoulder of the hill, soon going out of sight.

Rebel reached down, grabbed the corners of the blanket, and gathered the whole thing into a bundle with the leftover food inside. Conrad took the revolver out of the basket. Rebel crammed the blanket in to replace the gun.

"Let's get out of here," she said.

"Indeed," Conrad said. He tucked the Colt behind his belt. "Those men could still be lurking around."

Rebel shuddered. "Did you see the way they were looking at me? Especially that big, ugly one?"

"Not really," Conrad admitted. "I was watching their shoulders most of the time." That was where a tiny hitch could be seen just before most men went for their guns. Frank had taught him that. With some men, the tell was in their eyes, but experienced gunfighters could control that. Not the shoulder hitch, though.

"Well, it wasn't good," Rebel said. "I thought for sure they were going to—" She stopped and shook her head. "Let's just say I was trying to figure out how fast I could get to that Winchester in the buggy."

A grim laugh came from Conrad as he set the basket in the back of the buggy. "I must admit, the same thought was going through my mind, my dear."

Moments later, he had the vehicle rolling back down the hill toward Carson City, behind the big buckskin horse hitched to it. There was still no sign of the six riders. Conrad sighed with relief as he glanced over at his wife. That encounter had turned out much better than he had feared it might.

Although he was still disappointed that he and Rebel had been interrupted just at that particular moment . . .

"Damn it, Lasswell, we should've waited another few minutes before we rode up. Then we could've seen 'em goin' at it. That gal'd be worth watchin', I'll bet."

Clay Lasswell leaned to the side in his saddle and spat. "And then what would you fellas have done?" he demanded. "You're tellin' me you could've seen Mrs. Browning buck nekkid and not wanted to jump on her?"

The giant, moonfaced Carlson nudged the older man riding beside him and laughed. "Buck nekkid," he said. "I don't want to see that! You get it, Buck?"

"Shut up," Buck said without any real rancor. Carlson was an idiot most of the time. Buck had learned to make allowances for him. Julio Esquivel was the same way. He just shook his head at Carlson's comments.

Ezra Harker, the man who'd been complaining to Lasswell, said, "What would it have hurt if we'd gone ahead and shot the dude and taken the girl?"

Lasswell raked the fingers of his left hand through his ginger-colored beard. "Well, for one thing," he said, "that ain't what we're bein' paid to do. For another, did you see the way the boy kept eyein' that picnic basket? I'd bet a hat he had a gun in there."

"What if he did? You worried about bein' shot by some pasty-faced gent from back East?"

Lasswell squinted at Harker and said, "Do you just not pay attention to anything, Ezra? That boy didn't look too pasty-faced to me. And have you forgot that his pa's Frank Morgan?"

"Just because his pa's a gunfighter don't mean that he is. Anyway, Morgan's an old man now."

"Not that old," Lasswell said, thinking of some of the stories he'd heard about Frank Morgan in recent years. The Drifter might not be as young as he once was, but his gun hand hadn't slowed down any. He was still tough as whang leather and dangerous as a wounded wildcat. Sure, the boy was different, but if he'd inherited even part of his pa's skill with a gun and pure cussedness . . .

"We'll do things the way we were told," Lasswell went on. "That's the best way of bein' sure we get paid like we were promised."

The sixth man in the group, the dark, saturnine Ray Duncan, said, "We'd better get paid. If we don't, I'll be lookin' to even the score with some hot lead."

The riders kept moving gradually higher in the mountains. Off to the west, surrounded by pines, lay the blue depths of Lake Tahoe. It wasn't far from here to the California line. This was silver country, but large ranches abounded in the area, too. Several railroad lines passed through Carson City and Reno to the north. If a man wanted to rob a mine payroll or an ore shipment, hold up a train or rustle some cattle, this corner of Nevada was the place for him to be. Opportunities for lawlessness were everywhere.

Right now, those opportunities included kidnapping a rich man's wife.

"Anyway," Lasswell went on to Harker, "if we killed the boy, who'd pay the ransom for his wife?"

"Frank Morgan?" Harker suggested.

Lasswell spat again. "Morgan? You ever know a gunman to have a lot of money? Hell, it runs through our fingers like water, you know that. That's why we can't go too long between jobs. Not to mention the fact that if we was to kill Morgan's boy, I don't reckon he'd be too disposed to handin' over any ransom money to us. Likely, he'd come after us and try to kill us all instead."

"Well, then, what about the girl's family?"

Lasswell shook his head. "From what I understand, she

don't come from money. Browning's got all of it. And he'll pay handsomely to get her back once she's in our hands."

"A woman like that'd be worth damn near anything," Duncan said.

"Sí," Julio agreed. "She is very lovely."

Carlson said, "I don't care what else we do, long as I get a turn or two with her 'fore we send her back to the dude. Lord, I'm lookin' forward to that."

Lasswell frowned. He was going to have his hands full keeping this bunch of mangy coyotes under control, and he knew it. If he had to, he could afford to shoot one or two of them, he supposed. That would still leave him with enough men to do the job, assuming that the others were waiting like they were supposed to be.

A few minutes later, the six riders came to a large clearing. Lasswell had been smelling wood smoke for a while, so he wasn't surprised to see that the men waiting for them had built a campfire. They even had a pot of coffee brewing.

"Lasswell?" one of the men called as he strode forward to meet the riders. He was tall and barrel-chested, with a face that looked like it had been hacked out of an old log with a dull ax.

Lasswell reined in and nodded. "That's right."

The man stuck a hand up to him. "I'm Vernon Moss. You sent me a wire, told me to gather up as many good men as I could and meet you here."

Lasswell shook hands with Moss, then swung down from the saddle. The men with him dismounted as well. Lasswell looked around the clearing, saw that there were nine men in addition to Moss.

"That's Jeff and Hank Winchell," Moss said, pointing to two tall, skinny hardcases who looked as much alike as two peas in a pod. "Don't bother trying to tell them apart. That's Clem Baggott next to them, then Abel Dean, Jim Fowler, Titus Gant, and Spence Hooper. The old-timer's Rattigan, and the breed is called White Rock."

"You vouch for all of 'em, Moss?" Lasswell asked.

"I do."

Lasswell studied the men intently for a moment, then chuckled. "You're about as evil-lookin' a bunch of hombres as I ever seen. Good job, Moss."

"What is it we're after?" Moss wanted to know. "With sixteen men, we can hold up a train or knock over a bank easy."

"Our job will be even easier than that. We got to kidnap one woman."

Moss frowned at Lasswell, who heard several surprised mutters from the other men. "One woman?" he repeated. "Why do you need this many men to snatch one woman?"

"Because snatchin' her ain't the problem. Hangin' on to her until we get the ransom is."

"Must be one mighty special woman," Moss said. "Who is she anyway?"

"It ain't who she is. It's who her husband's father is. You ever hear of Frank Morgan?"

The worried look that suddenly appeared on Moss's face answered that question. "The woman we're after is Frank Morgan's daughter-in-law? The payoff had better be damned good! I won't take a chance on going up against Morgan if it's not."

"How does fifty thousand dollars sound?"

"Split between sixteen men?" Moss did some quick ciphering in his head. "That's a little over three grand apiece."

"It'll be even more if some of us don't live to claim a share," Lasswell pointed out.

"You reckon that's liable to happen?"

"If Frank Morgan gets involved," Lasswell said, "I think you can damned well count on it."

CHAPTER 3

Conrad didn't exactly forget about the encounter with the six men on the hillside, but he had plenty of other things on his mind, so he didn't dwell on it. Keeping up with all the far-flung Browning business holdings required a great deal of time and attention. When he and Rebel had first moved to Carson City, he had rented an office in one of the bank buildings downtown and hired a private secretary, as well as several bookkeepers and stenographers. All of them stayed busy as information flowed into the Carson City office over the telegraph wires from Boston, New York, Chicago, Denver, and San Francisco.

Conrad was at his desk a few days later when Edwin Sinclair, his secretary, came into the office. Most people thought of secretaries as frail and bookish, but Sinclair hardly fell into that category. He was taller and heavier than Conrad and fancied himself an amateur pugilist. The only thing typical about him was that he had to wear spectacles at times, as a result of years of doing close work on ledgers and files.

Sinclair had a stack of papers in his hands. Conrad groaned at the sight of them and said, "Not more reports?"

"The wheels of the business world are lubricated with ink, Mr. Browning," Sinclair said. "You know that."

Conrad chuckled. "You're right, of course, Edwin. Set them down here, and I'll start going through them." He pulled his watch from a vest pocket, flipped it open, and checked the time as Sinclair placed the stack of papers on the desk. "And a start is all I'll be able to make. There are too many to finish this afternoon. I wonder if I should take the others home with me."

"I'd be glad to come to your house and help you go through them this evening, sir," Sinclair volunteered.

Conrad considered the offer for a second, then shook his head. "I'm sure you have better things to do with your evenings than help me wade through paperwork," he said. "But I appreciate the offer."

"I really don't mind—" Sinclair began.

"No, that's all right." Conrad pulled the papers closer to him. "That's all, Edwin, thank you. And as late as it is, you and the boys might as well go on home."

"Well, all right, if you say so, Mr. Browning," Sinclair replied with a shrug of his broad shoulders. "I'll see you in the morning."

Conrad nodded, already distracted by the summaries of the business dealings conducted by the companies covered in the reports.

Not so distracted, though, that he didn't look up with a frown a few minutes after Edwin Sinclair had gone. He knew he was probably wrong to feel this way, but he didn't want Sinclair spending a lot of time around Rebel. The secretary had come to their home a few times in the evenings to help Conrad when the press of work threatened to become overwhelming. Rebel had insisted that he have dinner with them on those occasions. Western hospitality and all that,

Conrad supposed. And he had to admit that Sinclair had been as polite and charming as he could be. Conrad thought he had seen something in Sinclair's eyes, though, when the man glanced at Rebel . . . It was nothing overt, and of course he wasn't the least bit worried about Rebel ever being tempted to return the illicit affections of another man, but still . . . Conrad was just more comfortable keeping his dealings with Sinclair strictly at the office.

He worked a while longer, then finally pushed the papers away, rubbed his eyes, and yawned. When he stood up, it felt good to stretch muscles that had stiffened from long hours spent bent over a desk. As Conrad began getting ready to leave for the day, he thought about how good it would feel to climb up into a saddle and ride out into the mountains, to breathe some air that hadn't grown stuffy from being confined inside four walls, to see something besides those walls.

He had really enjoyed that excursion with Rebel a few days earlier, he thought, at least until those men interrupted them. They ought to spend more days like that.

His father would certainly be surprised to hear him say such a thing, he told himself with a smile as he gathered up the papers he was going to take home.

A few minutes later, carrying a case with the reports fastened securely inside it, Conrad left the building. His house was half a mile away. It was a good walk, and today he was looking forward to it. He thought about how Rebel had looked, stretched out on that blanket with an inviting smile on her beautiful face, and his stride lengthened in his eagerness to get home.

In a café located across the street from the bank building where Conrad Browning had his office, Edwin Sinclair watched through a window as Browning walked away.

Sinclair had a cup of coffee in front of him, but he had barely touched the brew. His hands clenched into fists on the table as he watched Browning.

"Something wrong, sir?"

The unexpected question made Sinclair give a little start. He looked up and saw that the waitress had paused beside him, a coffeepot in her hand. She looked slightly startled, too, and he supposed that was because of his reaction.

He forced a smile onto his face and said, "No, I'm fine, thank you."

"Some more coffee, Mr. Sinclair?"

She knew him because he ate lunch here fairly often. It was convenient to the office. But it had been a mistake for him to come in here this afternoon, he told himself. He didn't want the waitress or anyone else remembering—afterward—that he had been here today, watching Conrad Browning leave the bank building.

Still smiling, he shook his head and said, "No, thank you. In fact, I must be going."

"You hardly touched your coffee. Is there anything wrong with it?"

He wanted to yell at the stupid woman and tell her to stop badgering him with questions. Instead, he said, "No, it's fine as always. I guess I just wasn't thirsty after all."

What he was thirsty for was a shot of whiskey. That was all right. He could get one at the place he was going to next.

He left a bill on the table to pay for the coffee and placate the nosy waitress, then left the café and strode off in the opposite direction from Browning. His steps led into a rougher part of town. Although Carson City was the state capital and a bustling, modern city, it wasn't all that many years removed from the mining boomtown and cattle town it had once been. The frontier was still alive here, just not quite as visible as it used to be.

That was why Sinclair felt almost as if he were stepping into a dime-novel illustration as he entered the Ace High

Saloon a short time later. Frock-coated gamblers, cowboys in boots and spurs and tall hats, painted doves in gaudy dresses and rolled stockings . . . Sinclair was the one who was out of place here in his gray tweed suit and soft felt hat.

He spotted the man he was looking for at a table in the rear of the long, smoky room. He had met with the man once before, nearly a week earlier. At that time, Lasswell had been alone. Tonight, the gunman had a companion, a large man with a florid, rough-hewn face. A bottle and three glasses, one of them empty, sat on the table.

Sinclair tried to ignore the raucous talk and laughter around him as he made his way through the crowded saloon. When he was halfway across the room, one of the women who worked there blocked his path. "Buy me a drink, honey?" she asked as she smiled up at him. The heavy perfume she wore wasn't quite strong enough to cover up the smell of unwashed flesh. The neckline of her spangled dress gaped so low that he could see the upper edge of one nipple.

"No, I don't believe so," he replied with a shake of his head.

"You could buy something else if you wanted to," she said, putting a mock pout on her rouged face. "Big handsome fella like you, it'd be a pleasure, not just a chore."

Sinclair just wanted to get away from her. "Maybe later," he said, and reached around her to give her rump a squeeze. That made her laugh and jump and say, "Oh, you!" Mainly, though, it got her out of his way.

Lasswell grinned at him when he reached the table. "Thought you was gonna stop for a little slap an' tickle," he said.

Sinclair pulled back a chair, sat down, and nodded at the empty glass. "Is that for me?"

"Yeah." Lasswell picked up the bottle, splashed some of the amber liquid into the glass, and then pushed it across the table toward Sinclair. "Bottoms up."

Sinclair followed that suggestion, tossing back the drink

and savoring the fiery path it traced down his throat and into his stomach. He returned the empty to the table with a thump.

"Is it all set?" Lasswell asked.

Sinclair didn't answer. Instead, he asked a question of his own. He nodded toward the other man at the table and said, "Who's this?"

"Name's Vernon Moss," the man said, "and I can answer for myself and everything."

"I meant no offense, Mr. Moss. I simply wanted to know if it was all right to speak frankly."

"Vernon's in on the plan," Lasswell said. "I reckon you'd say he's my second in command. Anything you can tell me you can tell him." Lasswell leaned forward. "Now, is it set up? Are you gonna be at Browning's house tonight?"

"No," Sinclair said, aware of the bitter edge that crept into his voice. "He refused when I suggested that I come over to help him with the paperwork."

He had held back reports all day so that there would be a thick stack of them by late afternoon. He had done the same thing several times in the past, whenever he felt that it would be impossible to live through one more day without the sight of Rebel Browning. Since the trick had worked before, it should have worked again. Damn the luck anyway, Sinclair thought.

Lasswell frowned. "You was supposed to be there, so you could put Browning out of the picture."

"I know that," Sinclair snapped. He had played the scene over in his head time after time, figuring out how he would make some excuse to leave the room, then sneak back in behind Browning and knock him unconscious. Later, after Lasswell and his men carried off Rebel, he would have pretended that they had attacked him first, so that he had no idea what had happened while he was out cold. No one would have been able to dispute his story. But now it wouldn't happen that way.

Lasswell scratched at his beard. "That means we'll have to deal with Browning."

"For God's sake, you have at least a dozen men at your disposal, don't you? Isn't that enough to handle one man?"

"Me and some of the boys took a look at Browning the other day. I got a hunch he's tougher than you give him credit for, mister. When we bust in, there's liable to be shootin'."

"You can't kill him," Sinclair said. "You know that."

"I know what the orders are. I also know that bullets don't give a damn about orders when they start flyin' around. I can't guarantee that Browning won't be hit."

"That would ruin everything." Without waiting for Lasswell to pour, Sinclair grabbed the bottle himself and filled his glass. He drank half the whiskey and then said, "Let me think."

There had to be some way to salvage the plan. Everything had been carefully thought out. It couldn't collapse just because of one minor obstacle.

He wasn't sure who had come up with the scheme. His only contacts with his mysterious benefactor had been through letters, letters that he had been careful to burn after committing them to memory. So he had no idea why the man wanted Rebel Browning kidnapped. It was enough to know that he, Edwin Sinclair, was going to be her savior.

Once the ransom had been paid, he would slip into the isolated cabin where the outlaws had confined Rebel and "rescue" her before they could return to kill her, as they would make plain was their intention before leaving to collect the ransom. Then, grateful to him for saving her life, Rebel would finally see that she should be with him, not Conrad Browning. It was foolproof, Sinclair thought, even though certain elements of it did smack of a bad stage melodrama.

An idea began to come to him. He wrestled with it for a few moments while Lasswell and Moss drank and watched him with their dull eyes. Finally, he said, "How about this? I'll show up at Browning's house this evening with a telegram. I can tell him that it's an urgent wire from the San Francisco office or some such, and claim that the messenger delivered it to me rather than him by mistake. That will get me in the door, and then I can say that as long as I'm there, I might as well go ahead and give him a hand with all the paperwork he took home from the office."

Lasswell looked over at Moss. "What do you think?"

Moss's beefy shoulders rose and fell. "It might work, I reckon."

"It *will* work," Sinclair said. "For one thing, once I'm there, Mrs. Browning will insist that I at least stay and have a cup of tea with them. I'll find a way to get Browning alone and knock him out."

"That's the only way we can be sure he won't get ventilated," Lasswell said. "You better have it done by eight o'clock, though, because that's when we're comin' in the back. You're sure there won't be any servants there?"

"They only have a woman who does the cooking and cleaning, and she goes home by six. It'll be just the two of them . . . and me."

Lasswell nodded. "There's one more thing we been wonderin' about. Do you have any idea where Frank Morgan is these days?"

"Browning's father?" Sinclair asked with a frown. "Why do you want to know?"

"You know who Frank Morgan *is,* don't you?"

"Of course I do. He's some sort of dime-novel gunman."

Lasswell gave a harsh laugh. "Not hardly, mister. Morgan's the genuine article. If he's anywhere around these parts and hears that his daughter-in-law's been kidnapped, he'll come a-runnin' to get on our trail. And we don't want that. We don't want no part of it."

Sinclair suppressed the impulse to sneer. "You're that afraid of one man?"

"It's not a matter of bein' afraid. It's a matter of bein' careful."

Sinclair sighed. "I don't know where Morgan is, but I can tell you that not long ago he was in California, down around Los Angeles. Browning mentioned that his father was lending a hand to one of their lawyers."

"That don't make no sense at all," Lasswell said with a frown. "Morgan's a gunfighter, not a lawyer."

"All I know is what Browning said. It had to do with some sort of dispute over oil wells, or something like that."

"Oh," Lasswell said. "Some kind of ruckus. Gun work, more'n likely. I can see Morgan bein' mixed up in something like that."

Moss said, "California's too close. I wish he was over in Texas, or way the hell and gone up in Montana or the Dakotas."

"It'll be all right," Lasswell said. "The whole thing won't last long. It'll be over and done with, and we'll be gone before Morgan can ever get here."

"You hope," Moss said.

"Damn right I do."

"All right, it's settled," Sinclair said, not bothering to try to keep the impatience out of his voice. "I'll do my part. You do yours."

Lasswell poured himself a drink. "You can count on us."

"One last thing . . . Under no circumstances is Mrs. Browning to be hurt in any way, shape, or fashion, do you understand? No one lays a finger on her except to restrain her and bring her along."

"Sure, sure," Lasswell said. "We know we got to be careful with her."

"Good." Sinclair gave them his best steely-eyed glare. "Because anyone who harms her will answer to me."

* * *

When Sinclair was gone and Lasswell and Moss were sitting there polishing off the whiskey, Moss chuckled and said, “That young fool don’t have any idea what’s really goin’ on, does he?”

Lasswell shook his head as he emptied the last drops from the bottle into his glass. “No, he don’t,” he said. “Not one damn bit.”

CHAPTER 4

Conrad enjoyed dinner with Rebel, as he always did. A cloth of fine Irish linen covered the table in the dining room. The china and the crystal sparkled. The meal prepared by Mrs. O'Hannigan was delicious. But of course, it was Rebel's company that really made the meal special. She sat at the other end of the table in a white blouse and dark gray skirt, with her blond hair pulled up on top of her head in an elaborate arrangement of curls this evening.

Conrad could hardly wait to pull loose the pins that held Rebel's hair and allow it to tumble freely about her shoulders. *Bare* shoulders by that time, he hoped.

But of course, he had to show some restraint and decorum. He wasn't an animal after all, consumed by his lust. Almost, but not quite. And he had brought home that pile of work from the office, he reminded himself. He needed to get at least some of it done before he and Rebel retired for the evening.

He mentioned that as he lingered over a snifter of cognac following dinner. "If I don't take care of some of it, I'll be too far behind when I start in the morning," he said. With a smile, he added, "Then I'll never get caught up."

"You should have had Edwin come over to help you with it," Rebel said. "I'm sure he wouldn't have minded. He's such a hard worker."

Conrad hesitated. Over the past few years, he had learned a great deal about the sort of natural caution that most Westerners practiced. Living in an often harsh and unforgiving land ingrained that in a person. Rebel was no different. She was probably more suspicious of people as a rule than he was.

Like everyone, though, she had her blind spots, and Edwin Sinclair was one of them. She seemed never to have seen the things that Conrad had, and he had never mentioned them to her.

Now, he said, "He offered to help, but I told him it wasn't necessary."

"Why would you do that?" Rebel asked with a frown. "Helping with paperwork is part of his job."

"Not after office hours it isn't."

"Yes, but if he doesn't mind . . . Anyway, you could always pay him a little bonus for extra work like that, if he's not too proud to accept it."

"I suppose." Conrad didn't want to argue with her, not tonight, so he smiled and promised, "I'll certainly keep that in mind next time." He swirled the cognac left in the snifter, then tilted it to his lips and drank the last of it. As he got to his feet, he said, "I won't work for more than an hour or so."

"I suppose I can be patient," Rebel said. "I'll clear away these dishes and then go upstairs to read for a while."

On several occasions, Conrad had suggested that they ask Mrs. O'Hannigan to stay in the evenings until after dinner, but Rebel had insisted that she was perfectly capable of cleaning up. Not only that, she said, but Mrs. O'Hannigan needed to get home to her own family as well.

That was another point Conrad hadn't argued. He knew

that Rebel would be just as happy sitting next to an open campfire out on the trail as she was in the dining room of this big, two-story house on the outskirts of Carson City. Maybe even happier. So it was best, he thought, to let her do just as much as she wanted to do.

As he left the dining room and started down the hall toward his study, the image of Rebel in boots and jeans and a buckskin shirt drifted through his mind. Maybe if he could get ahead on his work, he could take some time off and they could head up into the high country on an extended trip. They could go on horseback, just the two of them, taking along enough supplies to last for a week or two. They wouldn't have to worry about fresh meat; the mountains were full of game, and Rebel was a superb shot with a rifle. Conrad could handle a long gun fairly well, too. They would be fine.

It was such an appealing prospect that Conrad stopped just outside the door to his study and sighed in anticipated pleasure.

A knock on the front door broke that reverie and put a puzzled frown on Conrad's face. They weren't expecting any visitors tonight. He had no idea who could be at the door.

"I'll get it," he called to Rebel as he started toward the front of the house. He didn't know if she had heard the knock, but in case she had, she would know that he was answering it.

When he swung the door open, the light from the foyer revealed Edwin Sinclair standing there on the porch, his hat in one hand and what appeared to be a yellow telegraph flimsy in the other. Conrad was surprised and not very happy to see Sinclair, especially after he had told the man not to come to the house this evening. But the telegram in Sinclair's hand meant that something important might have happened, so Conrad supposed he had to hear him out.

"Hello, Edwin," he said. "What are you doing here?"

Sinclair held up the yellow paper. "I received this wire that was intended for you, sir. I'm not quite sure how the messenger boy managed to make a mistake and deliver it to me instead, but that's what happened."

Conrad took the telegram and scanned the words printed on it in a bold, square hand. "Your name is on it as well as mine," he pointed out. "I'm sure that's what caused the mix-up." He continued reading as he spoke, then exclaimed, "What? Has Kirkson lost his mind? Did you read this, Edwin?"

"I did, sir. I was worried about the news, too."

"If Kirkson goes ahead with this plan, he'll cost us thousands of dollars." Ronald Kirkson was the manager of a steel plant in Pennsylvania owned largely by Conrad and his father. Conrad was no engineer, but even he could see that the changes in the manufacturing process Kirkson proposed would be tremendously inefficient.

"I imagine you'll want to wire him first thing in the morning to hold off on implementing the changes," Sinclair said. "In the meantime, since I'm already here, I'd be glad to help you go through some of that paperwork—"

"In the morning, hell!" Conrad broke in. "I'm going to wire Kirkson tonight. Right now, in fact. I'm going to write out a message, and you can take it to the Western Union office and send it as a night letter."

"That will cost more," Sinclair said.

"Penny-wise, pound-foolish," Conrad quoted. "Come with me."

"Where are we going, sir?"

"To my study. I want to sit down while I'm figuring out the best way to tell Kirkson that he's a damned fool."

"Oh. All right."

Conrad closed the door and then stalked down the hall toward his study. Sinclair was close behind him.

"What about that other work?" Sinclair asked as they entered the study. "Those reports?"

"They can wait," Conrad snapped. "They're nothing but an annoyance. This is a crisis, or at least it will be if we don't avert it." He went behind the desk. "Pull up one of those armchairs, Edwin. This may take a little while."

"Perhaps I should go out to the kitchen and brew some coffee for us."

"No, that's all right," Conrad said. Rebel was probably still in the kitchen, and the last thing he wanted was for her and Sinclair to spend even a few minutes alone in such an intimate setting. He was probably wrong to distrust Sinclair, but wrong or not, he wanted to keep the man where he could see him.

He sat down behind the desk, pulled a blank sheet of paper in front of him, took up a pencil, and started composing a strongly worded message. "What do you think about this?" he asked Sinclair, then read the sentences to the secretary as he scrawled them on the paper. He might not fully trust Sinclair where Rebel was concerned, but the man was a good secretary and knew the business.

"That's very good, sir."

"Do you think it's clear enough that Kirkson will regret it if he goes through with this?"

"Oh, I think so, Mr. Browning. Quite clear." Sinclair paused. "I hope all this uproar doesn't disturb Mrs. Browning."

Conrad shook his head. "It won't. She's upstairs." He didn't know if she had gone up or not, but he wanted Sinclair to think she had.

Sinclair started to look uncomfortable, shifting around in the chair like a man with something bothering him. Conrad frowned at him and asked, "What's wrong?"

"I'm sorry, sir, but, I'm not feeling well. If I could use the, ah . . ."

Conrad waved a hand toward the door. "Of course, of course. You know where it is." Despite not fully trusting Sinclair, Conrad couldn't deny him the use of the facilities. He stood up and began to pace back and forth, reading the message over to himself as he did so. "I'll have this ready to go by the time you get back."

"Of course." With a vaguely embarrassed expression on his face, Sinclair slipped out of the room.

The thought crossed Conrad's mind that Sinclair might run into Rebel while he was gone, but he decided that was unlikely. When she was finished cleaning up in the kitchen, Rebel would probably use the rear stairs to go up to their room. She'd said she was going to read while Conrad worked on the reports from the office.

He didn't care about the reports now. As he'd told Sinclair, they weren't really urgent. This telegram from Kirkson had upset him, and he wasn't going to worry about the paperwork anymore. As soon as he'd sent Sinclair off to the Western Union office with the scorching reply, Conrad intended to do his best to forget all about work for the rest of the evening.

He went back to the desk, stood in front of it, and leaned over to cross out several words and substitute others. There, he thought as he straightened. That made the message even stronger. All he needed to do now was recopy it with all the corrections made. Or perhaps he'd get Sinclair to do that. The man had excellent handwriting.

Suddenly, Conrad frowned. He put down the message he'd been writing and picked up the telegraph flimsy he had dropped on the desk. Something about the printing on it was familiar. He had assumed that a telegrapher from the Western Union office had printed the message, but something about the bold strokes of the letters reminded him of Sinclair's writing.

That made no sense. Sinclair had said that the message was delivered to his room at a boardinghouse several blocks away. He couldn't have written it.

The secretary had left the door partially open when he left the study. Conrad heard it swing open behind him now, and he started to turn so that he could ask Sinclair what was going on here.

He didn't make it. A swift step sounded behind him, and

something crashed into his skull. The blow's impact sent Conrad slumping forward. He dropped the telegram and caught himself by slapping his hands down flat on the desk. Groggy, half-stunned, he tried to push himself upright again.

The intruder hit him a second time, and this time his knees buckled. He couldn't hold himself up. The floor leaped up to smack him in the face. Conrad felt the rough nap of the rug in front of the desk scraping his cheek. He let out a groan that sounded to his ears as if it came from far, far away.

Then the sound faded out entirely, along with everything else, as Conrad lost consciousness.

It would have been easy to finish him off, Edwin Sinclair thought as he stared down at Conrad Browning, who lay on the study floor, out cold. A few more blows from the bludgeon he had carried into the house, concealed under his coat, and Browning's head would be a shattered, misshapen mess. He would never have Rebel again.

But he wouldn't be able to pay the ransom either, and without that, Lasswell, Moss, and the other hired gunmen wouldn't carry out their part of the plan. It was vital that Conrad Browning live through this night. That was why Sinclair had gone to the trouble of forging the message from Kirkson on a telegraph flimsy he had lifted from the Western Union office.

He didn't think that Browning would recognize his hand if he printed the words in as blocky a style as he could manage, and sure enough, the ruse had worked. Browning had accepted it as a genuine message from Kirkson. For a while, Sinclair had worried that there wouldn't be an opportunity for him to strike down Browning without being seen, but in the end, luck had been with him.

Now all that was left to do was to let Lasswell and the others into the house through the rear door. Sinclair slipped his watch out and checked the time. Five minutes until eight. He had almost shaved it too close.

As he put his watch away, he glanced down at Browning. Maybe it would be a good idea to tie him up. That was what real kidnappers would do, wasn't it? Of course, Lasswell and the others *were* real kidnappers, he reminded himself. They just had help that no one else would ever know about.

Sinclair yanked down one of the cords from the drapes and used it to bind Browning's hands behind his back. He wasn't any too gentle about it either, jerking Browning's arms around without worrying about whether or not he injured the bastard. He had hit Browning twice, so he didn't think there was any chance he'd regain consciousness any time soon, but just in case he did, this would take care of the problem. Sinclair used Browning's own handkerchief to gag him, tying the ball of cloth in place with another piece of drapery cord.

There, Sinclair thought as he straightened from his work, all trussed up like a pig on its way to market.

But now there was really no time to waste. He almost broke into a run as he hurried from the study and down the hall. His heart pounded heavily in his chest as he pushed open the door into the kitchen. He didn't know if it was from fear or anticipation or just sheer excitement at being part of something so audacious. He stepped into the room . . .

And his heart seemed to leap into his throat and freeze there as he saw Rebel standing at the foot of the rear stairs.

"Edwin!" she said, obviously surprised to see him. But then she smiled, like the sun coming up and chasing away the shadows of night, and went on. "I didn't know you were here. Did you come to help Conrad with all that paperwork after all?"

Before he could answer, a soft knock sounded on the rear door.

Judging by Rebel's expression, she was even more surprised by that than she was by Sinclair's unexpected appearance in her kitchen. She said, "Who in the world can that be at this time of night? Maybe Mrs. O'Hannigan forgot something."

She started toward the door, clearly intending to answer it.

Sinclair sprang forward. "Let me," he said. "You seemed to be on your way upstairs. You should go ahead. It's probably a tradesman at the door. I'll deal with him."

"Nonsense," Rebel said. "This is my house. I can answer my own—"

Lasswell must have run out of patience. A boot heel crashed against the door just below the knob, springing it open. The door flew back. Rebel let out a startled cry as she jerked herself out of its way.

"Edwin, run!" she shouted. "Get Conrad!"

Shocked, struggling to figure out what to do next, Sinclair stayed rooted to the floor. A couple of hard-faced men rushed into the kitchen with guns drawn. Sinclair had never seen either of them before, but he knew they must be some of Lasswell's men.

Rebel reacted with the sort of blinding speed that Sinclair would have expected from that gunfighter father-in-law of hers. She snatched up an empty coffeepot from the stove and swung it at one of the men, crashing it against the side of his head. He stumbled into his companion and dropped his gun. Rebel was on it like a hawk, scooping it up before it hardly had a chance to hit the floor. She shot the second man at such close range that the flame licking out from the gun muzzle scorched the man's shirt as the bullet punched into his chest.

Sinclair had made it clear to Lasswell and Moss that Rebel wasn't to be hurt, but he didn't know if the gunmen would be able to control themselves when someone started shooting at them. They might return her fire. He couldn't let that happen. He leaped toward her, wrapped his arms around her from behind, and said, "Rebel, no!" He got one hand on her wrist and forced the gun toward the floor.

More men burst into the room, among them Lasswell and Moss. Lasswell's bearded, leathery face creased into a grin as he said, "Looks like you decided to jump right in there and grab her yourself, Sinclair."

Sinclair bit back a groan of despair. Now everything really *was* ruined. He had hoped for a second that he could pass off his actions as merely fearing for her safety, but now Rebel had to realize that he was part of the plan. Otherwise, Lasswell wouldn't have known his name.

He would just have to make the best of it. If he disappeared along with Rebel, Browning and everyone else would believe that the intruders had kidnapped him, too. He could go with Lasswell and the others, and once the ransom was paid and he had his share, he could take Rebel and leave Carson City far behind. They would go to Mexico, he thought. She would go with him, and in time, she would learn to love him.

He twisted the gun out of her hand and threw it on the floor, then shoved her toward the outlaws. "Here," he snapped. "Get her on a horse, and let's get out of here."

Two of the men grabbed her. One of them was a giant with a moon face. Sinclair didn't like the leer the man wore as he looked at Rebel.

She twisted and struggled in their grip, but she had no chance of getting away. Turning her head, she looked straight at him and said, "You son of a bitch. Conrad will kill you for this, and if he doesn't, I will!"

Lasswell chuckled. "Better be careful, boys, she's a wildcat. Hurry up now. That shot means we ain't got time to waste."

One of the men pointed at the one Rebel had shot and said, "What about Ray?"

"Get him on his horse, too," Lasswell ordered. "Maybe he'll make it." He looked at Sinclair. "You talked like you was comin' with us, mister."

"Of course I'm coming with you," Sinclair snapped. "I can't stay here now. She knows I was part of it."

In fact, Rebel was still glaring murderously at him as the two men dragged her out of the house. Sinclair hoped they wouldn't treat her too rough.

"Well, here's the problem," Lasswell said. "We ain't got a horse for you."

"I'll ride double with someone, then." Sinclair took a step toward the door. "Let's go. As you said, there's no time to waste."

Lasswell put out a hand to stop him. "Sorry, Sinclair. Your part in this is over here and now."

"What? You're insane! I can't stay here. *She knows.*" Sinclair shook his head impatiently. "I realize we can't follow the original plan now, with me pretending to rescue her and everything—"

"That was never the plan," Lasswell said.

Sinclair frowned. "Of course it was. I was going to rescue her—"

"Nope. You were just here to knock out Browning, so we could grab the gal without havin' to worry about hurtin' him. Like I said, you're done."

"I most certainly am not!"

Lasswell looked past Sinclair and said, "Julio."

Sinclair hadn't realized that one of the men was behind him. He'd been so upset about his part in the plan being revealed to Rebel that he hadn't been paying much attention to anything else. Now as he started to turn, he felt a sudden, sharp, white-hot pain in his back. He gasped.

A second jolt of agony lanced through him. Someone had stabbed him, he realized as he stumbled forward. Then Moss stepped up and hit him in the belly, causing him to double over and fall to his knees. An icy chill that coursed through his entire body replaced the hot pain in his back.

"When Browning comes to and gets loose, he'll figure

you got yourself killed tryin' to defend his poor wife," Lasswell said as he loomed over Sinclair. "He won't know better until he gets her back . . . *if* he gets her back."

"You . . . you can't . . ." Sinclair gasped.

Lasswell looked past him again and nodded. Someone grabbed his hair and jerked his head back, and he felt something tug at his throat, followed instantly by a hot, wet gush.

"Your throat's just been cut, you damn fool," Lasswell told him. "You're so stupid, you had it comin'."

Sinclair blinked. He couldn't talk, couldn't breathe, and he suddenly felt incredibly sleepy. There was surprisingly little pain. Someone shoved him from behind, and he fell facedown. He wasn't sure, but he thought he smelled the coppery scent of his own blood pooling around his head.

It wasn't fair, he thought. He was going to die on the kitchen floor of Conrad Browning's house. He was going to die without ever seeing Rebel again. He was going to die . . .

He did.

CHAPTER 5

Conrad heard someone groaning, and gradually became aware that it was him. He was adrift in a deep, black sea, the waves jolting him back and forth. After what seemed like an eternity, he realized that the waves were actually the pulsing of blood in his head.

He was alive.

That knowledge brought strength and determination with it, but they seeped slowly into his body and brain. Finally, he tried to move his arms, but they were pulled behind him in an awkward position and wouldn't budge. Someone had tied him up, and the uncomfortable, soggy lump in his mouth was a gag of some sort. He moved his head and felt his chin scrape against something rough. He knew that he was lying on the rug in front of his desk.

Then it all came flooding back to him.

Sinclair. That bastard.

Sinclair had to be the one who had hit him and knocked him out. Conrad wasn't sure *why*, but he was certain it had been Sinclair. In that instant before everything had fallen in on him, he had realized that the writing on the telegraph form was his secretary's. Sinclair had printed the message in an attempt to disguise his hand, but it hadn't worked. Conrad had recognized those decisive strokes.

So the telegram was a lie. Kirkson wasn't going to change everything at the steel manufacturing plant. Sinclair had dreamed up the whole thing so he'd have an excuse to get into Conrad's house. But why?

Rebel!

The answer shot through Conrad's veins like a jolt of that newfangled electric current. And like that electric current, it galvanized his muscles into action. Conrad lurched up onto his knees, ignoring the fresh pain that pounded in his skull like the sound of distant drums and the agony in his shoulders. He leaned against the desk to brace himself and shoved with his legs until he was on his feet.

He had to free himself and get to Rebel.

Easier said than done. The room spun crazily around him as he turned his back to the desk. His hands had gone numb enough that he could barely feel them as he fumbled around for the letter opener he knew was on the desk. At last he found it, and struggled to turn the blade so that he could use it to saw through the cord binding his wrists. Luckily, the cord wasn't very thick and parted within a few minutes. Even so, those minutes seemed like an eternity to Conrad, because all he could think of was that something terrible might be happening to Rebel.

When his wrists were free, he pulled his hands in front of him again and took a moment to massage some feeling back into them. Then he ripped the gag out of his mouth and took a step toward the door.

He reeled, and would have fallen if he hadn't managed to grab the back of the chair where Sinclair had been sitting earlier. Conrad dragged a deep breath into his body and waited a few seconds. No matter what was going on, no matter what danger threatened, he couldn't do Rebel any good if he passed out again. He had to stay awake and on his feet.

Even though he stumbled a little, his stride was stronger when he started for the door again. He grasped the jamb to steady himself as he stepped out into the hall. "Rebel!" he shouted. His voice sounded distorted to his ears. "Rebel, where are you?"

No answer. In this case, maybe the worst answer of all.

She had said she was going upstairs. Conrad wasn't sure he could manage stairs just yet. If he took a tumble down them, he might break a leg, or hit his head and knock himself out again.

The rear stairs, he thought. They were narrower than the main staircase. He could press a hand against each wall and brace himself. He staggered toward the kitchen.

As soon as Conrad shoved the door open and stepped into the room, he recognized the smell in the air. He had seen enough gruesome death to know what freshly spilled blood smelled like. He stopped in his tracks and stared down stupidly at the figure lying on the floor in front of him.

It was Edwin Sinclair, Conrad realized. The secretary lay facedown. A large pool of reddish-black blood had formed around his head and was slowly soaking into the hardwood floor. Several large crimson stains marred the back of his suit coat. In the middle of one of those stains, the handle and part of the blade of a knife protruded from Sinclair's body.

And pinned to the corpse with that knife was a piece of paper.

Conrad lurched forward. He saw his name written on the paper and knew it was meant for him. He dropped to his knees beside Sinclair and reached for the knife. He wrapped his fingers around the handle and pulled it free. The blade made an ugly sound as it came out of Sinclair's lifeless flesh.

Conrad heard other sounds, but they meant nothing to him. A door slamming, voices shouting, heavy footsteps . . . He ignored all of them. Every bit of his attention was focused on the words crudely printed on the paper, which

Edwin Sinclair's blood had stained in places. Sinclair hadn't written this note.

> WE HAV YUR WIF. DO WHAT WE SAY OR WELL KILL HER. YULL HERE FROM US.

Rebel was gone, taken from their house by strangers, intruders who had killed the secretary. Had he been wrong about Sinclair? Conrad asked himself.

"Good Lord!" a gravelly voice exclaimed. "Put that knife down, mister. I've got you covered."

Numbly, Conrad looked around. Carson City had an actual police force now, not just a local marshal and deputies, as befitted the capital city of the whole state. Two uniformed officers stood just inside the kitchen, revolvers in their hands. They pointed the guns at Conrad, and he realized that he was still holding the knife. Not only that, but he was kneeling beside the bloody corpse of his own secretary.

"This isn't . . . what it looks like," he managed to rasp after a moment.

"What is it, then?" one of the officers demanded. "It looks to me like you stabbed that poor son of a gun."

Conrad held the paper out so the man could read it for himself. Suddenly, he was too tired to explain.

Too tired, and too filled with fear for his wife.

The presence of the note made it clear that Conrad hadn't killed Edwin Sinclair. The chief of Carson City's police force admitted that as he sat in Conrad's study an hour later.

"Your secretary must have tried to fight off the kidnappers," the chief said. "He paid for it with his life, but at least he tried."

Conrad rubbed his temples as he sat behind the desk. The dull, throbbing ache in his head hadn't gone away.

But it wasn't as bad as the ache in his heart.

"I misjudged poor Sinclair," he said. "To tell the truth, I wasn't sure I trusted the man. In business, yes, but not that much around my wife."

The chief raised his eyebrows. "You shouldn't say things like that, Mr. Browning," he advised. "Some folks might figure that was a motive for murder. Of course, in this case, we know the kidnappers are to blame for Sinclair's death."

"Chief, do you have any experience with things like this?"

"Well . . . no, sir, I don't. This is the first kidnapping I remember ever taking place in these parts. But I've heard about such things, and I reckon it's only a matter of time before you hear from those varmints again. They'll have to tell you how much money they want, and where and how you're supposed to deliver it."

"Do you think they'll want me to bring the money in person?"

The chief scratched his jaw. "That wouldn't surprise me. They'll figure you'd be less likely to try some sort of trick that way." He hesitated. "You *are* going to pay?"

"Of course," Conrad snapped. "I'd pay any amount of money to get my wife back safely."

But that didn't mean he was going to let those bastards get away with what they had done, he thought. They had to pay for taking Edwin Sinclair's life, and for the ordeal they were putting Rebel through.

Conrad wouldn't let himself think about what might be happening to her. Rebel was strong and smart. She would do whatever she needed to do in order to live through this. For the moment, her survival was all that mattered.

Vengeance would come later.

Even though he was willing to wait, Conrad had taken the first step toward settling the score with the kidnappers. He had written out a wire and prevailed on one of the police officers to take it to the Western Union office. The urgent message was addressed to Claudius Turnbuckle in San Francisco, a partner in one of the law firms that represented the Browning interests. The last time Conrad had seen his father, Frank Morgan had been on his way to Los Angeles to lend a hand to Turnbuckle's partner, John J. Stafford. Conrad didn't know if that affair had already been settled, but Turnbuckle would. The lawyer might have at least an idea of how to get in touch with Frank.

Because Conrad didn't mind admitting that he needed his father's help again.

"We'll do everything we can to help," the chief was saying now, "but our job is really keeping the peace here in town. You might want to give some thought to hiring the Pinkertons, or some outfit like that, if you want to track down the men who did this."

"I know someone who can find them," Conrad said, thinking of Frank.

The chief must have understood what he meant, because he nodded and said, "Oh. Yeah, you're probably right about that."

The problem was that it might take days to locate Frank, and even longer for him to get here. Conrad didn't think the kidnappers would wait that long to make their demands. They would move quickly, in hopes of getting their hands on the ransom and making their getaway before anyone had a chance to corral them. He would probably have to handle that part himself, without Frank's help.

The chief put his hands on his knees and pushed himself to his feet. "If there's anything I can do for you, Mr. Browning, don't hesitate to let me know," he said. "In the meantime, I don't reckon there's much any of us can do except wait. Maybe you should try to get some rest."

"Yes, of course," Conrad said, even though he had no intention of resting again until Rebel was at his side once more. He shook hands with the chief of police and thanked him. Then, the chief left, and he was alone.

He had never been alone in this house, he realized. Rebel

had always been with him. He felt a sharp pang of loss as that sunk in on him.

Staying busy would help, he thought. A cabinet on one side of the room held several Winchesters, a double-barreled shotgun, a long-range European sporting rifle, and half a dozen Colt revolvers. Checking and cleaning all those weapons would take time. Conrad wanted to be sure he had plenty of ammunition on hand for all of them, too.

There was no telling how many guns he might need before this was over.

By morning, Conrad still hadn't slept. The ache in his head had faded some but was still there. He went into the kitchen to make some coffee, but stopped short when he saw the large, dark stain on the floor. The undertaker's men had cleaned up the blood as best they could when they came to collect Edwin Sinclair's body, but nothing would get rid of that stain. The floor would have to be replaced. Once Rebel was back, the two of them could go on that trip to the high country, Conrad thought, and while they were gone, someone could come in here and do the work on the house that needed to be done to cleanse it of every reminder of what had happened.

A knock on the front door as he stood there contemplating the bloodstain made him jerk around. His long legs carried him quickly to the door. He had to force himself not to run.

When he opened the door, he found a boy about twelve years old standing on the porch. He looked like a typical frontier youngster in boots and overalls and with a round-brimmed hat. He gazed up at Conrad and asked, "Are you Mr. Browning?"

"That's right," Conrad said.

"An hombre told me to give this to you." The boy held out a folded piece of paper. "He said you'd give me a nickel."

Conrad took the paper. When he unfolded it, he saw that the words on it were printed in the same crude block letters as the message that had been left for him the night before. He recognized that before the actual meaning of the words sunk in on him.

BRING 50 GRAND TO BLACK ROCK CANYON TONIGHT MIDNIGHT COME ALONE.

Conrad's heart pounded hard in his chest. Fifty thousand dollars was an incredible amount of money. Most men wouldn't earn that much in a lifetime. He had it, though, and he didn't mind spending it if that would insure Rebel's safe return.

Unfortunately, there were no guarantees that the kidnappers would keep their word.

"How about that nickel, mister?" the boy who had delivered the message prodded.

Conrad reached in his pocket and brought out a double eagle. The boy's eyes widened at the sight of it.

"I'll do better than that," Conrad said. "This is yours if you can give me a good description of the man who gave you the message for me."

"Sure! He was older than you, and sort of skinny. He had a reddish-colored beard that sort of poked out from his chin."

"How was he dressed?"

The boy frowned. "Well, I never paid much attention to that. Like a cowboy, I'd say. I know he had on boots and an old Stetson."

"Anything else you can tell me about him?"

"Not really," the boy said with a shrug. "He was just a fella."

"Was anybody with him?"

"Nope. He was by himself. I know that."

"Where did you see him?"

The boy turned and pointed toward the road that led northwest out of Carson City. "He was up yonder, about half a mile, I reckon. He was just sittin' on his horse in some trees when I walked by and he called me over. He asked me if I knew you or where you lived. When I said I didn't, he told me how to find your house and gave me the paper."

"What about his horse?"

"It was a big chestnut gelding."

Conrad's heart had started to beat faster as the boy described the man who had given him the note. The description of the horse was the last bit of evidence Conrad needed. He remembered both man and horse from the encounter on the hillside overlooking the city several days earlier. He had no doubt that the kidnappers were the men who had interrupted the picnic he and Rebel had been enjoying.

Which meant that the encounter probably wasn't a coincidence. Those men had been following them, probably plotting their crime even then. Conrad suspected that they had wanted to get a good look at him and Rebel.

They must have decided it would be easy to steal her away from him, he thought bitterly.

"Mister?"

Conrad looked down at the boy and forced a solemn smile onto his face. He held out the double eagle.

"Here. You've earned this."

The youngster snatched the coin and bit it to make sure it was real, obviously a habit with him. He grinned and said, "Thanks, mister." He started to run away, then stopped and looked back at Conrad. "That note I brought you . . . was it bad news?"

"I don't know yet," he said honestly.

He wouldn't know—until midnight tonight.

CHAPTER 6

Despite the vow he had made to himself earlier about not resting until Rebel was safe again, Conrad knew he couldn't afford to be groggy tonight from lack of sleep. He would need to be alert, with all his senses functioning at top efficiency. For that reason, he went upstairs and forced himself to lie down on the bed in the guest room. He couldn't bring himself to stretch out by himself on the bed he normally shared with Rebel.

Exhaustion overwhelmed him, and he fell asleep with surprising ease even though he hadn't taken off his clothes. His dreams were haunted, though, by nightmares in which shadowy, faceless, evil figures were chasing Rebel through a dark, seemingly endless forest. More than once he jolted awake, only to fall back almost right away into a stupor that turned into yet another of the horrible dreams.

It was the middle of the day when he woke up and stayed awake. As he stumbled down the stairs, he spotted a Western Union envelope on the floor just inside the front door. He had sent instructions with the message to Claudius Turnbuckle that Western Union was to bring any reply to him right away, no matter what time it was, day or night. He supposed he had been sleeping so soundly that he hadn't heard the messenger knocking on the front door.

Conrad practically pounced on the telegram. He tore open the envelope and pulled out a yellow flimsy like the one Sinclair had brought to the house the previous night. This one read:

> MORGAN'S WHEREABOUTS UNKNOWN AT PRESENT STOP WILL ATTEMPT TO LOCATE WITH ALL URGENCY STOP ANYTHING ELSE I CAN DO TO HELP STOP TURNBUCKLE

Conrad heaved a sigh and suppressed the urge to crumple the telegram in his hand. That wouldn't do any good. He couldn't help but be disappointed, though. He had hoped that Frank was somewhere close by.

It looked like Conrad couldn't count on his father's help with this problem.

He took the telegram into his study and left it on the desk. Then he cleaned up a little, shaving and changing clothes. He had to pay a visit to the bank, and he didn't want to look like he had slept in his clothes—which, of course, he had.

Conrad did business with the bank in the same building where his downtown office was located. He went there now, hitching up the buggy horse and driving the half mile. When he walked into the bank, he carried a good-sized carpetbag with him.

A clerk ushered him into the bank manager's office without delay. The man stood up and shook hands with Conrad, smiling with the same eager affability that he used to greet any large depositor. "What can I do for you, Mr. Browning?" the man asked.

"I need fifty thousand dollars," Conrad said.

The manager prided himself on being unflappable, but even he gaped at that unexpected statement. For a moment, he couldn't speak. Then he said, "But . . . but that's a great deal of money, Mr. Browning!"

Conrad nodded. "I know that. I need it anyway."

"But why?"

Conrad allowed his tone to grow chilly. "No offense, but that's not really any of your business, is it?"

The bank manager clasped his hands behind his back and squared his shoulders. "Actually, it is," he said. "I have a responsibility to the depositors to protect their money. You don't have fifty thousand dollars in this bank, sir, so I'd be giving you other people's money."

"You know perfectly well I'm good for it," Conrad snapped. "You can wire my banks in Boston and Denver and San Francisco if you don't believe me."

"Oh, I believe you," the manager said quickly. He had been taken by surprise, but he didn't want to offend Conrad if he didn't have to. "It's just that there are procedures we normally follow—"

"I don't have time for normal procedures." Conrad placed the carpetbag on the manager's desk. "When I leave here, I need to have fifty thousand dollars in this bag."

The man ventured a nervous laugh. "You sound almost like a holdup man, Mr. Browning."

Conrad's face remained impassive as he said, "If that's what it takes."

The manager swallowed hard. "No . . . no, of course not. You're well known to be a man of sterling reputation. Of course you're good for the money. It won't be necessary to wire any of your other banks." He went to the door of his office, opened it, and called to the clerk who had announced Conrad a few minutes earlier. Quietly, the manager said, "Joseph, I want you to begin putting together a package of cash for Mr. Browning. Fifty thousand dollars. And be discreet about it."

The clerk's eyes widened. "Did you say—"

"You heard what I said," the manager snapped. "Hop to it!"

"Yes, sir!"

The manager closed the door again and turned back to Conrad. "We're more than happy to help you with this, Mr. Browning," he said. "But if there's anything else I can do . . . I mean, if you're in some sort of trouble . . ."

"What makes you think that?"

The manager looked solemn as he said, "Whenever someone needs a great deal of money in a hurry, there's always some sort of trouble."

The chief of police had promised to keep the news of Rebel's kidnapping quiet. Obviously, he had kept his word. If the story had leaked out, the bank manager would have heard about it by now.

Conrad smiled. "I appreciate your concern, but this is something I have to handle myself. I can promise you, I won't forget about how you're cooperating with me."

"We'll do anything we can to help, Mr. Browning. You know that."

A short time later, the clerk came back to the office carrying a box that contained bundles of twenty- and fifty-dollar bills. He placed it on the manager's desk and said, "Will there be anything else, sir?"

The manager looked at Conrad, who shook his head.

When the clerk was gone, Conrad and the manager both counted the money to be sure the amount was correct; then Conrad placed the bills in the carpetbag. The bag was fairly heavy when he was finished. He signed a receipt for the money, then said, "I'm sure that I can count on your discretion?"

"Of course," the manager answered. "No one will hear about this from me."

"I'll replace these funds, one way or another, within forty-eight hours." If the ransom payoff went off without a hitch and he got Rebel back safely, he would have fifty thousand sent to the Carson City bank from one of his other banks. If it didn't . . .

Conrad wouldn't allow himself to think about that.

As Conrad started to leave the office, the bank manager said, "Surely, you'd like one of our guards to go with you, Mr. Browning. That's a great deal of money to be carrying around with you."

"I'm aware of that," Conrad said. He pulled back his coat so that the manager could see the butts of the Colt .45s tucked behind his belt on each hip. "That's why I'm taking precautions of my own."

The manager didn't say anything to that. He just stared at the man in his office as if he had never seen Conrad before.

And it was true—he had never seen *this* Conrad Browning. This Conrad Browning had appeared only a few times in the past, when faced with danger to himself or someone he loved. This Conrad Browning was his father's son.

Conrad carried the carpetbag with him when he stopped at a clothing store on his way home. He came out half an hour later with a paper-wrapped bundle under his other arm. One more stop, at a local gunsmith's shop, and then he went back to his house to continue getting ready for that night.

Black Rock Canyon was northwest of the city, well off the road to Reno and not far from Lake Tahoe. Conrad had been there once, when he was investigating some land he was thinking about buying, just over the state line in California. One trail led through the canyon, which was steep-sided and covered with pines. No one lived there; it was dark and desolate, and above it loomed a huge bluff that gave the place its name. An appropriate lair for the sort of evil bastards who would abduct a man's wife, he thought.

When he had awoken from his troubled sleep earlier in the day, the beginnings of a plan had been in the back of his mind. First and foremost was Rebel's safety, of course, but once that was assured, he planned to go after the men who had taken her, with all the forces at his command. Also, he knew better than to assume that the gang would return her even if he paid the ransom. The chances that they would try to pull a double cross were high. If that happened, Conrad was going to be ready for them, or at least he was going to try to be. He would have felt a lot better about his chances if he'd had his father siding him.

But he had known for years that he wouldn't always have Frank Morgan to help him. The time had come for him to grow up and handle his own problems. Stomp his own snakes, as Frank would put it.

He opened the bundle he had brought from the clothing store and laid out his purchases on the bed in the spare room. He had bought a pair of black whipcord trousers and a black bib-front shirt, as well as a flat-crowned black Stetson. He already owned a pair of black, high-topped boots. At the gunsmith's shop, he had picked up a holster and cartridge belt of fine black leather. If it was necessary, he wanted to be able to blend into the shadows. The black outfit would make that easier. He planned to wear it underneath his regular clothes. The gunbelt would be in the buggy, along with a Winchester and his shotgun.

The kidnappers would be expecting a scared, inexperienced Easterner. That was what Conrad would give them—up to a point. But if they went back on the deal, or if Rebel was hurt in any way . . .

Then the man they would have to deal with would be someone else entirely.

Lasswell was beginning to wonder if the payoff would be worth it. He'd hardly had a moment's peace since they'd snatched that crazy bitch out of her house the night before.

At the moment, she was tied and gagged, the first time she had been quiet for more than a minute or two. For a gal who was married to a rich businessman from back East, she could cuss like a Texas cowboy who'd been following a trail herd and eating dust all the way to Kansas. Lasswell knew that for a fact, because he had been a cowboy just like that, years earlier as a kid, before he'd decided that following the owlhoot trail was more to his liking.

It was dangerous to get too close to her, too. Clem Baggott had made that mistake. Mrs. Browning had gotten her teeth fastened on his left ear and damn near ripped it off his head before Carlson pulled her away from him. Carlson had taken advantage of the opportunity to run his hands over her breasts, and she had repaid him by twisting around and kicking him in the balls. Howling in pain, Carlson had backhanded her and knocked her a good ten feet. When Abel Dean and Spence Hooper rushed over to grab her and keep her from getting away, she'd hauled off and punched Spence in the face hard enough to break his nose. Gant and White Rock had had to pile on as well to bring her under control.

And that was just getting her out of the house and onto a horse.

By the time they were able to ride away from there, Lasswell had gotten pretty worried that the law would show up. That didn't happen, though, and he started to think that maybe nobody had heard that shot after all.

Their camp was at the foot of the bluff that loomed over Black Rock Canyon. Finding the place in the dark was difficult, but Lasswell had been over the ground enough in the past few days so that he was able to do it. Once they got there, he had told Mrs. Browning that they would leave her legs untied and not gag her if she would promise to behave. Not only had she not made that promise, she had told him to go to hell and then do something physically impossible once he got there. Lasswell had never run into a woman quite like her.

Her hair had come loose from its upswept curls and hung in disarray around her face. Her eyes burned with anger and hatred, and Lasswell knew by looking at her that if she had been loose and had a gun in her hand, he'd be a dead man by now. They'd all be dead if she had her way.

If he had been thirty years younger, he thought, he could

come damn near falling in love with a woman like Rebel Browning.

Sure made him sorry about what was going to happen. But he had his orders, and he intended to carry them out; otherwise, he might not get paid. A man didn't have to be young to be in love with money.

All day long she had carried on, tied hand and foot and lying under a pine tree. Lasswell had finally gotten fed up and told a couple of men to gag her. Rattigan had almost lost a finger trying to follow that order.

Moss came over to Lasswell and said, "Duncan just died."

Lasswell grimaced. "Damn. Ray was a good man. He hung on longer'n I expected him to really."

"If he was a good man, he wouldn't have let a girl shoot him."

Lasswell felt a flash of anger toward Moss. "I rode with him for a long while, you didn't," he snapped. "I reckon I know how good he was. Anyway, that ain't no regular gal. She's a hellcat if ever I saw one."

Moss shrugged and then lowered his voice. "Carlson's gettin' some of the boys stirred up. He wants to have a go at her, and the others think they ought to have a turn, too."

"I never said anybody could do that."

"You never said they couldn't either."

Moss had a point. But Moss didn't know the rest of the plan. Nobody did except Lasswell. He was the only one who had actually talked to the boss. The orders he had were very specific, and they didn't include molesting Mrs. Browning. But he had allowed the other men to believe they might get a chance to have some fun with their captive, thinking that might make them more inclined to go along with what he wanted. He saw now that might have been a mistake.

"All right," he said with a weary sigh. "I reckon we'd better clear the air."

The sun was low enough in the sky so that thick shadows were gathering under the trees. Lasswell strode through them to the center of the camp and called, "Everybody gather 'round. I got somethin' to say."

The men formed a rough circle around him. Lasswell looked at them and thumbed his hat back on his head. Then he lowered his hand and hooked his thumb behind his gunbelt, so that his fingers hung near the butt of his Colt.

"There's been some complainin' around the camp because you fellas ain't had a chance to get more . . . friendly-like . . . with Mrs. Browning."

"Damn straight," Carlson said.

"Well, I'm here to tell you, that ain't gonna happen."

The men stared at him in surprise. Some of them, like Rattigan, didn't seem to care all that much. Others, like Titus Gant and the Winchell brothers, looked mad.

Carlson was the most upset, though. "What the hell are you talkin' about?" he demanded. He waved a big hand toward Rebel. "She's right there, and she can't do a damned thing to stop us. Why can't we take turns with her?"

"Because I say you can't," Lasswell said. "I'm the boss of this outfit, and what I say goes."

"Is it because you want her for yourself?" Gant asked. He wore a black frock coat and a string tie, and when he wasn't holding up banks or trains—or kidnapping women—he dealt faro in saloons. His voice was soft, but Lasswell recognized a dangerous quality in it. Maybe Carlson *wasn't* the one he ought to be worrying about the most.

"That ain't it," he said. "We took Mrs. Browning for the ransom money. That's all I'm thinkin' about."

"Her husband won't know that he's not getting her back in exactly the same condition as he saw her last until after he's paid the money," Gant pointed out.

"Yeah, well, what if he won't hand over the loot until he's talked to her? If she tells him that you fellas molested her, he might not pay."

Gant shook his head. "That's loco. He won't be calling the

shots. If he tries anything like that, we'll just kill 'em both and take the money anyway."

"Not if he's hidden it somewhere." Lasswell was trying to think of arguments he could use to convince them without having to tell them the truth. "I'm tellin' you, we got to be careful and cover all our bets."

Gant sneered and brushed his coat back. "And I'm telling you I intend to have that woman before we give her back to her husband."

Lasswell sighed. He read the challenge on Gant's face and in the gambler's stance, and he knew that he couldn't let it go unanswered.

With a flickering move that filled his hand and gave Gant no chance, Lasswell drew and fired.

He was close enough so that the bullet drove Gant back a couple of steps as it thudded into his chest. Gant tried to draw, but his body was no longer following his commands. He weaved to the side and then spun off his feet, crashing to the ground.

Lasswell stood there, apparently as casual as he had been a couple of heartbeats earlier, when Gant was still alive. Smoke curled from the barrel of the gun in his hand.

"Let's make it simple," he said. "None of you are gonna bother Mrs. Browning because I say you ain't. That plain enough for you?"

Nobody argued, not even Carlson. A few of the men muttered agreement, and the gathering broke up, the men drifting away to see to their horses or roll a smoke or get a card game going. Lasswell told the Winchell brothers to grab some shovels and start digging. They had both Gant and Ray Duncan to bury.

Moss came over to Lasswell, who had replaced the spent shell and pouched his iron. "I remember you now," he said quietly. "You were part of that big feud in Texas about twenty-five years ago. Seems like I recall hearin' something about a shoot-out in a saloon in Comanche. Fella named Lasswell downed four of the other bunch even though he had a couple of slugs in him."

"I'm still carryin' around one of those slugs," Lasswell said, "and it hurts like the dickens whenever it's about to rain."

"Hell, man, you're a gunfighter!"

Lasswell shook his head. "Not to speak of, not when there are men like Frank Morgan still alive. That's why I wouldn't go into this job with just me and the boys who'd been ridin' with me. Just the chance we might have to go up against Morgan is enough to make me mighty careful."

"Well, I reckon you won't have to worry about any of them comin' at you head-on," Moss said. "After seein' that draw, they won't want to do that. Gant was a pretty slick gun-thrower, and he didn't even clear leather." A shadow of a smile crossed Moss's granite face. "All you'll have to do is watch out behind you."

"I always do," Lasswell said.

CHAPTER 7

After night had fallen—after what had been the longest day of his life, without a doubt—Conrad went out to the carriage house and hitched the big buckskin horse to the buggy. The animal was more than just a buggy horse; Conrad had used him as a saddle mount before and knew the buckskin had plenty of speed and stamina. He stowed his saddle in the back of the buggy, along with the Winchester and the shotgun and the coiled shell belt.

He hoped he wouldn't need any of those things. He hoped that he would turn the money over to the kidnappers and that they would give him Rebel in return. But if it didn't work out that way, he was going after them. He would kill anyone who got in his way, until his wife was safe again.

It would take about two hours to reach Black Rock Canyon, Conrad estimated. He drove out of Carson City a quarter of an hour before ten o'clock, to give himself plenty of time. The carpetbag with the fifty thousand dollars in it was at his feet.

On his way out of town, he stopped at the Western Union office to see if there were any more messages from Claudius

Turnbuckle concerning Frank Morgan, but of course there weren't. Conrad had known there wouldn't be. But he had checked just to make sure.

The kidnappers had picked a good night for their evil purposes. The moon was only a thin sliver of silver in the sky, so the night was at its darkest, lit mostly by the millions of stars. They wouldn't do much good in Black Rock Canyon.

Conrad's thoughts were a confused, frightened jumble in his head. Most of the fright was for Rebel's safety, of course, but he knew he was nervous about how he would handle himself tonight as well. Danger had tested him in the past and he had always come through, but that was no guarantee he would again. He had big footsteps to follow, the footsteps of Frank Morgan.

That's loco, Conrad, he seemed to hear his father saying. *Follow your own trail, not mine, and don't walk in fear. You'll be all right. You'll do just fine. Do your best, and don't back down.*

Conrad took comfort from the words. A flesh-and-blood Frank Morgan would have been better, but right now he would take what he could get.

He was able to find the trail to Black Rock Canyon without much difficulty, although a time or two he worried that he had taken a wrong turn. Eventually, though, he spotted the huge rock formation that loomed above the canyon and knew he was in the right place. The bluff towered eighty or a hundred feet above the canyon floor, and formed a patch of even deeper darkness because it blotted out some of the stars. Conrad saw it above the tops of the pine trees that bordered the trail.

He didn't know when or how the kidnappers would stop him and demand the ransom, but he assumed they would whenever they were good and ready. He didn't bother taking out his watch to check the time. He would have had to strike a match in order to see it, and he didn't want to do that.

Every muscle in his body was taut with tension. His heart

pounded, causing the blood to pulse in a frantic drumbeat inside his head. He had trouble catching his breath. He imagined this must be what it felt like to be drowning.

Suddenly, a voice called out, "That's far enough, Browning!"

Conrad hauled back hard on the reins. He was glad the kidnappers were confronting him at last. Anything was better than just driving slowly along in the buggy and waiting for them to show themselves.

What happened next surprised him. Several torches blazed into life along both sides of the trail. The harsh light from them washed over the buggy so that Conrad couldn't make a move without the kidnappers being able to see what he was doing. They were smart. They didn't trust him any more than he trusted them.

A man stepped out into the middle of the trail, in front of the buggy. Conrad half expected to see the ginger-bearded man, but this fellow was one he'd never seen before. He was tall and burly, with a deeply tanned, rough-hewn face.

"Are you alone, Browning?" he asked.

"Your note said for me to come alone," Conrad snapped. "I'm cooperating. I want my wife back."

"You'll get her, if you do as you're told. If you don't . . ." The man waved a hand toward the trees alongside the trail. "There are a dozen rifles trained on you right now. Try any tricks, and you'll wind up ventilated."

Conrad looked toward the trees. Enough light from the torches penetrated into the shadows underneath them for him to be able to see the barrels of those rifles the kidnapper had mentioned. He also caught glimpses of some of the men holding the weapons. He recognized several of them from the previous encounter, including a huge, moonfaced man who was so big, he stuck out from both sides of the tree trunk he was using for cover, a bearded Mexican with a steeple-crowned sombrero, and an older, ugly man in a black vest and with black sleeve cuffs. Conrad stared at them over the barrels of their rifles and committed each face to memory in turn.

He would never forget any of them. Their images would be burned into his brain until the day he died.

Which might be today, he reminded himself. He was badly outnumbered, if it came down to a fight.

A wry smile tugged at his mouth. "You should hope your men are good shots," he said to the spokesman.

That comment put a frown on the man's face. "Why the hell do you say that?"

Conrad nodded to the right of the trail, then the left. "You've got six men on each side of the trail. If they shoot at me and miss, they're liable to hit some of the men on the other side."

The spokesman frowned. "Never you mind about that. You got the money?"

Conrad didn't even glance down at the carpetbag at his feet. Nor did he answer the man's question. Instead, he asked coolly, "Do you have my wife?"

"Oh, we got her, all right. Don't you worry about that."

"Let me see her." Conrad supposed that Rebel was somewhere back in the trees, with at least one of the kidnappers guarding her.

Instead, the kidnappers' spokesman took him by surprise by pointing at the sky and saying, "Look up."

For a terrible moment, Conrad thought the man was saying that Rebel was already dead and was pointing toward heaven, but then as he lifted his eyes, he saw another torch flare into life. This was on top of the rocky bluff that overhung the canyon. Conrad gasped as he saw the two figures illuminated by the torch's glare.

Rebel was one of them, standing perilously close to the bluff's edge. The other one, right behind her, was the bearded man Conrad had pegged as the leader of the kidnappers. He had hold of Rebel's arm with one hand. The other pressed the barrel of a revolver into her side.

"Oh, my God!" Conrad cried. "Rebel! Rebel, can you hear me?"

"I hear you, Conrad!" she called down to him. "And I love you!"

"I love you, too!"

The craggy-faced man in the trail said, "That's touchin' as all hell. Let's see the money, Browning."

Conrad had to tear his eyes away from Rebel. It wasn't easy. He glared at the man and said, "You don't get the money until my wife is safely in this buggy with me."

The man shook his head. "You ain't givin' the orders. Here's how it's gonna work. You give us the money and then stay right where you are. We leave, and our man leaves your wife up on top of that rock. There's a trail down. She can make it if she's careful. She climbed up there after all. Once we're gone with the money, she can climb down, and the two of you can go back to Carson City. You'll never see us again. Sound good?"

"The part about never seeing you again does," Conrad lied. He planned to see each and every one of them again, either at the end of a hangman's rope, or over the barrel of a gun.

But that would come later, after Rebel was safe.

"All right," he said. "I'll turn over the money. But I want your men to pull back, so that I don't have all those guns pointing at me." He paused. "They make me nervous."

The man thought it over, then shrugged. He drew his Colt and called, "All right, you fellas heard the man. Back off so it's just him and me. That all right with you, Browning?"

"Let's see them do it first," Conrad said.

One by one, the kidnappers stepped out from behind the trees and moved along the trail, withdrawing until they were about fifty yards behind their spokesman. That gave Conrad an even better look at their faces. He would know them when he saw them again, that was for sure.

"Now, damn it," the craggy-faced man said. "We've done what you wanted. Turn over the money, or we'll just kill you both and take it."

Conrad knew he had to risk it. He bent over and reached down to pick up the carpetbag, and as he did so he felt the pressure of the gun that was tucked into his trousers at the small of his back, under his coat. He hefted the carpetbag and stood up in the buggy. With a grunt of effort, he tossed it over the buckskin horse's head. Dust puffed up around the bag as it landed in the trail, almost at the man's feet.

He took an eager step forward and reached down to unfasten the catches on the bag. As he threw it open and saw the packets of bills inside, a grin creased his face.

"You can count it if you want," Conrad said coldly.

"I don't reckon that'll be necessary. You've played square with us. Now we'll play square with you." The man closed the bag, fastened it, and picked it up. He carried it over to where one of the torches was stuck upright in the dirt beside the trail. He wrenched the torch free and waved it over his head. Conrad supposed that was the signal to the man on the bluff with Rebel that they had the money.

Maybe now they would let her go, he thought. No tricks, he prayed. Please, no tricks.

"Browning!" the man on the bluff shouted.

Conrad's head jerked back as he gazed upward. He hoped to see the man let go of Rebel and retreat, but that didn't happen. Instead, as the man stepped behind her, he called, "What happens now is on your head! Welcome to hell!"

"Noooo!" Conrad screamed.

Rebel must have realized what was going to happen next. She twisted and tried to strike at the man, but she was too late. Muzzle flame spurted as the man fired. Rebel cried out in pain as the bullet tore into her and knocked her backward.

Right off the bluff.

Conrad couldn't believe his horror-stricken eyes as he saw Rebel stumble back into empty air and then plummet toward the base of the bluff so far below. Even though it took only the blink of an eye for her to disappear into the trees, the fall seemed to last an eternity.

Instinct sent Conrad's hand flashing to the gun at the small of his back. He whipped it out and tilted the barrel upward, blazing away at the man atop the bluff, the man who had just shot Rebel. The bastard was already gone, though, having leaped back out of Conrad's line of fire.

He jerked his eyes back down and saw that the man in the trail was still standing there, apparently dumbfounded by what had just happened. Evidently, it had taken him by surprise just as much as it had Conrad. But he recovered quickly from the shock and clawed at the gun on his hip.

Conrad grabbed the reins, yelled, "Hyaaah!" and sent the buckskin leaping forward. The kidnapper had to leap to one side to avoid being trampled by the big horse. He couldn't get out of the way of the buggy, though. The vehicle clipped him and sent him spinning off his feet. He screamed as he fell, and from the lurch Conrad felt, he was pretty sure one of the wheels had passed over the man's legs.

Standing in the buggy, holding the reins with one hand and the Colt with the other, Conrad sent the buggy racing toward the rest of the kidnappers. He emptied the revolver as he charged them, and between the flying lead and the racing horse and buggy, the men were forced to scatter. They fired back at Conrad as they scurried out of the way. He heard some of the slugs whine past his head, but he ignored them.

He didn't care if they killed him. He was sure that Rebel was dead. Shot at close range like that, followed by the fall off the bluff . . . There was no way she could have survived. So, actually, they had already killed him. His heart might still beat and his lungs might draw breath into them, but he was dead, right along with his beloved Rebel.

He charged through the kidnappers and kept the buggy moving, not stopping until he had gone a couple of hundred yards, well out of reach of the light from the torches that still blazed alongside the trail. Then he hauled the horse to a halt and leaped out of the buggy. He tore off his outer clothing, revealing the black garb that would be impossible to see in the shadows. Moving swiftly and efficiently, he reached behind the seat, picked up the gunbelt, and strapped it on. The holster already held a loaded Colt. The black Stetson was next, tugged down on his sandy hair. Then he retrieved the Winchester and the shotgun and loped off into the darkness, carrying one in each hand.

Shots roared, but the kidnappers had to be firing blindly because they couldn't see him in the shadows as he circled back toward them. After a moment, a man bellowed, "Hold your fire! Hold your fire, damn it!" Conrad thought the voice belonged to the ginger-bearded man. "Forget Browning! Leave him alive! *Just get that money!*"

They had all charged after him, determined to kill him, and had forgotten momentarily about the ransom. Conrad hadn't forgotten, though. That money was the bait that would bring them to him, so that he could kill them. He reached the trail and dashed out into the light. The carpetbag still lay there, close to the man he'd run over with the buggy. That man had pulled himself to the edge of the trail, dragging what appeared to be two broken legs behind him. He was whimpering in pain, but he let out a shouted curse as he saw Conrad coming.

"He's here! The son of a bitch is here! He's after the money!"

Men came running from the other direction, but they were too late. Conrad dropped the Winchester next to the carpetbag and whirled toward them, using both hands to brace the shotgun as he eared back the hammers and pulled the triggers. The double charge of buckshot exploded from both barrels with a thunderous boom.

Conrad heard yells of pain, but didn't know how many of them he'd hit or how badly they were wounded. He dropped the scattergun, snatched the rifle and the carpetbag from the trail, and darted past one of the torches into the trees again.

"Get that money!" the leader yelled. "But don't kill Browning!"

That was strange, Conrad thought. Why did the man want his life spared? So that he could be tormented that much longer by the knowledge that he had failed his wife, that she was dead because of him?

Before he could ponder that any further, a crackling in the brush near at hand warned him. One of the kidnappers burst from behind a tree and tackled him. Conrad went down hard, but he managed to hang on to both the carpetbag and the Winchester.

"I got him!" the man yelled as he tried to pin Conrad to the ground. "Over here! I got him!"

Conrad swung the carpetbag and smashed it against the man's head. The kidnapper fell off him and sprawled to the side. Conrad lurched to his feet and pressed the Winchester's barrel to the man's head. In the faint light from the torches, he saw the man's eyes widen with fear.

"Help! He's gonna—"

Conrad pulled the trigger.

This man had helped murder Edwin Sinclair, had helped kidnap Rebel. He was partially responsible for her being dead. There was no mercy in Conrad at this moment. Barely anything human remained inside him. He took no pleasure in blowing this bastard's brains out. It was just something that had to be done.

The sound of the shot set them off again, despite their leader's orders. Guns roared, and bullets whipped through the trees around Conrad, thudding into trunks and clipping off branches. Conrad crouched and ran, trusting to luck or fate to keep him safe, at least until he could kill the rest of them. After that, he didn't care what happened to him.

Something slammed into him and knocked him off his

feet. The carpetbag's handle slipped out of his hand as he fell. A burning pain in his side sent waves of weakness through him. He got a hand under him and pushed himself to his knees. He felt around for the carpetbag but couldn't find it.

As a young man back East, before he'd ever come West and met Frank Morgan for the first time, Conrad had taken part in several fox hunts. He was reminded of those times now as he heard the outlaws crashing through the brush toward him, yelling to each other like hounds baying after the fox.

And he was the fox.

He had no doubt they would tear him apart if they ever got their hands on him, just like the hounds did when they caught up with the fox. The wound in his side had put him at a disadvantage. He felt his strength deserting him, and since he no longer had the money, he couldn't use it to lure them on and kill them at times and places of his choosing.

They outnumbered him by too much. He had to admit it. He couldn't kill them all tonight. So he had to get away. Sooner or later they would die at his hand, but in order for that to happen . . .

He had to live.

That knowledge burned through him with a fiercer heat than the bullet that had gouged his side. The need for revenge that filled him could only be satisfied if he survived this night of blood and death.

He forced himself to his feet and stumbled through the trees. Behind him, somebody shouted, "Hey, it's the money! Hot damn, I found the money!"

"Let's get out of here!" That was the ginger-bearded man again, the one who had shot Rebel. It was all Conrad could do not to lift the Winchester and spray the remaining rounds in the direction of that voice as fast as he could work the rifle's lever.

But he couldn't hope to kill all of them, and even though

the bearded man was the one who'd pulled the trigger, they had all played a part in Rebel's death. He wouldn't be satisfied until all of them were dead.

"What about Hank?" another man demanded. "He killed Hank!"

"Sorry. There's nothin' we can do about it now. My orders were to leave Browning alive."

There it was again. Conrad huddled against a tree trunk and wondered who could have given such orders. He had seen the reaction of the man in the trail when the bearded man shot Rebel. He hadn't known that was going to happen, and Conrad thought that the rest of the kidnappers hadn't either. They had expected to collect the ransom and turn Rebel back over to him.

That meant the bearded man had been playing a different game, a game of his own. And only he had the answers that Conrad needed.

The voices faded. A few minutes later, Conrad heard hoofbeats in the night. They were leaving. Taking the money and riding away from the place where Rebel had died. Where a huge hole had been ripped out of Conrad's heart. No one could live with damage like that. *I'm dead,* he thought again. *Conrad Browning is dead.*

His head jerked up, and he realized that he had lost consciousness. He had no idea how long he'd been out. He blinked and looked through the trees, thinking that he might catch a glimpse of the torches if they still burned, but nothing met his eyes except darkness.

The canyon was quiet now. The place was far enough from town, isolated enough, that no one would have heard the shots. No one was going to come and help him. He shouldn't have tried to handle this alone, he thought. He should have asked for help, from the law or the Pinkertons or someone. But time had been short, and he had honestly believed that he stood the best chance of saving Rebel by following his instincts.

A sob wracked him. His instincts had betrayed him, and Rebel was dead.

He was no Frank Morgan, that was for damned sure. Frank wouldn't have let this happen. Frank would have found a way to save her, to save Rebel and kill all the bastards who had kidnapped her.

Conrad sat there stewing in self-loathing for long moments, before he finally braced his back against the tree trunk and began struggling to his feet. The least he could do was to find Rebel and take her body back to town so that she could have a proper burial. He owed her that much, after failing her so spectacularly.

The pain in his side had faded to a dull ache. He placed his hand against his shirt and felt the blood that had soaked into it. He couldn't tell how badly he was hurt, but he could walk, so he hoped the wound wasn't too bad.

Eventually, he stumbled onto the trail. He whistled, hoping that the horse was still somewhere around. A moment later, he was rewarded by the sound of hoofbeats moving toward him. A second after that, he heard the faint creaking of the buggy wheels.

The buckskin brought the buggy to him. Conrad caught hold of the horse's halter and leaned against him. The horse shied a bit, no doubt from the smell of blood. Conrad patted his shoulder, murmured to him until he calmed down. Then Conrad found the suit coat he had tossed behind the seat and dug out a box of matches from one of the pockets.

He made a torch of his own, ripping the lining out of the coat and wrapping it around a branch he found. Then, holding the torch above his head, he stumbled toward the spot where he thought Rebel's body had fallen. His head was spinning by now, and he couldn't be sure he was going in the right direction, but he would search all night if he had to.

His instincts were true this time. He found her only minutes later, lying in a huddled heap between two trees. Her body was broken from the fall, and her white blouse was dark with blood from the gunshot wound. Conrad fell to his knees beside her and jabbed the torch into the ground so that it would stand up as he gathered her into his arms. She was limp, lifeless. He cradled her against his chest and sobbed as he searched in vain for a pulse, a breath, even the faintest sign of life. But of course, there was none. Rebel was gone. And her last words, he realized, had been to tell him that she loved him.

That horrible, bittersweet thought was in his mind as he held her and cried, and then he felt the cold ring of a gun muzzle press against the back of his neck as a man said, "Don't move, Browning! I figured you'd come back for that bitch."

CHAPTER 8

Conrad stiffened as the man went on. "That was my brother you killed back yonder! My twin brother! Shot him like he was no better'n a damn dog! You know what that feels like?"

Forcing the words past the huge lump in his throat, Conrad said, "I'm holding my wife's dead body in my arms. And men like you and your brother killed my mother. So, yeah, I know what it feels like."

The response seemed to throw the kidnapper for a loop. He must have expected Conrad to beg for his life. It would be a cold day in hell before that happened, even though Conrad wanted desperately to live now, so that he could have his revenge on Rebel's murderers.

Even as he spoke, he was moving one hand carefully toward the makeshift torch stuck in the ground beside him. His fingers touched the branch. He pushed on it, gently and slowly, so the kidnapper wouldn't notice what he was doing.

"Well, now you're gonna find out what it feels like to get your brains blown out, just like my brother."

Before the man could pull the trigger, the torch tipped

over, falling straight at his legs. The flames coming at him caused him to jump back instinctively, and even though he jerked the trigger of his gun, Conrad had already rolled to the side, taking Rebel's body with him. The gun still blasted painfully close to Conrad's ear, but the bullet thudded harmlessly into the ground.

Conrad wound up lying on his back, with the kidnapper looming above him. He brought his right leg up and buried the toe of his boot in the man's groin. The kidnapper screamed in agony and doubled over, but he didn't drop his gun. He managed to get another shot off as Conrad flung himself to the side. The bullet plucked at the sleeve of the black shirt, but didn't touch Conrad's flesh.

Conrad whipped a leg around and caught the kidnapper behind the knees, sweeping the man's legs out from under him. The man fell heavily and curled up into a ball as he clutched at his injured privates. Conrad came up on his knees and pulled his Colt, then lunged forward. The gun barrel thudded against the man's head. He shuddered and then straightened out, unconscious.

Out cold like that, at least he wasn't thinking about how bad his balls hurt anymore.

A sudden glare caught Conrad's attention as he knelt there, breathing heavily. He looked around and saw that the carpet of dry pine needles on the ground had caught fire where he'd shoved the torch over. A fire like that would spread quickly in these woods, and for a second he thought about leaving the kidnapper there to roast alive.

Something inside him wouldn't allow him to do that. He had thought that all vestiges of his humanity had died with Rebel, but maybe that wasn't completely the case. He pushed himself to his feet, hurried over, and stomped out the flames before they could spread. That plunged the canyon into darkness again.

Conrad tried to ignore the pain of his own bullet wound as he knelt next to the unconscious kidnapper once more and used the man's own belt to lash his hands together behind his back. He didn't want the fellow going anywhere just yet. Conrad realized that he might be able to make use of him.

Then, using matches to light his path, he made his way back to the buggy and retrieved a blanket from the area behind the seat. The same blanket he had spread out on that hillside so they could sit on it to enjoy their picnic, he thought as another shred of his soul peeled away. He had never carried it back into the house. Now he took it into the woods and gently wrapped Rebel's body in it.

Once he had placed her in the buggy, he went back for the kidnapper, who was beginning to stir. Conrad hit him again with the gun to keep him still. He took hold of the man's feet and dragged him through the woods, back to the trail where the horse and buggy waited. He didn't worry about how scratched up the bastard got along the way either.

Conrad knew he had lost quite a bit of blood. He could feel the insidious weakness creeping through him. Grunting from pain and effort, he lifted the unconscious man and toppled him onto the buggy's floorboard, in front of the driver's seat. Conrad would have to ride back to Carson City with his feet resting on the man. It would be uncomfortable, but there was no way he was putting the kidnapper in the back of the vehicle with Rebel.

Conrad never remembered all the details of the drive back to town. By that time, he was functioning largely on instinct and sheer determination. He recalled that a time or two, the kidnapper started to move around a little, and each time, Conrad kicked him in the head. In the back of his mind, he hoped the man wouldn't die from the punishment before they got back to town.

The kidnapper knew things that he needed to know. Conrad intended to have answers.

The moon was down by the time the buggy reached Carson City. The darkest hour of the night lay over the town. No one was in the streets, and there was no one to challenge

Conrad or even see him as he drove around the house and into the carriage house.

The kidnapper was still breathing, but hadn't budged for a while. Conrad hauled the man out of the buggy and stood him up against one of the posts that supported the roof, tying him in place with some rope that was in the carriage house. Then, he lifted Rebel and carried her into the home that they had shared for all too short a time. Just having her in his arms seemed to give him strength, despite the wound in his side.

He took her upstairs and placed her on their bed, still wrapped in the blanket. Then, he went back downstairs and out to the carriage house, reeling like a drunken man as he did so. He paused just outside the carriage house and leaned against the wall for a moment in an attempt to regain some of his strength. It didn't really help.

He heard thumping and then a groan from inside the building. The kidnapper was regaining consciousness again. This time, Conrad didn't intend to knock him out. Not until he had the answers he wanted.

He drew his gun and shoved the door open, then heeled it closed behind him as he went in. He had left a lantern burning, and in its flickering light, he saw the kidnapper looking around wildly and pulling against the rope that held him to the post. Conrad took a deep breath and forced his stride to be steady as he walked toward the man. He lifted the gun as he advanced, and the kidnapper grew wide-eyed and still as he stared down the barrel of the Colt.

Conrad stopped in front of the man and rasped, "What's your name?"

For a second, he thought the kidnapper was going to be stubborn and refuse to answer, but the sight of a gun muzzle only inches from his face was a powerful persuader.

"It's Winchell," the man said sullenly. "Jeff Winchell." He grimaced. "What'd you do to me? My head feels like it's about to fall plumb off."

"You're lucky you've still got a head," Conrad said. "What was your brother's name?" He didn't have to know that to carry out his plan of vengeance, since the kidnapper's brother was already dead, but for some reason he was curious.

"It was Hank. Hank Winchell, you murderin' son of a bitch."

"You're a fine one to talk," Conrad snapped. "After the way you killed my wife."

"I didn't have anything to do with that! I swear it, mister. That was all Lasswell's doin'. As far as any of the rest of us knew, we were gonna let her go as soon as we had that ransom money."

"Lasswell?"

"Clay Lasswell. Some old Texas gunfighter. He was the ramrod of the bunch. He's the one who wired Moss and had him get together some men."

Conrad nodded as he made a mental note of the man. So the ginger-bearded man was Clay Lasswell, and he was the leader of the kidnappers, just as Conrad had supposed. Winchell's frightened words confirmed Conrad's earlier speculation that Lasswell had crossed up his own men by shooting Rebel.

He didn't let any of that show on his face, though, as he went on, "Who's Moss?"

"Vernon Moss. He's the one who was waitin' in the trail for you. You broke both his legs when you run over him with that buggy, you know."

"Good," Conrad said. "He had it coming. What about the others? What are their names?"

Winchell's eyes narrowed. "I know what you're doin'," he said. "You're tryin' to get me to sell out my pards. Well, I won't do it, damn you. I won't!"

"I think you will," Conrad said. He eared back the Colt's hammer so that only the slightest pressure on the trigger would be needed to send a bullet into the kidnapper's brain. "If you won't tell me what I need to know, then you're no good to me."

Winchell stared at him. The kidnapper's face paled, and beads of sweat popped out on his forehead. "You . . . you can't kill me," he said. "You're a businessman. You own banks and mines and railroads. You don't go around shootin' people!"

"You know who my father is, don't you?"

Winchell didn't answer with words, but he bobbed his head up and down, then winced at the fresh pain the movement must have set off inside his skull.

"What do you think Frank Morgan would do if he were here right now?" Conrad asked softly. "Do you think he'd hesitate to pull this trigger?"

Actually, at this very moment, Conrad figured that he was closer to being able to commit cold-blooded murder than Frank would have been. Although exterminating this vermin hardly qualified as murder.

Winchell's resolve broke. He twisted his head to the side and closed his eyes. "Don't shoot me," he said. "Please, don't shoot. I'll tell you what you want to know."

"Everything," Conrad said. "I want to know everything."

Winchell looked at him again. "You gotta understand. I don't know all of it. Lasswell was the only one who did. He was the only one who'd talked to whoever the boss was."

"Lasswell didn't come up with the idea of kidnapping my wife?"

"I don't think so. I think he was just a hired hand, like the rest of us, only he knew who was really pullin' the strings."

"Keep talking," Conrad said.

Winchell did, details spilling from him, although the kidnapper really didn't know much beyond the things Conrad had already deduced for himself. He knew the names of all the other men involved, though, and Conrad was careful to memorize each one of them. In some cases, he had only one name—Buck, Carlson, and Rattigan—but that was better than nothing.

"The only other hombre I'm sure was in on it was that dude," Winchell finally said.

"What dude?"

"The one who was supposed to let us in the house after he knocked you out."

"Edwin Sinclair?" Conrad asked in a hoarse whisper.

"I never heard his name. All I know is that he worked for you, and Lasswell had Julio cut his throat once we had your wife."

A chill washed through Conrad. So Sinclair hadn't been trustworthy after all. He had plotted with the kidnappers, and then been done in by the treachery of his own allies. He hadn't been killed trying to save Rebel. Conrad wished briefly that the kidnappers hadn't killed Sinclair. He would have liked to have done that himself.

But that part was finished. He looked over the Colt's barrel at Winchell and said, "You're certain that's all you know?"

"That's it, Browning. Except . . ."

"Go on," Conrad grated.

"I don't know if it makes any difference or not, but nobody laid a finger on your wife except to bring her with us. She wasn't, uh, molested or anything like that. I give you my word on that."

"Why should I accept your word?"

"Because I'm tryin' to convince you not to shoot me! Some of the fellas wanted to, uh, you know . . . but Lasswell wouldn't let 'em. He made it clear that we had to leave Mrs. Browning alone. I reckon that must've been part of his orders, too."

Conrad couldn't see the logic in that, but as a matter of fact, he did believe Winchell. The man was too frightened not to be telling the truth. And even though the knowledge that Rebel hadn't been assaulted was scant comfort at a time like this, it was better than nothing. At least she hadn't spent her final hours in terror and pain, being brutalized.

A moment of silence stretched by, and then Winchell said, "I've told you everything I know. I swear it, Browning. What are you gonna do now?"

Conrad's lips drew back from his teeth in a grimace as he stared at the kidnapper. He said, "I know what I ought to do, what I want to do . . ."

Winchell swallowed hard.

Conrad tilted the Colt's barrel up and let down the hammer. He lowered the gun and slid it into its holster. Winchell sagged forward against the rope.

"I'm not going to kill you," Conrad said. "I'm going to turn you over to the police and let the law deal with you. You'll probably hang anyway, but I'm not going to be your executioner."

Winchell licked his lips. "I'm much obliged. I'm mighty sorry about what happened to your missus. I really am, Browning. I never wanted to hurt nobody." He began to sob. "I'm sorry, I'm so sorry . . ."

"Shut up," Conrad snapped. He turned away. His right arm was limp from holding up the gun as he interrogated Winchell, and his head was still spinning. He knew he needed medical attention. But not yet. First, he had to find someone to summon the police, so they could arrest Winchell, and then he had to deal with making the arrangements for Rebel's funeral.

He was stumbling toward the buggy when the buckskin horse suddenly threw his head up in alarm. Conrad started to turn, but before he could, something crashed into him from behind. He couldn't keep his feet. He went down hard, and Winchell landed on top of him. The belt Conrad had used to tie the man's wrists looped around his neck, and Conrad barely got a hand up in time to keep the belt from closing tightly on his neck. His fingers gave him a little room to breathe, but Winchell planted a knee in the small of his back and heaved harder and harder, cutting off Conrad's air. The wound in his side had stopped bleeding earlier, but now he felt the hot, wet flow once again.

"Threaten me, will you?" Winchell rasped. "Kill my brother, shove a gun in my face, lord it over me . . . You'll pay for that, you son of a bitch!"

Conrad had no idea how the man had gotten loose, and it didn't matter. The only important thing at the moment was that Winchell was on the brink of strangling him to death. Conrad fought back desperately, driving the elbow of his free arm behind him, into Winchell's belly. That bought him a little respite. Conrad shoved hard with his knees and arched up off the floor. Winchell toppled off him and the belt around Conrad's neck came loose.

He wanted to stop and drag air into his lungs, but there was no time for that. Winchell came at him, flailing punches. Conrad lowered his head and bulled forward, tackling Winchell. They rolled across the floor, winding up almost under the buggy horse. The animal danced away skittishly as Conrad grappled with the kidnapper. Hatred mixed with desperation allowed him to find the last bits of strength remaining in his body, and he grabbed Winchell's shirt and heaved the man against one of the buggy wheels.

Winchell's feet slipped out from under him, and he went down. Conrad reached up and slapped the horse's rump. The buckskin leaped forward, and since he was still hitched to the buggy, the vehicle lurched ahead as well.

The iron-tired wheel rolled right over Winchell's throat, cutting short the terrified scream that had started to well from the kidnapper's mouth.

Conrad looked away as the wheel crushed the man's throat. The horse backed up, but the damage was done. Winchell thrashed wildly as he tried to get air into his lungs. His face turned purple, then blue. Then his spasms subsided and he lay still, except for a few twitches as his muscles caught up to the fact that he was dead. For the second time tonight, Conrad had used the buggy as a weapon, and this time it had been lethal.

He reached up, caught hold of the buckskin's harness, and pulled himself to his feet. Winchell had choked to death, he thought as he looked down at the body, but not at the end of a rope. Conrad didn't care. One more of the kidnappers was dead; that was all that mattered.

And as he gazed at the corpse, an idea began to form in his mind, an offshoot of things that had happened earlier. The remaining kidnappers might worry that he would come after them and try to avenge his wife, but they wouldn't think that if they believed he was dead. In fact, they might even let their guard down a little if they thought he was no longer a threat.

For the first time since this terrible night began, a smile touched Conrad's lips. An agonized, haunted smile, to be sure, but still . . .

He pulled Winchell's body clear of the buggy and then unhitched the horse and turned it into its stall. He picked up the rope he had used to tie Winchell to the post and saw that it was badly frayed. Running his fingers over the back of the post, Conrad found the rough spot where Winchell must have worked the rope back and forth until it parted. Even before that, he had worked his hands free from the belt. That had been going on all the time he was questioning the man, Conrad thought, and he hadn't even noticed because he was so light-headed from loss of blood and had been concentrating on what Winchell was telling him.

Weaving, Conrad walked back into the house and went to his study. He barely had the strength to pull out some paper and a pen, and the letters he scratched onto the paper wavered and blurred. That was all right; he wanted people to think that he had written the letter in a state of great emotional distress. Actually, he was cold inside just then, numb to everything except the need for vengeance.

Leaving the letter in the middle of his desk where someone was sure to find it, he went upstairs and stepped into the bedroom. He had to say good-bye to Rebel. For the next several minutes, he spoke from the heart, telling her how much he loved her and how sorry he was for everything that had happened, then finished by saying, "I promise you that they'll all pay for what they did. Each and every one of them." He knew that if the situation were reversed, she would have devoted the rest of her life to hunting down his killers. He could do no less for her, and he knew she would understand.

"I love you," he whispered one last time, and as he turned away, he thought he heard a whisper saying the same thing, brushing across him like a warm breeze.

Although not an overly religious man, Conrad prayed for strength to finish this as he went downstairs. He had a small supply of cash for emergencies in the desk. He stuffed the bills under his shirt, on the side that wasn't soaked with blood. He planned to take only one revolver and the Winchester with him, so he left the spare Colt on the desk, holding down the letter that explained how he couldn't go on living after what had happened to Rebel.

Dawn wasn't far off now. The eastern sky was gray as he walked behind the house to the carriage house, taking with him a jug of kerosene he'd picked up in the kitchen. He went inside and saddled the buckskin, then led the horse out and tied the reins to an iron bench that sat beside the path between the house and the carriage house.

"Be back in a minute, big fella," he whispered as he patted the horse's shoulder. He went inside and began splashing the kerosene around the interior of the carriage house. The building was far enough away from any other structures that Conrad was confident a fire wouldn't spread beyond it. When he was finished, he tossed the empty jug aside and walked over to Jeff Winchell's body.

Kneeling next to the dead kidnapper, Conrad slipped the Colt from its holster and pressed the muzzle to Winchell's right temple, the same place a man would hold a gun if he intended to blow his own brains out. He pulled the trigger.

Then he stood, holstered the gun, and took a match from his pocket. He went to the doorway, rasped the match alight against the jamb, and tossed it into a puddle of kerosene, which went up with a fierce *whoosh!*

Conrad turned his back and walked away. Now that Rebel was gone, his only living relative was Frank Morgan. He would have to stop somewhere and send a wire to Claudius Turnbuckle, advising the lawyer that he was really still alive and swearing him to secrecy. Conrad wanted Turnbuckle to let Frank know that he wasn't dead; he didn't want his father grieving over him. Let Frank grieve over Rebel. That was enough.

Conrad untied the buckskin's reins and climbed into the saddle. He knew he was on his last legs, but he wanted to get well away from Carson City before he stopped to seek medical attention. Maybe he could find a sawbones in some small settlement up in the mountains.

He didn't look back as he rode away, but he could hear the flames crackling behind him, consuming the body that everyone would believe was his. He wouldn't be here for Rebel's funeral, and he deeply regretted that, but he could come back some day and visit her grave. He would tell her that he had avenged her death, that everyone responsible for what happened to her was gone.

Everyone but him.

He forced that bitter thought out of his mind. As of tonight, Conrad Browning was dead, too, another victim of whatever he had become. Yeah, Conrad was dead, he told himself as he swayed in the saddle. Long live . . . long live . . .

Well, he would work on that. Later.

CHAPTER 9

Conrad didn't know where he was or how long he had been unconscious. He didn't even recall passing out. The last thing he remembered was riding alongside a tree-lined, sun-dappled creek in the foothills somewhere north-west of Carson City. It was the middle of the day. He had been riding for hours after leaving the city and the burning carriage house behind him, floating in and out of awareness and trusting that the buckskin would continue following the trail.

He didn't remember when he had last eaten, but he had no appetite. As he rode along beside the stream, though, he was suddenly achingly thirsty. The sight of the water dancing and bubbling along the rocky creek bed prompted him to dis-mount. The merry chuckling of the stream drew him like a siren's song. Conrad dropped to his knees at the edge of the water and leaned forward, longing to plunge his head into the crisp, cold stream.

That was the last thing he remembered until this very mo-ment.

Slowly, he became aware of several things. He was lying

on something soft and comfortable, and when he moved his fingers, he felt a sheet under them. Another sheet covered him. Something tight around his midsection made it a little difficult to breathe. His eyes were closed, but he saw light through the lids. Light and shadow. Someone was moving around near him. He heard music, far enough away that it had to be coming from another room. Someone playing the piano?

And closer, someone humming softly, keeping time with the tune.

Conrad forced his eyes open. He winced against the glare of sunlight slanting in through a window with gauzy yellow curtains over it. A shape moved between him and the light. He squinted as his vision tried to adjust.

The other person in the room with him was a woman. A young woman, Conrad thought, although her back was to him and he couldn't see her face. The way she moved as she opened a drawer in a chest and placed some folded linen inside it seemed to indicate youth, though. So did the long, thick auburn hair that hung down her back. She was still humming along with the music as she closed the drawer and turned away from it, but the humming stopped abruptly as she saw him looking at her.

"You're awake," she said.

That seemed pretty obvious to Conrad. He started to say, *That's right,* but his voice didn't work very well. What came out of his mouth was more of an incoherent croak.

"Don't try to talk just yet," the woman said as she came toward the bed. "Let me get you some water."

He could tell for sure now that she was young, just as he had thought, and the part of his brain that still recognized such things realized that she was pretty, a fair-skinned, green-eyed redhead with a faint dusting of freckles across her nose.

She picked up a pitcher and a glass from a table beside the bed. She poured a little water in the glass, then leaned over the bed and slipped her other hand behind Conrad's head, lifting it and supporting it as she brought the glass to his lips.

"Not too much now," she said. "As weak as you are, you don't want to rush anything."

He was weak, all right. Every muscle in his body was limp. He didn't think he could get out of this bed if it was on fire.

He drank eagerly, but she gave him only a little water, not enough to ease the parched condition of his mouth. After a moment, she let him take another sip. Then she carefully lowered his head to the pillow.

"That's enough for now," she said. "I'm going to go tell my father that you're awake."

This time when he tried to speak, he could form words in a husky whisper, but he barely had enough strength to get them out. "Wh . . . where . . . am . . ."

"Where are you? A little settlement called Sawtooth."

"N-Nevada . . . ?"

She shook her head. "No, it's over the line in California. We're not far from Nevada, though."

Conrad managed to nod. With a sigh, he closed his eyes as the young woman hurried out of the room, but he didn't pass out again. So he had managed to ride across the border into California. That didn't surprise him all that much. He hadn't known where he was, and he had no specific destination in mind. He'd just wanted to get away from Carson City and the great tragedy he had left behind him.

Except he would never really leave it behind him, he realized as the image of Rebel's broken, wounded body filled his brain. He shuddered and felt like he ought to cry, but no tears came. Maybe the large amount of blood he'd lost had caused them to dry up.

Or maybe they were just frozen solid, like his heart.

The music in the other room had stopped while the young woman was giving him a drink, but now it started again. As

Conrad listened to it, he realized that it wasn't coming from a piano. The notes had a slightly tinny quality to them. He decided that they came from a Gramophone cylinder. It was somewhat unusual to find one of the newfangled machines in some backwater frontier settlement, he thought, but he had heard them before and was convinced that was what it was.

Footsteps approaching the bed made him open his eyes again. He saw a gray-haired man in a rumpled shirt and vest, with a string tie around his neck, looking down at him. "So you're awake," the man said.

Whoever these people were, they sure had a grasp of the obvious, Conrad thought. He nodded and husked, "I could . . . use some more water."

The man gestured to the young woman, who had followed him into the room. "Go ahead and give him some, Eve," he said. "It's not going to hurt him. Burning up with fever like he is, he can use all the fluid he can get."

"All right, Pa." The glass on the table beside the bed still held some water. She supported Conrad's head again and helped him drink. Greedily, he sucked down the rest of the water in the glass.

His voice was a little stronger when he spoke again. "You say I've got fever?"

The man nodded. "That's right. The wound in your side had festered by the time you got here. I cleaned it up the best I could, but the infection had spread. You're still trying to fight it off, and I'll be honest with you, there's not much I can do to help you, other than keeping you comfortable and seeing that you get some nourishment. Your own body will have to do the rest."

Conrad didn't think his body was capable of doing much of anything right now. The effort of lifting his head a couple of times to drink had exhausted him. He wasn't sure he could move again.

"Are you . . . a doctor?"

The man nodded. “That’s right, son. My name’s Patrick McNally.” He inclined his head toward the young woman. “My daughter Eve.”

“Thank you . . . for helping me,” Conrad said. “How long have I . . . been here?”

“Three days,” McNally replied.

That answer surprised Conrad. He had supposed it was later in the same day on which he had passed out beside the creek. He was lucky he hadn’t fallen into the stream and drowned.

“I’ve been . . . unconscious . . . for three days?”

“Oh, no,” Eve McNally said. “You’ve come to several times. But you were never as clearheaded then as you seem to be now. That’s a good sign, isn’t it, Pa?”

McNally nodded. “A very good sign. When a man’s mind starts working again, a lot of times his body follows along. You regained consciousness enough so that we could give you water and a little broth, but this is the first time you’ve talked. Coherently anyway.”

A sudden worry struck Conrad. He wanted everyone to think that he was dead, but from the sound of it he’d been babbling away to the McNallys.

“What did I . . . say?”

Eve smiled. “You must be a student of history. You kept talking about the War Between the States.”

“I . . . what?”

“You went on and on about the rebels.”

A pang like a knife struck deep in Conrad’s chest. He was glad they hadn’t realized what he was really talking about, but the reminder of his loss was painful.

“You mentioned the name Lasswell, too,” McNally added. “A lot of other names as well, but that was the one you talked about the most. Is that your name, son? Are you Lasswell?”

Conrad closed his eyes for a second and shook his head. “No,” he whispered. “I’m not Lasswell.”

"What is your name, then?"

He hesitated, then said the first thing he thought of. "It's Morgan."

"Is that your first name or your last name?"

"Just . . . Morgan."

Eve touched her father's sleeve. "Pa, you know it's not polite to pry too much into a man's business. Anyway, he needs more rest, doesn't he?"

"He does," McNally admitted with a nod. He leaned over the bed and rested his hand briefly on Conrad's forehead. "Still got fever."

"I'll get a cloth and bathe his face."

"That's a good idea. It'll help him rest."

Both of them went away. A few minutes later, Eve came back with a basin and a rag. She pulled up a chair beside the bed, dipped the rag in the water in the basin, wrung it out, then wiped the wet cloth over Conrad's face. It felt wonderfully cool and soothing. He closed his eyes and let himself concentrate on the sensations.

Somewhere along the way, the music had changed again. Conrad didn't recognize the song, but it held more than a hint of melancholy. "That music," he whispered without opening his eyes. "Where does it . . . come from?"

"Oh, that's just . . . my mother."

Conrad heard the slight hesitation in her answer, but he was too tired to ask her about it. And, he supposed, it was really none of his business.

He faded off to sleep without really being aware of it.

When he woke again, night had fallen. Or maybe it was several nights later, for all he knew. The sky outside the window, on the other side of the yellow curtains, was dark. The lamp on the table was turned so low that Conrad could barely see.

After looking around the room for a moment, though, he

spotted Eve McNally sitting in a rocking chair in the corner. Her head was tilted back and her eyes were closed. She seemed to be asleep. Conrad watched her for a moment, then cleared his throat.

The swiftness with which she came alert in the chair told him that she was accustomed to sitting vigil with sick people. She had probably handled that duty for her father's patients many times. She stood up, came over to the bed, and rested her hand on Conrad's forehead.

"You still have fever," she told him. "You're burning up."

He knew that from the chills that ran through him, causing him to shudder. All his senses seemed a little distorted as well. "Water," he whispered.

Eve gave him a drink. As she lowered his head to the pillow, she said, "I should go get my father."

"Is he . . . asleep?"

"That's right, but I know he'd want me to wake him."

Conrad found the strength to give a tiny shake of his head. "No need. He said . . . there was nothing he could do . . . but what you're . . . already doing."

"Well . . . I suppose that's true." She pulled the straight chair closer to the bed and reached for the basin and the rag.

"Is it . . . the same day?"

Eve smiled. "You mean the same as when you were awake before? Well, technically, no, I suppose, since it's after midnight. But I know what you mean, and yes, it's only been about ten hours since you were awake."

"Have I . . . babbled any . . . since then?"

She shook her head as she started wiping his face with the wet cloth. "No, you just moaned every now and then. You haven't been trying to fight the Civil War over again." She paused, then went on. "Your father must have told you about the war. You're not old enough to have fought in it yourself."

As a matter of fact, Frank Morgan had been in the war. Conrad knew he'd fought for the Confederacy. But Frank had never really talked much about the experience, and Conrad hadn't pressed him for details.

He didn't confirm or deny Eve's speculation. After a moment, she said, "My father worked in a Union field hospital. He wasn't old enough then to be a doctor, so he was an orderly. All the terrible things he saw there were what convinced him to study medicine. He said there had to be something better that doctors could do."

Conrad felt too bad to really care that much about what Eve was saying, but the sound of her voice was soothing, like the wet rag on his heated face. He wanted to keep her talking, so he murmured, "How did you wind up . . . in Sawtooth?"

"Father practiced for a long time in Sacramento. That's where I was born and raised. But then my mother . . . got sick, and he wanted to go someplace where he wouldn't have as many patients or be as busy, so he could devote more time to taking care of her. My uncle owns the Sawtooth general store, so he suggested that we move out here. He said the town needed a doctor."

"It's a . . . mining town?"

"Mining and ranching," Eve said with a nod. "It's a nice place to live. Nothing like Sacramento, of course."

Conrad thought he heard a trace of wistfulness in her voice. That wasn't surprising. A young, vibrant woman, raised in a bustling city, was bound to find a little frontier settlement like this somewhat confining.

He wondered what was wrong with Eve's mother. Nothing that would keep her from playing a Gramophone, obviously. But he didn't think it would be courteous to ask, and old habits died hard.

"What about you, Mr. Morgan?" Eve asked. "Where are you from?"

Conrad smiled. "Thought you told your pa . . . it wasn't polite to pry."

"Yes, but turnabout is fair play, as the old saying goes."

"Boston," he said. "I was . . . raised in Boston."

Her eyebrows went up. "Really? I thought you didn't sound like you'd been a Westerner all your life."

"I've only lived out here . . . a short time."

"I hate to admit it, but the way you were dressed when Bearpaw brought you in, I thought you might be a desperado of some sort. Those black clothes and the guns, I mean."

"Bearpaw?" Conrad repeated with a frown.

Eve took the cloth and dipped it in the basin again. "Oh, that's right, you don't know how you got here, do you?" she asked as she wrung it out. "Phillip Bearpaw found you lying next to Sawtooth Creek, unconscious. He thought you were dead at first, but when he saw that you were still alive and had been wounded, he put you on your horse and brought you here. I'm sure he saved your life."

"I suppose he did. Phillip Bearpaw, eh?"

"That's right. He's a Paiute, but an educated one. He and my father are friends."

Conrad nodded. "I reckon I'm his friend now, too, since he saved my life. I'll have to thank him. And you and your father, too."

"No thanks are necessary. Pa's business is helping people after all."

That might well be true, Conrad thought, but as much money as he had, he could well afford to repay his debt to Dr. Patrick McNally—

That thought came to a sudden halt as he remembered that it was Conrad Browning who had all that money, and he was no longer Conrad Browning. His name now was Morgan, and Morgan was a penniless drifter.

Well, maybe not penniless, he corrected himself. He had brought a few hundred dollars with him from the house in Carson City, although it was possible that money was now in the pockets of one Phillip Bearpaw—if the Paiute hadn't already spent it on liquor.

"You said Mr. Bearpaw brought my horse in, too?"

Eve nodded. "That's right. It's out back in our barn, along with Pa's buggy horse. I've been taking care of it. It seems like a fine horse."

"He is," Morgan agreed. "Seems like . . . you take care of a lot of things around here."

"I do my best. Pa has his hands full with . . . well, with his patients and all."

Morgan sensed that she meant something more than that. Something to do with her mother, more than likely, he guessed.

"I washed your shirt and got the blood out of it as best I could," she went on. "Luckily, you can't really see the stain on a black shirt like that. And I was able to mend the bullet hole."

"I'm obliged."

"It wasn't much trouble. Your gun and gunbelt are in one of the drawers, and your rifle is leaning in the corner. You won't need any weapons as long as you're here, of course. And if you're worried about the money that was inside your shirt, don't be. It's all safe."

Morgan didn't want to admit that he'd been wondering about that very thing a few moments earlier. He just nodded and said, "Thank you."

"You know," Eve said as she looked down at him, "even though you're still running a fever, I think you're better tonight. You're more alert, and you're making more sense. If that fever would just break, I think you'll have turned the corner."

"Maybe it will."

"I'm sure it will. It's just a matter of time."

Unfortunately, time was something he didn't have a lot of, Morgan thought.

There were still a dozen men out there he had to kill, and chances were, they'd be getting farther away with each day that passed.

CHAPTER 10

Sometime during the night, the man who had been Conrad Browning dozed off again. When Morgan woke up, he was drenched with sweat. It must have run off him in rivers, because the bedclothes underneath him were soaked. They were cold and clammy and uncomfortable. He was going to call out, but then he heard a shuffling sound, as if someone were coming across the room toward him. He pried his eyes open, expecting to see Eve McNally, but in the dim light coming from the lamp, a totally different vision in a long, white nightgown presented itself to him.

The woman who leaned over him was much older than Eve, although her face was relatively unlined. White hair flew out wildly around her head. She looked down at Morgan out of wide, staring eyes but didn't say anything. Startled by her, he instinctively tried to jerk away, but he was so weak and the bandages around his midsection were so tight that he could barely move. He succeeded in causing fresh jolts of pain to shoot through his wounded side, however.

"Eve!" he called. "Eve!"

He must have frightened the old woman. Her eyes widened even more for a second, and then her face twisted as she started to cry. She blubbered like a child. Big tears rolled down her cheeks.

With a rush of footsteps, Eve hurried into the room. "Mama!" she said as she took the old woman's arm. "Mama, you shouldn't be up wandering around. You could hurt yourself!"

Mrs. McNally tried to pull away. Eve hung on to her arm, gently but firmly. The old woman lifted her other arm and pointed at Morgan in the bed.

"Joseph!" she said. "Joseph's come back!"

Eve slipped an arm around her shoulders and turned her away from the bed. "Mama, you know that's not Joe," she said. "I wish it was, but it's not. Joe's not here right now."

"But . . . but he's coming back sometime, isn't he?" Mrs. McNally asked between sobs.

"Of course he is. We just have to wait for him."

"I . . . I sit and wait for him all day."

"That's right. You sit and wait and play your Gramophone."

The old woman sniffled and said, "Joseph loved those old songs."

"We'll play all of them for him when he comes back," Eve promised.

Dr. McNally appeared in the doorway, wearing a nightshirt and a worried expression. "Dear Lord," he muttered. "I thought she was sound asleep."

Eve steered her mother across the room. "Mama, you go with Pa, all right? You need to get some rest."

"Will Joseph be back in the morning?" Mrs. McNally asked.

"I don't know," Eve said. "We'll have to wait and see."

The doctor took hold of his wife's other arm and led her

from the room, glancing back at Eve as he did so and shaking his head sorrowfully. Eve sighed and eased the door closed behind them.

Then she turned to the bed and said, "I'm so sorry, Mr. Morgan. We try to keep a close eye on her. Sometimes at night, she gets up and roams around the house, looking for my brother."

"Joseph," Morgan guessed.

Eve nodded. "That's right. He . . . died a couple of years ago. That's what made my mother . . . like she is."

"I'm sorry," Morgan said, and meant it. These people had helped him, quite possibly saved his life. That meant that because of them, he was still alive to kill Clay Lasswell and the other men he intended to hunt down.

Eve sank down wearily on the straight-back chair near the bed. She wore a high-necked blue nightgown, and even though the part of Morgan that might have appreciated the fact she was an attractive young woman was numb with grief and loss, he still took note of it.

"For a while Pa hoped that she would come out of it," Eve said. "He thought that once the shock of losing Joe wore off, she would be herself again. But I guess it never has." She looked at Morgan with a sad smile, then suddenly exclaimed, "Oh, my Lord! Look at you. Your face is covered with sweat! Your fever's broken, hasn't it?"

"I reckon so," Morgan said in a husky voice.

"And here I was, babbling on." She stood up and leaned over the bed, cupping his face between her hands. "Yes, you're a lot cooler than you were. Thank God for that. You're going to be able to fight off the infection after all." She felt the bed around him. "These sheets are soaked. I'll need to change them. You'll need a fresh nightshirt, too."

Morgan felt a sudden and unexpected surge of embarrassment. "Don't you think you, uh, ought to get your father to do that?"

"Pa's going to have his hands full getting Mama settled

down again. I can take care of this." She straightened and put her hands on her hips. "I've been working as my father's nurse for quite a while, Mr. Morgan. I don't think I'll be seeing anything I haven't seen before."

In general, maybe, Morgan thought, but not specifically. But he didn't argue. He was too tired and weak for that. He lay back, closed his eyes, and let Eve do what she needed to do. When she was finished, he had to admit that it felt a lot better lying on dry sheets and wearing a clean, dry nightshirt.

"With any luck, you'll be ready for some real food again tomorrow," she said. "We won't rush it, though. It'll take quite a while for you to regain your strength after what you've been through."

"How long?" Morgan asked.

She frowned at him. "How long what? Until you're up and around?"

"Yeah."

"I imagine it'll be a couple of weeks before you're able to get out of bed at least."

Morgan shook his head. "A week," he said.

"Don't be silly. You won't be strong enough by then."

"Yes, I will be."

"My, aren't you the stubborn one? Is there somewhere you have to be?"

"Yes," Morgan said. "And something I have to do, the sooner the better."

"Yes, well, if you rush it, you'll be taking a chance on having a relapse. You had a really close call, Mr. Morgan. You don't want to die now just because you insisted on doing something foolish."

Morgan heaved a sigh. "No," he whispered. "I don't want to die now."

But after Lasswell and the others were dead, it wouldn't really matter, now would it?

* * *

Morgan slept late the next morning. When he woke up, a man he had never seen before was sitting in the rocking chair, puffing on a pipe and watching him.

Even though the stranger was sitting down, Morgan could tell that he was big. The man wore a black hat with a rounded crown. A couple of eagle feathers were stuck in the band. He wore a blue shirt over fringed buckskin leggings, as well as high-topped moccasins. As if Morgan needed anything else to guess the identity of his visitor, the coppery shade of the man's skin was a dead giveaway.

"You're Bearpaw," Morgan said. "The man who saved my life."

The man took the pipe out of his mouth and said, "Phillip Bearpaw. You can call me Phillip."

Morgan nodded. "I'm pleased to meet you. And I'm mighty obliged to you for helping me. I'd likely have died out there if not for you."

Bearpaw grunted. "No likely about it. You would have drowned. I heard the splash and came to see what had happened. You were facedown in Sawtooth Creek."

"You were that close? I didn't see anybody around."

"People only see me when I want to be seen," Bearpaw said. He chuckled. "In this case, I was just around the next bend in the creek, fishing and reading John Milton's *Paradise Lost*. Ever read it?"

Morgan shook his head. "I'm afraid not. My father's an avid reader, though. He may have."

Bearpaw clamped his teeth on the pipe stem and gave a solemn nod. "You should try it sometime. It'll give you a new understanding of the condition of man's immortal soul."

Morgan frowned a little and said, "I haven't run into many Paiutes, but you're not like any of them."

"Bearpaw heap sorry. Ugh."

Morgan laughed out loud, then felt a sudden twinge of

guilt. It had been less than a week since Rebel's murder. He shouldn't have ever laughed again, let alone this soon.

"Anyway, I'm grateful to you for saving my life, Phillip. I'd be glad to—"

Bearpaw frowned, and Morgan stopped short as he realized that the Paiute might take any offer of a reward as an insult. Instead, Morgan said, "If there's anything I can ever do for you, it would be my pleasure."

Bearpaw nodded. "I'll remember that." He took the pipe out of his mouth again. "How are you feeling this morning?"

"I reckon I'll live." Frank would have said something like that in a similar situation, and Morgan thought that if he was going to succeed in making everyone think that Conrad Browning was dead, he would have to stop talking like him.

"Eve said your fever broke last night. That's good."

"Where is Eve?"

"Getting some rest."

"I'm glad," Morgan said. "She deserves it. I have a feeling she's been spending most of her time watching over me for the past few days."

Bearpaw nodded. "That girl's good at being a nurse, all right. She'd make a good doctor, too, one of these days, if that's what she wanted to do. She's too busy taking care of her folks, though, and helping out with Patrick's patients. You hungry?"

The sudden shift took Morgan a little by surprise. "Actually, I am. Starving, now that I think about it."

"Another good sign." Bearpaw stood. "I'll go get you something to eat."

He left the room, and came back a few minutes later with a plate and a cup of coffee. The plate had a couple of biscuits smeared with molasses on it. Bearpaw set the cup and plate on the table beside the bed and helped Morgan sit up, propping the pillow behind him. Moving like that caused pain to shoot through Morgan's side, and the room spun around him a little from his head being upright again. Both of those reactions settled down quickly, however, and he grasped the cup eagerly when Bearpaw handed it to him.

"Careful," the Paiute cautioned. "The coffee's hot."

Morgan took a sip. He couldn't remember the last time he'd tasted anything as good as the strong, black brew. Then he took a bite of biscuit, savoring the sweetness of the molasses, and that was even better.

"Don't wolf it down," Bearpaw cautioned. "Your stomach may not be used to solid food yet."

Morgan took it slow and easy, but he ate every bite and drained the cup of every last drop of coffee. His stomach protested a little, but overall he felt strength flowing back into his body from the food.

Drowsiness began overwhelming him even before he finished eating. As he polished off the last of the meal, he yawned prodigiously. Bearpaw took the plate and cup and set them aside, then said, "You'd better get some more sleep."

"I really ought to . . ."

Morgan's voice trailed off as he realized there really wasn't anything he *could* do right now. His only mission in life was to bring justice to the men responsible for Rebel's death. He didn't care about business anymore; Conrad Browning's lawyers were more than capable of keeping the various enterprises humming along smoothly. He was realistic enough to know that he was in no shape to face any of his enemies right now. Recovering from his injury was really the only job he had at the moment.

"All right," he said as he allowed Bearpaw to help him stretch out again. "I guess a nap wouldn't hurt anything."

"Someone will be here when you wake up," the Paiute promised.

That was the beginning of a long week for the man who now called himself Morgan. He slept and ate and gradually grew stronger. When he was awake, Eve McNally was usually there to bring him food and drink and make sure he was comfortable, although from time to time Bearpaw or Dr. McNally spelled her in those duties. Sometimes, Bearpaw sat in the rocker and read from his battered copy of *Paradise Lost,* his deep, resonant voice a perfect match for the English poet's high-flown words. At other times, Morgan just lay there and listened to the Gramophone music coming from elsewhere in the house. As was often the case in frontier settlements, the doctor practiced medicine in the same house where he and his family lived. The bedroom where Morgan was recuperating was on the side of the house, close enough to the front so that occasionally he heard horses passing by on the road.

One afternoon when he was dozing, the sound of shots rang out somewhere not far away, coming in clearly through the open window. By now, Morgan was strong enough to sit up on his own, even though he hadn't tried to get out of bed and walk yet. When the gunshots startled him out of his half sleep, he bolted up in the bed and cried, "Rebel!"

No one else was in the room, but Eve hurried in a few seconds later. "Don't be alarmed, Mr. Morgan," she said as she came to the bedside. "There's no war. The rebels aren't attacking."

He fell back with a groan. She didn't understand, and he couldn't explain it to her without revealing who he really was. "Sorry," he said. "I didn't mean to yell."

"You must have been dreaming, and then when you heard those shots . . ." She made a face.

"Who was doing the shooting?"

Eve shook her head. "Just a couple of men riding by on the road. Troublemakers. They've been around town for the past few days. Trash like that drifts in from time to time and hangs around town for a while annoying everybody, but then they get bored and ride on. It's nothing to concern yourself with, Mr. Morgan."

Morgan wasn't concerned, now that he knew what was

going on. For a moment, though, the sound of the shots had carried him back to that awful night full of blood and death that had stolen everything from him, even his own identity.

But losing his identity was his own idea, he reminded himself. He had given it up in hopes that it would make it easier for him to deliver justice to Rebel's murderers. He didn't really mourn the loss of Conrad Browning, not for a second.

The next day, he said to Eve, "It's time for me to get up."

"I don't know about that," she replied with a frown. "You've only been here a week. I don't think you're strong enough yet."

"I'm getting up," Morgan said.

She held out a hand to stop him. "Let me at least go ask Pa what he thinks."

Morgan considered that, then nodded and leaned back against the pillow propped up behind him. "All right . . . but I'm getting up."

"You are the stubbornest man. Wait right there." She paused in the doorway to point a finger at him. "I mean it."

A couple of minutes later, Dr. McNally came in with Eve following him. "My daughter tells me you're ready to get up," the doctor said.

Morgan nodded. "It's time."

"You know, most people with a gunshot wound like that would be laid up for a couple of weeks, maybe even a month."

Most people couldn't have been shot like that and gone on to do everything he had afterward, Morgan thought. Thinking of his father, he said, "I come from good stock."

Eve crossed her arms and said, "I told him it was a bad idea."

McNally rubbed at his chin. "Oh, I don't know. He's young, and he was obviously in good health before he got shot. Plus he's been eating like a horse for days now."

That was true. Morgan's appetite had come back stronger than ever.

"I think it'll be all right to give it a try," McNally went on.

Morgan threw back the sheet and started to swing his legs out of the bed.

"Now, don't rush things," McNally said. He moved to Morgan's side and took hold of his right arm. "Eve, get his other arm. Take it slow and easy. Try standing up first, and see how that makes you feel."

With the two of them helping him, Morgan stood up. His legs were a little unsteady at first, but he was able to stiffen the muscles and straighten to his full height.

"I'm not dizzy," he said.

"That's a good sign," McNally agreed. "Take a step."

Morgan had a bad second or two when he thought his legs weren't going to obey his commands, but then he moved his right leg forward, braced himself, and took a step with the left. "I'm walking across the room," he said.

"Don't get in a hurry. Eve, hang on to him."

"I've got him," Eve said grimly.

With slow and methodical steps, Morgan walked across the room. Then he walked back to the bed, and by the time he got there, he was exhausted. As they helped him lie down, he sank gratefully onto the mattress.

"Guess I'm not . . . as strong as I thought I was," he said.

"Just stronger than most of the folks I've ever seen," McNally said with a smile. "You did just fine, Mr. Morgan. You'll be up and around in no time."

"I'll hold you to that," Morgan said.

By the time a couple more days had gone by, McNally's prediction was proven true. Morgan could stand up by himself, walk around the room, and even venture out into the rest of the house. The first time he walked into the family's parlor, with Eve at his side, he saw where the music had been coming from.

Mrs. McNally sat in a rocking chair with a lace doily over the back of it. Her hair was neatly combed and braided now, and she wore a simple housedress. Next to the rocking chair was a table, also covered with a doily, and on the table sat the Gramophone, a polished wooden box with a crank handle on the side, a turntable for the shellac discs on which the music was recorded, and a needle arm connected to a large, brass, trumpet-shaped horn that angled into the air. The turntable was revolving at the moment, and as the needle followed the grooves etched into the disc, the vibrations were transmitted to a diaphragm in the base of the horn that converted them to music. Morgan had seen several of the machines before and was fascinated by the process.

Mrs. McNally looked up at him and exclaimed, "Joseph!"

"No, Mama," Eve said quickly, going to the chair to keep her mother from getting up. "This isn't Joseph. It's one of Pa's patients, Mr. Morgan."

"Oh." The old woman sat back in the chair and seemed to lose interest in Morgan. The Gramophone needle reached the end of the grooves. She moved it aside, took the disc off the turntable, and replaced it with another one she took from a box that sat on the table next to the Gramophone. She turned the crank on the side of the machine until the turntable was spinning smoothly, then placed the needle at its outer edge. Music filled the room again.

"She sits there and does that all day?" Morgan said under his breath as Eve came back to his side.

She nodded. "All day," she replied, and he plainly heard the sorrow in her voice. "But when people lose something so precious to them as Joe was to her, they do whatever they have to in order to keep going."

Morgan understood that all too well. Mrs. McNally clung to the hope that someday her lost boy would return.

Morgan's hope was that he would live long enough to see all the bastards who'd murdered Rebel die.

CHAPTER 11

The next afternoon, Morgan was sitting in the parlor with Bearpaw and Mrs. McNally when Eve came hurrying in from outside. Morgan knew she had walked down to the general store owned by her uncle to pick up a few supplies. She clutched a bundle in her arms, but as Morgan looked at her, he could tell that something was wrong. Her face was flushed and she was breathing heavily, as if she'd been running.

And she looked scared, too. Morgan recognized the expression right away.

He stood up and said, "What is it?" As long as he didn't try to move too quickly, he could get around fairly well now.

"Nothing," Eve said, but the answer came too fast. Morgan knew she was lying, and so did Bearpaw.

"Something is wrong," the Paiute said. "You might as well tell us, Eve."

She glanced at her mother and then inclined her head toward the door that led into the kitchen. "Not here," she said.

Morgan realized that she didn't want to explain in front of

Mrs. McNally. He nodded and followed her into the kitchen, along with Bearpaw.

Eve set the package of supplies on the table and turned to Morgan and Bearpaw. "There's no reason for either of you to get involved in this," she said. "It's over and done with, and nobody was hurt. You don't have to worry about me."

"Why don't you tell us what happened and let us be the judge of that?" Bearpaw said.

Eve grimaced. "All right. I was in Uncle Ned's store when those two troublemakers came in."

"Garrity and Jessup?" Bearpaw asked.

She nodded. "That's right." With a glance at Morgan, she added, "Those are the two men who've been hanging around town the past week or so, the ones who fired those shots."

"I figured as much," Morgan said.

"Anyway, they came up to me and started . . . saying things. Making rude comments. You know, the way some men do around women."

"A man who doesn't treat women with respect isn't worthy of the name," Morgan snapped. Another lesson he had learned from Frank.

"I can't argue with that," Eve said. "I tried to ignore them, but they wouldn't go away. Then Uncle Ned heard what was going on and got the shotgun he keeps under the counter. He told them to get out of his store and not set foot in there again."

"Did they leave?" Morgan asked.

"They did, but not before cursing Uncle Ned and telling him that he'd be sorry. That scared me even more than the things they'd been saying to me. But when they were gone, he told me not to worry about it. He said they were just full of hot air and bluster."

Morgan wasn't so sure about that. He had seen hardcases like those two before. Sometimes they'd back down if one of their victims stood up to them, but sometimes challenging them just made them more dangerous. You had to be prepared for whichever way it went.

"I went ahead and got the supplies and started to walk home," Eve continued, "but then I saw Garrity and Jessup following me on their horses."

Morgan stiffened with anger. "Did they bother you again?"

She shook her head. "No. They stayed back. But just seeing them following me like that, walking their horses along the road and grinning . . . well, it frightened me. I started running."

Bearpaw said, "That's probably all they wanted, just to scare you and upset you."

"Then they succeeded," Eve said. "I'm scared and upset. But like I said starting out, it's over now, and no harm was done."

"Let's hope that's right," Morgan said.

He wasn't convinced that Garrity and Jessup would give up that easily, though.

Bearpaw lived in a shack on Sawtooth Creek, about a mile from the settlement. He had gone home that evening, while Morgan sat in the parlor with the McNallys. Mrs. McNally played the Gramophone and rocked slowly back and forth. Dr. McNally dozed in a chair, the copy of the Sawtooth *Gazette* he had been reading spread out in his lap. Eve worked on some mending, while Morgan tried to read the copy of *Paradise Lost* that Bearpaw had loaned him. The words that had flowed so well off the Paiute's tongue weren't nearly as easy to read. Morgan couldn't get too interested in the poem's story either. He had already been to hell, and he had no real hope of heaven.

A knock on the door made McNally start up from his nap, sputtering and fumbling with the newspaper. "A doctor never gets to take it easy for very long," he said as he got to his feet. He went to the door and opened it.

The man who stood there didn't appear to need a doctor. He seemed to be hale and hearty. The badge pinned to his vest told Morgan that he was a lawman of some sort.

"Hello, Zeke," McNally said. "Is somebody sick at the jail?"

"No, but you better come downtown with me right away, Doc," the man said. "Somebody jumped your brother Ned while he was lockin' up his store and beat the hell out of him." The lawman glanced at Eve and Mrs. McNally and added, "Beg your pardon for the language, ladies."

Eve had cried out softly as the lawman broke the news. She put a hand to her mouth for a second, then stood up and said angrily, "It was those two drifters, Garrity and Jessup! It had to be, Marshal."

The man frowned at her. "Why's that, Eve?"

"Because Uncle Ned had trouble with them this afternoon." In a few hurried words, she told him about the encounter in the store. "They warned him he'd be sorry for pointing that shotgun at them. They came back and attacked him, Marshal. It had to be them!"

"Well, I haven't had a chance to ask Ned about it yet. Maybe he got a good look at them."

Dr. McNally had grabbed his hat, coat, and medical bag. "I'm ready to go, Zeke," he said as he came back to the door. The two men hurried out.

Morgan felt the urge to go with them, but he knew there was nothing he could do to help. Also, even though he was a lot stronger than he had been, he wasn't up to a walk of several blocks.

Besides, he didn't think the two women ought to be left here alone.

"I'm sure your uncle will be all right," he told Eve. "Your pa's a mighty good doctor."

"Of course he is," Eve said. She clasped her hands together. "I'm just upset because this is all my fault."

Morgan stared at her. "How in the world do you figure

that?" he asked. "You're not the one who jumped your uncle and beat him."

"No, but it's because of me that it happened. Uncle Ned wouldn't be hurt now if he hadn't been defending me from those two . . ."

"Varmints is a good word," Morgan suggested.

"I was thinking of something a little stronger," Eve said with a glance toward her mother, who was still rocking and playing the Gramophone, seemingly oblivious to what was going on.

Morgan stood up and went over to Eve. "Look," he said, "you're not to blame for any of this. The ones responsible are the ones who actually did it. Nobody else."

"I know that, but still—"

"No buts about it," Morgan said. "That's the way it is. Blaming yourself for something when it's not your fault isn't going to do anybody any good. Blaming yourself when it *is* your fault doesn't do any good either, unless you try to set things right."

He knew that from bitter experience.

"I suppose you're right," Eve said with a sigh. "I wonder if I should go down to the store."

"Might be better to stay here, in case your mother needs you." That was true enough. Morgan didn't particularly want to be left alone with Mrs. McNally either.

Eve paced worriedly until her father returned an hour later. "Ned's going to be all right," he said as soon as he came in. "They gave him a good thrashing, and he's got a broken rib and a busted nose. But he'll recover. We took him home and patched him up. Your Aunt Charlene will look after him."

"Thank God," Eve said. "It was Garrity and Jessup, wasn't it?"

McNally shrugged. "Ned couldn't say for sure. It was dark, and they jumped him from behind. He said he never got a good look at their faces."

"You *know* it had to be them," Eve insisted.

"I'm sure it was," her father agreed, "but knowing something and being able to prove it are two different things. Still, Marshal Chambliss said he was going to run Garrity and Jessup out of town anyway. They've stirred up enough trouble in other ways to justify that."

"I hope he's careful," Eve said. "Those two are loco. Crazy mean. You can tell it by looking in their eyes." She crossed her arms and shuddered.

A short time after that, when one of the Gramophone discs reached its end, Mrs. McNally said, "I'm tired. I'm going to bed. I want to be rested in the morning, because I think that's when Joseph will be back."

"You never can tell," McNally said, humoring her as he and Eve always did. He went to her and took her arm as she stood up from the rocking chair. "Come along, dear. I think I'll turn in, too."

They went into their bedroom, leaving Morgan and Eve alone in the parlor. Eve sat on the divan, Morgan in an armchair near the fireplace that was cold at this time of year.

"Another week or two and you'll be able to ride again," Eve said. "What will you do then, Mr. Morgan?"

"I'll have to be moving on. I told you, I have places to go and things to do." He didn't offer any details, and Eve didn't press him for them.

In fact, she said, "I'm not sure I want to know what sort of things you have to do. I have a feeling that they're not very pleasant."

Morgan shrugged. He didn't expect to get any pleasure out of killing Lasswell and the other kidnappers. It was just something he had to do, as he'd told Eve.

She stood up and said, "I'll help you get ready for bed."

"I can take care of myself," Morgan said. "Things are different now. I'm not helpless anymore."

"I suppose you're right about that. I'll say good night, then—"

Eve stopped short and Morgan's head lifted as the sound of shots drifted in from the night. These were farther away than the ones he'd heard before, Morgan thought, but still close enough to be clearly audible.

"That came from downtown," Eve said as she stood up from the divan and turned anxiously toward the door.

Morgan got to his feet as well and said, "Hold on. You're not thinking about going down there, are you?"

"Someone could be hurt."

"Yeah, and maybe some drunk was just firing into the air, or somebody was blowing off steam like those two drifters yesterday. If anybody's wounded, I'm sure the marshal will come to fetch your father."

"Well . . . I suppose you're right. Still, I just hate to hear shots. I hope Mama didn't hear them. Things like that can really upset her."

The vehemence with which she spoke surprised Morgan a little, and he wondered if there was some special reason Eve didn't like the sound of gunshots.

"I'm not going to bed yet," she went on. "I'm going to wait up a little while and make sure nobody needs medical help before I turn in."

"I'll wait up with you," Morgan said.

"You need your rest—"

"I've been getting plenty of rest. Probably more than I ever have in my life."

That was true, Morgan thought, at least to a certain extent. Since he'd been an adult and been forced by his mother's death to take over the management of the Browning financial interests, he had worked long hours, and even when he was at home instead of the office, he spent too much time worrying about the business.

That was one thing about overpowering grief—it swept away all the other concerns and made a man realize just how petty so many of his worries really were. And getting shot and losing a lot of blood wore a man out to the point that he had no choice except to rest.

He and Eve sat down again. A couple of minutes of awkward silence went by, and then both of them sat up straighter as they heard horses outside.

"Someone *was* hurt," Eve began. "I'll fetch Pa—"

"Hey!" a man shouted outside. "There in the house? Are you there, Red?"

Eve's hand went to her mouth. Her face paled in shock. "That's one of them!" she said to Morgan in a half whisper. "Garrity or Jessup! That's what they were calling me in Uncle Ned's store this afternoon."

The two troublemakers showing up at the McNally house so soon after those gunshots didn't bode well, Morgan thought. He got to his feet and blew out the lamp, then told Eve, "Don't answer them."

A second man shouted, "We know you're in there, Red! Blowin' out the lamp ain't gonna do you no good! C'mon out here and talk to us!"

The door to the elder McNallys' room opened. The doctor said, "Eve, what's going on? What's all that yelling?"

"It's Garrity and Jessup, Pa," she told him. Morgan heard her moving across the room toward her father. Eve knew the furnishings so well she didn't need any light in order to be able to get around.

"I thought I heard some gunshots a few minutes ago," McNally said worriedly. "Thank God your mother is already sound asleep."

"There were shots downtown," Morgan said. "Then those troublemakers showed up here."

"Oh, Lord," McNally mumbled. "I'd better see if I can find my gun—"

Morgan snapped, "Don't do it. You'd just be giving them an excuse to shoot you."

From outside, one of the men shouted, "You'd damn well

better listen in there! We just shot your marshal! Ain't nobody comin' to help you! Send out that redheaded gal, or we'll torch the place!"

"Yeah!" the other hardcase agreed with glee in his voice. "We'll burn it to the ground!"

"What are we going to do?" Eve asked in a terrified whisper. "They've already murdered Marshal Chambliss!"

Morgan moved toward them in the darkness. He reached out, touched Eve's shoulder. She gasped and tried to pull away from him, but his fingers tightened on her.

"Listen to me," he said. "You and your father go back in your parents' room and stay there. I'll handle this."

"But you're wounded, son," McNally objected.

"I'm strong enough to deal with a couple of skunks like those two," Morgan declared. He hoped he was right about that. Otherwise, these people who had done so much to help him might be in bad trouble. He wasn't going to show them any doubts that he might have, though. Instead, he went on. "It'll be all right. You have my word on that."

Outside, one of the men howled, "Come on out, you redheaded bitch! If you're nice enough to us, maybe we'll let you and your folks live!"

"Why doesn't somebody come and help us?" Eve asked in an anguished voice.

"They gunned down the marshal," Morgan reminded her. "Before that, they attacked your uncle. Everybody in town probably knows that. They're scared. Garrity and Jessup have Sawtooth buffaloed."

McNally asked, "What are you going to do, son?"

A cold smile touched Morgan's lips in the darkness. "With any luck . . . buffalo them right back."

They had to be curious about what he meant by that, but he didn't explain as he hustled them into the bedroom and closed the door. Outside, the two hardcases were still yelling at the house, their words growing angrier and more obscene as they went on. Morgan went back into the room where he'd been recuperating, and felt around until he found the chest of drawers where Eve had put his gunbelt.

He opened the top drawer, reached inside, and felt the smooth walnut grips of the Colt. He pulled out the belt and buckled it around his waist. He still wore the tight bandages around his midsection, which caused him to move a little stiffly, but he was able to reach down far enough to tie the holster's thong around his leg. Then he opened the Colt's cylinder and explored the chambers to see if the gun was still loaded.

Morgan grimaced as he felt the empty chambers. Eve must have unloaded it. He reached into the open drawer again and brushed his hand over the bottom. Cartridges rolled across the wood. Morgan gathered them up and thumbed them into the Colt. He had carried out this task enough times so that he could do it without any light, although it would have been easier if he could see what he was doing.

Then he closed the cylinder, slid the revolver back into the holster, and took a deep breath.

"I'm warnin' you, girl!" one of the men outside shouted as Morgan reached the front door. "If you don't come out now, we're gonna start shootin'! We'll ventilate that house and everybody in it!"

Morgan opened the door, stepped out onto the porch, and said, "You're not going to do anything except either get the hell out of here—or die!"

CHAPTER 12

His sudden appearance on the porch took them by surprise. Both men fell silent. Morgan could feel them staring at him.

After a couple of heartbeats, one of the troublemakers demanded in a loud, angry voice, "Who the hell are you?"

"The man telling you to leave these people alone."

"Do you know who we are?" the other man asked. "We just killed this town's marshal!"

"Do you know who *I* am?" Morgan shot back. If he was going to run a bluff, he knew it had to be a good one. Without waiting for them to answer, he went on, "They call me Kid Morgan."

"Never heard of you," one of the men said with a sneer in his voice.

"I'll bet you've heard of Wolf Dunston," Morgan said, plucking the name out of his memory. "I killed him last year in Santa Fe. And what about Linc McSween?" he hurried on, not giving Garrity and Jessup too much time to think. "He drew on me in Tucson, and he's dead now. Hardy Williams? Mart Dooley? Ed Cambridge? All notches on my gun, boys."

Every one of those names was fictional. Morgan had gotten them from dime novels he had read about his father. To Frank's great chagrin, he was the hero of dozens of those gaudy pamphlets, all of them featuring lurid stories made up by scribblers who probably kept bottles of whiskey on their desks so they could take slugs of hooch whenever what they were writing started to make too much sense. Although the man who used to be Conrad Browning probably wouldn't have admitted it, he'd read quite a few of those dime novels, and some of the names of the vicious outlaws and gunslingers who appeared in them had stuck with him.

Garrity and Jessup looked at each other. "You ever hear of any of those fellas?" one of them asked the other.

"Yeah, I think I have. They're supposed to be bad hombres."

Morgan heard a trace of nervousness edging into their voices. He added, "The last two men I killed were the Winchell brothers, Jeff and Hank." That much was true.

"I *know* I've heard of them. Damn it, Jessup, what the hell've you got us into?"

"I don't care who he is!" Jessup said. "There's two of us and one o' him! We can take him! You want to have some fun with that pretty little redheaded gal or not?"

"There were two of the Winchell brothers, too," Garrity pointed out, "and he killed them."

"So he says. All we got is his word for that!"

"It's true," Morgan said calmly. "Turn around and ride away, or you can ask them about it yourselves, once you meet up with them in hell."

"You're a big damn talker."

That was true. Talk was Morgan's best weapon right now, because he had no idea whether or not he could beat these men to the draw. Considering that they outnumbered him two to one, it was mighty unlikely he could kill both of them before one of them got him.

But they had already gunned down Marshal Chambliss,

he reminded himself. They had nothing to lose. If he didn't stop them somehow, they would carry off Eve McNally and do God knows what to her. He couldn't allow that to happen. If he could bluff them, make them ride off, that was his best chance. He didn't like the idea of letting them get away after they'd killed the marshal, but once they were gone from here, the law could go after them and deal with them. That wasn't his job.

"I'm done talking," he said now. "Anything else I've got to say, I'll let my gun do it."

For a second, he thought it was going to work. He really did. But then Jessup yelled at his companion, "Kill him!" and grabbed at the gun on his hip.

In that moment, Morgan became a creature of pure instinct. Without thinking about what he was doing, he reached for his gun, closed his hand around the grips, lifted the weapon from its holster, tipped up the barrel, and fired. The double-action Colt .45 was in excellent shape. Its mechanism worked smoothly. Morgan continued pulling the trigger as he raised the gun, extending his arm. Flame lanced from the muzzle again and again as the Colt bucked against his hand. Garrity and Jessup fired back at him from their saddles. What felt like a gust of hot wind fanned his face. The roar of gunshots was so loud and overpowering, Morgan felt like he was trapped in the center of the world's worst thunderstorm.

Approximately three seconds after Morgan drew his gun, the hammer fell on an empty chamber. He had turned sideways without even realizing it, making himself a smaller target, and now he stood there on the porch with his right arm held out straight from the shoulder, the empty revolver in his hand.

Garrity and Jessup were dark, motionless shapes on the ground. Their horses stampeded off down the road, the empty stirrups flapping as they ran.

A pounding roar still filled Morgan's head. After a moment, he realized it was the sound of his own pulse. Slowly, he lowered the gun.

He had fired all the rounds in the Colt, he told himself. The smart thing to do now would be to reload, as quickly as possible, just in case one or both of the gunmen weren't dead. Did he have any bullets? Or was the rest of his ammunition in the house?

The gunbelt had loops on it so that cartridges could be carried in them, he remembered. That was why some people called a belt like this a shell belt. He reached around to his back and felt the loops. Sure enough, there were bullets in them, although at this moment he didn't recall putting them there. He pulled out five of them—the hammer always sits on an empty chamber, unless you're reloading in the middle of a fight, his father had taught him—and opened the cylinder to let the empties fall out. He thumbed the fresh rounds into the gun.

A dark figure loomed up beside him. Morgan snapped the cylinder closed and turned quickly. The figure stuck his arms into the air and said, "Whoa! Take it easy, Kid. It's just me, Phillip Bearpaw."

Morgan lowered the gun and heaved a sigh of relief. "Phillip," he said. "What are you doing here?"

"I heard there was trouble in town," the Paiute answered, "and came over in case Patrick needed anybody to stay with Lucinda. I figured he and Eve might be busy tending to the wounded."

"I think the only person who was shot was Marshal Chambliss." Morgan nodded toward Garrity and Jessup. "Except for those two."

"I saw the fight as I came up," Bearpaw said. "I heard some of what you told them, too, Kid. We'll have to talk about that . . . later."

Morgan frowned. What did Bearpaw mean by that?

"Right now," Bearpaw went on, "we'd better make sure

those two miscreants are dead. I'll go inside and get a lantern."

The front door opened then, and Dr. McNally stepped out. "No need for that, Phillip," he said. "I've got one right here."

The doctor scratched a match into life and lit the lantern. As its glow washed over the porch, he went on. "Are you all right, Mr. Morgan?"

"I reckon." Morgan hadn't really thought about it, but now as he took inventory of himself, he realized that he hadn't been hit. Some of the bullets fired by Garrity and Jessup had come close to him, but not close enough to do any damage.

"What about that wound in your side? Does it feel like it's opened up again?"

Morgan shook his head. "I really think I'm fine."

The three men walked down the steps. McNally held the lantern high so that its light spread out over the bodies of the two gunmen. Bearpaw was carrying an old Sharps rifle, Morgan saw. The Paiute kept the weapon trained on Garrity and Jessup as he used a toe to roll them onto their backs.

Morgan felt a twinge of surprise as he saw the dark stain on the chest of each man's shirt. From the looks of it, he had hit them dead center.

"They won't bother any more young women or gun down any more marshals," he said.

"No, they won't," Bearpaw agreed. "They've gone west of the divide."

Morgan holstered the Colt. As he did so, he heard a rush of footsteps behind him. He turned, and Eve threw her arms around him.

"Are you all right, Mr. Morgan?" she asked as she hugged him tightly—tightly enough, in fact, to make a tiny twinge of pain go through his side.

"I'm, uh, fine," Morgan said. He lifted a hand and awkwardly patted her on the back. "Just fine."

He had been a widower for a little less than two weeks. He had no business having an attractive young woman in his arms, even one who was just hugging him out of gratitude. He put his hands on Eve's shoulders and gently moved her away from him. In the lantern light, he thought he saw a hurt expression flicker across her face.

"Doc! Doc McNally!"

The shout drew everyone's attention. They turned to see half a dozen townsmen hurrying toward them. As the men panted up and stopped, one of them went on. "Zeke Chambliss is hurt, Doc. He needs your help."

"Garrity and Jessup said they killed him," McNally exclaimed.

The townsman shook his head. "No, Zeke ain't dead, but he's got a busted shoulder and a crease on his head that bled like a stuck pig. Can you come help him?"

"Of course I can. And thank God he's still alive," McNally added as he handed the lantern to Bearpaw. "Let me get my bag." As he started to turn toward the house, he paused and said to Morgan, "If you're sure you're all right . . . ?"

"I'm fine," Morgan said again. "Go tend to the marshal."

The townies were gawking at Garrity and Jessup. "Who killed these two?" one of the men asked.

Bearpaw nodded toward Morgan. "The Kid here did that. He's Kid Morgan, the famous gunfighter."

"Wait a minute—" Morgan began.

"Kid Morgan!" another of Sawtooth's citizens repeated. "I think I've heard of you. You're the fella Bearpaw found in the creek, all shot up."

"What happened?" a third man asked eagerly. "Did you get wounded in a gunfight, Kid?"

Morgan opened his mouth to explain that the whole thing was a pack of lies. His father was the famous gunfighter, not him. All he'd been doing was trying to scare off Garrity and Jessup so they'd leave the McNally family alone.

But then a realization struck him, and he stopped the explanation before he started it. He wanted everybody to believe that Conrad Browning was dead back in Carson City. The best way to insure that was to create a totally new identity for himself, and if these people wanted to believe some yarn he had made up that contained only a few shreds of truth, then so be it. Kid Morgan, he thought. It had a ring to it.

The townsmen were still clamoring for answers. Morgan hooked the thumb of his right hand in his gunbelt and raised his left hand to silence them.

"I don't talk too much about what's happened in the past," he said. "That's sort of a rule of mine."

"We understand," Bearpaw said. "Let's leave him alone, fellas. He needs some rest. He's still recuperating."

One of the men laughed and jerked a thumb at Garrity and Jessup. "Looks to me like he's healed up just fine."

Dr. McNally emerged from the house with his medical bag. "Let's go," he said briskly. "Phillip, would you mind staying here to keep an eye on things? Not that it's really necessary, I guess, with Kid Morgan staying with us."

"Yeah, I can stick around," the Paiute replied with a nod.

"And I'll send the undertaker back for those bodies," McNally added over his shoulder as he hurried away.

Morgan turned wearily toward the house. He still had a little difficulty believing that he had actually killed those two men in a gunfight. Their bullet-riddled bodies were vivid proof of it, though.

He stopped in surprise as he saw the way Eve was looking at him. Her eyes were wide and staring, and from the expression on her face, she had just seen something ugly wiggle out from under a rotten log.

"Eve," Morgan said with a frown. "What's wrong?"

"Is it true?" she asked. "Are you a gunfighter?"

"Well . . ." It seemed like it was a little late to start denying it now.

Eve turned and ran back into the house without another word.

Morgan turned to look at Bearpaw. "What the hell was that all about?"

Bearpaw tucked the Sharps under the same arm he was using to hold the lantern, then clapped his other hand on Morgan's shoulder. "Maybe I'll tell you about it," he said, "but not until you've told me what all that Kid Morgan bull-shit was about."

"So you knew I was making it all up?" Morgan asked a short time later as he and Bearpaw sat at the table in the kitchen of the McNally house. He kept his voice down so that they wouldn't be overheard.

"Yeah, I just played along until I got a chance to talk to you in private," Bearpaw said. "Your name may really be Morgan, for all I know, but like I told you, I got here in time to see that fracas, and I know you're not a professional gun-fighter. I don't recall ever hearing about any gunslinger named Kid Morgan either, no matter what the other folks around here have talked themselves into believing. The only Morgan I know of who's a fast gun is Frank Morgan."

Since Bearpaw already knew some of the truth, Morgan figured the only thing to do was to tell him the whole story. The Paiute was too smart to be taken in by lies.

"I come by the name honestly. Frank Morgan is my fa-ther."

Bearpaw's eyebrows rose. "I never knew The Drifter had a kid."

"The fewer people who know about it, the better. I realize I already owe you my life, but now I have to ask you for an-other favor. I have to ask you not to tell anybody about this."

"I can't make a promise like that without knowing what the truth is," Bearpaw replied with a shrug. "But if you're not out to hurt the McNallys or any of my other friends, I don't suppose I'd have any reason to break your confidence."

Morgan clasped his hands together on the table in front of him. "All right," he said. "It's like this."

He spent the next fifteen minutes telling Bearpaw everything that had happened, from that interrupted picnic on the hillside above Carson City, to riding away from his old life while the carriage house burned behind him with Jeff Winchell's body in it. Bearpaw listened in silence for the most part, breaking in only to ask an occasional question.

When Morgan was finished, Bearpaw frowned across the table at him and said, "You never considered telling the McNallys the truth? Don't you think you owe them that much?"

"I thought about it," Morgan replied with a curt nod, "but I decided not to."

"Because you don't want anything to interfere with this vengeance quest of yours?"

"Don't you think I deserve some vengeance?" Morgan shot back. "Those men took away everything that was precious to me. They ripped my heart out and left me a walking dead man."

Bearpaw grunted. "A little melodramatic, don't you think?"

"No," Morgan said quietly. "I don't think so at all. Anyway, the reason I decided not to tell the McNallys the truth is that I thought it would be safer for them that way."

"Safer?" Bearpaw shook his head. "I don't understand."

"Think about it," Morgan said. "Lasswell's orders were to make me think that Rebel would be safe if I paid the ransom, then kill her right in front of my eyes. His job was to make me suffer as much emotional pain as possible. Someone gave him those orders, and whoever it was has one hell of a grudge against Conrad Browning."

Bearpaw thought it over and then nodded slowly. "So if

word got around that Patrick and his family had helped Conrad Browning, then whoever was really behind the kidnapping might try to hurt them, too, just to get back at you."

"That's the way I figure it," Morgan said. "But nobody is going to connect Conrad to some obscure gunfighter called Kid Morgan. There'll be nothing to make anybody suspect that Conrad didn't die a suicide in that carriage house."

"You've got a tricky mind, Kid . . . but I think maybe you're right about this. It'll be safer for these folks if they don't know the truth."

"So I can count on you to keep my secret?"

Bearpaw nodded again. "Yes. I won't reveal what you just told me."

"Now," Morgan said, "you have to tell me how you knew I wasn't telling the truth out there. If I'm going to keep up this pose, it'll have to be as good as I can make it."

"First of all, tell me this. How do you intend to go about killing Lasswell and the other men who kidnapped your wife?"

Morgan frowned. "Well, I don't really know yet. I suppose I'll have to fight them . . ."

He stopped as Bearpaw solemnly shook his head.

"If you go up against anybody who's halfway decent with a gun, Kid, you'll just get yourself killed."

"I managed to take care of the Winchell brothers, and then Garrity and Jessup."

"You killed Hank Winchell by blowing his brains out when he was stunned," Bearpaw said with brutal honesty, "and it was a fluke that his brother fell so you could make the horse pull that buggy wheel over his neck. That was some fast thinking on your part, mind you, but you were still damned lucky."

"What about Garrity and Jessup? I outdrew them."

"Again, you were lucky. You came up against a couple of fellows who were slow as mud on the draw and terrible shots to boot. They thought they were dangerous gunmen, but they really weren't. I've seen some real gunfighters in my time, and those two weren't anywhere in the same league."

Morgan stared at the Paiute, dumbfounded. "But I hit them," he protested. "Shot them right out of the saddle."

"Yeah, each of them had one bullet wound to the chest. Not bad. But how many shots did you fire?"

Morgan recalled that he had emptied the Colt, and as he answered Bearpaw's question, he realized what the other man was talking about. "Five shots," he said. "Which means that three of them were clean misses."

"Sixty percent, to be mathematically precise. Hitting what you're shooting at less than half the time will get you killed in a hurry if you're going up against someone who's actually good with a gun. Maybe some of those kidnappers aren't any good. Maybe some of them aren't any better than Garrity and Jessup. But I'll bet some of them are. I *know* Clay Lasswell is a lot better. He'd kill you in the blink of an eye, Kid."

The bitter, sour taste of defeat and despair came up under Morgan's tongue. "Are you saying that I should just give up? That I shouldn't go after the men who are responsible for my wife's death?"

Bearpaw shook his head. "Not at all. I'm saying that you need to get a lot better before you face any of them."

"How am I going to do that?"

Bearpaw chuckled and leaned back in his chair. "Did you ever hear of a man called Preacher?"

"I don't think so," Morgan replied with a puzzled frown.

"How about Smoke Jensen?"

"Of course. He's as famous as Wild Bill Hickok or—"

"Or Frank Morgan?" Bearpaw finished. "It's a toss-up who was really faster in his prime, Smoke Jensen or your father, and I suppose it's a question that will never be settled. Preacher was an old mountain man who taught Smoke everything he knew about gunfighting. Smoke had the natural ability, the vision and reflexes he was born with, and Preacher provided him with the know-how to use them. I knew Preacher, and he told me once that as soon as he saw Smoke handle a gun, he knew that the boy had the potential to be one of the best, if not *the* best." Bearpaw folded his arms across his chest. "I saw you draw on Garrity and Jessup tonight, and I tell you, Kid, I saw something similar to what Preacher must have seen with Smoke. You were born with a talent for gun-handling. I don't think you'll ever be at quite the same level as Smoke—or your father—but with practice and a good teacher, you could be better than just about anybody else."

"How much practice are you talking about?"

Bearpaw shrugged. "Months? Years? The really good ones never stop practicing."

"I don't have that long," Morgan declared with a shake of his head. "That gang has already had time to scatter to the four winds. The more time that goes by, the harder it'll be to track them all down."

"Maybe so, but you still can't afford to rush it."

"Anyway, where can I find a teacher like you were talking about?"

The Paiute glared at him and said, "White man heap hurt Bearpaw's feelings. Ugh."

"Stop that," Morgan snapped. "Are you talking about teaching me yourself? You're not a gunfighter."

"No, but I told you, I knew Preacher, and that old man liked to talk. He could go on for hours about all the things he taught Smoke Jensen. Didn't your father ever mention any of the little tricks he'd learned over the years?"

"As a matter of fact, he did," Morgan admitted. "I reckon I learned a few things without even being aware of it."

"I reckon you did, too. And I can teach you more. Most of it is really just common sense, and the first thing is, you have to hit what you shoot at. Being fast on the draw isn't worth a plugged nickel if you can't hit anything. That's why you work on accuracy first. The speed is already there. You were born with it. You just have to develop it once you've mastered the accuracy."

"Why would you want to take the time and trouble to help me?" Morgan asked.

"I pulled you out of that creek, didn't I? The way some cultures see it, once you've saved a man's life, you're responsible for him from then on. Anyway, you helped Patrick and his family, and since they're my friends, I figure I owe you. What do you say? Take a little time anyway to get better before you go after those men."

Morgan thought it over for a long moment, then nodded. "I reckon I can wait a little while. But not too long. If I don't catch up to those men fairly soon, someone else is liable to kill them first."

"Would that be so bad?" Bearpaw asked. "If they're dead, does it matter whether or not they died by your hand?"

"Yes," Morgan said. "It does."

CHAPTER 13

Marshal Zeke Chambliss came to the McNally house the next morning. The lawman's left shoulder was heavily bandaged, and that arm was in a sling. He had a bandage around his head as well, but he seemed fairly strong.

"Kid, I just wanted to thank you for what you did last night," Chambliss said as he shook hands with Morgan in the McNallys' parlor. "For all you knew when you braced those two hellions, they really had killed me."

"I'm glad they didn't," Morgan said with a faint smile.

"Oh, so am I!" Chambliss laughed. "Anyway, another reason I'm here is to make you a proposition. How'd you like to pin on the marshal's badge while I'm healin' up?"

"Wait a minute, Zeke," Dr. McNally protested. "Mr. Morgan's not yet fully recuperated from his own wound."

Morgan glanced at the doctor. "I thought you said when you changed the bandage this morning that the bullet hole looked like it was almost completely healed."

"Almost," McNally insisted. "I said *almost* completely healed."

"You said that after today, you didn't think I'd need to wear the bandage anymore."

McNally frowned. "You shouldn't use a man's own words against him."

"It doesn't matter," Morgan said, smiling again. He turned back to Chambliss. "Sorry, Marshal. I appreciate the offer, but I have to say no. I'm not cut out to be a lawman."

Chambliss looked disappointed. "Are you sure, Kid? I'm thinking that with a famous gunfighter wearing the badge, troublemakers will steer clear of Sawtooth."

The citizens of Buckskin had thought the same thing when they offered the marshal's job to Frank Morgan. But it hadn't really turned out that way, and as a result, Frank's relatively brief stint as a star packer was over.

Morgan shook his head and told Chambliss, "I've got business of my own elsewhere as soon as I'm fit to ride. And that's not going to be very long. I reckon your deputies will have to hold down the fort until you're better."

"Well, we'll muddle through, I guess," Chambliss said with a sigh. "If you change your mind, though . . ."

"No chance," Morgan said.

"In that case . . ." Chambliss put out his hand again. "I'll wish you good luck and say so long."

Morgan had noticed that Eve wouldn't meet his gaze this morning. When the marshal was gone, he waited until he got a chance to speak to her alone, then asked, "What's bothering you, Eve? Did I do something wrong?"

She shook her head, but again she wouldn't look at him. "No, of course not," she said. "You saved us from those two gunmen. There's no telling what they might have done if not for you, Mr. Morgan."

"Well, that's what I thought, but you seem like you're angry with me."

"I don't know what you're talking about," she insisted. "Now, if you'll excuse me, I have work to do."

Morgan could only stare after her as she bustled off to prepare her father's examination room for the day's patients.

Giving up any attempt to figure her out as a bad job, he stepped out onto the porch instead and looked down the road toward downtown. Sawtooth really wasn't a very big settlement, but this was his first good look at it. The road entered the town from the south. Dr. McNally's house was on the edge of the settlement. To the north, the road turned into a broad main street with businesses lining it for several blocks. Most of the residences were on the cross streets. The town was located in a valley between a line of wooded hills to the east and a range of more rugged mountains to the west. The mines were located in those mountains, Morgan knew, while beyond the eastern hills sprawled a vast plain cut up into large ranches. Sawtooth Creek twisted out of the mountains about a mile south of the settlement and provided water for those ranches.

Farther to the east lay the mostly arid Humboldt Basin, which wasn't good for much of anything, but this area around Sawtooth was nice country. A man could be happy here, Morgan thought as he leaned on the porch railing, especially if he had a woman like Eve McNally at his side.

He stiffened in surprise. Where had *that* come from? He had no feelings for Eve other than gratitude. He wasn't capable of anything else right now, and suspected that he never would be again. But that didn't stop him from recognizing that some other young man would be lucky to have Eve fall in love with him.

He hoped like hell that she hadn't fallen for him.

He went back inside and got his hat. As he settled it on his head, he paused to look into the mirror on the wall of his room. He hadn't really paid that much attention to the way he looked since he'd been here. He'd lost weight; his face was thinner than it had been before. Not surprisingly, his eyes had a solemn, almost haunted look to them. Eve had shaved him several times, but he thought that maybe he ought to let his beard grow. That would be one more thing to separate him from the clean-shaven Conrad Browning.

"Where are you going?" Dr. McNally asked as Morgan walked through the front room.

"I just want to get out and move around a little. I don't mean to sound ungrateful, Doc, but I've been cooped up here for long enough that I'm getting restless."

McNally chuckled. "I'm not so old that I don't remember that feeling, son. Go right ahead. Just don't overexert yourself. Remember, you don't have all your strength back yet."

Morgan left the house and walked down the road into the main part of the settlement. As he did, people on the street saw him and gave him friendly nods. Some of them spoke to him, shaking his hand and welcoming him to Sawtooth. Word had gotten around about what had happened with Garrity and Jessup.

But for that very reason, other citizens seemed leery of him, looking at him from the corners of their eyes and even crossing the street so they wouldn't have to greet him. They believed he was a famous gunfighter, Morgan realized, so they were afraid of him.

He had never really thought about it before, but now he realized that was the sort of thing his father had been forced to put up with for years and years, being admired and feared at the same time.

The blood on a man's hands was mighty hard to wash off.

Morgan didn't spend much time in town. He had nothing in common with these people. When he walked back to the McNally house, he found Phillip Bearpaw sitting in one of the rocking chairs on the front porch.

"How are you feeling this morning?" the Paiute asked.

"All right, I suppose," Morgan answered with a shrug.

"No lingering effects from that shoot-out last night, either physical or . . . ?"

"If you're asking if I lost any sleep over killing those two, the answer is no. I gave them a chance to ride away. It was their decision to go for their guns. But I don't take any real pleasure in killing them, any more than I would have if they'd been a couple of rabid skunks. It was just something that needed doing."

Bearpaw nodded. "That's a good attitude to take, I guess. It's the sort of thing that Preacher or Smoke Jensen would say. Don't look for trouble, but don't back down from it when it finds you. Don't brood about it either."

"Waste of time, as far as I'm concerned," Morgan said.

Bearpaw pushed himself to his feet. "Feel like taking a ride?"

"Actually, I do. And I'll bet my horse is even more anxious to stretch his legs. Where are we going?"

"I thought we'd go out to my cabin," Bearpaw said. "It's far enough away from town that the sound of gunshots shouldn't bother anybody. I picked up a box of cartridges at Ned's store. There's no time like the present to get started on that practice."

They walked around to the back of the house. Bearpaw's horse, a shaggy Appaloosa, was tied up at the shed where Morgan's buckskin and Dr. McNally's buggy horse were housed. Morgan started to get his saddle out of the shed and put it on the buckskin, but Bearpaw stopped him.

"Let me do that," the Paiute suggested. "If Patrick were to see you doing something like lifting a saddle, he wouldn't be happy. And Eve would be positively livid that you were risking opening up that wound again."

Morgan hesitated, then agreed. He didn't like having somebody taking care of a chore he could handle himself—just another example of how much he had changed since he was a young man—but he knew Bearpaw was right.

Eve must have heard them talking, because she appeared at the back door, looked at them for a second as Bearpaw saddled Morgan's horse, then came outside and strode toward them.

"Where do you think you're going, Mr. Morgan?" she asked.

"Out to Phillip's cabin," Morgan said with a nod toward Bearpaw. "He asked me to visit." He didn't see any need to explain that he was going out there to practice his gun-handling.

"Did you ask my father if it was all right for you to ride?"

"Well . . . no, I didn't. But it's not far—"

"Only about a mile," Bearpaw put in. "And we'll take it slow and easy, won't we, Kid?"

Morgan saw something flicker in Eve's eyes when Bearpaw called him "Kid." She said, "If you tear that wound open, you'll lose all the progress you've made since you've been here."

Morgan nodded in acknowledgment of the warning. "I know that. That's why I intend to be mighty careful."

Eve blew her breath out in an exasperated fashion and said, "All right. Go ahead. Just don't say I didn't tell you it was a mistake."

Carefully, Morgan put his left foot up in the stirrup and swung up onto the buckskin's back. It felt good to settle into the saddle. He smiled down at Eve and said, "So far, so good. That didn't hurt at all."

She said, "Hmmph," and turned to walk back to the house.

Bearpaw mounted up as well, and the two men rode slowly away from the house, following the trail to the south. When they were well out of earshot of the house, Morgan said, "You know, you never did tell me why Eve's so upset with me. I tried to convince myself it was just my imagination, but that's obviously not the case."

"It's not really my place to talk about Eve's feelings," Bearpaw said. "You should ask her yourself."

"I did. She insists that everything's fine."

Bearpaw shrugged. "It's her decision what she does . . . or doesn't . . . want to tell you."

"Yeah, I reckon you're right," Morgan admitted.

That didn't mean he had to like it, though.

They reached Bearpaw's home, which was a sturdy-looking log cabin, a short time later. Morgan frowned at it, causing Bearpaw to chuckle and say, "What were you expecting, a wickiup or a tepee?"

"I thought the only Indians who lived in houses were the Cherokee and tribes like that back East."

"I happen to like an actual roof over my head, and a good solid wall between me and the cold wind in the winter. Plus I need better light to read by than a campfire. These eyes of mine aren't as young as they used to be."

"You're not like any other Indians I've run into."

"I never met a gunfighter with a Boston accent either," Bearpaw responded. "Although the accent does seem to be fading a little. You may never sound like a real Westerner, though."

"I'd better learn how to act like one."

"Amen to that." Bearpaw turned his horse. "Come on, let's go over by the creek."

They rode along the stream in which Morgan had almost drowned until they came to a large, open field bordered by a rocky bluff twenty feet high. Bearpaw reined in and told Morgan to dismount. They tied their horses to a couple of saplings. Then Bearpaw pointed to a large pine tree about twenty feet away, at the base of the bluff.

"Draw and fire at that tree," he said. "Hit it as many times as you can."

Morgan faced the pine and reached for the Colt, pulling the gun and bringing it up as fast as he could. He emptied all five rounds at the tree. The shots sounded like thunder as they rolled together, one after the other.

As Morgan lowered the gun, Bearpaw said, "Do you see any marks on the tree?"

Morgan gave a disappointed shake of his head. "No."

"How about on the bluff right behind it?"

A sigh came from Morgan as he counted. "I see five places where bullets hit the bluff. I missed with every shot."

"And that tree wasn't even shooting back at you like Garrity and Jessup were. You see, I told you you were lucky."

"You were right," Morgan admitted. "What did I do wrong?"

"You didn't listen. I told you to draw and fire at the tree. I didn't tell you to do it fast." The Paiute gestured toward the gun in Morgan's hand. "Reload and let's try it again."

This time Morgan understood what he was supposed to do. He holstered the revolver, faced the tree, and drew the gun again. He didn't waste any time about it, but he didn't rush either, as he lifted the gun and aimed at the pine. A second elapsed between each shot, giving him time to line his sights again.

This time chunks of bark and splinters flew in the air as the bullets chewed into the tree. Only one round missed and thudded into the bluff behind the pine.

"That's more like it," Bearpaw said.

"But way too slow to beat anybody to the draw," Morgan pointed out.

"What if the man you're facing is faster than you but a terrible shot? If he gets off three rounds and misses with all of them, and you just fire once but hit your target, you're going to win."

"And what happens if I face somebody who's faster than me and just as accurate?" Morgan wanted to know.

"Oh, well, in that case . . . you'll die."

Morgan laughed. He couldn't help it. As he shucked the empties from the Colt and started reloading, he said, "I'm going to try again."

"Of course you are. I didn't expect any less from you."

For the next hour, the two men stood beside the creek while Morgan practiced, pausing from time to time to let their ears have a break from the roar of gunshots. Morgan concentrated on hitting the tree, but even so, his draw became faster and smoother the more he repeated it. By the time Bearpaw said, "All right, I think we've burned enough powder for today," Morgan felt like he had made some real progress. It was just a start, of course, but still, he was pleased.

He was glad to stop, though, because his arm *was* getting tired. Drawing and firing a Colt .45 took quite a bit of effort. As Morgan reloaded for the final time, Bearpaw said, "Those arm muscles are probably going to be sore tomorrow."

"I can put up with it."

"How about your side? Any pain from that wound?"

"It aches," Morgan admitted. "Not so much that I can't stand it, though. I'm more interested in knowing how you thought I did today."

"Like I said, you have a considerable amount of natural talent. I didn't see anything today to make me doubt that."

"How long do you think it'll be before I'm ready to tackle Lasswell and the others?"

Bearpaw rubbed his chin and shook his head. "Now, that I couldn't tell you. You're not ready yet, I know that."

"You'll tell me when I am?"

"Sure, Kid."

Morgan wasn't sure whether to believe him. He wondered if Bearpaw would keep on insisting that he wasn't ready yet, in an effort to keep him safe. If that was the case, it wasn't going to work.

His shattered soul was still crying out for vengeance, and he could deny it for only so long before he had to answer its call.

Dr. McNally was waiting for them when they got back that afternoon. With a worried frown on his face, he said to Morgan, "I don't know if gallivanting around all over the country is good for you in your condition, son."

"We just rode down to Bearpaw's cabin," Morgan explained. "I told Eve that's where we were going."

"How's your side?"

"It's fine. A little achy, but not bad." Morgan didn't mention that his right arm ached a lot worse from the workout he had given it today.

"You youngsters are just too restless for your own good," McNally groused. "All I can do is tell you to be careful . . . and that I'm not going to be very happy with you if you undo all the hard work Eve and I have put in to get you healed up as much as you are."

"I'll be careful," Morgan promised.

Over the next two weeks, Morgan rode down to Bearpaw's cabin every day to practice with the Colt. Eve still seemed bothered by having him around, so he thought it was better to get away from the place for a while each day. Sometimes, Bearpaw came to the McNally house to get him; other times, Morgan just showed up at the Paiute's cabin, ready to do some shooting.

Nor was Bearpaw content just to help Morgan with the Colt. He wanted to see how the young man handled a Winchester, too. Morgan's sure eye and steady hand made him an excellent shot with the rifle.

One day, Bearpaw handed Morgan his old Sharps. "Try this buffalo gun," the Paiute suggested. "It's got a mighty powerful kick, though, so be ready for it."

"I can handle it," Morgan said confidently as he took the rifle.

"You're going to need something farther away than that tree to shoot at," Bearpaw mused. "A Sharps like that has quite a range. I've heard stories about how one of *your* people once used a Sharps to knock one of *my* people off his horse at distance of about a mile down in the Texas Panhandle." He squinted off across the field and then pointed. "See that white blaze on that pine yonder, where the bark's been peeled off? It's only about two hundred yards away, so I'm sure you can hit something that close."

"Close?" Morgan repeated. "I can barely see it, let alone hit it!"

"What happened to that confidence of yours? Give it a try. You might want to find a branch or something to rest the barrel on first, though. A Sharps is pretty heavy."

Morgan found a branch low enough on one of the pines to support the rifle barrel while he drew a bead on the distant target. He eared the Sharps's hammer back as Bearpaw instructed him, took a deep breath, lined up the sights, and gently squeezed the trigger.

What felt like the kick of a mule slammed against his shoulder and knocked him back a couple of steps.

"Son of a—" Morgan exclaimed.

Bearpaw grinned at him. "I told you it had a heck of a kick. I saw wood fly on that tree, though. Not bark. Wood."

"You mean I hit the mark?"

"You sure did."

Morgan felt a surge of pride. The marksmanship by itself meant nothing to him, but it was important because it might someday help him in his quest to avenge Rebel's death.

"A Winchester is a mighty fine gun," Bearpaw went on, "but when you need to make a long-range shot, nothing is better than a Sharps. You might want to think about getting one."

Morgan nodded. "I'll do that. Can I try again with this one?"

"If you think your shoulder can stand it. Here, let me show you how to reload . . ."

Late that afternoon, Morgan headed back to Sawtooth. The sun had dipped halfway behind the mountains to the west when he reached the McNally house. He started around the house, intending to put the buckskin in the shed and tend to the horse, when a rider moved out of some nearby trees and hailed him.

"Morgan? Kid Morgan?"

"That's right," Morgan replied as he reined in. A bad feeling caused his muscles to tense. "What can I do for you?"

"My name is Duke Garrity," the man said, "and that was my little brother you killed a couple of weeks ago. So you can fill your hand, you bastard, because you're about to die!"

CHAPTER 14

Garrity didn't give Morgan a chance to explain, or even to say a single word. He just reached for his gun, his hand moving to the Colt on his hip with blinding speed.

Morgan knew his life hung by a slender thread. Impulse cried out for him to rush his own draw, but the lessons hammered into his head by Phillip Bearpaw counteracted that urge. Even though he drew fast, he stayed under control. Garrity's gun roared first, but Morgan's blasted a fraction of a second behind it, the shots coming so close together that they were barely distinguishable from each other.

Garrity cried out and went backward out of the saddle to land on the ground with a heavy thud. His horse moved skittishly away from him.

Morgan threw his left leg over the buckskin's back and slid to the ground, coming to rest in a crouch with his gun still trained on Garrity. The man rolled onto his side and reached ahead of him, trying to get his hand on the Colt he had dropped when he toppled off his horse. His fingers fell short of the gun butt. He struggled mightily to reach the weapon, but failed. With a gasp, he slumped face-first onto the ground. His outstretched fingers twitched a time or two and then were still.

Morgan moved forward and kicked Garrity's gun well out of reach. At that moment, the rear door of the McNally house burst open and the doctor rushed out, brandishing a shotgun. "What in blazes happened?" he demanded. "What were those shots?"

"That hombre rode out of the trees and threw down on me," Morgan explained with a nod toward Garrity's body as he replaced the spent shell in the Colt. "He was the older brother of that fella Garrity I had to kill a couple of weeks ago."

Eve had followed her father out of the house. She stopped behind McNally and listened to Morgan's explanation. Morgan holstered the Colt and moved toward her, saying, "It's all right, I'm not hurt—"

Without warning, she threw herself at him and started pounding his chest with her fists as she screamed, "Go away, go away, go away! We don't want you here! We don't want your kind around!"

Morgan stood there stunned, not even trying to stop her from hitting him. He knew she had seemed upset ever since the night of that first gunfight, but never in a million years would he have expected a reaction like this from her.

After a moment, Eve's fury seemed to run out of steam. She stumbled back a step, raised her trembling hands and covered her face with them, then said in a broken voice between sobs, "Please, just . . . just go away . . ."

Inside the house, Gramophone music played. Morgan wasn't sure if Lucinda McNally had even heard the shots, lost as she was in her own world.

McNally lowered the shotgun and moved to his daughter's side. As he slid an arm around Eve's shoulders, he urged gently, "Come on back inside, honey. You don't need to be out here right now."

"M-make him go away, Pa," she said as she allowed him

to turn her toward the house. "Make him understand we don't want him here."

After everything that had happened, Morgan would have thought it impossible for his heart to harden any more, but at the sound of those anguished words, it did. He felt it happen, the chill stealing over him like frost creeping across the grass on a cold morning. "Eve, I'm sorry—" he began, but Dr. McNally looked back over his shoulder and shook his head, signaling for Morgan to leave it alone.

As father and daughter went inside, Morgan sighed heavily and caught up the reins of his horse. He collected the dead man's horse as well and led them both to the shed. By the time he got there, Marshal Zeke Chambliss arrived to check out the gunshots, accompanied by one of his deputies. The lawman still wore his left arm in a sling, but according to McNally, his injuries were healing well.

"What happened here, Kid?" Chambliss asked as he and his deputy stood there in the gathering dusk, looking down at the body of Duke Garrity.

Morgan explained about Garrity forcing the shoot-out. Chambliss scratched his jaw and said, "That name's familiar. I think I've seen a few reward dodgers on him come through. Didn't put the name together with that fella you ventilated a couple of weeks ago, though. This one's a bad hombre. Got three or four killin's to his credit, if I'm rememberin' right, as well as some holdups."

"He was fast," Morgan said with a nod. "Faster than his brother."

The deputy chuckled. "But not fast enough to beat Kid Morgan."

Morgan didn't say anything to that. The body on the ground spoke for itself.

But it didn't say as much as Eve had before her father took her in the house.

* * *

McNally came back out a short time later while Morgan was tending to the buckskin, giving the horse some grain and water. He had already unsaddled the buckskin and rubbed him down. Chambliss's deputy had led Duke Garrity's horse up the street to the livery stable, where it would be cared for for the time being. Garrity's body had been loaded into the back of the undertaker's wagon and carted off as well.

The doctor didn't have his shotgun with him this time. He stopped in front of the shed and jammed his hands in his pockets. Even in the gloom now that the sun was down, Morgan could see the unhappy expression on McNally's weathered face.

"I'm sorry about what happened, son," McNally said. "I've been afraid that Eve was building up to something like that ever since that other night."

"The night I saved her from those hardcases, you mean?" Morgan asked coolly.

"Don't think for a second that we're not grateful to you, Eve and me both. She was scared to death that night, especially when the shooting started, and she was mostly scared for you, I think. Her gratitude was real. But so was what she felt when she found out that you're a gunfighter."

"What's that got to do with anything?"

McNally sighed. "You know my son Joe died a couple of years ago."

"Of course," Morgan said with a nod. "I'm sorry."

McNally took one hand from his pocket and rubbed his jaw. "My wife's never recovered from what happened to that boy," he said. "You know that. You've seen it for yourself."

"I'm sorry about that, too," Morgan said quietly.

As if he hadn't heard, McNally went on. "But in her own way, Eve's never recovered either. She works so hard helping me and taking care of her mother so that she's too busy to think about what happened. That's what I believe anyway."

"I mean no offense, Doctor, but . . . what *did* happen?"

McNally looked squarely at Morgan and said, "My boy was killed in a fight. A gunfight."

A sort of understanding dawned inside Morgan. He couldn't have picked a worse identity to assume as far as Eve was concerned than that of a gunfighter. Having him around reminded her too much of what had happened to her brother.

McNally went on. "The thing of it is, Joe wasn't even involved in the trouble. He was just walking down the street in Sacramento when two men arguing about which one was faster on the draw decided to pull their guns and start blazing away at each other. They were both fatally wounded, but as one of them went down, he fired a final shot that missed the other man and hit Joe instead. Joe never had a chance to make it to cover when the shooting started. The bullet hit him in the head. Killed him instantly, I expect, like a bolt out of the blue."

"I'm sorry," Morgan said, and meant it. "No offense, Doctor, but that didn't have anything to do with me."

"Maybe not, but in Eve's mind, you're the same sort of man as the ones who killed her brother and caused her mother to be . . . the way she is. You can't expect her to forget. She sees too many reminders of what happened every day. Every time Lucinda plays that Gramophone . . ." McNally's voice trailed away as he shook his head. "I think she was afraid from the start that you'd turn out to be a gunman. It wasn't until she heard, though, that you're this notorious Kid Morgan that it got to be too much for her."

Morgan felt a strong impulse to tell the doctor that it was all a lie, that he wasn't really a gunfighter, just a businessman from back East named Conrad Browning. He wanted to tell Eve, so she would see that she was wrong about him.

And yet, doing that had the potential to ruin his plan. He wasn't even sure that it was true anymore either. Conrad Browning had killed the Winchell brothers, and maybe there had still been a little of Conrad left the night he faced down Garrity and Jessup.

But Conrad couldn't have killed Duke Garrity. The man was too slick with a gun for Conrad.

It had taken Kid Morgan to do that.

Knowing that it was too late for him to change the path he had chosen—or the path that had chosen him, some might say—he sighed and said, "I reckon the best thing for me to do is leave."

McNally shook his head. "I won't turn out an injured man. Never have and never will."

"I'm all right, Doctor," Morgan said. "Maybe not at full strength yet, and maybe that wound hasn't completely healed, but I'm strong enough to travel."

"You know that a wound like that would put most men flat on their backs for at least a month. It hasn't even been three weeks."

"Long enough is long enough," Morgan said.

"But where will you go?"

Morgan peered off into the night. "Like I've told you, I have business to tend to. I don't know exactly where it will take me."

"At least wait until morning to leave," the doctor urged. "You can't ride off at night like this."

Morgan thought it over for a moment and then nodded. "I reckon I can do that. I'll try to stay out of Eve's way while I'm still here. I don't want to upset her any more than I already have."

McNally put a hand on Morgan's shoulder and squeezed. "You couldn't have known."

But he should have, Morgan thought. After all, didn't gunfighters always carry death and suffering with them, wherever they roamed?

Eve had gone to her room when she went inside the house, so Morgan didn't see her again that night. He slept fitfully and woke early. He thought it might be a good idea to get the buckskin ready to ride and leave before Eve had a chance to see him and get upset again.

She was in the kitchen when he walked in, though, already preparing breakfast even though dawn was still at least an hour away. "Good morning," she said without looking around at him as she stood at the stove putting biscuit dough in a pan. "Pa tells me you're leaving today."

"That's right," Morgan said. "I reckon it's time."

Eve didn't try to talk him out of it. She just said, "I hope you'll take care of yourself."

"I'll try," he said. If she wanted to act like her outburst the night before hadn't happened, that was all right with him. He wasn't comfortable talking about anybody's feelings. He never had been, even before the tragedy that had befallen him.

"I'll pour you a cup of coffee."

She handed him the coffee, still not meeting his eyes, and he sat down at the table to sip on the steaming brew while she went on getting ready for breakfast. After a few moments of silence, she surprised him by asking, "Where will you go?"

"I don't know yet."

That was true. He would have to pick up the trail of Lasswell and the other kidnappers, but he wasn't quite sure how to go about that. Frank would have known, he thought, and that reminded him that he'd never had a chance to send a telegram to Claudius Turnbuckle in San Francisco explaining the situation. It was possible that Frank had heard by now about what happened in Carson City. He might believe that his son was dead. The Kid hated that idea, but there was nothing he could do about it right now. Sawtooth didn't have a telegraph office, and he didn't know how long it would be before he came across one.

Dr. McNally came bustling into the kitchen and stopped short, seemingly a little surprised to see Morgan there. But he smiled and nodded and said, "Good morning," then went over to kiss Eve on the cheek. "Your mother is still sleeping soundly," he told her.

"That's good," she said. She turned and brought a plate of biscuits and bacon over to the table and set it in front of Morgan. Now he understood. She was trying to get him out of here, and she thought that the sooner she fed him, the sooner he would be gone.

The back door opened while Morgan and the doctor were eating. Phillip Bearpaw came in, his Sharps rifle tucked under his arm. "Good morning, all," he said with a grin. He looked at Morgan. "You're up early, my friend."

"I'm riding on today," Morgan said.

A puzzled frown replaced Bearpaw's grin. "So soon? I thought you'd be around for a while yet."

"No, it's time for me to move on." Morgan glanced toward the stove. Eve stood there with her back toward him, but he could tell that she had stiffened as the conversation went on. He hoped Bearpaw wouldn't press him for details about why he was leaving now.

With the easy familiarity of a frequent visitor to the house, the Paiute poured himself a cup of coffee and then sat down at the table with Morgan and McNally. He looked like he was thinking something over, and after a moment, he said, "How would you like to have some company, Kid?"

Morgan's eyebrows rose. "You want to go with me?"

"I thought I might." Bearpaw looked over at McNally. "I'll miss you and your family, Patrick, but it's not like I'd be gone forever."

"What you do is your own business, Phillip. We'd miss you, of course, but you do whatever you think is best."

Bearpaw looked at Morgan again. "How about it, Kid?"

Morgan figured he had a pretty good idea what Bearpaw was thinking. Bearpaw thought Morgan wasn't ready to face down Lasswell and the others yet, and the Paiute was probably right about that. He wanted to keep on working with Morgan while they hunted down the kidnappers.

That wasn't a bad idea, Morgan realized. Bearpaw knew a lot more about surviving on the frontier than he did, although Morgan thought he was learning fairly rapidly. Bearpaw might be a big help in getting on the trail of his quarry, too, Morgan told himself. He wasn't even sure where to start, but he was willing to bet that Bearpaw would have some ideas.

One thing was certain, though. When it came time to face his enemies, Morgan intended to do that alone. He wasn't going to put Bearpaw in danger, although he had a hunch the Paiute would have been willing to back him up, no matter what the play.

They could hash that out later. For now, Morgan nodded and said, "I think I'd like that."

Eve turned and stalked out of the kitchen.

"Uh-oh," Bearpaw said when she was gone. "Why is she so upset this morning?"

"A man named Duke Garrity was waiting for me under the trees out back when I rode in yesterday evening," Morgan explained.

"Garrity," Bearpaw repeated. "Related to that fellow from a couple of weeks ago?"

"His brother."

"I take it there was gunplay?"

"They're supposed to bury Garrity this morning."

Bearpaw let out a tiny whistle. "How fast was he?"

"Pretty fast. Marshal Chambliss said that this Garrity had killed several men."

McNally said, "I guess all that practice down at Phillip's cabin paid off, Kid."

Morgan and Bearpaw both glanced at him in surprise.

"Did you think I didn't know what was going on?" McNally asked. "I have two eyes, and I'm pretty good at figuring things out. I know you've been working with the Kid here, Phillip. How's he doing?"

"Pretty good," Bearpaw admitted. "Good enough so that he's still alive this morning."

"But you don't think he's ready to go after the men he's looking for, especially not alone."

Bearpaw shrugged.

McNally looked at Morgan and asked, "Are they the ones who shot you, Kid?"

"They did a lot worse than that," Morgan said. "But it's not anything I want to go into right now."

"I suppose I can respect that." McNally picked up his coffee cup. "I think I can talk Eve into fixing up some supplies for the two of you."

"We'd appreciate that, Patrick," Bearpaw said. "Living off the fat of the land isn't as easy as it used to be when my ancestors roamed this land and game was abundant." He pushed his chair back and stood up. "I'll go get my gear together, and I'll be back here ready to ride in an hour, Kid. Will that be all right?"

"Sure," Morgan replied. "I'll be ready, too."

It wouldn't take him that long to get his things together, he thought. He didn't have all that much. The clothes on his back . . . and his guns.

Couldn't forget the guns.

CHAPTER 15

When it came time to ride away, Eve surprised Morgan by coming out of the house and putting her arms around him. "Take care of yourself, Mr. Morgan," she whispered as she hugged him. "I'd hate for anything bad to happen to you."

"Thanks, Eve. And thank you for everything you did to help me when I was hurt."

She stepped back and looked down at the ground. "I would have done as much for any of Pa's patients."

Somehow, Morgan didn't believe that. Even though a large part of him didn't want to admit it, he knew there had been a connection between the two of them that went beyond that of nurse and patient. If things had been different . . . if they had met at another place, in another time . . .

He shoved those thoughts out of his brain. They had no place in his head, not now, not ever.

Eve turned to Bearpaw and hugged him as well. "You be careful, too," she told him.

"Oh, I intend to," he said.

"And come back soon."

Dr. McNally and his wife came out of the house then, the doctor keeping a hand protectively on her arm. He offered his other hand to Morgan and said, "We'll be keeping you in our thoughts and prayers, son."

"Thanks," Morgan said. "I reckon I can use them."

Mrs. McNally turned to her husband and said, "Patrick, why is Joseph leaving again? He just got here."

McNally opened his mouth to try to explain, but before he could say anything, an impulse seized Morgan. He gave in to it, taking his hat off and stepping forward to put his arms around Mrs. McNally. He gave her a firm but gentle hug.

"Don't worry about me, Ma," he told her. "I'll be back soon."

She patted him on the back and then reached up to stroke his sandy hair, which had gotten fairly long. "Oh, Joseph," she said. "I'll miss you so much. I'll be waiting for you. I love you."

"I love you, too, Ma," Morgan said. "Listen, I really don't want you worrying about me, and you don't need to sit around all day waiting for me to get back either. You just go on living. Take care of Pa and Eve and yourself, and I'll see you when I see you. All right?"

She looked up him and nodded as he used his thumb to wipe a tear away from her cheek. "All right," she whispered. "If you say so, Joseph, that's what I'll do."

He nodded, stepped back, and put his hat on his head again. "So long, everybody," he said as he took hold of the buckskin's reins.

"Good-bye, son," McNally said. Tears glistened in his eyes, and in Eve's as well. "Take care. You, too, Phillip."

Morgan and Bearpaw swung up into their saddles. As they started to turn their horses, Eve stepped forward and put a hand on Morgan's leg. She looked up at him and mouthed the words *Thank you.*

Morgan nodded, then heeled the buckskin into a trot as

Eve stepped back. Bearpaw rode alongside him on the Appaloosa.

"That was a mighty nice thing you did back there for those folks," the Paiute said quietly.

"No more than they deserve," Morgan said. "It was the least I could do."

The two men fell silent as they rode south, putting the settlement of Sawtooth behind them.

"How do you plan to go about finding the men you're looking for, Kid?" Bearpaw asked later.

"To tell you the truth, I don't know," Morgan answered. "I was hoping maybe you'd have some ideas."

Bearpaw chuckled. "It's a good thing I decided to come along, then. You said you know all their names?"

"That's right. At least, I know the names they were going by a few weeks ago. Some of them may be aliases."

"This may come as a shock to you, since you know me only as the educated, cultured individual that I am now, but there was a time when I . . . how shall I put this? . . . rode some rather dark and lonely trails."

Morgan looked over at him. "You were an outlaw?"

"Not to the extent that Lasswell and those others are," Bearpaw said quickly, "but from time to time some cattle or horses that didn't exactly belong to me may have wound up in my possession. As a result of that time in my life, I know some of the places frequented by men who have heard the owl hoot. We can start by asking questions in those places. We'll have to be careful how we go about it, though. We don't want it getting back to the men we're looking for that someone is on their trail."

That made sense to Morgan. He said, "I'll follow your lead."

"In that case, I think we should circle around Carson City—"

"That sounds good to me," Morgan declared. He had no desire to go back there now.

"And head for a trading post I know down where Nevada, Arizona, and Utah all come together," Bearpaw went on. "Chances are, the members of that gang scattered after what happened, rather than staying together. From what you told me, they didn't all ride together on a regular basis, but came together more for that one job."

It caused a twinge deep in the Kid's chest to hear Bearpaw talking so matter-of-factly about Rebel's kidnapping and murder, but he told himself that was how it had to be, not only for the Paiute, but for him, too. He couldn't allow his emotions to rule him. He remembered a quote—from Shakespeare, he thought—about revenge being a dish best served cold. Giving in to hot-blooded rage could lead a man into making mistakes, and those mistakes could doom his entire effort.

"Some of them may have headed for Mexico," Bearpaw continued, "and they may have stopped at this place I'm thinking of. If we can track down two or three of them, then maybe they can tell us where to find some of the others."

"So you're saying we'll find them two or three at a time."

Bearpaw nodded. "That's our best bet. The whole bunch isn't going to fall right into your lap, Kid."

"The problem will be convincing the ones we find to tell us where to look for the others."

"Oh, there are ways to persuade people to talk," Bearpaw said with a slight smile. "I *am* one of those dirty, torturin' redskins after all."

"At least you didn't say 'heap' and 'ugh' this time," the Kid said.

As Bearpaw suggested, they circled wide around Carson City and then headed southeast, keeping the various mountain ranges that ran along the Nevada-California border on their right hand. The Great Basin, broken up by a few smaller ranges, stretched out seemingly endlessly to their left. A couple of days into the journey, Morgan gazed off to the west and knew that the mining town of Buckskin lay in that direction. Conrad and Rebel had visited there while Frank Morgan was the marshal, and the Crown Royal Mine, owned by the Browning Mining Syndicate, still operated near Buckskin, although its output of silver ore had begun to dwindle, the Kid recalled.

All that was part of another life, he told himself. Someone else's life. He turned his face forward again and concentrated on the trail in front of them.

Bearpaw called a halt early enough every day so that they could make camp and then Morgan could practice with his gun for an hour or so. The muscles in his arm had strengthened so that drawing and firing the Colt time and time again no longer wore them out. Whenever he washed up in the icy streams that flowed down out of the mountains, he checked the scar on his side where the bullet had torn out a large chuck of flesh. The red, puckered scar was ugly, but the wound had healed cleanly and Morgan wasn't worried about it anymore. From time to time it ached a little, but nothing he couldn't handle. Dr. McNally had done a fine job of patching him up.

Dr. McNally—and Eve . . .

It took the two men a week to reach their destination, a week of riding through starkly beautiful, sparsely populated country. Arid desert flats alternated with rugged, rocky mountain ranges and the occasional grassy valley. Isolated ranches were located in those valleys. Bearpaw pointed out some of the squat, adobe ranch houses and said, "Twenty years ago, those folks had to worry all the time about my people, or the Apaches, attacking them and wiping them out. Now the Paiutes have made peace, and so have most of the Apaches. The few bands of renegades left have moved across the border into Mexico and never raid this far north anymore."

"Is that why you don't mind us having a campfire at night?" Morgan asked.

Bearpaw grinned. "That's right. It wasn't all that long ago that being so careless might have cost you your life. Now, the main thing the ranchers have to worry about is their herds dying of thirst. Same thing is true for pilgrims like us. You need to know where the water holes are when you travel through this part of the country. Lucky for you that I'm with you. I know where every spring and *tinaja* is."

"Is there anything you *don't* know?"

"Not much," Bearpaw said with a chuckle. "And if I don't know it, I'll probably lie about it and say that I do."

"Now you tell me how unreliable you are," the Kid drawled.

Late in the afternoon, they came to a place where two trails crossed. Several buildings were scattered around, the largest of them built partially of logs and partially of adobe. A long porch ran along the front of it. A latticework roof attached to the *vigas* that stuck out from the top of the wall provided shade. About a dozen horses were tied up at the hitch rails in front of the place. The other buildings were adobe shacks.

"A German named Immelmann owns the trading post," Bearpaw told Morgan as they approached. "The Mormons used to have a settlement here, thirty or forty years ago. They abandoned it, though, and all the buildings fell into ruin except that one. It was in pretty bad shape but still standing when Immelmann came along and fixed it up. A few wagon trains used to pass through, but those days are pretty well over. Now, most of his business comes from men like the ones we're looking for."

"Outlaws," the Kid said.

"Men who don't want to be found, for one reason or another," Bearpaw amended. "After Immelmann got the trading post going, a few other folks moved in. They've started calling the place Las Vegas. Some of them think there'll be a regular town here one of these days, but I doubt it. If Immelmann ever dies or leaves, the settlement will dry up and blow away without the trading post to keep it going."

Morgan didn't doubt that. He didn't care about the future of Las Vegas, though, only the present. And then only if he and Bearpaw could find a clue here to the men they were looking for.

They added their horses to the ones tied up at the hitch rails and stepped onto the porch. The shade, even though it was dappled by the sun coming through the latticework, was a welcome relief from the heat. Morgan thought it was considerably cooler on the porch.

The front and back doors stood open to let any stray breezes blow through the building. As Morgan and Bearpaw headed for the front door, three men started through it from inside, on their way out. The men stopped short as they saw the two newcomers.

"Oh, no, Injun," one of them said with a frown. "You ain't goin' in there where white men are drinkin' and playin' cards."

The Paiute looked down at the porch and shuffled his high-topped moccasins. "Bearpaw heap sorry," he said. "Injun mighty thirsty. Not cause trouble."

Morgan forced himself not to stare in disgust.

One of the other men laughed, a loud, braying hee-haw like a donkey. "The last thing a filthy ol' redskin like you needs is firewater," he said. "You get a snootful, and you'll be liable to go on the warpath. Where'll us poor white folks be then? You'll probably scalp us all!"

"Let us by," the Kid said tightly. "We're not looking for trouble."

"You travelin' with this redskin, mister? Hell, ain't you got no pride? Ain't you got nothin' better to do than hang around with a savage?"

Morgan thought about all the times Bearpaw had quoted Milton and Shakespeare and John Donne from memory, for hours at a time. Chances were, the Paiute knew more poetry by heart than these three louts had read in their entire lives combined.

But that wasn't the sort of thing that Kid Morgan would be thinking about, he reminded himself. Instead, he forced himself to stoop to their level and said, "Don't worry, I'll keep an eye on the redskin. I won't let him get into the whiskey, just regular water."

The first man sneered. "That's fine as far as it goes," he said, "but what about the stink?"

"Oh, I reckon he can put up with it. It ought to fade after a while anyway, since you fellas are leaving."

Bearpaw turned his head slowly and stared at Morgan. He didn't know where the words had come from. Just a few seconds earlier, he'd been trying to be conciliatory. But then something had snapped inside him. He was tired of everybody's bullshit. Right now, Phillip Bearpaw was the best friend he had in the world, and he was damned if he was going to let these sorry-ass bastards talk about his friend that way.

The three men weren't quite as quick on the uptake as Bearpaw was, but it didn't take them long. Then Donkey-Laugh looked offended and exclaimed, "Hey! He's sayin' we stink worse'n an Injun!"

"You got a big mouth, boy," the first man growled.

"You can try to close it if you want," the Kid said.

Something about his stance and his cold, level eyes must have warned the men. None of them made a move toward a gun. But their leader, who was also the biggest of the trio, said, "You need a lesson in manners, you son of a bitch. And I'm just the man to give it to you!"

He lunged across the porch and swung a malletlike fist at Morgan's head. Morgan leaned quickly to the side. As long as he didn't let any punches land where that bullet had wounded him, he ought to be all right, he thought.

Of course, that might be easier said than done.

Morgan's swift move made the man's fist miss. As the man stumbled forward, off balance, Morgan grabbed the front of his shirt and heaved as he turned. The man flew past him and sailed off the shallow porch to go rolling and sprawling in the dust.

Donkey-Laugh yelled, "Hey!" again, and charged. Morgan met the attack by stepping in and hooking a hard left into the man's belly. Donkey-Laugh doubled over as the blow knocked the wind out of him. Morgan grabbed the back of his head and shoved it down as he brought his knee up. His knee cracked into Donkey-Laugh's jaw with stunning force. As the man crumpled, Morgan thought that he wouldn't be letting loose with any more of those braying laughs for a while. Not with a jaw that was either broken or was going to be pretty sore for a while at the very least.

That left the third man, but as Morgan turned toward him, he saw that the hombre was backing away, hands held at shoulder level. "Take it easy, amigo," the man said. "This ain't my fight. I *know* I stink."

A few feet away on the porch, Bearpaw suddenly lifted his Sharps and eared back the hammer. The Kid looked over his shoulder and saw that the first man was on his feet again. His hair and face and clothes were covered with dust. So was the hand that had started to reach for the gun on his hip. That hand had frozen where it was as the man found himself staring down the ominously large barrel of the Sharps.

"They say that discretion is the better part of valor, my friend," Bearpaw told the man. "You'd be wise to heed that advice."

The man gaped at Bearpaw and muttered, "What the hell—?" But he slowly moved his hand away from the butt of his gun.

"I told you we weren't looking for trouble," Morgan said. "We still aren't. Why don't the two of you pick up your friend and head on to wherever you were going when you stopped to harass us?"

"You're lucky you got that redskin watchin' your back, mister," the man said between clenched teeth. "I was about to blow a hole in you."

"You were about to try," Bearpaw said. "The way I see it, I just saved your life. You were going to draw on Kid Morgan."

"Who?" the man asked with a frown.

"Kid Morgan. The man who killed the Winchell brothers and Duke Garrity, not to mention Garrity's little brother and a man called Jessup."

The third man put in, "Say, I've heard of Duke Garrity. He's pretty fast."

"*Was* pretty fast," Bearpaw said.

Morgan saw the nervousness in the first man's eyes now. He was starting to realize that he might have bitten off too big a chunk. He said, "Look, Kid, let's just let this go, all right?"

Morgan nodded. "Fine by me."

The man motioned to his companion, and together they picked up the half-conscious Donkey-Laugh, who started moaning as they helped him to his horse. They got him into the saddle and then mounted up themselves. Flanking their injured pard, they rode off. Morgan and Bearpaw watched them go, just to make sure the men didn't try to double back and attack again.

"Was ist los?" a voice asked from the doorway. "What is this disturbance on my porch?"

They turned to see a tall, gaunt man with a white spade beard. The man's lean, leathery face creased in a sudden grin as he recognized the Paiute.

"Bearpaw!" the man said. "I thought I recognized your voice. If you had started spouting poetry, I would have known for sure, *ja*."

Bearpaw shook hands with the man. "It's good to see you, too, you old Dutchman. How long has it been, seven or eight years?"

"*Ja,* about that. Who is your friend?"

"This is Kid Morgan."

The Kid nodded and said, *"Guten tag, Herr Immelmann."*

"Ah! Sprechen sie Deutche?"

"Ein bischen." Morgan hoped he hadn't make a mistake by greeting the trading post's proprietor in German. He had about exhausted his knowledge of the language when he told Immelmann he spoke only a little.

"Come in, come in," Immelmann urged them. He waved a knobby-knuckled hand toward the retreating riders. "Don't worry about those three. They think they are tough hombres, but they are really not."

As Morgan and Bearpaw stepped into the trading post, which was even cooler because of its thick log and adobe walls, the German went on. "You must tell me what brings you here, if such a question will not be considered impolite."

"Things got a mite too warm for us where we were," Bearpaw said.

Immelmann let out a laugh that sounded too hearty for his slender frame. "The more things change, the more they stay the same, eh, my old friend? Come. The beer is cold, and the women are warm! What more does a man need?"

Vengeance, the Kid thought. That was what some men needed—and he was one of them.

CHAPTER 16

Immelmann had a Mexican bartender working for him, so he was able to sit with Morgan and Bearpaw at a round table in the rear of the big, shadowy barroom half of the trading post instead of serving drinks. The three men nursed beers. Bearpaw explained to Morgan that while he couldn't handle whiskey, like most of his people, beer never muddled his mind.

Immelmann said, "The two of you are on the dodge, *ja*?"

"Not exactly," Bearpaw said. "I don't think there's any paper out on us, so you don't have to worry about any bounty hunters showing up to look for us. We'd just as soon avoid any lawmen, though, just to be on the safe side."

Immelmann nodded sagely. "I understand."

The German thought he understood anyway, the Kid mused. That was what he and Bearpaw wanted.

"Have you seen an hombre called Moss pass through these parts lately?" Bearpaw went on. "We heard that he's looking for some men for some sort of job up north, and we thought we might try to sign on with him." He and Morgan had decided that would be a safe enough question to ask, grounded in truth as it was.

"Do you mean Vernon Moss?"

"Yeah, that's the fellow's name."

Immelmann gave a solemn shake of his head. "Have you not heard what happened to him?"

Bearpaw leaned forward and frowned. "No. He get shot up or something?"

"Both of his legs were crushed in an accident. I'm told that he will be a cripple for the rest of his life. And this happened while he and some other men were engaged in that job you mentioned."

"You mean we missed out on it?"

A sour look appeared on Immelmann's face. "You would not have wanted to be part of this, old friend. It was an ugly business, nothing like rustling or stealing horses. Moss and some other men kidnapped a woman."

"Yeah, that's pretty bad," Bearpaw agreed with a frown.

"It was even worse than you think. They held the woman for ransom, and even though her husband agreed to pay, they murdered the poor woman. Clay Lasswell shot her. Do you know Lasswell?"

Bearpaw shook his head. Across the table, the Kid kept a stony expression on his face, but it took an effort to do so.

"I thought better of Lasswell, to tell you the truth," Immelmann went on. "He has killed a number of men in gunfights, true, and I suspect he may have shot a few in the back from long range while he was working as a regulator in Wyoming, but I would not have guessed that he would murder a woman in cold blood." The German shrugged. "I suppose as we get older and more tired, the list of things we will not do for money grows shorter and shorter."

"How do you know about all this?" Bearpaw asked, still making it sound like he was only idly curious.

"Julio Esquivel told me. You remember Julio? Short, has a beard, very good with a knife?"

Bearpaw shook his head. "I don't think I ever crossed his trail. How about you, Kid?"

Morgan said, "Nope."

"Well, Julio stopped here about a week ago with a couple of other men." Immelmann made a face. "One of them was a huge brute who treated one of my whores badly. I was glad to see them go."

Morgan remembered Esquivel and the big, moonfaced man from that awful night. Trying not to sound like he was prying, he said, "Who was the third man?"

"I hadn't seen him before," Immelmann replied. "They called him Buck."

So Buck, Esquivel, and the giant Carlson had ridden through here a week earlier, Morgan thought. "Did they say where they were headed?" he asked.

Immelmann frowned, and the Kid saw a warning look flash in Bearpaw's dark eyes. He might have pushed things too far by asking such a direct question. But after a moment, Immelmann shrugged and said, "I might not tell you if that monster had not been so rough on my girl, but when they left here they were riding east. I heard them say something about going over to the Four Corners."

"We're obliged," Bearpaw said.

Immelmann looked back and forth between Morgan and the Paiute. "You had no interest in joining up with Moss," he said coldly. "You're looking for him and the men who rode with him on that job." It wasn't a question.

"You and I go way back, my friend," Bearpaw said. "I know we can count on your discretion."

An angry frown creased the German's face. "You used me," he accused. "Played on our friendship."

"As you said, those men did a very bad thing."

"I think perhaps you two are the bounty hunters now. Such men are not welcome at my trading post."

"I'm sorry you feel that way," Bearpaw said. "But you won't mention to anybody that we were here, will you?"

"Doing so might make people suspect that I gave you information." Immelmann shook his head. "I will say nothing. But I would ask you to leave now."

Morgan and Bearpaw started to get to their feet. The Paiute paused and said, "For what it's worth, if anything, there's no blood money involved in this hunt, Immelmann. It's personal."

Immelmann held up a hand to stop him. "I don't wish to hear any more. Anyway, any time you set out to kill a man, it is personal, is it not? How can it be any other way when you end another life and risk your own?"

Those were good questions, the Kid thought. And from the way Immelmann was looking at him, he wondered just what the German was thinking. He would have been willing to bet, though, that Immelmann didn't suspect Conrad Browning and Kid Morgan were one and the same.

As he and Bearpaw rode away from the trading post a short time later, Morgan said, "Sorry. I know I pushed too hard back there. I should have waited and let you get the information out of him at your own pace."

Bearpaw shrugged. "It doesn't matter. We found out what we needed to know."

"Can we trust Immelmann?"

"Maybe. I think so. Like he said, he can't tell anybody too much about us without making them suspect that he gave us the information we were looking for. He's better off keeping his mouth shut, like he would have if it had been anybody but me asking. He owed me a favor."

"And now I've ruined your friendship," Morgan said.

"Justice doesn't come without a price."

"This isn't your fight, you know," Morgan pointed out.

"Maybe it didn't start out that way, but after everything you did for the McNallys, and the way you stood up for me back there . . . I reckon I've made it my fight."

The silence that fell between them was awkward, since

neither was the sort of man who expressed emotion all that well. After a moment, the Kid asked, "What's the Four Corners?"

"That's the area where Colorado, Utah, Arizona, and New Mexico all come together," Bearpaw explained. "Some of the most desolate country you'll ever see. A fitting place for the sort of men we're after."

"We've got some ground to make up on them," Morgan said. He heeled the buckskin into a faster pace. Bearpaw followed suit, and soon the trading post at Las Vegas fell far behind them.

Bearpaw had warned him that they were heading into some desolate country, and the Paiute was right. As they traveled almost due east over the next two weeks, Morgan didn't know if they were in northern Arizona or southern Utah. It didn't really matter, Bearpaw told him. One was just about as ugly as the other, seemingly never-ending wastelands of dirt, sand, and rock.

And yet, here and there, great beauty existed, such as the long line of sandstone cliffs that shone a brilliant red in the sunlight. Wherever there was water, grass grew and flowers bloomed, little bits of paradise among the desert vastness.

They came to such an oasis a couple of days after leaving Las Vegas, late in the afternoon, and when Morgan spotted an adobe ranch house among the cottonwoods that lined a small creek, he was eager to ride on in and find out if the people who lived on this isolated ranch had seen the three men they were after.

But as Morgan lifted the reins and started to heel his horse into a trot, Bearpaw reached over and grasped his arm, stopping him.

"Take it easy, Kid," the Paiute said. "Something's wrong up there."

"What do you mean?" Morgan asked. Then, black shapes circling in the sky caught his eye, and he answered his own question. "Damn. Those are vultures, aren't they?"

"Buzzards, some call them. They're bad news, regardless of the name." Bearpaw pulled the Sharps from the saddle sheath in which he carried it. "Unlimber that Winchester of yours. We'll ride in, but we're going to be careful about it. Slow and easy."

That was how they approached the ranch, which consisted of the adobe house, an adobe barn, and a pole corral. The lack of a bunkhouse meant the family that owned this place worked it by themselves, without any hired hands. As Morgan and Bearpaw drew closer, Morgan expected at least one dog to come running out to meet them, barking its head off. Instead, an ominous silence hung over the sun-blasted day.

"If this was twenty years ago, I'd say the Apaches had been here," Bearpaw commented quietly. "I don't know what to make of this yet, except that it can't be good."

The Kid spotted a dark shape on the ground inside the corral. "Is that a horse?" he asked, pointing toward it with the barrel of his Winchester.

"No. Milk cow more than likely. Another bad sign."

"Bad how?"

"A ranch with a milk cow usually has kids around."

Morgan grimaced. He hadn't thought about that.

"In the door," Bearpaw said a moment later. His voice was bleak, and his face looked like it had been carved out of the same red sandstone that had formed those cliffs a ways back.

Morgan saw the body lying across the threshold of the ranch house door. The man lay facedown, a large black stain on the back of his shirt. That stain shifted as the riders drew closer, and Morgan heard a loud buzzing. His stomach twisted in sick revulsion.

"Those are flies," he said.

Bearpaw nodded. "That's right. They're after the blood on the man's shirt. Quite a feast in surroundings like this."

Another huddled shape between the house and the barn turned out to be the family dog. Morgan averted his eyes, thinking of the big cur that traveled with his father. He had a soft spot for dogs. He was sure he and Rebel would have gotten one sooner or later if . . .

Those thoughts wouldn't do any good. The Kid forced them out of his head.

"So we've got a man, a dog, and a cow," he said. "Where is everyone else?"

"Inside, I suppose." Bearpaw reined to a stop in front of the house. "Why don't you stay out here, Kid? I'll have a look."

"I can stand it," Morgan said. "I've already seen things worse than any man should ever have to see."

"I reckon you have, at that." Bearpaw nodded. "Come on then, if you're sure."

Both men dismounted. Holding their rifles at the ready, in the unlikely event that any danger still lurked inside the ranch house, they stepped over the body of the man who sprawled in the doorway. Morgan felt sick as he heard flies buzzing again. It took a moment for his eyes to adjust to the dimness inside the house—and when they did, he almost wished that they hadn't.

A boy about eight or nine lay on his back on the hard-packed dirt floor, staring sightlessly at the ceiling. He appeared to have been shot once in the chest. The flies had been at him, too.

"Baby's over there in the crib," Bearpaw said, gesturing toward a little bed on curved rockers that sat in one corner. "Don't look, Kid."

This time, Morgan followed the advice.

"Where's the mother?" he asked.

Bearpaw nodded toward a doorway leading into another

room. "She'll be in there, I expect. That's probably the bedroom."

He was right on both counts. The woman lay naked on the bed, arms and legs spraddled out, the sheets around her head dark with dried blood from the hideous wound in her neck. Someone had cut her throat almost from ear to ear.

"Esquivel," the Kid breathed.

"That Mexican traveling with Buck and Carlson?"

The Kid nodded. "He cut Edwin Sinclair's throat the same way."

"I don't see how you could really tell something like that . . . but I'm sure you're right, Kid." Bearpaw stepped over to the bed and reached down to close the woman's staring eyes. She had been pretty, with short blond hair that curled around her head, until her face had frozen in lines of agony and torment.

Bearpaw jerked his head toward the door. "I need some air," he said.

Morgan knew just what the Paiute meant. He felt the same way himself.

They had to step over the dead man in the doorway again, but once they did, they were back in the open air, with the hot sun blazing down on them. Morgan said, "Maybe we can find a shovel around the place so we can bury them."

"Yeah, there's bound to be one. Come on. I want to have a look at the corral."

The Paiute opened the gate and walked into the corral, circling around the bloated corpse of the milk cow. Numerous piles of horse droppings littered the dirt. Bearpaw hunkered on his heels next to one of them and studied it for a moment, then reached out to pick up some of it and rub it between his fingers.

"This isn't more than seven or eight hours old," he said.

Morgan frowned. "What does that mean?"

Bearpaw wiped his fingers in the dirt. "Those three left Immelmann's place a week ahead of us. Even given the fact that we've been pushing our horses and they probably weren't, they must have arrived here at least four days ago. And they only left this morning."

Morgan frowned and shook his head. "I still don't understand."

Squinting against the sun, Bearpaw nodded toward the ranch house. "The man's been dead the longest. Three days, maybe a little more. But the woman and the kids were killed a lot later, maybe as late as this morning."

Morgan tried to figure out what that meant, and as he did so, he felt horror growing inside him. "Those three we're after rode in here, and the family offered them food and water for their horses and a place to spend the night," he said, putting it together in his head.

Bearpaw nodded. "Yes, and then they got up the next morning and murdered the man. They probably told the woman that if she cooperated, they would spare her and the children. She had to know that was unlikely, but she had to try to save her kids any way she could. So she went along with whatever they wanted."

Morgan took a deep breath. He knew that Buck, Carlson, and Esquivel must have put that poor woman through three days of hell and degradation. They had assaulted her in her own bed, again and again, with her children in the next room and her husband's body lying only yards away.

And then, when the bastards were tired of their sport, they had brutally slaughtered all three members of the family and ridden away as if the whole blood-drenched business meant nothing. Morgan hoped that Esquivel had slashed the woman's throat before her children were killed, so she hadn't had to hear the shots that ended their lives. But he wouldn't have wanted to bet on that. That would have been one last bit of torture to end things on.

He forced his mind on to more practical considerations. "They're less than a day ahead of us now. If we push on, we'll be able to catch up to them tomorrow for sure."

Bearpaw came out of the corral and closed the gate behind him, even though there was nothing alive in there to get out. "What about the burying?" he asked. "If we do that, it's going to be so late that we can't push on today. We'll have to wait until tomorrow."

A part of Morgan didn't want to accept any delay. The need for vengeance was stronger than ever in him after seeing what had happened here.

But he knew he couldn't just ride away and leave these poor people as bait for the scavengers. "We'll bury them," he said, "and we'll let our horses get a little extra rest while we're doing it. Because tomorrow . . . we're going to ride like hell."

CHAPTER 17

The sun was almost down before Morgan and Bearpaw finished scraping out a single grave big enough for all four members of the luckless ranching family as well as their dog. There was nothing they could do about the milk cow. The two men took turns using a shovel they found in the barn. Digging in the hard ground was backbreaking work, and neither of them could do it for very long at a time.

Morgan's side ached quite a bit when they were finished. If Eve had been here, she would have warned him that he was going to damage that wound and undo all the healing he'd done, he thought with a grim smile. He knew he was all right, though. He just needed some rest.

He would get that rest once they were done. They wrapped each body in a blanket and carried them out one by one, placing them carefully in the grave. Then they had to cover it up again. The sun was down and night was falling when they finished that. A dwindling arc of orange and gold light remained in the western sky as Morgan tamped down the mounded dirt.

They had removed their hats and shirts while they were

digging. Now, the breeze that sprang up felt chilly on the Kid's bare, sweat-soaked torso. He drew his shirt back on and buttoned it up, then stood by the grave with his hat in his hand. Bearpaw followed suit.

"Are you saying the words, Kid, or am I?" the Paiute asked.

"You know better words than I do, Phillip. You should do it."

Bearpaw nodded solemnly. He held his black hat over his heart and intoned, "The Lord is my shepherd; I shall not want." Morgan closed his eyes, and as he listened to Bearpaw continue with the Twenty-third Psalm, he wondered what words had been said at Rebel's funeral.

It didn't matter, he told himself. No words on earth held the power to bring her back, and that was all he would have wanted if he had been there.

"Surely goodness and mercy shall follow me all the days of my life," Bearpaw concluded, "and I will dwell in the house of the Lord forever. Amen."

"Amen," Morgan murmured. He hoped these poor people were at peace now.

They didn't spend the night at the ranch. It was too ghost-haunted a place for that. Instead, they followed the creek for about half a mile and found a good place to camp. That night, as they sat by the embers of the fire, Bearpaw asked, "What are we going to do when we catch up to them, Kid? That's going to be tomorrow or the next day, if I don't miss my guess."

"*We're* not going to do anything," Morgan said. "I'm going to confront them."

"I don't know if you're ready for that," Bearpaw replied with a frown.

"You've been working with me for more than a month now. How much more do you have to teach me?"

"A man never stops learning, not if he's wise," Bearpaw said.

"But you know I'm fast," Morgan insisted. "And I hit nearly everything I aim at."

"*Nearly* can get you killed."

"So can getting up in the morning."

The Paiute shrugged. "I suppose you can look at it that way. What you're asking me, Kid, is if you're good enough to face three hardened killers. And what I'm telling you is . . . I don't know. But between the two of us—"

"No," Morgan said.

"Listen, Kid, be reasonable. Three against two is better odds than three against one. I can hold my own in a fight."

"You said yourself that you're not a gunfighter," Morgan pointed out. "I won't have your blood on my conscience, too, Phillip. When I face them, it'll be alone."

"Then you're a damned fool," Bearpaw said hotly.

Morgan shrugged. "I've been called worse. I've called myself worse."

With a surly expression on his face, Bearpaw said, "We'll talk about this in the morning. I'm turning in."

"Fine. But things won't be any different in the morning."

As a matter of fact, though, things were different, because Morgan and Bearpaw had visitors in the morning. The sun wasn't up yet when they heard a dog barking, and then a moment later, bells ringing.

Morgan rolled quickly out of his blankets and snatched up the Winchester from the ground beside him, but Bearpaw said, "Take it easy. I've heard sounds like that before. Listen closer."

Morgan frowned as he heard some sort of bleating. "What *is* that?"

"Sheep," Bearpaw said. "Some sheepherder is bringing his flock down to the creek to give them water before he turns them out on their graze."

The sheep came in sight a few minutes later, fifty or sixty of the woollies being herded along by an old Mexican man in a sombrero and serape, aided by a long-haired, black-and-white dog that dashed back and forth with seemingly endless energy, keeping the sheep bunched up.

The Mexican stopped short at the sight of Morgan, Bearpaw, and their horses. A worried look stole over his face, which was as brown and wrinkled as a walnut. Bearpaw greeted him in Spanish, though, and although Morgan wasn't fluent in the language, he was pretty sure the Paiute was telling the sheepherder not to worry, that they meant him no harm and had simply camped here for the night.

"Ask him if he's seen the men we're looking for," Morgan suggested.

For the next few minutes, Spanish flew back and forth between Bearpaw and the Mexican, the conversation going too fast for the Kid to keep up with it. Then Bearpaw turned to him, nodded, and said, "He saw them yesterday, over east of here. He moves the sheep around every day, bedding them down in a different place along the creek each night so they'll have fresh grass. Sheep are hell on the grass."

"What about those three bastards?" Morgan prodded.

"Emiliano—that's this fellow here—says they were headed toward Gomez's place. According to him, that's a cantina in a village about twenty miles east of here. I hadn't heard of it before, but evidently it's the same sort of place as Immelmann's trading post, where a man can get what he wants without too many questions being asked."

"How does he know that's where they were going?" Morgan asked.

"He overheard them talking about it. He savvies some English, even though he doesn't speak it very well. He was afraid when he saw them coming, so he took his dog and hid in an arroyo until they had ridden past. He was lucky; they didn't notice his sheep."

Morgan nodded as he thought about the information Emiliano had given them. "They'll probably stay for a while at Gomez's," he said. "A few hours anyway."

"They'll stay the night more than likely."

"That should give us plenty of time to get there today."

"And what are you going to do then, eh?" Bearpaw asked.

Morgan gave him an honest answer. "I don't know yet," he said. "But I know I won't ride away from there until I've dealt with them . . . and found out where we need to go next."

And that was the way it had played out, the Kid thought now as he rode away from what had been Gomez's cantina.

Bearpaw had continued to argue fervently that Morgan ought to let him come along, but in the end he had sighed and agreed to stay out of the fight.

"I'm warning you, though," he had told Morgan, "if you make me go back to Sawtooth and tell Eve McNally that you're dead, I'll find you in the happy hunting ground one of these days and make you wish you had listened to me."

"The happy hunting ground?" Morgan had said with a raised eyebrow.

"Ugh," Bearpaw had said.

As Morgan rode back toward the spot where he had left the Paiute, he raised his right hand and looked at it. He saw it tremble, just slightly. He had felt no fear when he faced the three killers, only a cold desire to see justice done. Now, however, a little reaction was setting in. A tiny case of nerves. He would have to work on that. One of these days, he hoped, he would ask his father if he felt the same way after a gunfight.

Luck had been with him today. Skill, too, of course, but no man survived such a battle without at least a smidgen of luck on his side. And there was more at stake than just survival. He really *had* been a damned fool, just as Bearpaw had warned him. He had come within a whisker of killing all three of his enemies without finding out where any of the other kidnappers had gone. If Julio Esquivel hadn't clung stubbornly to life for a few minutes, until Morgan realized his mistake . . .

But despite everything, Esquivel had lived long enough to tell him that Clem Baggott and Spence Hooper had been headed for Gallup, New Mexico Territory. According to the Mexican knife artist, Baggott's sister ran a whorehouse there, and the two men planned to stay with her for a while, until they decided what they wanted to rob next.

Bearpaw must have been watching for Morgan. The Paiute came galloping out of the little canyon where he had stayed while Morgan rode into the village. "Kid!" Bearpaw greeted him anxiously. "Are you all right? I heard the shots from down there."

"I'm fine," Morgan assured him. "They came close . . . but not close enough."

"They're dead?"

Morgan nodded.

"All three of them?"

"That's right. But before he died, Esquivel told me that two of the others were on their way to Gallup."

Bearpaw heaved a sigh of relief. "I was afraid you might forget we needed to question one of them."

"When they started shooting at me, I almost did forget," Morgan admitted with a slight smile. "Lucky for me, I didn't kill Esquivel right off."

Bearpaw's shaggy black brows drew down in a frown. "How'd you get him to talk? I thought I was supposed to be the one in charge of torture."

"I had something he wanted," the Kid said. "A quicker death than a bullet in the gut."

Bearpaw let out a little whistle. "Yeah, that would loosen a man's tongue, all right. You'll have to tell me all about it."

"On the way to Gallup," Morgan said. "And that is . . . which direction?"

Bearpaw pointed south.

* * *

Gallup was a railroad town, and in less than ten years of existence, it had become noted for two things. One was its high Indian population, which was no surprise because it was located in the middle of several reservations. The other was that it was rough as hell, also no surprise, because most settlements that sprang to life along the railroads were that way. The term "Hell on Wheels" had originated with the railroad towns, and Gallup certainly fit the description. It had a multitude of saloons, gambling dens, and whorehouses.

One of those whorehouses was called Rosa's, and according to what Julio Esquivel had said, Rosa was Clem Baggott's sister. The first thing Morgan and Bearpaw did when they rode down out of the mountains north of the settlement was to stop a man walking along the street and ask him if he knew where the brothel was located.

The hombre frowned indignantly and demanded, "Do I look like the sort of man who would know anything about a house of ill repute?"

As a matter of fact, the man had been weaving slightly as he made his way down the street, and his nose was red from drink. So yeah, the Kid thought, he looked exactly like the sort of man who might know such a thing.

But the Kid just said, "Sorry, mister, didn't mean any offense. I just thought I might stand you to the price of a drink if you could help us out."

"Oh." The man hiccupped softly. "Well, in that case . . . you go down this street a couple of blocks, then turn right just past the railroad tracks. Rosa's will be on the left, four blocks down."

Morgan dug a coin out of his pocket and flipped it to the drunk. "Much obliged."

"They may not let the Injun in, though," the man warned. "Depends on what kind of mood Rosa's in."

"Bearpaw take his chances," the Paiute intoned.

As they rode away, Morgan said, "You like doing that, don't you?"

"People expect it. If you give people what they expect, then they don't get suspicious. And if a fellow thinks that I don't speak much English, he's not going to be as careful about what he says around me."

That made sense, the Kid thought. It had been a lucky day for him in more ways than one when Bearpaw heard that splash and came along to pull him out of the creek.

Rosa's was a large, two-story clapboard building across the street from the railroad tracks and down a ways from the depot. A balcony ran along the front of the building so that the soiled doves who worked there could stand outside in their skimpies and wave to passengers as eastbound trains pulled in. The hope was that some of those passengers would disembark from the trains and hurry back up the street to take advantage of the local hospitality. It probably worked, at least some of the time.

A corral stood next to the whorehouse. Morgan and Bearpaw led the buckskin and the Appaloosa into it, unsaddled the horses, and placed the saddles on the corral fence along with seven or eight others. Morgan wondered which of the other horses in the corral belonged to Baggott and Hooper, if indeed any of them did. Since the two outlaws were staying a while, they might have stabled their mounts somewhere else.

It didn't matter, Morgan told himself. Baggott and Hooper weren't going to have any need of horses for much longer.

They went up the steps onto the porch underneath the balcony. A large black man sat in a wicker chair next to the door. He wore a derby hat and a dusty black suit over a collarless white shirt. "Afternoon to you, sir," he said to Morgan. He looked at Bearpaw and added a noncommittal grunt, then went on. "Lookin' for some fine ladies, are you?"

"That's right," Morgan said.

"You can go right on in, and welcome. The Injun's got to stay out here, though."

"But he's my friend," Morgan objected.

The black man shook his head. "Don't matter. Miss Rosa says no Injuns today, and what Miss Rosa says goes."

Bearpaw thumped himself lightly on the chest with a fist and said, "No worry 'bout Bearpaw, friend Morgan. Bearpaw sit on step, wait for friend."

"No, you can't sit there either," the black man said. "Mosey on down to the train station, why don't you? There'll be a westbound in soon; you can probably cadge some money for firewater."

Bearpaw nodded. "Bearpaw do like dark man say." He turned away, and one eye opened and closed quickly in a wink that Morgan could see, even though the bouncer couldn't.

The Paiute shuffled off down the street while Morgan stepped inside the whorehouse. As a younger man, well before his marriage to Rebel, he had been inside a few such establishments in Boston, but those had been high-class enterprises, nothing like this shabby, squalid brothel. The rug on the floor in the parlor was threadbare, and some of the overstuffed furniture around the room was losing its stuffing.

The same was true of most of the women waiting in the parlor for customers. They were getting on in years, blowsy in soiled shifts, and more than one smile was missing some teeth as they grinned at Morgan in what was supposed to be an enticing manner. He didn't feel the least bit tempted. He couldn't imagine any circumstances in which he would. Maybe if he hadn't actually *seen* a woman for fifteen or twenty years . . .

One of the whores caught his eye, though. She was younger than the others, around twenty years old, and even though her skin lacked any reddish hue, her raven hair and high cheekbones testified to at least some Indian blood in her. She was even slightly pretty, in a coarse way.

A woman in a crimson gown, with graying blond hair piled high on her head, came into the parlor through another door. She had a cup of coffee in one hand, and Morgan guessed she had been out in the kitchen heating up the brew. She stopped short at the sight of Morgan and said, "Howdy, mister. I didn't know anybody had come in."

"He's a pretty one, ain't he, Rosa?" one of the whores purred.

The madam moved toward Morgan. "You looking for some female companionship, cowboy?"

Morgan hesitated. He was going to have to spend some time here, more than likely, until he got a line on Baggott and Hooper. He wasn't sure how to go about this, but he knew that he couldn't stay if he didn't act like he wanted to partake of the dubious pleasures offered by the house.

"That one," he said as he pointed to the youngest whore, the one with Indian blood.

The other soiled doves looked disappointed. Rosa smiled and said, "Good choice. Tasmin, take our guest upstairs and show him a fine old time."

The young woman stood up from the divan, sidled over to Morgan, and took hold of his arm with both of her hands, pressing herself against him so that he felt the warm mound of her breast prodding his side.

"You come with me, mister," she said as she smiled up at him. "I promise, you won't ever be sorry that you picked me."

Morgan felt a surge of panic inside him. He didn't want this woman. He didn't want any woman—except the one he could no longer have.

At that moment, the door from the parlor to the kitchen opened again, and a man came into the room. Morgan glanced at him, saw a middle-aged hombre with a battered Stetson shoved back on his head and a close-cropped, salt-and-pepper beard. He said, "Rosa, how's about frontin' me some more money? There's a poker game down at the saloon tonight, and I reckon I can clean up in it."

The young whore started tugging Morgan toward the stairs. Rosa turned to the man who had just come into the room and snapped, "Damn it, Clem, I've told you not to bother me while I'm working."

Clem Baggott. The name rang in Morgan's mind. This was one of the men he and Bearpaw had come here looking for. Morgan turned his head to look closer at the man, and recognized him from that awful night in Black Rock Canyon, even though he had only seen Baggott for a moment by the glaring light of those torches alongside the trail.

Morgan wasn't the only one who recognized somebody, though. Even though Morgan looked quite a bit different now, Baggott's eyes bulged out in shock. He yelled, "Son of a bitch! You're that bastard from Carson City!"

Then he reached for the Colt on his hip, even as the whore called Tasmin screamed and tightened her two-handed grip on Morgan's gun arm.

CHAPTER 18

Morgan knew he had only an instant to act. He reached over with his left hand, grabbed Tasmin's shift, and hauled hard on it. The garment tore a little, but held together enough to pull her away from him. He swung her around and slung her right into Rosa. The two women collided with startled yells and fell to the floor, out of the line of fire.

At the same time, Morgan lunged the other way. Baggott's gun blasted, flame licking from the muzzle. Morgan couldn't hear the whine of the bullet past his head because all the women in the room were screaming by now, but he felt the hot wind-rip of its passage.

His Colt had flickered into his hand. It roared and bucked as he squeezed the trigger. Baggott grunted in pain and spun halfway around. He tried to catch himself on the back of a divan, but his groping hand missed. He pitched to the floor, dropping his gun as he did so.

Morgan had time to hope that Baggott wasn't fatally wounded, since he didn't know yet where Hooper was, and then the front door crashed open and the huge black bouncer came into the room like an avalanche, bellowing angrily.

"Get him, Hyde!" Rosa screamed from the floor. "He killed Clem!"

Morgan hoped again that wasn't the case, that Baggott wasn't dead. Then the bouncer called Hyde was on him, reaching for him with long, tree-trunk-like arms.

Morgan could have shot the man, but as far as he could tell, Hyde was unarmed. Anyway, he wasn't sure bullets would stop the charging behemoth. Morgan tried to twist away, knowing that if those arms ever trapped him in their circle, he would be in for some rib-crushing.

He managed to avoid the bear hug, but Hyde grabbed the back of his shirt and threw him at the wall. The planking vibrated as Morgan's right shoulder slammed into it. He cried out in pain as that arm went numb. A thud sounded as the gun slipped from his fingers and fell to the floor.

He had been hoping to wallop Hyde over the head a few times with the Colt and maybe slow him down that way. Now he was unarmed, and definitely out of his class as far as weight, reach, and rough-and-tumble ability were concerned. As Hyde charged him again, he dropped into a crouch and threw himself at the big man's knees, hoping to chop Hyde's legs out from under him.

The maneuver was only partially successful. Morgan hit Hyde low, and the bouncer fell. But he landed on top of Morgan, who was pinned to the floor by Hyde's weight. Hyde got one hand on Morgan's throat and closed it, cutting off his air. Morgan's vision started to blur as he tried to gasp, but he could still see Hyde looming above him, raising a giant fist and getting ready to bring it down like a sledgehammer into the middle of Morgan's face.

Even over the roaring of blood in his ears, Morgan heard a solid thump. Hyde's eyes rolled up in his head until only the whites showed; then he pitched forward senselessly. He was still on top of Morgan, though, so all the Kid could do was stare over Hyde's shoulder at Bearpaw, who stood there with the Sharps clutched in his hands. Morgan figured it was the butt of the rifle he had heard connecting solidly with the back of Hyde's skull.

"Get him . . . off me!" Morgan managed to croak.

Bearpaw looked like he wanted to laugh, but he kept a straight face as he bent down and grasped the collar of Hyde's coat. "You'll have to help me," he said. "I'm not sure I can budge this big fellow by myself."

Morgan got his hands against Hyde's shoulders and shoved while Bearpaw heaved. After a moment of grunting struggle, they were able to roll the big man off Morgan.

"Check on . . . Baggott," Morgan said as he sat up and tried to catch his breath. "I had to . . . shoot him . . ."

Bearpaw turned toward Baggott, and as he did so, Morgan heard a small popping sound. Bearpaw grunted again and took a sudden step back.

"I'm shot," he said.

Morgan surged to his feet and saw Rosa swinging an over-and-under derringer toward him. "You son of a bitch!" she screamed. "You killed my brother!"

Morgan leaped and swatted the little pistol aside just as it popped again. That emptied it, but he closed his hand over it and twisted it out of Rosa's fingers anyway, so she couldn't reload and try again to shoot him. He was worried about Bearpaw, so he gave the madam a shove that sent her stumbling backward to sit down hard on her ample rump.

Morgan swung around and saw that Bearpaw had sunk onto the arm of a ratty divan. The whores had all scurried away and vanished except for Tasmin, who stood huddled in fear against one of the walls.

Bearpaw slipped a hand inside his shirt, pulled it out, and looked at the crimson stains on his fingertips. "Yeah, I'm shot, all right," he said.

Then he toppled over backward onto the divan.

Morgan started toward him, but he had taken only a single step when another gun blasted from somewhere above him.

The slug whipped past him. He looked up and saw a man standing at the top of the stairs, smoke curling from the barrel of the gun in his fist.

Morgan recognized this man from Black Rock Canyon, too, and knew he had to be Spence Hooper. As Hooper fired again, Morgan launched himself in a dive toward the Colt he had dropped a few moments earlier while battling with Hyde. The feeling had returned to Morgan's arm, so he was able to snatch up the gun as he slid across the threadbare rug. He came to a stop at the bottom of the stairs and fired up at Hooper.

Hooper screamed and listed sideways as blood and bone exploded from his left kneecap. He pitched forward, squeezing off another shot as he did so. The bullet chewed splinters from the stairs halfway down. Still screaming from the pain of his shattered knee, Hooper tumbled on down the stairs, coming to a stop just a few steps up from Morgan.

The Kid scrambled to his feet. Hooper had dropped his gun, and Morgan didn't see any other weapons. He turned so that he could cover Hooper while checking on Rosa, Tasmin, and Hyde. Rosa had crawled over to her brother, and now lay half on top of him, sobbing and wailing. Baggott hadn't moved since he went down, so Morgan thought there was a good chance he really was dead. Tasmin still stood against the wall, watching wide-eyed.

Bearpaw rolled onto his side and started trying to struggle to his feet. "I'm all right," he said as Morgan hurried over to help him. "That bullet just nicked me. Keep an eye on the other one."

Morgan ignored what Bearpaw said, got an arm around the Paiute, and helped him stand up. Morgan looked at Tasmin and asked, "How quick will the law get here?"

"Wh-what?"

"The law," Morgan repeated. "The local sheriff, police, whatever they have here. How long?"

She shook her head. "I don't know. They leave this end of town alone mostly. But with that many shots, they'll have to come see what it's about. Five or ten minutes maybe?"

Morgan hoped that would be long enough. "Hooper's still alive," he said to Bearpaw. "We need to question him."

Bearpaw nodded. "Help me over there, then stand back and keep an eye out for trouble."

The two men went to the foot of the stairs. Hooper lay there whimpering. Bearpaw reached down, rested a hand on the outlaw's thigh just above the shattered knee, and pushed hard.

Hooper shrieked.

"That was just to get your attention," Bearpaw said as the cry died away. "Where are the others?"

"Wh-what . . . others?" Hooper gasped.

"The other men who rode with you when you kidnapped Conrad Browning's wife."

Hooper blinked up at the Paiute. "I . . . I don't know what . . . you're talkin' about . . . I never kidnapped no woman—"

Bearpaw didn't let him go on. Instead, he pushed on Hooper's leg again. Hooper gobbled in pain.

But when the agony eased a little, words began to spill from Hooper's mouth. "I don't know where they all went, but Rattigan and that breed, White Rock, were gonna do some prospectin' in Colorado! Rattigan said he knew a place up in the Sangre de Cristos where he thought there might be some gold! I think it was called Blue Creek, or something like that. God, don't do that again, redskin. I can't stand it."

"What about the others?" Bearpaw insisted.

"I don't know! I swear! Vernon used to talk about someplace down on the border, but I don't know any more than that. And nobody else told me anything about where they were goin' when we split up." Hooper sobbed. "You gotta get me to a sawbones. I'm hurt bad."

"You're sure you don't know where we can find any of the others?"

"No, I swear! That's all I know."

"Then you don't have to worry about a sawbones," Bearpaw said. His arm and shoulder moved.

Morgan saw Hooper give a little jerk. The man's eyes widened. Morgan looked down in time to see Bearpaw let go of a knife with a staghorn handle that protruded from Hooper's chest. The thrust must have gone right into the outlaw's heart. Hooper opened his mouth, but no more words came out before his head fell back on the steps. He kept staring as the life faded from his eyes.

On the other side of the parlor, Hyde groaned as he began to stir.

"Help me up," Bearpaw said. "We'd better get out of here."

It was too late for that. Heavy footsteps sounded on the porch, and three men crowded into the room, each of them carrying a shotgun. Morgan started to lift his gun, then stopped as he spotted the badges the men wore pinned to their coats.

"Arrest them, Marshal!" Rosa screamed. "String 'em up! They murdered my brother!"

The lawmen leveled their Greeners at Morgan and Bearpaw. "Shuck your irons, boys," one of the men growled. "We got some sortin' out to do here."

"I hope that telegram you sent does some good, Kid," Bearpaw said an hour later as the two of them sat on an iron cot in a cell in the Gallup city jail. "Otherwise, things don't look too promising for us. 'Therefore never send to ask for whom the bell tolls,' John Donne said. 'It tolls for thee.'"

"And just what does that mean?"

"It means that if you hear them hammering together a gallows, it's probably going to be for us."

Morgan took a deep breath. It had taken a lot of talking to

convince Marshal Davis to let him send a telegram to Claudius Turnbuckle in San Francisco. The message had been a short one.

STILL ALIVE STOP NEED LEGAL HELP GALLUP NMT STOP
CONRAD

Rosa had insisted, tearfully and at the top of her lungs, that Morgan and Bearpaw had burst into the whorehouse and started shooting for no reason. They had gunned down her brother, and then they had shot Spence Hooper and caused him to fall on his own knife. That was the only explanation that made any sense to the marshal, since the knife in Hooper's chest belonged to him. Even Rosa admitted that. She had been too busy grieving over her brother—who was indeed dead, shot cleanly through the heart—to realize that that version of events didn't make complete sense. Hooper wouldn't have lived long enough for Bearpaw to question him if that had been the case.

But they already had one murder charge hanging over their heads, Morgan thought, so why complicate matters even more?

"You didn't have to kill him," Morgan whispered now as he sat beside Bearpaw. "I would have done it, once we found out everything we could from him."

"You mean you would have shot him in cold blood?" the Paiute asked.

"That's the way I killed Hank Winchell."

"There was nothing cold-blooded about that night," Bearpaw said with a shake of his head. "You had just seen your wife murdered. You were in a state of shock. Pulling the trigger on a man weeks later is different."

"I shot Esquivel."

"You put him out of his misery. He would have died anyway from that bullet in his guts, and he would have suffered a lot more. You were merciful to him, Kid. That wasn't murder. Me, I've already got plenty of bad things on my conscience. Taking care of one outlaw who needed killing won't cause me to lose any sleep."

Morgan didn't say anything. Despite the hatred and the need for vengeance that had consumed him since leaving Carson City, he was coming to realize that there was a difference between killing a man in a fair fight and snuffing out the life of someone who couldn't fight back.

After a few minutes, Morgan asked, "How's your shoulder?"

Bearpaw started to shrug, then stopped as the motion caused him to grimace in pain. "It hurts like the devil," he said, "but I'll live. That little popgun of Rosa's didn't have much punch. The bullet wasn't more than a couple of inches under the skin."

A doctor had come to the jail after Morgan and Bearpaw were locked up and tended to the Paiute's wound, which was messy but not life-threatening. A bulky bandage showed now as a lump under Bearpaw's shirt.

"Kid, I'm sorry things got out of hand," he went on. "I never figured on Baggott recognizing you like that."

"Neither did I," Morgan said. "I guess he's got a good eye for faces, because I've changed a lot since that night. We just didn't have any luck."

"A man's always got luck. It's just that sometimes it's good . . . and sometimes it's bad. Mostly, it's some of both. We're still alive, aren't we?"

"For now," Morgan said. He had visions of a trial, and a judge passing sentence, and a long walk up thirteen steps to the gallows . . .

The door into the cell block opened, and Marshal Davis came in with another man, a tall, imposing, white-haired gent in an expensive suit and Stetson. Morgan and Bearpaw were the only prisoners at the moment, other than a couple of drunken Navajos sleeping off a bender, but the marshal pointed at them anyway and said, "There they are, Colonel."

"Thank you, Marshal," the man said in deep, powerful tones. Morgan had heard voices like that before, and they were nearly always in courtrooms. He got to his feet and went over to grasp the iron bars in the door as Marshal Davis went back into the jail office and the stranger came over to the cell.

"Did Turnbuckle send you?" Morgan asked tensely.

The man smiled and said, "Colonel Theodore Binswanger at your service, sir. My old friend from law school, the esteemed Claudius Turnbuckle, did indeed communicate urgently with me this afternoon via the telegraphic wires. He asked that I render any possible aid to you, and, I suppose by extension, to your ruddy companion there. It's quite fortunate for you that Claudius is acquainted with someone who practices law here. Marshal Davis tells me that the charge will be quite serious when you're arraigned. Murder."

"It wasn't murder," Morgan snapped. "Baggott fired first, and so did Hooper. It was self-defense in both cases."

"The story told by the proprietress of the establishment varies considerably from that version, Mr. . . . Morgan, is it?"

"That's right." Morgan didn't know how much Turnbuckle might have told Colonel Binswanger in his telegram, so for now he was going to keep his connection with Conrad Browning to himself.

"Oh, by the way," Binswanger said as he reached into his coat, "Claudius sent a private wire for you as well." He held out a folded, sealed paper. "I've honored the sanctity of your communication."

"Obliged," Morgan said as he took the telegram and tore it open to read the words printed on it.

WHAT IN THE BLAZES STOP THOUGHT YOU WERE DEAD STOP WILL TRY LOCATE FRANK AND TELL HIM STOP TRUST BINSWANGER STOP FULL OF HOT AIR BUT HONEST STOP

Morgan folded the message and slipped it into the pocket of his black shirt. He was glad he had finally gotten in touch with Turnbuckle. At least, he had started the process of letting his father know that he was still alive. It had taken a lot longer than Morgan had intended.

"Now, what can you tell me about the fatal incident?" Binswanger asked.

Morgan rubbed his jaw. He had been thinking about how to play this.

"Bearpaw and I just stopped at the whorehouse for . . . well, you know."

The lawyer sniffed. "I am aware of the establishment's unsavory reputation naturally, though I have no, ah, personal knowledge of what goes on there."

"Bearpaw was outside, and I was just standing there in the parlor when that first fella came in, yelled something about Carson City, and started blazing away at me. All I can figure is that he thought I was somebody else, somebody he had a grudge against."

"Have you ever been to Carson City?"

"Yeah, but I never saw that hombre before," Morgan lied. "He didn't have any reason to throw down on me."

"What happened then?"

Morgan told the rest of the story just the way it had happened, leaving out only the part about Bearpaw questioning Spence Hooper—and then putting Hooper's own knife in the outlaw's chest.

Binswanger nodded and said, "That does indeed sound like classic, clear-cut cases of self-defense. Unfortunately, it's your word against that of this . . . Rosa. And I'm relatively certain that the, ah, ladies in her employ will corroborate her testimony." The lawyer lowered his voice. "However, I happen to know that there's a move afoot among the city fathers to clean up some of the more unsavory sections of town. I have a feeling that if there was even one witness to support your claims, the judge could be persuaded to drop the charges against you before the case proceeds any further . . . on the condition, of course, that the two of you depart from our fair city posthaste."

"We'd be glad to," Morgan said, thinking of what Hooper had told them about Rattigan and White Rock prospecting in the Sangre de Cristos up in Colorado, "if the marshal would just let us out."

Binswanger sighed. "I'll see what I can find in the way of a witness," he said. "But to be honest with you, sir, I don't hold out much hope of success."

Neither did Morgan. He knew that the soiled doves who worked for Rosa weren't going to contradict her story.

Binswanger left the jail, and Morgan sat down on the cot next to Bearpaw again. He picked up his hat, which was lying on the cot next to him, and looked at it idly. After a moment, he said, "Well, damn."

"What is it?" Bearpaw asked.

Morgan held up the hat and poked his finger through a hole in the crown. "There's a matching one on the other side," he said. "My hat fell off when I was tussling with Hyde, and then when Hooper took that shot at me, the bullet must have hit the hat while it was lying on the floor."

"Pure luck once again. Good luck, in this case."

"How can you say that? I've got a hole in my hat!"

"Better than a hole in your head," Bearpaw said.

Morgan laughed. "You're right about that."

They watched the light fade in the cell's single, barred window. It faced west, so they could see a slice of sky as it turned orange and crimson from the setting sun. Some of those brilliant hues still remained in the sky when Colonel Binswanger appeared again, bustling into the cell block when the marshal unlocked the door. A smile wreathed the old attorney's face.

"Superlative news," Binswanger said as he came up to the cell door, followed by the marshal, who was jingling a ring of keys. "A witness came forward to support your story. I didn't even have to locate her. She came to me when she heard that I was representing the two of you."

"She?" Morgan repeated.

Binswanger waved off the question as Davis unlocked the cell door and swung it open. "Judge Applewhite has dismissed the charges."

"We weren't even arraigned yet," Morgan said, not wanting to look a gift horse in the mouth, but puzzled by the turn of events.

"You were arraigned in absentia, and then the charges were dismissed. Simple really. Informal, but effective. The only caveat, as I said, is that the two of you are now expected to depart as soon as possible. You are henceforth persona non grata in Gallup."

"He means light a shuck outta here," Marshal Davis growled.

"We intend to," Morgan said as he retrieved his Stetson from the cot. "Just as soon as I buy a new hat."

"Make it quick," the marshal warned. "Rosa's gonna pitch a fit when she hears about this. And she's still got some influential friends in this town. Men who use the back door when they visit her place, if you know what I mean."

Morgan did. He wasn't surprised to hear that some of Gallup's leading citizens were also secret patrons of the whorehouse.

He and Bearpaw followed Binswanger out of the cell block, with the marshal bringing up the rear. Binswanger led them through the jail office. They stepped out onto the porch, and Morgan was surprised to see the young whore Tasmin standing there, wearing a simple brown dress.

"You?" he said. "You're the one who told the law what really happened?"

She nodded. "That's right. I couldn't let you and your friend be railroaded for something you didn't do."

She stood there while Binswanger shook hands with Morgan and nodded civilly to Bearpaw. "I'll bid you gentlemen farewell. Claudius instructed me to submit the bill for my services to Turnbuckle and Stafford, and he would see to taking care of it."

"Thanks," Morgan said. "You were a big help, Colonel."

Binswanger shook his head. "I didn't do all that much." He gestured toward Tasmin. "It was mostly this young lady here."

He tipped his hat to her and then walked away.

"You know you're not going to be able to work for Rosa anymore after this," Morgan told her. "I don't know how we can thank you for what you've done."

"I do," Tasmin said. "I heard what that bastard Hooper told you." The loathing in her voice told Morgan that she'd probably had a few unpleasant experiences with Hooper while he and Baggott were staying at Rosa's. "You're going to Colorado to look for those two men he was talking about, aren't you?"

Morgan glanced at Bearpaw, who inclined his head as if to say that it was pretty obvious they were, but he was leaving the decision of what to tell Tasmin to Morgan.

"That's right," Morgan said to her. "I reckon we are."

"Then if you want to pay me back for helping you . . . take me with you."

CHAPTER 19

Morgan and Bearpaw both stared at the young soiled dove. "Take you with us?" Morgan repeated after a moment, thinking about the danger he and the Paiute would be riding into for the foreseeable future. "We can't do that."

"Well, I can't stay here in Gallup," Tasmin said. "Do you think Rosa's going to let me get away with helping you? At the very least, she'll have Hyde beat me. She might even order him to kill me." She shook her head. "No, I've got to get out of town, and since I got in trouble helping the two of you . . ."

"She has a point, Kid," Bearpaw said.

Morgan struggled with the decision facing him. When he rode away from Carson City, he'd had in mind tracking down the kidnappers on his own, so that no one else would be endangered. Then he had wound up traveling with Bearpaw. That had worked out all right so far, other than the fact that the Paiute had been wounded. Now this young woman—little more than a girl actually—was asking to join them on their journey as well.

Tasmin seemed somehow different now that she was out

of the whorehouse. She had scrubbed the paint off her face and was dressed more modestly, of course, but she also sounded more intelligent when she spoke. Morgan supposed that most men didn't go to a place like Rosa's for the conversation . . .

His thoughts were straying, and Tasmin still stood there on the jail porch waiting for an answer. Morgan took a deep breath. Considering what she had done for him and Bearpaw, he didn't see how he could deny her request. All she wanted was a chance to be safe from Rosa's revenge.

"All right," he said. "You can come with us . . . for now. But if we find a good place for you to stay, that's it. You'll need a horse, too—"

"I have one. How do you think I got here to Gallup?"

"I don't have any idea. And don't take that as a request to tell me your life story." Morgan knew he was being a little rude, but he didn't like being forced into things. "We'll be leaving in about ten minutes. Can you be ready to ride?"

"I can," she replied without hesitation. "I don't have much in the way of belongings, and I brought it all with me when I slipped out of Rosa's and went to look for Colonel Binswanger. My bag is down at the livery stable with my horse."

"All right. We'll meet you there in ten minutes."

"Thank you. You won't be sorry, Mr. Morgan."

She had said something similar when she was about to take him upstairs in the whorehouse, but it sounded entirely different now.

Tasmin hurried off, while Morgan and Bearpaw angled across the street toward a general store so that Morgan could buy a new hat. He still had quite a bit of the money he had brought with him from Carson City. As plentiful as game was, they hadn't had to spend much on supplies.

The store didn't have a black hat like the one Morgan had been wearing. He settled on a brown one instead, with a lighter brown band. The crown was slightly higher than his old hat, but still flat.

"Looks good on you," Bearpaw said. "Why don't you get that buckskin jacket there to go with it?"

Morgan frowned as he looked at the jacket Bearpaw indicated. It was the sort that pulled over the head, with a neck opening that laced up with a rawhide thong. Fringe decorated the shoulders and arms of the garment.

"Sort of gaudy, isn't it?" he asked. "And this weather's too hot for a jacket."

"Sure, it's hot now," Bearpaw admitted, "but it won't be long before the northers start blowing down through these parts. You can be sweating at noon and shivering by the time the sun goes down. Besides, that rawhide fringe comes in mighty handy for mending saddles or harness."

Morgan thought it over for a moment, then shrugged and nodded. "All right, you've talked me into it. I don't reckon it would hurt to be prepared for cooler weather."

He paid the storekeeper for the purchases, then walked out wearing the brown hat, with the buckskin jacket thrown over his left arm. He still thought it was a little gaudy—but he had to admit it was the sort of thing a notorious gunfighter might wear, at least in dime-novel illustrations. And since Morgan had been basing a lot of his new personality on those very dime novels, he supposed he ought to dress the part.

Give people what they expected to see, Bearpaw had said. Morgan was willing to do that.

Their horses were still in the corral next to Rosa's. Morgan kept a wary eye on the place as they retrieved the buckskin and the Appaloosa, in case Rosa spotted them and sent Hyde after them. The door was closed and the shades were pulled on the windows, though. It looked like the house was closed down, maybe because Rosa was mourning her brother.

Tasmin was waiting in front of the livery stable when they walked up, leading their horses. She had changed into a man's work shirt with the sleeves rolled up a couple of turns on her forearms, as well as a pair of denim trousers.

Morgan glanced at her saddle and asked, "You're going to ride astride?"

Her chin lifted defiantly. "I reckon you already know that I'm not exactly a lady. I never cared for a sidesaddle."

"That's fine with me," Morgan said. A faint smile touched his lips as he recalled all the times he had seen Rebel riding that way. She didn't have any use for a sidesaddle either.

The three of them mounted up. Tasmin had a canvas bag tied to her saddle horn. She reached inside it and brought out an old hat with a floppy brim. She jammed it down on her head and heeled her horse into motion. Morgan and Bearpaw exchanged quick grins as they let her take the lead.

"Where exactly are we going?" Morgan called after her as they reached the edge of town.

"Colorado, right? Somewhere in the Sangre de Cristos?"

"You know how to get there?"

Tasmin slowed her horse and looked back at the two men. "Well . . . no," she admitted. "I just wanted to get out of Gallup as quickly as I could." She gave Morgan a challenging look as she went on. "Do *you* know how to get there?"

"Just a general idea. I reckon Bearpaw does, though."

"Heap right," Bearpaw said. "Know-um way to mountains."

Tasmin's expression was withering as she said, "You've forgotten that I heard you talking back at Rosa's place. Don't try to pull that on me."

Bearpaw chuckled. "Sorry. You get in the habit of doing something and it's hard to stop."

"Not me," Tasmin said as she faced forward again. "I'd just as soon break all of my habits, and the sooner the better."

* * *

Bearpaw was right about the weather. As they traveled eastward across the rugged New Mexico landscape, the first couple of days remained warm, even hot, but then on the third morning, a strong wind started blowing out of the north. It carried more than a hint of a chill in it.

"I told you," Bearpaw said as they got ready to break camp. "Tonight, it'll be cold enough to make your breath fog."

Morgan wondered what that would mean for the sleeping arrangements. The first two nights, there had been a minimum of awkwardness because Tasmin took her bedroll and carried it a good distance away from the men before she spread it out. Tonight, she would probably want to be closer to the fire.

By noon, he had taken the buckskin jacket out of his saddlebags and slipped it on to help shield him from the chilly wind. Tasmin wore a flannel coat, and Bearpaw had a small buffalo robe draped around his shoulders. The sky was clear, but the Paiute frowned as he squinted up at it.

"Snow in less than a week," he announced with serene confidence.

"How can you tell that?" Morgan asked.

"My people live in harmony with nature. We know these things."

Tasmin laughed. "One of my grandfathers was a Hopi medicine man. He always said things like that."

"And he was right, wasn't he?" Bearpaw asked.

"Usually," Tasmin admitted with a shrug.

That night, the air was frigid. As Morgan expected, Tasmin spread her blankets near the fire. He made sure there was a little distance between them when he laid out his own bedroll. He went to sleep with the sound of the north wind howling in his ears.

When his eyes snapped open sometime later, the wind

had died down. Unsure what had woken him, he gazed up into a crystal-clear sky in which the stars seemed like they were about to tumble down around him.

Then, something moved against his back. His muscles tensed. His hand moved toward the Winchester that lay on the ground beside him.

"It's just me," Tasmin said in a sleepy voice as she snuggled closer to him. "I got cold, so I moved my blankets over next to yours. All right?"

Morgan grunted, then said, "Fine. I wouldn't want you to freeze. Go back to sleep."

She didn't, though, and neither did he. After a few minutes, she said in a small, tentative voice, "Kid?"

"What?"

"The other day at Rosa's place, when you picked me to take upstairs . . . you didn't really want to go up there with me, did you? You were just looking for Baggott and Hooper, right?"

"That's right," Morgan said. He tried not to be curt or cruel about it, but he wasn't going to lie to her.

"And you don't want me now either, do you?"

Morgan hesitated, not because he was unsure of the answer, but rather because he didn't want to hurt her feelings. Finally, he said, "It's not that I don't want you, Tasmin. I don't want any woman right now. I have other things I have to deal with first before I can even think about anything like that."

She squeezed his shoulder. "You have so much sadness in you, Kid. I'm sorry for whatever caused it. If there's anything I can do to help . . ."

"Just stay out of the way if there's trouble."

That came out more abruptly than he'd intended. He felt her flinch as if she'd been struck. But she said, "Fine. I won't be a bother."

Then she turned over and pressed her back against his,

rather than spooning with him. That was probably better, he thought.

Craggy peaks, lushly timbered valleys, arid wastelands all passed under their horses' hooves as they continued eastward, angling somewhat to the north toward Colorado as they did so. The cold weather passed by, the wind turned out of the south again, and the temperatures warmed. This was a volatile time of year, though, Bearpaw pointed out. There might be another blue norther at any time, and he hadn't backed off on his prediction of snow.

They avoided large towns, traveling north of Albuquerque and south of Taos and Santa Fe, then turned in a more northerly direction to follow the mountains. The Sangre de Cristos were in the northeastern corner of the territory, running north and south from New Mexico into southern Colorado. Raton Pass was on the border between the two. Bearpaw explained all this to Morgan and Tasmin, and since he seemed to know where he was going, they were content to let him take the lead.

"Is there anywhere west of the Mississippi you *haven't* been?" Morgan asked as they approached the towering pass.

"I'm sure there is," Bearpaw replied with a grin, "but I can't think of any place right now."

"How did you wind up in Sawtooth?"

The Paiute could shrug now because the minor bullet wound in his shoulder was almost healed up. He did so and said, "Everybody's got to be somewhere. I'd lived a pretty eventful life, and Sawtooth seemed like a nice quiet place to settle down and live out the rest of my years in peace. It was, too . . . until Kid Morgan showed up."

Tasmin looked over at Morgan. "I know you're supposed to be a famous gunfighter," she said, "but I don't think I'd ever heard of you."

"You just don't travel in the right circles," Bearpaw told her. "The Kid's famous, all right."

She looked like she wasn't sure whether she believed him or not. Morgan didn't say anything. He still felt a little uncomfortable about the whole business of pretending to be somebody else, somebody who didn't really exist.

Although Kid Morgan was becoming more and more real with every gunfight, he realized.

The view from the top of the pass was one of the most spectacular they had seen so far, with majestic mountains rising on either side of them, and behind them plains stretching away for scores of miles to the south and east. Up ahead, in Colorado, the mountains continued, although they were higher and more rugged to the west, falling off into rolling hills to the east.

The climb to the pass was steep, so Bearpaw reined in to rest his mount when they reached the top, and the Kid and Tasmin followed suit. They swung down from their saddles and stood there for long minutes, looking out over the impressive landscape.

"This is a lot prettier than the pueblo where I grew up," Tasmin commented.

"You said you're Hopi?" Morgan asked.

"Only a fourth. My other grandparents were white." Her mouth quirked in a bitter smile. "Missionaries, in fact, who came out here from the East to save the heathen savages. They must not have done a very good job of it, considering the way I turned out."

"I'm not sure I'd go that far," Morgan told her.

"You don't know just how heathen I am." She gave a defiant toss of her head. "And you never will, Mr. Kid Morgan. All that is behind me now."

That was fine with him, he thought.

Bearpaw's attention was focused on their backtrail, and when Tasmin went off into the brush to take care of some personal business, he motioned Morgan over to him and said quietly, "I think somebody's following us, Kid."

Morgan's eyes narrowed as he scanned the landscape below the pass. He didn't see anything moving except a couple of hawks soaring on the wind currents, but he trusted Bearpaw.

"How many?"

"Three, I think. They're a long way back, and I can't even see them right now. But I've caught several glimpses of them today, and I'm pretty sure they're back there."

"How do you know they're actually following us?"

"I don't, of course," Bearpaw admitted. "They could be pilgrims who just happen to be going the same direction we are. A lot of people use this pass. But I slowed down, and they slowed down. I pushed a little harder, and they pushed a little harder."

Instinctively, Morgan's hand dropped to the butt of his gun. "Who'd have a reason to follow us?"

"That madam back in Gallup could have hired some gunwolves to come after us and settle the score for her brother," Bearpaw suggested.

Morgan nodded. That was a possibility, all right. But it didn't seem likely to him. "We'll keep our eyes open. If they're following us, when do you think they'll make their move?"

"No telling. They're close enough they can catch up to us tonight, if they want to."

Tasmin was coming back. Morgan glanced at her and said, "I wish we'd found a place to leave her."

"I'm not sure she would have stayed. That girl's got ideas in her head about you, whether she'll admit it or not . . . and whether you like it or not."

That was one of the last things Morgan wanted to hear, but he was afraid Bearpaw might be right. "If there's trouble, I'm counting on you to keep her safe," he told the Paiute.

"What are you going to be doing?"

"Killing whoever's giving us that trouble," Morgan said.

CHAPTER 20

Later that afternoon, Bearpaw pointed to a dark blue line on the northern horizon and said, "That's a storm coming. Remember that snow I told you about?" He nodded toward the distant clouds. "It's up there. We'll need to find a good place to camp where we can get out of the weather."

"Maybe we should make for the nearest town," Morgan suggested.

Bearpaw squinted at the sky. "That'd be Trinidad. But I'm not sure we've got time to make it that far before nightfall." He hitched the Appaloosa into a faster pace. "We'll give it a try."

The horses were tired after a long day on the trail, though, so Morgan and his friends could only push them so hard. The dark blue line on the horizon seemed to rush southward toward them, and it wasn't long before it turned into looming, bluish-gray clouds. The wind picked up, and the chill was back.

"If you see a good place to camp," Morgan called to Bearpaw, "we'll go ahead and stop."

The Paiute nodded. It was hard to tell because his face

was usually impassive anyway, but Morgan thought he looked more concerned than usual. Between the weather and those three riders following them, this might turn out to be a long, dangerous night.

A short time later, Bearpaw pointed to a ridge to the left of the trail and said, "I think we'd better go over there and see if we can find somewhere to hunker down. A nice overhang would give us a place to get out of the weather."

Morgan nodded. "Lead the way. We'll be right behind you."

It took about half an hour for them to locate a suitable place. A granite bluff jutted into the air and sloped inward to a cavelike area at its base. It would provide shelter from the north wind and block at least some of the snow, if Bearpaw was right about that being on the way as well.

Morgan and Bearpaw tended to the horses while Tasmin gathered wood and built a fire. Ever since they had left Gallup, she had been good about helping out around camp and had done her share of the work without any complaints. She soon had a nice little fire blazing away merrily, the smoke rising to spread out against the overhanging rock and then dispersing.

By now, the sky was completely overcast. Dark gray clouds scudded swiftly overhead. The temperature dropped steadily. As Morgan and Bearpaw hunkered next to the fire, Morgan said, "It looks like you were right, Phillip."

Bearpaw grunted. "I just hope we're not in for a full-fledged blizzard. We may be stuck here for several days if the snow gets too deep."

"Do you expect that to happen?"

"Not really," Bearpaw replied with a shake of his head. "It's too early in the season for that. But when you're talking about the weather, Kid, you can't really take anything for granted. It does what it wants to do, and there's not a blessed things we humans can do about it except try to adapt."

They had some dried venison plus the makings for biscuits. Bearpaw prepared supper, and the three of them sat by the fire and ate the meager meal. While they were eating, Morgan saw snowflakes begin to fall, whipped along by the wind.

"There's your snow," he told Bearpaw with a grin. "I guess you knew what you were talking about after all."

"I told you. Never argue with a redskin about the weather."

The light had begun to fade. Morgan went to the front of the cavelike area underneath the overhanging bluff and looked out across the hills he could see from there. He was especially watchful for any signs of motion, but didn't see any. Maybe the riders who had been behind them earlier had sought shelter from the storm, too. If they had any sense, that's what they had done, whether they were following Morgan and his companions or not.

Morgan turned and went back to the fire. Behind him, the snowfall grew thicker.

If the circumstances had been different, they would have put out the fire so that anyone tracking them wouldn't be able to see it. As it was, though, without the fire it would get mighty cold before morning. They would let it burn down to embers, but wouldn't extinguish it completely.

During the time they had been traveling together, Morgan had gotten a little more comfortable having Tasmin around. She didn't make any pretense of separating her bedroll from his anymore. She was huddled against him for warmth as the flames died down. During a brief, private conversation earlier in the evening, Morgan and Bearpaw had agreed to take turns standing watch tonight, just in case anything happened. Bearpaw took the first turn.

Morgan dozed off, feeling a chill seeping into his bones from the rocky ground despite the blankets underneath him. Outside their little sanctuary, the wind howled and the snow blew almost horizontal to the ground.

* * *

"Wake up, Kid."

The voice penetrated Morgan's sleep-fogged brain. It took a second before he realized that it didn't belong to Bearpaw. Nor was it Tasmin's voice. The tones were male, harsh and angry.

Morgan lunged up from his blankets and reached for the gun on his hip.

Something crashed into his face and sent him sprawling onto his back before he could grab the Colt. A second later, there was another jarring impact, this time on his left side. Somebody was kicking him, he realized.

The faint glow from the embers, reflected back from the overhanging bluff, showed him a dark shape looming above him. He rolled away as the man tried to kick him again. That took him past the Winchester he had placed beside his blankets when he turned in. He snatched up the rifle and started swinging the barrel around to bear on his attacker.

"Hold it, Kid, or I'll blow the whore's brains out!"

Morgan froze, and not from the frigid chill in the air. Somebody snapped a match into life, and its harsh glare revealed a shocking scene. Bearpaw lay huddled near the horses while the man with the match stood over him, holding a gun on him. Another man had jerked Tasmin to her feet and had an arm looped around her throat while his other hand pressed the barrel of a revolver to her head. The third man, the one who had been trying to stomp the Kid to death, was Hyde, the giant black bouncer from Rosa's place in Gallup. He pushed some fresh wood into the fire, and after a moment it caught and grew brighter.

Hyde wasn't the only one of the trio Morgan recognized. The other two hombres had been members of the gang that had kidnapped Rebel. He hadn't seen them since that night in Black Rock Canyon, but their images were still fresh in his mind, preserved perfectly by the hatred he felt.

"Put the rifle down, Kid," warned the man holding Tasmin. "I ain't gonna tell you again."

Morgan grimaced and tossed the Winchester aside. On the other side of the fire, Bearpaw moaned and stirred. The bastards must have snuck up on him under the cover of the storm and knocked him out, Morgan thought.

"Reach over with your left hand and take the Colt out," the man holding Tasmin ordered.

"Once he's unarmed, I'm gonna bust him into little pieces," Hyde rumbled.

"Not until we have a talk with him," the other man said. "Do what I told you, Kid. Shuck that iron."

Carefully, Morgan reached over with his left hand and slipped the Colt out of its holster. He wondered for a second just how good a shot he was with that hand. Not good enough, he decided. He bent over and placed the revolver on the ground next to the Winchester.

"Now back away from them."

Morgan did so reluctantly. Tasmin was watching him with a fearful expression on her face. He knew from some of the things she had said during the trip that she was terrified of Hyde. Rosa had run the house with an iron fist, and Hyde was her enforcer. The beatings he doled out on Rosa's command had seriously injured some of the soiled doves.

"I guess Rosa sent you after us to settle the score for her brother," Morgan said. He didn't say anything about recognizing the other two men from Black Rock Canyon. He didn't want them to know about that just yet.

"We got scores of our own to settle," the man said. "Clem Baggott and Spence Hooper were friends of ours. We came to see them and found out they'd been shot dead by some fancy gunslinger. Clem's sister was glad to send this big darkie with us to help track you down."

Even after splitting up, most of the gang seemed to have converged on Gallup, Morgan thought. He supposed that wasn't so surprising. Baggott's sister ran a whorehouse after all. These hardcases probably had thought they could lie low there as well as anywhere else.

"What's your game, mister?" the man went on. "Why'd you come gunning for Clem and Spence?"

"We weren't gunning for them," Morgan said. "I explained it all back in Gallup. I just stopped off at Rosa's for a little slap-and-tickle, and that fella Baggott came into the parlor and started shooting at me."

The man shook his head. "Clem was a pretty level-headed sort. He wouldn't have blazed away like that and put his sister in danger without a good reason. He recognized you."

Morgan shook his head. "He mistook me for somebody else, if anything. I never saw him before."

The man sneered and pressed the gun barrel against Tasmin's head hard enough to make her cry out softly in pain and fear. "I don't believe you," he said.

"It's the truth," Morgan insisted. He was looking desperately for some way to turn the tables on these men, but so far he hadn't found any.

The other man, the one guarding Bearpaw, frowned as he stared at Morgan. "Abel, there's somethin' familiar about this hombre," he said suddenly. "I'd swear I've seen him before."

Abel . . . That had to be Abel Dean. Morgan plucked the name out of his memory. Dean squinted at him and said, "Yeah, Jim, I think maybe you're right. He looks familiar to us, and Clem recognized him . . . Who the hell can he *be*?"

"All I know is he's Kid Morgan," Hyde said, "and I'm gonna kill him."

Jim Fowler—that was the other man's name, Morgan recalled—took a step forward. "Maybe I'm goin' loco," he said, "but I'd swear this fella looks like the one from Carson City. The one whose wife we took out to that canyon—"

"Son of a bitch!" Dean exclaimed. "It *is* him!" He jerked the gun away from Tasmin's head. "Kill him!"

Before either of the kidnappers could fire, Bearpaw suddenly lunged hard against Fowler's legs. The Paiute had regained more of his senses than he had let on. Fowler stumbled to the side as he pulled the trigger. The blast was deafeningly loud as it echoed back from the overhanging bluff.

At the same time, Tasmin turned her head and sank her teeth into Dean's throat under the shelf of his jutting jaw. His yell was one more of surprise than pain, but she kept him from firing at Morgan while he tried to knock her loose.

Morgan dived for the Colt on the ground. Hyde moved with surprising speed for such a big man and rammed into him, knocking him away from the gun. Blood streamed down the side of Hyde's face from his ear, and Morgan realized that the wild shot fired by Fowler must have clipped him. Hyde swung a sweeping backhand at him. Morgan ducked under it.

He wasn't going to make the mistake of trying to tackle Hyde again. That hadn't worked too well the first time. Instead, he lunged behind the horses, using the animals to shield him from Hyde's charge and from Dean's and Fowler's guns. The shot had spooked the horses, so they were dancing back and forth.

Morgan tore the buckskin's picket rope loose and leaped onto the horse's back. He banged his boots against the horse's flanks and sent him leaping forward. The buckskin's shoulder collided with Hyde. The big man had more than met his match. He went sailing off his feet from the impact.

Morgan leaped off the buckskin and tackled Dean, knocking him away from Tasmin. Both of them went down hard. Morgan crashed a fist into the outlaw's face and used his other hand to grab the wrist of Dean's gun hand. He slammed that hand against the rocky ground a couple of times, and the second time, the gun came loose. Morgan hit him again.

He didn't have time to do anything else before Hyde grabbed him from behind, lifted him into the air, and threw him against the bluff. Pain shot through Morgan as he crashed into the unyielding surface. Hyde came at him again.

Shots began to roar. Hyde's eyes widened as bullets punched into his back. He stumbled forward, reaching behind him and trying to paw at the wounds like a maddened beast. The shots continued until the hammer fell on an empty cylinder. Hyde lost his footing and fell to his knees, then pitched forward on his face, revealing Tasmin standing behind him, both hands wrapped around the butt of Morgan's Colt as smoke curled from the muzzle.

"Kid, watch out!" Bearpaw yelled.

Morgan whirled around and saw that Fowler had broken away from the Paiute, who had been wrestling with him while Morgan had his hands full with Dean and Hyde. Fowler snapped a shot at him. The bullet whined off the rock as Morgan dove and rolled, grabbing the Winchester as he did so. He came up on one knee and fired the rifle from the hip. Flame lanced from the barrel. Fowler jerked backward as the bullet drove into his chest. Morgan worked the Winchester's lever and cranked off two more shots. The impact of the slugs sent Fowler stumbling away from the fire. The wind whipped snow around him, hiding him from sight.

Morgan sprang to his feet and grabbed Tasmin's arm. "Are you all right?" he asked. When she nodded, he shoved her toward the horses. "Get behind them and stay there!"

He stepped over to Bearpaw and bent down to help the Paiute to his feet. "How about you? Are you hurt?"

Bearpaw shook his head. "No, this old skull of mine is too hard for it to be dented easily. Better keep an eye on that one," he added, nodding toward Dean.

"What about the one I shot?"

"You put three rifle slugs in his chest, Kid. I don't think we need to worry too much about him."

Morgan hoped Bearpaw was right about that. He wasn't going to venture out into the storm to look for Fowler, though.

Dean was still only half conscious. Morgan made sure he was disarmed, then tied his hands behind his back.

Hyde was dead. Even as big as he was, five .45 slugs in his back had been enough to put him down for good. As Morgan checked him to be sure, Tasmin asked from behind the horses, "Did I kill him?"

"You sure did."

A couple of seconds of silence passed. Then she said, "Good. He had it coming to him. You don't know all the things he did back there at Rosa's."

Bearpaw built the fire up. As its flickering light filled the area under the bluff, Morgan knelt in front of Dean and lightly cuffed the man back to consciousness. Dean groaned and then lifted his head, staring at Morgan with pure hatred. His lips were bloody and swollen from Morgan's punches.

"You're him, aren't you?" Dean said thickly. "Browning."

"I don't know what you're talking about. My name is Kid Morgan."

Dean shook his head. "I don't care what you call yourself. You're him."

Morgan had reloaded and holstered his Colt after taking it back from Tasmin. He slipped it out now and placed the barrel under Dean's jaw. He eared back the hammer and said in a quiet, dangerous tone, "If you believe that, then you know you'd better tell me what I want to know."

Dean looked like he wanted to tell Morgan to go to hell. Defiance burned in his eyes. But that defiance faded under the steady, level gaze of the Kid, and finally he swallowed hard and said, "What is it you want?"

"Rattigan and White Rock are supposed to be prospecting somewhere up here at a place called Blue Creek. Is that true?"

Dean managed to nod. "As far as I know, it is. I remember them talking about it."

"Do you know where Blue Creek is?"

"From the way Rattigan talked, it's about fifteen miles west of Trinidad."

"All right. Where are Clay Lasswell, Ezra Harker, and Vernon Moss?"

Dean's mouth twisted bitterly. "You crippled Moss. He'll never walk on those legs again. Lasswell and Harker got a wagon and put him in it. They were gonna take him back where he came from, somewhere down in Texas. Some little town called Diablito."

"Little Devil," Bearpaw translated.

Morgan nodded. He understood that much Spanish. He asked Dean, "You know where to find that town?"

The outlaw shook his head. "Not really. I just know that it's somewhere on the Rio Grande, right across the river from Mexico."

The Texas-Mexico border was pretty long, Morgan recalled, but he would travel every mile of it if he had to in order to find Lasswell, Harker, and Moss. He didn't care if Moss was crippled. The man hadn't yet paid the price for the crime he'd helped commit. Not by a long shot.

As Morgan took the gun barrel away from Dean's neck, the man looked around and said, "Where's Fowler? Where'd he go?"

"He stumbled out into the storm after I shot him," said Morgan.

"Damn it! You're gonna leave a wounded man out there in that blizzard?"

"I'm not going to go out there looking for him if that's what you mean."

"You can't just leave him to die!"

"He's probably dead already," Bearpaw put in. "The Kid hit him three times in the chest with that Winchester."

Dean closed his eyes and began to curse in a low, bitter voice. Morgan ignored him, stood up, and went over to Tasmin. "You'd better crawl back in your bedroll and try to get some more sleep," he suggested.

"What about you?" she asked.

"I'll turn in after a while."

"What are you gonna do with me?" Dean demanded in a shaky voice. "Are you gonna kill me, too?"

Bearpaw hunkered beside him and grinned evilly at him. "I'd say you've got it comin' for what you did, mister."

"It wasn't my idea," Dean protested. "Lasswell and Moss were the ones behind it. The rest of us were just hired hands."

Lasswell and Moss had been hired hands, too, Morgan thought. For the first time in a while, he pondered the question of who had hired Lasswell and given him his orders.

But the snowy night held no answers.

CHAPTER 21

The storm blew itself out during the night. The sky was still overcast the next morning, but the wind had died down and no more snow fell. During the blizzard, the wind had scoured the flatter terrain so that only an inch or two of snow remained on it. The white stuff had piled up in deep drifts, though, against rocks and other barriers.

It had drifted against Jim Fowler's body during the night and eventually spilled over it, so that now the corpse appeared to be a long, white, low mound about fifty feet from the camp. Fowler had made it that far before collapsing.

Morgan went out and brought in the body, dragging it by its heels. Abel Dean glared at him in hatred as he left Fowler's body sprawled under the bluff next to Hyde's corpse.

"Damn it, at least you could bury them!"

"Or you can, if you want to try to dig a grave in this cold ground with your fingers," Morgan said. "We didn't bring along a shovel."

Dean frowned. "Well, it just don't seem right to leave them for the wolves."

Bearpaw said, "Wolves have to eat, too. And it may be a long, hungry winter."

Dean shuddered, but didn't say anything for a moment. Then he asked, "What are you gonna do with me?"

"I guess we'll have to take you with us," Morgan replied. "You'll have to walk, though, unless we happen to find the horses the three of you were riding. I'm hoping they pulled loose from wherever you tied them up last night and found someplace to get in out of the storm. Hate to think about good horseflesh freezing to death for no good reason."

"But you left Jim out there to freeze," Dean snapped. "He was a human being, not an animal."

"That's debatable," Bearpaw said.

They got ready to ride. Morgan tied a length of rope from Dean's bound wrists to his saddle horn. "We'll turn you over to the law in Trinidad," he said. "To tell you the truth, I planned to kill you, but I reckon I'm not as cold-blooded as I thought I was."

"You mean you don't have the guts."

Morgan turned and looked at Dean, who paled at what he saw in the younger man's eyes. Dean didn't say anything else.

As long as they avoided the drifts, the going wasn't too hard. The horses had no trouble with a couple of inches of snow. There was no sign of the other horses, so Dean had to stumble along behind Morgan's horse. It would be a long walk to Trinidad for him, but it wouldn't kill him.

Bearpaw found the trail that ran between Raton, New Mexico, and Trinidad, and the four of them headed north again. They would reach the settlement before the day was over, Bearpaw said.

"When we get there, it'll be time for us to say so long," Morgan told Tasmin. "You can't go with us after that."

"I've held up my own end so far, haven't I?" she shot back at him. "I'm the one who killed Hyde when he was about to beat you to a pulp."

"And I appreciate that. But we weren't planning on those three jumping us like that. We *know* that once we leave Trinidad we'll be riding into trouble."

She looked over at him. "I heard enough, last night and back in Gallup, too, to know that you're hunting down a group of men. What did they do to you, Kid?"

Morgan shook his head. "It wouldn't change anything for you to know."

"Dean called you Browning. Is that your real name?"

"I'm just Kid Morgan. That's all."

Tasmin blew out her breath in frustration. It fogged in the chilly air in front of her face. "You're the stubbornest man I ever did see."

"You'll be staying in Trinidad," Morgan said again. That ended the discussion.

They stopped at midday to gnaw on some leftover biscuits and to let the horses rest. Morgan didn't untie Dean. The man sat on a log and glared at his captors as he ate.

When they were almost ready to go, Morgan walked over to the buckskin. Suddenly, Tasmin cried out behind him, a cry that was choked off abruptly. When he spun around, he saw that Dean had lunged up from the deadfall, gotten some slack in the rope that connected him to Morgan's saddle, and whipped that slack around Tasmin's neck from behind. She must have strayed too close to him. Morgan had warned her to keep her distance from the prisoner, but obviously she hadn't been careful enough about following that order.

"Drop your guns!" Dean shouted at Morgan and Bearpaw. "Drop 'em now or I'll choke her to death, I swear I will!"

"Take it easy," Morgan urged. He didn't want the commotion to spook his horse. If the buckskin got nervous and bolted, even for a short distance, it would tighten that rope and squeeze the life out of Tasmin in a matter of seconds.

"Drop your guns and back away from them!" Dean screamed.

Bearpaw looked at Morgan, who nodded grimly. "I guess we'd better do what he says."

He eased his Colt from its holster and bent to place it on the snowy ground. A few yards away, Bearpaw did the same with the Sharps. The Paiute didn't carry a handgun.

"The knife, too, redskin!" Dean ordered.

Bearpaw took his knife from its sheath and tossed it on the ground next to the Sharps. He and Morgan backed away from the weapons.

Dean forced Tasmin forward. Morgan knew that if Dean ever got his hands on a gun, the three of them were dead.

The outlaw grinned and said to Tasmin, "You're not gonna bite me this time, you little bitch. I'll be lucky if I don't come down with hydrophobia, bein' bit by a slut like you."

They reached Bearpaw's rifle and knife. Dean paused and bent down, trying to pick up the knife and keep the pressure on the rope around Tasmin's neck at the same time. Morgan guessed he wanted to cut the rope so he'd be free from the horse.

That was fine with Morgan. Dean might not realize it, but once he cut the rope, Tasmin would be in less danger. Maybe then one of them could make a move.

Morgan and Bearpaw stood there tensely while Dean sawed on the rope. As soon as it parted, Dean dropped the knife and shoved Tasmin toward the revolver. As she stumbled forward, she seemed to accidentally thrust a leg behind her, so that it went between his legs. Suddenly, their feet were tangled, and Dean let out an angry curse. He threw Tasmin aside and lunged for the gun.

Morgan knew he couldn't beat the outlaw to the Colt. But the knife was closer, so he made a dive for it. His fingers wrapped around the handle just as Dean snatched up the gun. Dean wheeled around as Morgan scrambled to his feet. They were still too far apart. Morgan couldn't reach him with the knife.

Bearpaw leaped between them as flame gouted from the

muzzle of the gun. The bullet struck the Paiute in the body and spun him around. He had occupied Dean's attention for only a second, but that second was long enough for Morgan to leap forward and slam the blade into Dean's chest. With his other hand, he knocked the gun aside as Dean fired again.

Dean took a step back and fumbled at the handle of the knife protruding from his chest. Morgan hit him hard with a right to the jaw. Dean went down, and the gun flew out of his hand. He spasmed as he tried to pull the blade out of his body, but then he went limp, his hands falling away from the knife. Blood welled from his mouth as he kicked a final time.

Seeing that Dean was dead, Morgan whirled around and ran to Bearpaw's side. The Paiute had fallen on the snowy ground, which was now speckled with crimson droplets in places. Morgan went to a knee and lifted Bearpaw's head.

"How bad is it?"

"Bad enough to . . . hurt like blazes."

"You'll be fine," Morgan said. "We'll get you to a doctor. It can't be much farther to Trinidad." He fumbled with the buffalo robe and the shirt underneath it, finally pulling them aside so that he could see the wound. The bullet had ripped into Bearpaw's side and then torn out his back. Blood was everywhere. Morgan wasn't sure how serious the wound was. He told himself that Bearpaw would be all right. He had to be.

Tasmin knelt on Bearpaw's other side. She had removed the rope from her neck and seemed to be fine, except for a welt where the rope had scratched her skin. "How bad is it?" she asked.

"I don't know." Morgan answered honestly because Bearpaw had passed out. "Help me get something tied around these wounds."

They labored frantically for the next few minutes, tearing strips from a blanket and winding them tightly around Bearpaw's midsection after Morgan pressed more wads of cloth into the wounds to try to stop the bleeding. Then they lifted him into his saddle. Thankfully, Bearpaw roused enough to grab hold of the saddle horn with both hands and help keep himself mounted.

Then Morgan and Tasmin swung up into their saddles as well and set off for Trinidad with Bear-paw riding between them. None of them looked back at Abel Dean, who lay motionless in the snow behind them.

The doctor, a tall, balding, rawboned man, came out of his surgery rubbing his bloody hands on a rag. He gave an anxious Morgan and Tasmin a nod and said, "It looks like you got him here in time. I got the bleeding stopped, cleaned out the wounds, and stitched them up. He's got a good chance to pull through, but he'll be laid up for quite a while. A month maybe."

Morgan thought back to what Dr. Patrick McNally had said about him, which was pretty much the same thing. He had beaten that prediction because he had the need for revenge driving him. Bearpaw didn't have to do that. The Paiute had helped Morgan this far.

From here on out, The Kid would go it alone.

He turned to Tasmin and said, "You'll stay here in Trinidad and make sure that he gets better."

"But, Kid—" she began with a frown.

Morgan shook his head. "I owe my life to Phillip."

"Then why don't *you* stay here and take care of him?"

"Because there are still things I have to do, things that won't wait." He looked in her eyes and went on. "Tasmin, I need you to do this. For him . . . and for me. I need to know that both of you are safe."

"While you're off risking your life on some sort of . . . of vengeance quest?" she whispered.

"Don't mind me," the doctor said behind them. "I think

I'll go have a cup of coffee. The two of you can hash out whatever you need to. Just remember there'll be a bill for my services."

"You'll get your money," Morgan said. "I'll see to that."

The doctor nodded and went out, leaving Morgan and Tasmin looking squarely at each other. After a moment, Tasmin sighed and said, "I'm not going to be able to budge you, am I?"

Morgan shook his head. "I'm afraid not."

"You know, most of the time men do whatever I want. It's not fair that you're not like them. Who was she?"

Tightly, Morgan asked, "What do you mean?"

"The woman who left you in such pain."

"She didn't leave me," he said. "She was *taken* from me."

"By the men you're hunting down?"

Morgan shrugged.

Tasmin reached out, rested a hand on the chest of the buckskin jacket Morgan wore. "I'll take care of Bearpaw," she promised. "I'll see to it that the doctor does everything that needs to be done. What are you going to do?"

Morgan glanced at the window. Night had fallen outside. It had taken them most of the rest of the day to reach Trinidad, which at the moment was a picturesque little settlement with snow on the roofs of its buildings and the mountains looming up in the west.

"It's too late to leave now. In the morning, I reckon I'll head for Blue Creek."

"Where there are two more men you need to kill."

Morgan shrugged again. There was no need to put it into words.

The doctor came back into the room, carrying a cup of coffee. He said, "I had to give Mr. Bearpaw some laudanum, so he'll probably sleep the rest of the night. I'll keep an eye on him. You don't have to worry. You can both go have something to eat and then get some rest. The Trinidad Hotel ought to have a room for you."

Neither Morgan nor Tasmin corrected the doctor's assumption that they would just need one room. Tasmin said, "I'll be back in the morning to check on him and help out any way I can."

"Is there a Western Union office in town?" Morgan asked.

The doctor nodded. "Two blocks down the street on the left."

"Much obliged for everything."

They left the doctor's house, stepping out into another frigid night. Morgan spotted a café, so he and Tasmin stopped and had an actual meal, which tasted good after long days of making do on the trail. Then they went to the Trinidad Hotel, where Morgan rented two rooms and used most of the rest of his money to pay for a couple of weeks in advance on Tasmin's room.

"I'll see you later," he told her. "Go on up and get some rest."

"Where are you going?"

"I need to send a wire."

He found the Western Union office and sent another telegram to Claudius Turnbuckle, asking that the lawyer arrange to pay for the doctor and any other expenses Tasmin and Bearpaw might have. He wanted both of them to have money in the bank in Trinidad to take care of any emergencies, too.

With that taken care of, he returned to the hotel and stopped at the desk to get the key to Room Seven. Tasmin was across the hall in Room Eight.

The clerk gave Morgan a puzzled frown. "The young lady already took the key to your room, sir. She said she would take care of both of them."

Morgan hadn't told her to do that, but he supposed that no harm was done. He nodded his thanks and went upstairs. Pausing in front of Tasmin's door, he knocked softly on it, intending to ask her for the key to his room.

There was no answer.

Morgan knocked again and called, "Tasmin?" Maybe she was already so sound asleep that she couldn't hear him, he thought. He turned and stepped across the hall to try the door to his room, hoping that she had unlocked it before turning in.

The knob twisted easily in his hand. He swung the door open, and saw that the lamp on the table next to the bed was already burning with its flame turned low.

The bed was occupied, too. Tasmin sat there with her back against a pillow propped between her and the headboard. She wore a simple white nightgown, and her dark hair was loose and flowing around her shoulders.

"Oh, no," Morgan said as he began to shake his head.

"Why not?" she asked. "It doesn't have to mean anything. I *am* just a whore after all."

Tears shone in her eyes as she spoke.

Morgan stepped into the room and eased the door closed behind him. "I never thought you ought to . . . I mean, you don't have to feel any obligation to . . . I never expected—"

"Shut up," she whispered. "We both need this."

Morgan shook his head. Maybe someday, but not now. Not yet.

"I can't."

Her hands clenched into fists. "I'll bet you can. You just won't."

"That's not true. I just can't be with any woman right now."

"Until you've finished killing the men who took the last woman from you?"

Morgan dragged a deep, ragged breath into his body. "If you must know," he said, "that's right. And maybe not even then. Maybe not ever."

She leaned forward in the bed. "Then for God's sake, at least *tell* me about it. Tell me the truth for a change, Kid. If you don't, then I'll think it's just because I'm a cheap whore."

"That's not true," Morgan insisted. "I swear, Tasmin, ever

since I've gotten to know you, I never think of you that way. That's all in the past."

Her lips curved in a thin smile. "So, you can put what I used to be behind you without any trouble, but you can't put your own past behind you, too?"

Morgan just stared at her, unsure what to say. He didn't think anything would make a difference.

"Did you ever stop to think that if you talked about it, it might be easier to let go?"

"I don't want to let go. Not yet." He struggled with the thoughts that filled his head. "I . . . I need to hang on to the pain for now. It keeps me going. When I'm done with . . . what I have to do . . . maybe then things will be different. Maybe I can start looking ahead again, instead of looking back."

Tasmin looked at him for a long moment, then sighed and shook her head. "You might as well go across the hall and get some sleep," she said.

Relieved, he turned and reached for the doorknob.

"You'll need to be well rested to do all that killing," she said to his back.

CHAPTER 22

The log cabin sat against the snowy, timbered slope of a hill. The little stream known as Blue Creek twisted along at the base of the hill. Morgan supposed that was where the two men who occupied the cabin did their panning for gold. He saw an old-fashioned sluice box at the edge of the creek. The odds of them finding much dust like that, in this day and age when modern mining methods had replaced those old ways, was mighty slim, Morgan thought as he hunkered behind a boulder on the opposite slope and watched the place. A die-hard prospector always had hope, though, even when he didn't have much of anything else.

Smoke curled from the cabin's stone chimney. Both men were in there, Morgan knew. He had seen them moving around a short time earlier, right after he got here. They had tended to the horses in the little corral and shed out back, then gone into the cabin. It was late in the afternoon. They might not emerge again until the next morning.

Morgan didn't intend to wait that long.

It had taken him most of the day to get here from Trinidad. The clouds had finally broken up during the day, so the sun was shining brightly now as it dipped toward the peaks behind the cabin. With the weather clearing like that and the wind dying down, the night would be really cold. Morgan's eyes narrowed as he looked at the stack of firewood beside the cabin.

Could be that one of the men would decide to bring in some more wood before nightfall, just so they'd have plenty. He began working his way toward the cabin, circling so that he could come in from that direction. If neither of them came out to fetch wood, he'd have to think of some other way to lure them out.

He crossed the creek upstream, leaping from rock to rock in order to do so, then headed for the cabin. It didn't have any windows on this side, but Morgan used the trees for cover anyway. When he reached the cabin, he pressed his back to its rear wall, just around the corner from the stack of firewood.

He could hear Rattigan and White Rock moving around inside and talking, and the knowledge that he was this close to two more of the men responsible for Rebel's death gnawed at his guts. He wanted to go around to the front of the cabin, kick the door open, and go in shooting. If it came down to it, that was exactly what he would do. But he hoped there would be a better way.

The sun had touched the mountains to the west and shadows had begun to gather when Morgan heard the cabin door open. He slipped the Colt from its holster and waited.

Booted feet crunched in the snow as one of the men came around the cabin to the stack of firewood. Morgan heard him muttering to himself. He waited until the man had gathered up several pieces of wood and turned back toward the front of the cabin before he sprang out of concealment and brought the Colt crashing down on the man's head.

The man dropped the firewood and toppled forward. From inside the cabin, a voice yelled, "White Rock? What was that racket? You all right out there?"

White Rock wasn't going to answer. He was out cold. Morgan moved quickly past the unconscious half-breed. He reached the front corner of the cabin just as Rattigan came out the door, gun in hand.

Morgan hesitated for a second as he saw how old Rattigan was. The man's face was lined and leathery, and the beard stubble dotting his angular jaw was pure white. For that second, Morgan was reminded of his grandfather, and his finger froze on the trigger.

Then Rattigan's face twisted in an evil grimace, and flame erupted from the barrel of the gun in his hand. Morgan felt a tremendous impact on his left hip that slewed him around. Rattigan fired again. This slug burned past Morgan's ear, and he didn't waste any more time thinking about Rattigan's age. Old or not, the outlaw was as vicious and evil as any of the others Morgan had faced. Maybe more so, because he'd had more time to practice. Morgan snapped his gun up and triggered it as his left leg folded up beneath him.

Because he was falling, his aim was a little off. His bullet caught Rattigan in the left shoulder and knocked the old man back a step. Rattigan kept his feet and hung on to his gun, though. He threw a third shot at Morgan. The bullet plowed into the snow-covered ground only inches away. The Colt bucked in Morgan's hand for a second time. This bullet punched into Rattigan's chest and knocked him down. When he tried to raise his gun, Morgan shot him again. Rattigan went over onto his back, the revolver slipping from his fingers as he slumped.

Boots crunched in the snow. Morgan rolled over and saw that White Rock had regained consciousness and was coming at him, a piece of firewood held high over his head. The breed's face was contorted with hate as he yelled, "You son of a bitch!"

Morgan knew that White Rock intended to crush his skull with that firewood. He tipped up the barrel of the Colt and fired. The bullet struck White Rock in the throat and ripped through at an upward angle into his brain. Blood fountained as he stumbled forward another step. The firewood slipped from his fingers and fell to the ground as White Rock pitched forward, landing on the crimson spray that had come from his ruined throat and stained the snow.

Unable to stand because his left leg was still numb, Morgan scooted backward so that he could cover both men. He was pretty sure that Rattigan and White Rock were both dead, but injured as he was, he didn't want to take any chances.

Neither man moved. Morgan could tell they weren't breathing anymore. He reached for the loops on his gunbelt, intending to take some cartridges from them and reload.

The belt was surprisingly loose around his hips, he discovered. He moved his hand to the place where he'd been hit, and found that the thick leather was torn almost completely apart. He didn't feel any blood, though, and after a second, he realized that Rattigan's bullet had hit the gunbelt and glanced off, ruining the belt but failing to penetrate Morgan's body. His leg had gone numb from the impact; that was all.

Relief washed through him. He had worried that he might bleed to death out here, far from town. Now he knew that the numbness in his leg ought to wear off after a while. He'd be bruised and sore, but if the bullet hadn't broken any bones, he would be able to get back to Trinidad.

Morgan reloaded the Colt, then untied the holster thong from his leg and took off the ruined gunbelt. He tossed it aside and crawled over to the cabin, dragging his injured leg behind him. When he made it to the wall, he reached up with his free hand and found a good grip between a couple of the logs. He was able to pull himself up and lean against the cabin.

As he did that, feeling began to come back into his leg. He waited until he trusted his muscles to obey him, then limped toward the door, which stood open. Rattigan hadn't closed it behind him before he started shooting. By the time Morgan made it to the door, he was confident that the bullet hadn't broken his hip. Everything seemed to be working, albeit painfully.

He stepped inside and shoved the door closed to trap the heat from the fireplace. As he warmed up, the stiffness in his leg eased even more, although the place where the bullet had struck the gunbelt was still very tender to the touch. A coffeepot was on the stove. Morgan found a cup on a crude shelf and filled it with the strong black brew, then sat down in a rough-hewn chair at an equally rough table to sip from the cup and rest his leg.

After a while, he felt strong enough to limp outside and drag the bodies of Rattigan and White Rock around to the back of the cabin. He left them there and crossed the creek to head back up the hill to the place where he'd left his horse. The buckskin was still there. He tossed his head, obviously glad to see Morgan.

"Sorry," the Kid muttered. "Let's get you down to that shed."

By the time he'd finished tending to the horse, night had fallen. Morgan went inside, taking some firewood with him, and built up the blaze in the fireplace. The two outlaws had enough supplies on hand so that he was able to scrape together some supper without much trouble. Not wanting to use either of the bunks in the cabin where Rattigan and White Rock had slept, he had brought in his bedroll. He spread it out in front of the fireplace and crawled into the blankets to sleep, using his saddle as a pillow.

But between his painful hip and the knowledge that two dead men lay on the cold ground just on the other side of those logs, Morgan was a long time dozing off.

He wouldn't have been surprised if wolves had dragged off the corpses during the night, but Rattigan and White Rock were still there the next morning. Morgan's hip and leg were pretty sore, but he was able to get around fairly well.

He hauled both bodies into the cabin, one at a time, and dumped them on the bunks. He planned to leave them there, a mystery for whoever stumbled on this cabin next.

Although he didn't like stealing from the dead, he needed a new gunbelt, and Rattigan wore one with a brown, buscadero-cut holster attached to it. Morgan took it off the body and tried it on. It fit fairly well around his lean hips. He slipped the Colt into the holster, worked it up and down a few times, and nodded in satisfaction. The belt and holster would do.

He left the corral gate open as he rode away. The outlaws' horses would have to fend for themselves. If he showed up in Trinidad with a couple of extra horses, the law might start asking too many questions.

It was late afternoon by the time he reached the settlement. He went straight to the doctor's house and tied the buckskin outside. When he limped into the front room, he found it empty, but voices came from the room where he had left Bearpaw the day before.

The Paiute was propped up in bed when Morgan came in. He grinned and said, "Kid!"

Tasmin sat in a straight chair beside the bed. She looked at Morgan and smiled in relief, but didn't say anything.

"Are you all right?" Bearpaw went on. His grin disappeared and was replaced by a frown as Morgan limped across the room to get another chair and pull it up beside the bed.

"I'm fine," Morgan said. "A little gimpy, that's all."

"That's a new gunbelt you're wearing. A different one anyway."

"My old one got ruined."

"By a bullet?" Bearpaw didn't wait for Morgan to answer. He continued. "What about Rattigan and White Rock?"

"We don't have to worry about them anymore."

Bearpaw heaved a sigh of relief and nodded. "Good. That

just leaves the three down in Texas. As soon as I'm able to travel, we'll head down that way—"

"I'm going now," Morgan broke in. "Well, first thing tomorrow anyway."

"By yourself? You don't need to do that, Kid."

Tasmin said, "You're wasting your breath, Phillip. He's as stubborn as a mule. He can barely walk, and he's talking about starting to Texas tomorrow."

Morgan smiled faintly and pointed out, "I'm not going to walk there."

"Yeah, but you don't need to take on those three by yourself," Bearpaw insisted. "I ought to come with you."

"The doctor said you'd be laid up for a month."

"Patrick said the same thing about you. You were up and around in a couple of weeks."

Morgan shook his head. "I can't wait even that long. Lasswell and Harker were going to take Moss home. There's no telling if they stayed there in Diablito. I may have to track them somewhere else."

Bearpaw studied him intently for a moment, then asked, "You think you're ready to go it alone?"

"I went it alone yesterday," Morgan said, "and I'm still alive."

Bearpaw's head went up and down in a slow nod. "I suppose you're right about that. The proof is in the pudding, as they say. But Lasswell's probably the most dangerous of the whole bunch. We don't really know about Harker and Moss."

"Moss is crippled."

"Doesn't mean he's not still dangerous. A broken-backed rattler can still sink its fangs in you, Kid."

Morgan didn't want to continue this argument. He leaned forward in his chair, squeezed Bearpaw's shoulder, and said, "I'll see to it that all your expenses are taken care of while you recuperate, yours and Tasmin's both. And I'll tell you who to wire in San Francisco if you ever need anything after that. When you're ready to travel, the two of you can head back to Sawtooth." He smiled at Tasmin. "It's a good place to live. You'll be able to make a new life for yourself there."

"Where no one will know I used to be a whore?" she asked.

Morgan inclined his head. "Everybody can use a fresh start now and then, I reckon."

"What about you, Kid? When does your fresh start come along?"

"Not yet," he replied, thinking about Clay Lasswell, Ezra Harker, and Vernon Moss. "Not yet."

He stood up. Bearpaw held up a hand and said, "Wait a minute, Kid. I can see that I'd be wasting my time trying to talk you out of this."

Morgan smiled again, signifying agreement.

"I want you to take my Sharps with you," Bearpaw went on. "One of these days, you'll need to make a long shot, and you won't find a sweeter rifle for it than that one."

"The Sharps is yours," Morgan protested.

"That's right. So it's mine to give away if I want to. Take it, Kid. Otherwise, I might just have to follow you to Texas."

"I'll buy a wagon," Tasmin said. "We can load you in it and probably travel now."

"The hell with that," the Kid said sharply. "You try something crazy like that and it's liable to kill you, Phillip."

"Then take the Sharps. Make a loco old redskin feel better."

Morgan sighed. He could see that he wasn't going to win this argument. "All right," he said. "If it'll help, I'll take the Sharps. Between that and the Winchester and my Colt, I reckon I'll be armed for bear."

"My knife, too," the Paiute said. "I want you to have it."

Morgan nodded. "All right." He had already decided that he would stop at one of Trinidad's general stores and make arrangements to have a new Sharps and the best knife they had in stock delivered to the doctor's house for Bearpaw when he was well away from the settlement.

"You'd better come to see me in the morning before you ride out," Bearpaw warned.

"I can do that . . . as long as you promise not to give me any more trouble."

"Trouble?" Bearpaw repeated with mock indignation. "More often than not, *I'm* the one who's *saved* you from trouble."

"No argument there," Morgan said. "I owe you my life several times over."

He left the room, saying that he needed to take his horse down to the livery stable. Tasmin followed him out onto the porch. It had warmed up quite a bit during the day, and some of the snow had melted. The rest of it would be gone in another day or two, Morgan thought.

"Are you really all right?" Tasmin asked as they paused on the porch.

"I'm fine," Morgan assured her. "My hip is bruised, but that's all."

"And it'll probably be healed up by the time you reach the Rio Grande."

"I'm counting on that," Morgan said.

She folded her arms across her chest. "Did you ever stop to think that all this you're doing won't bring her back, Kid?"

He looked off into the distance and answered honestly. "Every day of my life."

CHAPTER 23

Texas was a far cry from Colorado, in more ways than one. Over the course of several weeks, Morgan had traveled more than a thousand miles from those snow-dappled mountains to this hot, dry, dusty plain along the Rio Grande. Though autumn storms continued to bring snow and cold winds to more northern climes, weather like that seldom penetrated to this chaparral-covered border country southeast of Laredo.

If everything he had learned since leaving Colorado was correct, the border village of Diablito was now only a mile or two ahead of him. His journey was almost at an end. That was the good news.

The bad news was that two men were following him.

Morgan had no idea who they were, but they had been back there for a couple of days, never coming too close, always staying far enough back to keep him in sight without crowding him. Bearpaw had taught him to watch his backtrail, and that lesson was paying off now.

Morgan thought about trying to set up an ambush for the men following him, but he had decided that as long as they didn't make a move against him, he would press on toward his destination. They had to have a reason for dogging his trail, and maybe he would find out what it was once he reached Diablito.

In the meantime, and without taking his attention off what was in front of him and behind him, a portion of his thoughts drifted back to Trinidad. He would never forget the look on Bearpaw's face as he gripped the Paiute's hand and bade him farewell. Frank Morgan was his father, and the Kid had come to accept that. But Bearpaw was like the uncle he'd never had.

Nor would he forget the sadness in Tasmin's dark eyes as she stood there on the front porch of the doctor's house, a shawl around her shoulders, her dark hair blowing in the wind. When they were standing there together on the porch, before he mounted up and rode away, she had made a move like she was about to kiss him, then stopped abruptly as if realizing that it wouldn't do any good. It would just deepen the pain for both of them.

"Life has damned bad timing, doesn't it?" she had whispered.

Morgan thought about how things might have been different, first with Eve McNally, then with Tasmin, and knew that was true. Life had damned bad timing, and there wasn't a thing anybody could do about it.

Nothing except ride on and look to the future, not the past.

That is, as soon as the past was laid to rest.

Vernon Moss wheeled himself toward the open door, groaning in pain as he did so. He didn't figure he would ever get used to this damned chair. He was starting to think the agony from his crushed legs would never fade either. But it wasn't quite as bad when he could sit outside in the shade of the vine-covered porch. There might be a little breeze, and maybe the young Mexican girl he paid to take care of the place would rub his useless legs through the blanket that was spread over them. Sometimes that made them feel better.

Moss was still several feet from the door when the tall figure of a man appeared in it, dark and featureless against the bright sunlight outside. Moss took his hands off the chair's wheels and said, "Who the hell are you?"

"I'm looking for Vernon Moss," the stranger said.

"You found him . . . or what's left of him," Moss said bitterly.

"Where are Clay and Ezra?"

The stranger sounded like he knew them. It was hard for Moss to think because of the pain in his legs, so he said, "They've gone down to the cantina. They'll be back in a little while. You used to ride with them or something?"

The man chuckled, but there wasn't any humor in the sound. Instead, it struck Moss as something that might have come from an open grave. He didn't know why that bizarre thought passed through his mind, but it made him shiver.

"Started in a cantina, and now it's going to end in one," the stranger muttered to himself.

Moss slipped a hand under the blanket. "Damn it, mister, I want to know who you are."

"You don't remember me? From Black Rock Canyon?"

The stranger moved a step into the room, so that Moss could see him a little better. Moss recognized his face, just like he recognized the reference to Black Rock Canyon. He would never forget that night, or the face of the man who had run him down with that buggy and crippled him for life.

"Damn you!" Moss screamed as he jerked the pistol from under the blanket.

The gun in his hand roared, but not before flame licked from the muzzle of the stranger's Colt, which had appeared with blinding speed. Moss felt a giant fist punch him in the chest. The impact made the chair lurch back. The gun trickled from his fingers and fell onto the blanket. Many's the time he had thought about taking that gun and putting the barrel in his mouth or pressing it to his temple and then pulling the trigger to put himself out of his helpless misery—but in the end, he hadn't been able to do it. He'd been too gutless.

Now, even though blood had begun to fill his mouth, he managed to croak, "Thank you," to the stranger before he died. Those words, and the sudden pound of hoofbeats, were the last things Vernon Moss heard on this earth.

Morgan whirled around as he heard the horses coming up fast behind him. Just as he had expected, the shots had drawn the men who'd been following him into the open. So he wasn't surprised to see the two riders galloping toward him.

He was shocked, though, that he recognized them—and they were two of the last people he would have expected to see here in this sleepy border village.

One was tall and lanky, with a thatch of dark hair under his Stetson. The other was shorter and stockier, with a round face and sandy hair. Despite those obvious differences, they bore a distinct resemblance to each other—and to Morgan's late wife.

They were Rebel's brothers, Tom and Bob Callahan.

As surprised as Morgan was to see them, they appeared to be even more shocked to recognize him as they reined their horses to sliding halts. Bob Callahan, the shorter of the brothers, yelped, "Conrad!" Even in the gunfighter garb, they knew their brother-in-law.

Morgan figured the fight wasn't over. Diablito was small enough so that Lasswell and Harker would have heard those shots and might come to investigate. He replaced the spent cartridge in the Colt and slid a round into the normally empty sixth chamber. Then, as he snapped the cylinder closed, he said, "What are you boys doing here?"

"We've been following you," Tom said as he swung down from the saddle. Beside him, Bob did likewise. Tom went on. "We picked up your trail up in the Four Corners. We were lookin' for the bunch that kidnapped and killed Rebel. Figured if anybody was gonna settle the score for her, it'd have to be us . . . since as far as we knew, you'd killed yourself in Carson City."

Morgan nodded. "That's what everybody was supposed to think."

"Then . . . then, damn it, *you're* the mysterious gunfighter who's been killin' off those bastards one by one?" Bob asked in amazement.

"We knew somebody else was after 'em," Tom added, "but we figured it didn't have anything to do with what happened to Rebel."

"It had everything to do with it," Morgan said. "And it's not over—"

Before he could finish that sentence, a shot blasted from down the street. The bullet whined past his ear and thudded into the adobe wall of Moss's house. Morgan wheeled around and spotted Lasswell and Harker splitting up, taking cover behind buildings on opposite sides of the street as they continued throwing lead at Morgan and the Callahan brothers.

"Hunt some cover!" Morgan snapped as he triggered a shot back at Lasswell and Harker and ducked behind a corner of the adobe shack.

Tom and Bob slapped their horses on the rump and sent the animals running out of the line of fire as they scurried for cover of their own. Slugs kicked up dust around their feet, but they made it to safety, Bob behind the house across the street, Tom behind a shed.

Lasswell and Harker must have moseyed out of the cantina to see what the shooting was about, noticed the three men standing in front of Moss's shack, and figured that trouble had caught up to them at last. Now it was going to be a cat-and-mouse game, the two outlaws against Morgan and his unexpected allies. Morgan had his enemies outnumbered for a change.

He wasn't sure he liked that. He had placed Bearpaw in danger, and the Paiute had paid the price. Tasmin had come close to dying, too. Morgan didn't want anything to happen to Tom and Bob. They had already suffered enough, losing their sister like that.

But he also knew that the Callahan brothers were tough, seasoned hombres who had been in more than one fight. He caught Bob's eye across the street and gestured to him, signaling that he was going to work around behind the buildings and try to get the drop on Lasswell. Bob nodded and motioned that he and Tom would do the same with Harker.

As Morgan moved in a crouching run behind the buildings, he hoped that the people who lived here in Diablito would keep their heads down while this little war was going on. He didn't want any other innocents getting hurt.

The guns had fallen silent for the moment while everyone jockeyed for position. Morgan moved carefully, using every bit of cover he could find and darting across the open areas as fast as he could. Sweat trickled down his back. His heart pounded, either from nerves or from the anticipation that his long quest would soon be over—or both. He jerked a little as shots from across the street suddenly shattered the tense silence.

"Tom!" Bob Callahan yelled in alarm.

Morgan's jaw clenched. Tom must be hit, he thought. He dashed up a narrow alley between two buildings, and reached the street in time to see Ezra Harker drawing a bead on Bob as Bob tried to drag his wounded brother to safety.

"Harker!" Morgan shouted.

The outlaw whirled toward him. Flame stabbed from Harker's gun. At the same time, the Colt in Morgan's fist roared and bucked. Harker staggered, but didn't go down. He fired again, sending shards of adobe flying as the bullet struck the corner of the house next to Morgan.

The next second, Harker was riddled with lead as Morgan fired three more times and both Callahan brothers blazed away at him, too, even the wounded Tom, who lay propped up on one elbow as he fired with his other hand. Harker went backward in a macabre dance with blood exploding from him as the bullets ripped through him.

In the eerie silence that fell as the thunderous echoes rolled away, Morgan heard a gun being cocked behind him.

"That's six," Clay Lasswell said. "You've gotta be empty."

Lasswell didn't realize he had replaced the bullet he had used to kill Moss, Morgan thought as he stiffened. The gunman didn't know that there was still one round in the Colt.

"Turn around," Lasswell went on. "I want to see who I'm about to kill."

Morgan let his arm sag to his side in an air of defeat. He turned slowly and faced Lasswell. The ginger-bearded gunman said, "So you're the bastard who's been trackin' down those fellas who rode with me. Yeah, I know about it. I heard through the grapevine about how you killed Baggott and Hooper and Buck and Julio and the rest of 'em. What I want to know is why."

"Take a good look at me," Morgan rasped. "Then you'll know."

Lasswell's eyes narrowed, then widened in shock. "Browning! But you're supposed to be—"

He didn't finish. He pulled the trigger instead.

But even as Lasswell's finger closed on the trigger, Morgan's gun came up again with speed the likes of which he had never achieved before. So fast that it all seemed to happen in the same shaved heartbeat, both Colts roared, Morgan felt the hot breath of a slug as it passed his ear, and Lasswell was rocked back by Morgan's bullet driving into his body.

Now Morgan's gun really was empty, and he couldn't defend himself if Lasswell got off another shot. But Lasswell didn't fire again. He staggered to the side, then dropped his gun and fell to his knees.

Morgan suddenly cried, "Wait! Don't die yet!" and leaped toward him.

Lasswell crumpled onto his left side.

Morgan dropped to his knees as well and grabbed Lasswell's shoulders. "Damn you, don't die!" he said as he shook the outlaw. "Who hired you to kill my wife? Tell me!"

Blood dribbled from the corner of Lasswell's mouth as he looked up at Morgan with an expression that was half smile, half grimace. "You'll . . . never know," he gasped out.

Then his head drooped to the ground and all the life went out of his body.

Morgan looked up at the hot Texas sky and howled, *"Nooooo!"*

It wasn't over.

Maybe it never would be.

Four days later, wearing the fringed buckskin jacket against the dank, chilly wind coming off the Pacific, Kid Morgan walked into the San Francisco building that housed the offices of Turnbuckle and Stafford. A law clerk greeted him, saying, "Mr. Turnbuckle is expecting you, Mister, ah, Kid. He said to show you right into his office when you got here."

"Thanks," Morgan said with a nod. He followed the man to a heavy door of polished, engraved wood. The clerk swung it open, and Morgan stepped inside.

He stopped short at the sight of the two men standing by the window. Claudius Turnbuckle was a stout, balding man with bushy eyebrows and muttonchop whiskers. Morgan expected to see him. It was the other man who came as a surprise.

"Hello, Conrad," Frank Morgan said.

The Drifter was a medium-sized, deceptively powerful man with graying dark hair. He wore range clothes and a holstered six-gun. He stepped forward, put his arms around his son, and gave him a hug that the Kid returned awkwardly.

"Claudius has just been telling me what you've gone through these past few months," Frank went on. "I wish I'd found out sooner. I'd have given you a hand."

"That's . . . all right," the Kid said. "I handled it."

At least, he'd handled it as much as he could, he thought.

"I was up north in timber country. Claudius didn't know where to find me." Frank put a hand on the Kid's shoulder and squeezed. "I'm so sorry about Rebel. She was as fine a gal as anybody will ever see."

The Kid nodded. The pain of his loss was still there inside him, as sharp as ever, but he had learned by now to keep it tamped down, to not acknowledge it unless he had to. That was the only way he could keep going.

After the shoot-out in Diablito, he and the Callahan brothers had ridden to San Antonio, where a real doctor took over caring for the wounded Tom Callahan. Morgan had patched him up as best he could, and the sawbones said that Tom ought to be all right. Then Morgan had sent a wire to Turnbuckle, letting him know what had happened, and gotten a speedy message in return asking him to come to San Francisco as soon as possible. He'd been able to catch a westbound Southern Pacific train in San Antonio, and now here he was in San Francisco, reunited with his father.

"I have a particularly good bottle of brandy I've been saving," Turnbuckle said. "I'll break it out, and then we can all sit down and you can tell us what you've been doing, Conrad."

"We already know some of what he's been doing," Frank said with a slight smile. "Raising hell from here to Texas. I have to say, Conrad, I knew you'd changed a mite, but . . ." He looked the Kid over. "Maybe not this much."

As glad as he was to see his father, Morgan wasn't in any mood to sit around and reminisce. He still had things to do. But he supposed he owed Frank and Turnbuckle an explanation, so he took off his hat and sat down as the lawyer suggested, accepted a snifter of brandy, and launched into a recitation of everything that had happened in the past few months. It was a dark and bloody tale, and that was reflected in the faces of Frank and Turnbuckle.

"Is Tom going to be all right?" Frank asked when the Kid was finished.

"I think so."

"What about that fella Bearpaw?"

Morgan nodded. "I've already sent a wire to Tasmin and gotten one back from her saying that they're fine. They're still in Trinidad, but they'll be starting back to Nevada soon. She wants me to visit them in Sawtooth . . ." Morgan shrugged. "But I doubt if I ever will. I still have things to do."

"Returning to take over the management of the Browning financial interests, you mean?" Turnbuckle asked.

"No," the Kid replied, not bothering to keep the harshness out of his voice. "Those days are over. Too much has happened for things to ever go back to the way they were before."

The lawyer frowned. "But surely you don't intend to continue with this . . . this . . ." He waved at the Kid's fringed jacket and the buscadero gunbelt and holster. "Masquerade!"

"It's not a masquerade anymore. I'm Kid Morgan now." He paused. "I might have one more use for Conrad Browning, though."

"To help you find out who hired Lasswell to kill Rebel and put you through hell?" Frank guessed.

"That's right." The Kid drained the last of his brandy and reached for his hat. "Whoever sicced Lasswell and his bunch on me has a grudge against Conrad, not Kid Morgan, so if I'm going to draw the bastard out, Conrad has to live again. The Callahan boys told me that Rebel is buried in New Mexico, down close to where she and I first met." He stood up, nodded to Frank and Turnbuckle, and said, "It's time for Conrad Browning to pay a visit to his wife's grave."

Turn the page for an explosive preview!

JOHNSTONE COUNTRY. THE ULTIMATE KILLING GROUND.

There a million ways to die in the Black Hills of Dakota Territory—but only one way to make it out alive if your name is Buchanon: with guns blazing . . .

THE HILLS HAVE EYES

The Buchanons are no strangers to hard times—or making hard choices. After losing a hefty number of livestock to a killer grizzly, Hunter Buchanon is forced to sell a dozen broncs down in Denver for some badly needed cash. Everything goes smoothly—until he's ambushed on the way home. The culprits are a murderous bunch of prairie rat outlaws, as dangerous as any Buchanon has ever tangled with. But Hunter is hell-bent on getting his money back. Even if means pursuing the thieves into Dakota Territory—where even deadlier dangers await . . .

Meanwhile, Angus Buchanon has agreed to guide three former Confederate bounty hunters into the Black Hills, on the trail of six cutthroats who robbed a saloon and killed two men in Deadwood. This motley trio of hunters are as cutthroat as the cutthroats they're after. And it doesn't take long for Angus to realize they mean to slaughter him as well at the end of the trail . . .

One family of ranchers. Two groups of cold-hearted murderers. So many ways to die.

National Bestselling Authors
William W. Johnstone
and J.A. Johnstone

CHAPTER 1

Hunter Buchanon whipped his hand to the big LeMat revolver jutting from the holster around which the shell belt was coiled on the ground beside him. In a half-second the big revolver was out of its holster and Hunter heard the hammer click back before he even knew what his thumb was doing. Lightning quick action honed by time and experience including four bloody years during which he fought for the Confederacy in the War of Northern Aggression.

He didn't know what had prompted his instinctive action until he sat half up from his saddle and peered across the red-glowing coals of the dying campfire to see Bobby Lee sitting nearby, peering down the slope into the southern darkness beyond, the coyote's tail curled tightly, ears pricked. Hunter's pet coyote gave another half-moan, half-growl like the one Hunter had heard in his sleep and shifted his weight from one foot to the other.

Hunter sat up slowly. "What is it, Bobby?"

A startled gasp sounded beside Hunter, and in the corner of his left eye he saw his wife Annabelle sit up quickly, grabbing her own hogleg from its holster and clicking the hammer back. Umber light from the fire danced in her thick, red hair. "What is it?" she whispered.

"Don't rightly know," Hunter said tightly, quietly. "But something's put a burr in Bobby's bonnet."

Down the slope behind Hunter, Annabelle, and Bobby Lee, their twelve horses whickered uneasily, drawing on their picket lines.

"Something's got the horses' blood up, too," Annabelle remarked, glancing over her shoulder at the fidgety mounts.

"Stay with the horses, honey," Hunter said, tossing his bedroll aside then rising, donning his Stetson, and stepping into his boots. As he grabbed his Henry repeating rifle, Annabelle said, "You be careful. We might have horse thieves on our hands, Hunter."

"Don't I know it." Hunter jacked a round into the Henry's action, then strode around the nearly dead fire, brushing fingers across the top of the coyote's head and starting down the hill to the south. "Come on, Bobby."

The coyote didn't need to be told twice. If there was one place for Bobby Lee, that was by the side of the big, blond man who'd adopted him when his mother had been killed by a rancher several years ago. Hunter moved slowly down the forested slope in the half-darkness, one hand around the Henry's receiver so starlight didn't reflect off the brass and give him away.

Bobby Lee ran ahead, scouting for any human polecats after the ten horses Hunter and Annabelle were herding from their ranch near Tigerville deep in the Black Hills to a ranch outside of Denver. Hunter and Annabelle had caught the wild mustangs in the Hills near their ranch, and Annabelle had sat on the fence of the breaking corral, Bobby Lee near her feet, watching as Hunter had broken each wild-eyed bronc in turn.

Gentled them, rather. Hunter didn't believe in breaking a horse's spirit. He just wanted to turn them into "plug ponies," good ranch mounts that answered to the slightest tug on the reins or a squeeze of a rider's knees, and could turn on a dime, which was often necessary when working cattle, especially dangerous mavericks.

Hunter and Annabelle needed the money from the horse sale to help make up for the loss of several head of cattle to a rogue grizzly the previous summer. Times were hard on the ranch due to drought and low stock prices, and they were afraid they'd lose the Box Bar B without the money from the horses. They were getting two hundred dollars a head, because they were prime mounts—Hunter had a reputation as one of the best horse gentlers on the northern frontier—and that money would go far toward helping them keep the ranch.

Hunter wanted desperately to keep the Box Bar B not only for himself and Annabelle, but for Hunter's aged, one-armed father, Angus, and the boy Hunter and Annabelle had adopted—Nathan Jones, who after his doxie mother had died had ridden with would-be rustlers, including the boy's scoundrel father, whom Hunter had killed.

The boy was nothing like his father. He was good and hard-working, and he needed a good home.

Hunter moved off down the slope but stopped when Bobby Lee suddenly took off running and swinging left toward some rocks and a cedar thicket, growling. The coyote disappeared in the trees and brush and then started barking angrily. A man cursed and then there were three rocketing gun reports followed by Bobby's mewling howl.

"Damn coyote!" the man's voice called out.

"Bobby!" Hunter said and took off running in the direction in which Bobby Lee had disappeared.

"They know we're here now so be careful!" another man called out sharply.

Running footsteps sounded ahead of Hunter.

He stopped and dropped to a knee when a moving shadow

appeared ahead of him and slightly down the slope. Starlight glinted off a rifle barrel and off the running man's cream Stetson.

"Hold it right there, you son of a bitch!" Hunter bellowed, pressing his cheek to the Henry's stock.

The man stopped suddenly and swung his rifle toward Hunter.

The Henry spoke once, twice, three times. The man grunted and flew backward, dropping his rifle and striking the ground with another grunt and a thud.

"Harvey!" the other man yelled from beyond the rocks and cedars.

Harvey yelled in a screeching voice filled with pain, "I'm a dead man, Buck! Buchanon got me, the rebel devil. He's over here. Get him for me!"

Hunter stepped behind a pine, peered out around it, and jacked another round into the Henry's action. He waited, pricking his ears, listening for the approach of Buck. Seconds passed. Then a minute. Then two minutes.

A figure appeared on the right side of the rocks and cedars, moving slowly, one step at a time. Buck held a carbine across his chest. Hunter lined up the Henry's sights on the man and was about to squeeze the trigger when something ran up behind the man and leaped onto his back. Buck screamed as he fell forward, Bobby Lee growling fiercely and tearing into the back of the man's neck.

Hunter smiled. Buck screamed as he tried in vain to fight off the fiercely protective Bobby Lee. Buck swung around suddenly and cursed loudly as he flung Bobby Lee off him. The coyote struck the ground with a yelp and rolled.

"You mangy cur!" Buck bellowed, drawing a pistol and aiming at Bobby.

Hunter's Henry spoke twice, flames lapping from the barrel.

Buck groaned and lay over on his back. "Ah, hell," he said, and died.

"Good work, Bob," Hunter said, walking toward where the coyote was climbing to his feet. Hunter dropped to a knee, placed his hand on Bobby Lee's back. "You all right?"

The coyote shook himself as if in an affirmative reply.

"All right," Hunter said, straightening. "Let's go check on—"

The shrill whinny of horses cut through the silence that had fallen over the night after Hunter had shot Buck.

"Annabelle!" Hunter yelled, swinging around to retrace his route back to the camp. "Come on, Bobby! There must be more of these scoundrels!"

The coyote mewled and took off running ahead of Hunter.

Only a minute after Hunter and Bobby had left the camp, the horses stirred more vigorously behind where Annabelle sat on a log near the cold fire, her Winchester carbine resting across her denim-clad thighs. She'd just risen from the log and started to walk toward the string of prize mounts when a man's voice called from the darkness down the hill behind the horses.

"Come here, purty li'l red-headed gal!" The voice was pitched with jeering, brash mockery.

Annabelle froze, stared into the darkness. Anger rose in her.

Again, the man's voice caromed quietly out of the darkness: "Come here, purty li'l red-headed gal!" The man chuckled.

Several of the horses lifted their heads and gave shrill whinnies.

The flame of anger burned more brightly in Annabelle, her heart quickening, her gloved hands tightening around the carbine she held high across her chest. She knew she shouldn't do it, but she couldn't stop herself. She moved slowly forward. Ahead and to her left, thirty feet away, the horses were whickering and shifting, pulling at the ropes securing them to the picket line.

Annabelle jacked a round into the carbine's action and moved toward the horses. She patted the blaze on the snout of a handsome black, said, "Easy, fellas. Easy. I got this."

She stepped around the horses and down the slope and stopped behind a broad-boled pine.

Again, the man's infuriating voice came from down the slope beyond her. "Come here, purty li'l red-haired gal. Come find me!"

Annabelle swallowed tightly, said quietly, mostly to herself: "All right—if you're sure about this, bucko . . ."

She continued forward, taking one step at a time. She had no spurs on her boots. Hunter's horses were so well-trained they didn't require them. She made virtually no sound as she continued down the slope, weaving between the columnar pines and firs silhouetted against the night's darkness relieved only by starlight.

"Come on, purty li'l red-headed gal," came the jeering voice again. "Wanna show ya somethin'."

"Oh, you do, do you?" Annabelle muttered beneath her breath. "Wonder what that could be."

She headed in the direction from which the voice had come, practically directly ahead of her now, maybe thirty, forty feet down the slope. That she was being lured into a trap, there could be no question. Hunter had always told her that her red-headed anger would get the best of her one day. Maybe he'd been right.

On the other hand, the open mockery in the voice of the man trying to lure her into the trap could not be denied. She imagined shooting him, and the thought stretched her rich, red lips back from her perfect, white teeth in a savage smile.

She took one step, then another . . . another . . . pausing briefly behind trees, edging cautious looks around them, knowing that she could see the lap of flames from a gun barrel at any second.

"That's it," came the man's voice again. "Just a bit closer, honey. That's it. Keep comin', purty li'l red-headed gal."

"All right," Annabelle said, tightly, loudly enough for the man to hear her now. "But you're gonna regret it, you son of a b—"

She'd smelled the rancid odor of unwashed man and raw whiskey two seconds before she heard the pine needle crunch of a stealthy tread behind her. She froze as a man's body pressed against her from behind. Just as the man started to wrap his arm around her, intending to close his hand over her mouth, Annabelle ducked and swung around, swinging the carbine, as well—and rammed the butt into her would-be assailant's solar plexus.

The man gave a great exhalation of whiskey-soaked breath, and folded.

Annabelle turned further and rammed her right knee into the man's face. She felt the wetness of blood on her knee from the man's exploding nose. He gave a wheezy, *"Mercy!"* as he fell straight back against the ground and lay moaning and writhing.

Knowing she was about to have lead sent her way, Annabelle threw herself to her left and rolled. Sure enough, the rifle of the man on the slope below thundered once, twice, three times, the bullets caroming through the air where Annabelle had been a second before. The man whom she'd taken to the proverbial woodshed howled, apparently having taken one of the bullets meant for her.

Annabelle rolled onto her belly and aimed the carbine straight out before her. She'd seen the flash of the second man's rifle, and she aimed toward them now, sending three quick shots their way. The second shooter howled. Annabelle heard the heavy thud as he struck the ground.

"*Gallblastit!*" he cried. "You like to shot my dang ear off, you wicked, red-haired bitch!"

"What happened to 'purty li'l red-haired gal'?" Annabelle spat out as she shoved to her feet and righted her Stetson.

She heard the second shooter thrashing around down the slope, jostling the branches of an evergreen shrub. He gave another cry, and then Annabelle could hear him running in a shambling fashion downhill.

"Oh, you're running away from the 'purty li'l red-haired gal,' now, tough guy?"

Anna strode after him, following the sounds of his shambling retreat.

She pushed through the shrubs and saw his shadow moving downhill, holding a hand to his right ear, groaning. He'd left his rifle up where Anna had shot him. "Turn around or take it in the back, tough guy," she said, following him, taking long, purposeful strides.

"You're crazy!" the man cried, casting a fearful glance behind him. "What'd you do to H.J.?"

"What I started, you finished."

"He's my cousin!"

"*Was* your cousin."

He gave another sobbing cry as he continued running so awkwardly that Anna, walking, steadily gained on him as she held the carbine down low against her right leg.

"You're just a bitch is what you are!"

"You were after our horses, I take it?"

The man only sobbed again.

"How'd you get on our trail?"

"Seen you passin' wide around Lusk," the man said, breathless, grunting. "We was huntin' antelope on the ridge."

"Market hunters?"

"Fer a woodcuttin' crew."

"Ah. You figured you'd make more money selling my and my husband's horses. At least you have a good eye for horse flesh."

The man gained the bottom of the ridge. He stopped and

turned to see Anna moving within twenty feet of him, gaining on him steadily—a tall, slender, well-put-together young lady outfitted in men's trail gear, though, judging by all her curves in all the right places, she was all woman. He gave another wail, sunlight glinting in his wide, terrified eyes, then swung around and ran into the creek, the water splashing like quicksilver up around his knees.

He'd likely never been stalked by a woman before. Especially no "purty li'l red-headed gal."

Anna followed the coward into the creek. "What's your name?"

"Oh, go to hell!"

"What's your name?"

He shot another silver-eyed gaze back over his shoulder. "Wally. Leave me be. I'm in major pain here!"

Now that Anna was closing on him, she could see the man was tall and slender, mid- to late-twenties, with long, stringy hair brushing his shoulders while the top of his head was bald. He had small, mean eyes and now as he turned to face her, he lowered his bloody right hand to the pistol bristling on his right hip.

"You stop there, now," he warned, stretching his lips back from his teeth in pain. "You stop there. I'm done. Finished. You go on back to your camp!"

Anna stopped ten feet away from him. She rested the Winchester on her shoulder. "You know what happens to rustlers in these parts—don't you, Wally?"

He thrust his left arm and index finger out at her. "N-now, you ain't gonna hang me. You done blowed my ear off!" Wally slid the old Smith & Wesson from its holster and held it straight down against his right leg. "Besides, you're a woman. Women don't behave like that!"

He clicked the Smithy's hammer back.

"You're right—we don't behave like that. Not even we 'purty li'l red-headed gals'!" Anna racked a fresh round into the carbine's action, raised the rifle to her shoulder, and grinned coldly. "Why waste the hemp on vermin like you, Wally?"

Wally's little eyes grew wide in terror as he jerked his pistol up. "Don't you—!"

"We just shoot 'em!" Anna said.

And shot him.

Wally flew back into the creek with a splash. He went under and bobbed to the surface, arms and legs spread wide. Slowly, the current carried him downstream.

Anna heard running footsteps and a man's raking breaths behind her. She swung around, bringing the carbine up again, ready to shoot, but held fire when she saw the big, broad-shouldered man in the gray Stetson, buckskin tunic, and denims running toward her, the coyote running just ahead.

"Anna!" Hunter yelled. "Are you all right, honey?"

He and Bobby stopped at the edge of the stream. Both their gazes caught on the man bobbing downstream, and Hunter shuttled his incredulous gaze back to his wife. Raking deep breaths, he hooked a thumb over his shoulder. "Saw the other man up the hill. Dead as a post." Hunter Buchanon planted his fists on his hips and scowled his reproof at his young wife. "I told you to stay at the camp!"

Anna strode back out of the stream. She stopped before her husband, who was a whole head taller than she. "We purty li'l red-headed gals just need us a little blood-letting once in a while. Sort of like bleeding the sap off a tree."

She grinned, rose up on her toes to kiss Hunter's lips then ticked the brim of his hat with her right index finger and started walking back toward the camp and the horses. "Come on, Bobby Lee," she said. "I'll race ya!"

CHAPTER 2

The next day, late in the afternoon, Hunter had a strange sense of foreboding as he rode into the Arapaho Creek headquarters.He stopped his horse just inside the wooden portal in the overhead crossbar of which the Arapaho Creek brand—A/C—had been burned. He curvetted his fine grullo stallion, Nasty Pete, and took a quick study of the place.

The house sat off to the right and just ahead of him—a large, two-and-a-half story stone-and-log affair. A large, fieldstone hearth ran up the lodge's near wall shaded by a large, dusty cottonwood, its leaves flashing silver in the breeze blowing in from the bastion of the Rocky Mountain Front Range rising in the west. A couple of log barns and a stable as well as a windmill and blacksmith shop sat ahead on Hunter's left, beyond a large corral.

The wooden blades of the windmill creaked in the wind, and that hot, dry, vagrant breeze kicked up finely churned dirt and horse apples in the yard just ahead of him; they made a mini, short-lived tornado out of them. The breeze brought to Hunter's nostrils the pungent tang of sage and horse manure.

Likely impressive at one time, the place hard a time-worn look. Brush grew up around the house and most of the outbuildings. Rusted tin wash tubs hung from nails in the front wall of the bunkhouse. Also, there were few men working around the headquarters. Hunter spotted only four. Only one was actually working. A big, burly man in a leather apron, likely the blacksmith, was greasing the axle of a dilapidated supply wagon, the A/C brand painted on both sides badly faded.

One man sat on the corral fence to Hunter's left, rolling a sharpened matchstick from one corner of his mouth to the other with a desultory air. Two others sat outside the bunkhouse between the stable and the windmill, straddling a bench and playing two-handed poker.

Of course, most of the hands could be out on the range, tending the herds, but Hunter had spied few cattle after he, Annabelle, and the ten horses they would sell here, had ridden onto Navajo Creek graze roughly twenty miles north of Denver, near a little town called Javelina. The graze itself was sparse. It was a motley looking country under a broad, blue bowl of sky from which the sun hammered down relentlessly.

It was all bunch grass and sage, a few cedars here and there peppering low, chalky buttes and meandering, dry arroyos. It was, indeed, a big, broad, open country with damn few trees, the First Front of the Rocky Mountains cropping up in the west, some of the highest peaks showing the ermine of the previous winter's snow. This dry, dun brown country lay in grim contrast to those high, formidable ridges that bespoke deep, lush pine forests and roaring creeks and rivers.

What also appeared odd was that three of the four men Hunter could see appeared old. Late fifties to mid-sixties. Only the man sitting with his boot heels hooked over a corral slat to Hunter's left appeared under forty. He regarded Hunter blandly from beneath the weathered, funneled bridge of his once-cream Stetson that was now, after enduring much sun, wind, rain, and hail of this harsh country—a washed-out yellow.

The man slid his gaze from Hunter to the main house and said, tonelessly, "Looks like the hosses are here, boss."

Hunter followed the man's gaze toward where an old man with thin gray, curly hair and a long, gray tangle of beard stood on the house's front porch. He had to be somewhere in his late-sixties—hard-earned years, judging by the man's slump and general air of fragility.

He appeared to be carrying a great weight and was damned weary of it. He wore wash-worn, broadcloth trousers, a thin cream longhandle top, and suspenders. He squinted at Hunter, his bony features long and drawn. He looked as though he might have just woken from a nap.

"Hunter Buchanon?" the man called raspily.

"Rufus Scanlon?" Hunter countered.

The man dipped his chin, his long beard brushing his flat, bony chest.

"We have the horses up on the ridge," Hunter said, hooking a thumb to indicate the low, pine-peppered ridge behind him. "I rode down to see if you were ready for 'em."

He glanced into the corral where only three horses stood still as stone save switching their tails at flies, hang-headed, regarding the newcomer dubiously.

The man beckoned broadly with a thin arm; his lips spread an eager smile, giving sudden life to the otherwise lifeless tangle of beard. "Bring 'em on down!"

Hunter glanced around the yard once more. He was selling his prized horses for two hundred apiece. He had a hard time reconciling such a price with such a humble looking headquarters. He hoped he and Anna hadn't ridden all this way for nothing.

"All right, then," he said.

He neck-reined Nasty Pete around and galloped back out through the portal. He followed the trail across Navajo Creek and up to the crest of the ridge where Anna was holding the horses in scattered pines. They stood spread out, calmly grazing, Anna sitting her calico mare, Ruthie, among them.

When they'd stopped here on the ridge, Bobby Lee had disappeared. Likely sensing they'd come to the end of the trail, the coyote had lit out on a rabbit or gopher hunt. Seeing Hunter, Anna booted the mare over to him, frowning incredulously beneath the brim of her dark green Stetson, its horsehair thong drawn up securely beneath her chin. The Rocky Mountain sun glinted fetchingly in her deep red hair.

"What is it?" she asked, the mare nuzzling Nasty Pete with teasing affection.

"What's what?"

"I know that look. What's wrong?"

Hunter shrugged and leaned forward against his saddle horn. "Not sure. Humble place, the Navajo Creek. Doesn't look like the kind of outfit that can afford these hosses. I told Scanlon in my letter that this was a cash deal only. That's two thousand dollars. Just a might skeptical that old man down there has two thousand dollars laying around, lonely an' in need of a home." The big ex-Confederate gave his wife a pointed look. "I'll guaran-damn-tee you, though, I'm not goin' home without the cash he agreed to pay or without the horses he agreed to buy if he can't buy 'em!"

"You should've had him put cash down."

"Yeah, well, I've never had to do that before."

"That's because you've always known the men you were selling to."

Hunter sighed and raked a thumb through a two-day growth of blond beard stubble. "I gotta admit I ain't the shrewdest businessman."

"No, you're not. You're a simple, honest ex-rebel from Georgia." Anna sidled Ruthie up next to Nasty Pete, thumbed Hunter's hat up on his forehead, and kissed him. "And that's why this Yankee girl loves you. Not sure I could've fallen in love with a shrewd businessman. My father was one of those."

Hunter smiled.

Annabelle frowned with sudden concern. "You don't think he might try to take them from us, do you? The horses."

Hunter shook his head. "Doesn't seem the type. Besides, not enough men around, and those who are, all but one, don't look like they could raise a hogleg. Nah, he's probably one of those tight Yankees who let his place go to pot because he was too cheap to hire the men to keep it up. He probably has a mattress stuffed with money somewhere in that old house. He's likely ready to spend some of that cash on horses, maybe try to build up his own remuda. Hope so, anyways." Hunter glanced around, again seeing no sign of a herd. "Looks like he might be out of the cattle business."

Anna straightened in her saddle. "Let's go see. With any luck, we'll be in Javelina by sundown, flush as railroad magnates and sitting down to a big surrounding of steak and beans!"

"Mrs. Buchanon, you are indeed a lady after my own heart."

"Oh, I think you've known for a while now that you have that, dear heart." Anna narrowed an eye at him and hooked her mouth in a crooked smile, jade eyes shimmering in the late afternoon light. "Lock, stock, and barrel!" She started to rein her calico around, saying, "Let's go drive these broomtails down to—"

Hunter touched her arm. "Hold on."

She turned back to him, frowning. "What is it?"

"Whatever happens down there." He gave her a commanding look and jerked his chin to indicate the humble headquarters at the base of the ridge. "Don't go off half-cocked like you did last night."

"Oh, I went off fully cocked last night, dear heart."

"Anna!"

But she'd already reined away from him and was working Ruthie around to the far side of the herd.

Hunter stared after her, shaking his head in frustration.

But wasn't it his own damn fault—letting himself tumble for a fiery Yankee girl, a redhead spawned and reared by the equally stubborn and warrior-like Yankee Black Hills Rancher, Graham Ludlow, who'd become Hunter's blood enemy when the man had tried to keep his prized daughter from marrying into the Confederate Buchanon family?

In fact, the two families had nearly destroyed each other in the feud that had followed.

But after the smoke and dust had cleared, Hunter had found himself with the prize he'd lost two brothers, and nearly his father, old Angus, in winning. Annabelle's father had been ruined, his ranch, nearly reduced to ashes, now defunct. Hunter had to admit, as he watched Anna now, expertly working the mustangs, that she'd been worth it.

If anything had, she had . . .

He chuckled wryly. "You romantic fool, Buchanon."

He rode out and joined his young wife in gathering the herd and hazing them on down the trail, across the creek, and into the Navajo Creek headquarters, where the man who'd been sitting on the corral fence stood holding the gate wide. When Hunter and Anna had all the horses inside the corral, obscured by a heavy cloud of roiling, sunlit dust, Rufus Scanlon strode over from the main lodge, grinning again inside the tangle of beard.

He wore a corduroy jacket over his underwear top—a concession to having guests, especially one of the female variety, Hunter silently opined—and rested his bony arms on the top corral slat, inspecting his new remuda.

"Nice, nice," he said, blinking against the dust. "Say that brown and white pinto looks to have some Spanish blood. Look at the fire in his eyes!"

Hunter and Anna sat their horses behind him.

"Most of these do," Hunter said, surveying the fine-looking remuda, all ten stallions stomping around, skirmishing, nosing the air, getting the lay of the new land. A lineback dun tried to mount a steel-dust with a long, black snout and black tail and nearly got into a fight for his trouble. Others gazed off into the distance, wild-eyed, wanting to be free once more. "Some very old bloodlines in this string. Old Spanish an' Injun blood. You'll have some good breeders here, Mister Scanlon. Get you a coupla fine mares, an' you'll have one hell of a remuda."

"Were they hard to break?"

"Oh, they're not broke," Hunter said with a dry chuckle. "Do they look broke to you? Nah, their spirits are intact. But you try to throw a saddle on any of the ten, an' they'll give you no trouble. Now, when you try to mount . . ."

"That's when you'll have trouble," Anna cut in. "They'll test any one of your riders"—she grinned beautifully, gazing at the herd fondly and with a sadness at the thought of parting with them—"just to make sure they're man enough."

"Or woman enough?"

Hunter turned to see a young woman striding over from the main house—a well setup brunette in a white blouse and long, black wool skirt and riding boots. She took long, lunging strides, chin in the air, a glowing smile on her classically beautifully face.

Her hair hung messily down about her shoulders, blowing back in the wind, strands catching at the corners of her mouth. She was olive-skinned, likely betraying some Spanish blood of her own, and there was a wild clarity and untethered delight in her eyes as brown as a mountain stream late in the day—as late as the day was getting now, in fact.

"Or, yeah," Anna said uncertainly, cutting a territorial glance at Hunter whom she'd no doubt spied eyeing the newcomer with keen male interest, "woman enough. Even gentled, they'll throw you for sure if they sense you're afraid of them." She glanced at Scanlon who stood packing a pipe he'd produced from the breast pocket of his worn corduroy jacket. "Who's this, Mr. Scanlon? The lady of the house?"

Scanlon merely chuckled as though at a private joke, eyes slitted, as he fired a match to life on his thumbnail and touched the flame to the pipe bowl.

"Lucinda Scanlon," said the young lady, somewhere in her early twenties, Hunter judged while trying not to scrutinize her too closely, knowing he was under his wife's watchful eye. She extended a hand to Anna. "The lady of the house and the whole damn range!" Chuckling, she added, "Pleased to meet you . . . Mrs. Buchanon, I assume?"

"Annabelle," Anna said, returning the young lady's shake, regarding her dubiously, as though a wildcat—tame or untamed, was yet to be determined—had so unexpectedly entered the conversation.

"Annabelle, of course," said Lucinda Scanlon, casting Anna a broad, warm smile before turning to Hunter whom she also offered a firm handshake and welcoming smile. Her eyes were not only as brown as a mountain creek but as deep as any lake up high in the Rockies, Hunter found himself noting. "And you're Mr. Buchanon."

"Hunter." He felt a sudden restriction in his throat at this sudden newcomer's obvious charms and forthright, refined, open, and friendly manner. Appearing so suddenly out of nowhere here at this humble, going-to-seed headquarters, she was definitely a diamond in the rough. A bluebird in a flock of crows.

"Indeed, Hunter. I enjoyed your letters describing the remuda."

"Well, uh," Hunter said, hiking a shoulder in chagrin. "Anna helped me with it. I can ride all day, but I ain't . . . *haven't* . . . exactly perfected my sentences." He chuckled self-consciously. "Letters but not always my sentences."

Annabelle cut him a sharp look as though silently throwing a loop over his head and reining him in. He realized he'd removed his hat and quickly donned it.

Scanlon saw the interplay and laughed.